ILFANTI

and the

Orb of Prophecy

MARCELLA LEALY

This has the makings of a great tale. The realm in peril; a kidnapped damsel in distress; and the old adventurer coming out of retirement for one final quest to find an artifact that will reveal the location of the Empress, bring her back, confront Zoldex, and then usher in a new era of peace and prosperity for all races.

No pressure.

- Ilfanti

The Imperium Saga

Also by Clifford B. Bowyer

Fall of the Imperium Trilogy
The Impending Storm
The Changing Tides
The Siege of Zoldex

The Adventures of Kyria
The Child of Prophecy
The Awakening
The Mage's Council
The Shard of Time
Trapped in Time
Quest for the Shard
The Spread of Darkness
The Apprentice of Zoldex
The Darkness Within
The Rescue of Nezbith

Ilfanti and the Orb of Prophecy
Continuing the Passion

The Imperium Saga

ILFANTI

and the

Orb of Prophecy

Clifford B. Bowyer

HOLLISTON, MASSACHUSETTS

Ilfanti and the Orb of Prophecy
Copyright © 2010 by Clifford B. Bowyer

Cover Art by David Michael Beck

First printing February 2010
10 9 8 7 6 5 4 3 2 1

ISBN # 0-9787782-7-8
ISBN-13 # 9780978778279
LCCN # 2009908182

Silver Leaf Books, LLC
P.O. Box 6460
Holliston, MA 01746
+1-888-823-6450

Visit our web site at www.SilverLeafBooks.com

In loving memory of my grandparents.
May the tales that they told and the lessons they taught
live on inside those of us that they have touched.

CAST OF CHARACTERS

Ilfanti, dwarven male from Mage's Council
Kabilian, human male from Dartais
Crick, hobgoblin male from Dartie
Rhyne, wraith male from Falestia
Osorkon, dwarven male from Memtorren
Khonsu, dwarven female from Memtorren
Inorus, dwarven male from Memtorren

Crew of the *Soaring Mist*:
    Captain Augustus, human female from Dartais
    Krimdor, aquatican male from Mage's Council
    Brondolfr, barbarian male from Falestian Plains
    Kemocay, adlesian male from Adlai
    Fasbender, gnomish male from Underwood
    Jin Fe, aezian male from Aezea
    Green, raspler male from Tenalong
    Beige, raspler male from Tenalong
    Shimada, aezian female from Aezea
    Palisha, human female from Falestia

Crew of the *Passion*:
    Captain Glynn, avarian male from Vysellius
    Buoen, avarian male from Vysellius
    Felch, avarian male from Vysellius
    Rossis, avarian male from Orastius
    Stavn, avarian male from Vysellius
    Wien, avarian male from Vysellius

ILFANTI

and the

Orb of Prophecy

PROLOGUE

For most citizens of Egziard, the nights were a form of salvation and reprieve. The scorched dry lands of the desert were harsh and unforgiving. The temperatures during the day were amongst the highest in the world, often peaking at 150 degrees Fahrenheit on what would be considered a cool and breezy day for that region.

The night was a respite for the people that lived in or roamed the desert. The temperatures dropped considerably without the raging sun baking down on them. Many animals that populated Egziard were nocturnal for this very reason, seeking shelter during the dry sunlit hours.

The nomads who wandered the desert were no exception. They never remained in the same spot for long, always moving from one place to another in search of food and water. The centuries had honed their senses—it was said that a desert nomad could sense the presence of water from a mile away, or more. Once they came upon it, a nomad could even drink a single drop of water from the desert sand.

The wanderers traveled in small groups, usually consisting of members of an extended family unit, or several families together that had forged an alliance. The larger groups were more developed and stronger, but this was not the norm for the nomads. Each group, or tribe, had a single leader: the sheikh. This individual—who was always a man—would determine the migration patterns and all activities for his tribe, including interactions and negotiations with other nomads.

Ptahmose was the sheikh of the Ptahhemat-Ty tribe. The group had been forged when his great-grandfather, Ptahhemat, had forged an unlikely alliance with Ty, a well-known raider who butchered anyone that his tribe encountered. Ty was in the elder years of his life, and all his children were women, and as such, unable to lead the tribe. He then forged an agreement with Ptahhemat in which the two wed their eldest children and combined their separate nomadic groups, creating the largest tribe in Egziard.

The size and strength of the Ptahhemat-Ty tribe had never been more formidable. Ptahmose, though not a direct descendent of Ty, was as ruthless and bloodthirsty as the tyrant had ever been. He had expanded his power over the past three decades, and not even the pharaohs were willing to challenge him on the open sands.

The Ptahhemat-Ty tribe currently consisted of over six hundred able-bodied warriors. An additional thousand members of the tribe were the revered elders, the wives, and the children who were not yet old enough to join their fathers. They also boasted the possession of a herd of camels that could carry all of the warriors, as well as ninety massive abuephas—the rampaging beasts that could topple a stone wall with ease.

Even with all of his power and the prosperity of his tribe, Ptahmose was unwilling to accept that the Ptahhemat-Ty tribe could not further increase their station. There were legends of an ancient temple known as Ramahatra that contained within untold secrets and powers. According to the legend, not only did this temple have unfound riches, weapons, and more power than anyone could ever dream of, but it also contained the Orb of Prophecy.

The Orb was reputed to be a mystical artifact that many had sought over the years, but none had managed to uncover. The question of whether it even existed added to the legends and the enthusiasm of those brave enough to wander the desert searching for it. According to the legends, if the Orb of Prophecy were in your possession, then it would reveal the answer to any question you could ask. The future was already a written book for the Orb, and the bearer could use it to alter his own destiny by seeing what was to come.

Ptahmose was certain that the Orb existed. He had, of course, heard the legends since childhood, but recently the tribe had uncovered a small compass of unique origins during a raid. Those on the expedition claimed that the compass would lead them to Ramahatra and the treasures within, if even a fraction of the legends were true. Ptahmose demanded that Ramahatra be discovered and its treasure possessed solely by him. The power of the Orb had to be his alone. With it, he would be able to expand his power and rule all of Egziard, even going so far as to overthrow the mighty pharaohs.

His brother and trusted confidant, Ptahetep, had cautioned him about following the compass directly. Not only did Ramahatra supposedly have these untold treasures, but it was also cursed and protected by an evil that had not been known to the world for many millennia.

Though Ptahmose did not believe in curses, he respected his brother's advice. He had sent ten scouting parties of fifteen men each out into the desert to seek the location of the ancient temple in the direction that the compass was pointing. But that was over a fortnight ago, and his patience was now growing very thin.

For Ptahmose, remaining idle too closely resembled death. He wanted to be always moving, but the advantages of carefully planning the plunder of Ramahatra were too great for rash action. As the days passed, he sent smaller groups out into the barren wastes of Egziard to search not for the lost temple, but for his scouting parties. None ever returned.

He stood at the edge of the small encircled area where his tribe had erected their tents. Most of the people were huddled around fires and talking amongst themselves. Ptahmose could not rest, though. His people were out there, and he wanted to be able to do something about it.

That was when he saw them. They were too far away for him to see clearly, especially in the darkness, but he could just make out a trio of men running towards their encampment. There were no camels or weapons in sight, only the three men. Ptahmose wondered if they could be part of one of his scouting parties, but if so, where were their mounts and equipment?

He drew his scimitar and emitted several long calls that sounded like the word "la" in varying harmonic tones. Hundreds of men rushed to his call, their weapons also drawn and facing the oncoming trio. Whoever they were, friend or foe, they would find the Ptahhemat-Ty tribe waiting for them.

❋ ❋ ❋ ❋ ❋

The three men found no solace in the breeze of the night. Their hearts were pounding, their lungs were straining for air, and their chests felt as if they would explode. Their exposed skin was red, blistered, and cracked. Each step was excruciating agony, but their terror of what was behind them kept them moving—pushing them far beyond their limits.

There had been fifteen of them to start. Fifteen fully garbed and heavily armed members of the Ptahhemat-Ty tribe. Even with such a small number, other groups of nomadic wanderers that more than tripled their numbers would flee before them. They were the strong, the powerful, and the ones to be feared.

Now, these men trembled with the mere memory of what they had observed. Their only thought was that if they could reach the encampment of their people, perhaps, just perhaps, they would live to see another sunrise. Finally, after running without rest for days, the last three survivors saw their destination. They could see the strong and proud warriors of the Ptahhemat-Ty tribe moving out to meet them. Ptahmose, their relentless leader in front, would be first to come upon them.

A scream from behind jolted two of the runners. They did not even need to turn to know that another of their party had fallen victim to the dark-skinned witch and her minions. This was not the first companion they had lost. When the first of their group had fallen the others had searched for the attacker, but could only find the skeletal remains of their companion; as if all of his flesh and organs had been devoured. Many joined the first, and those that survived learned that the one that fell would at least provide a slight distraction so that the survivors could try to push on.

The fire was close. The two would be there soon. They desperately hoped that they would make it in time. All they needed was a few more minutes. With their bodies feeling like they were about to burst, both water-starved men ran harder toward their salvation.

Another scream of agony pierced the night, and Bek knew that he was alone. He tightened his grip on the artifact that they had claimed from Ramahatra and pushed forward. He was almost there. He could see Ptahmose clearly now.

"My Sheikh!" he cried out.

"Bek!" Ptahmose called in return.

Then he heard it. It was not the beating of his heart, but the silent rumble that signaled the end. "Beware the witch!" he cried out as he stopped and tossed the artifact to Ptahmose.

"Bek?" Ptahmose questioned as he caught the item. Before his eyes, Bek began convulsing and screaming in agony. The sand around him burst skyward and the scout began clawing at his skin as if something was crawling on him that he was desperate to get off.

Then he saw it. They were small orange and black snake-like creatures. They were no bigger than the size of a finger, but hundreds of them were swirling all over Bek's body. They moved like quicksilver, never stopping as they crawled around him.

"What madness is this?" Ptahmose gasped, taking a hesitant step toward his scout.

In moments, Bek's body fell to the ground, only dried and crusted skeletal remains left behind. The creatures dropped back within the sand in which they had come, and Ptahmose watched as the sand moved with hundreds of tiny bulges until they dropped down to the normal desert calmness.

"What madness is this?" he repeated, glancing around at his people in hopes that someone would have an answer. "What just happened?"

Ptahetep stepped forward cautiously and jabbed the skeletal remains of Bek with his saber. The bones disintegrated with his touch. "The curse," he spat as he jumped back.

Ptahmose looked down at the item in his hand. It resembled the compass that allegedly pointed to Ramahatra. It was a triangular black piece of onyx with golden markings around the edge and a single golden serpent in the middle. Clutching the item in his hand, he turned away from Bek and returned to the encampment. Ramahatra had been found.

ILFANTI'S LOG

"Be careful and don't be too cocky."

Those were her words. Cala's words. Cocky? Me? That is something that I would never even have thought of back in my Paladin years. Back then life was a constant adventure, one grand scheme after the other, each more dangerous than the last. How I miss those days.

Most Mages go out in their Paladin years and visit the races of their origins. They have a deep need to find their roots and learn what makes them truly tick; not just what they had learned sitting in a classroom, but also seeing what it meant to be an elf, a dwarf, a wraith, or whatever; what one truly acts like and is. That held no allure for me. Perhaps I was just strange.

I am a dwarf. I don't intend it as a slight to my people, but they will spend their centuries on this planet working in a mine, crafting armor and weapons, or waging war. They feel that this existence is glorious, and if they were to die in battle, then it would be a good death. Sure. That's fine. But that's not for me.

I think dwarves are honorable and noble. I think that there is no better ally in the entire world—and I have visited a great many places beyond the boundaries of the Seven Kingdoms, so I would know. If a dwarf becomes an ally, it is for life. He would die by your side and never question that decision.

It is not a bad code to live by. I too forge friendships that transcend time. I would die fighting beside Cala or Herg without regrets and feel that it would be an honorable death. I would gladly sacrifice myself if it would mean that they survive to see another day. I am a dwarf.

But then in some ways, I am not. I cannot be happy mining for precious gems and elements. I have no desire to become a blacksmith or craftsman and forge weapons, armor, and artifacts so glorious that they would stand the test of time. No, that life is not for me.

That life may be good for a normal dwarf, but I am also a Mage. I was raised since infancy to be what I have become. I have learned history, mathematics, science, literature, and more. I cannot look at the *face of a cliff and see potential gems locked inside. To me, that is time-consuming and boring. Perhaps that is why after I met my first dwarves in Tregador during my Paladin years, I decided to shave my beard and never allow even a single day to pass without making certain that I was clean-shaven.*

I prefer exploration. I want to find the unknown. I want to broaden my horizons. If something has been lost for centuries, I will seek it out. If it is something that others claim does not exist, I will journey to the corners of Terra to prove that is does. In short, I am an adventurer. Life, to me, is more meaningful when I believe in what I am doing, and there are constant perils and obstacles that must be overcome.

Unlike most Paladins, my time away from the Council lasted two hundred years. I have never felt as alive or as energetic as I felt during those two centuries. Though I have grown in fame in the Council, have trained dozens of Apprentices, and have even become a member of the Council of Elders, nothing has ever compared to my Paladin years.

Perhaps I never should have stopped. Who knows where I would be now. Probably on a ship somewhere seeking the next grand adventure or discovery. But I'm about to do that anyway.

No, I do not regret returning to the Council. It was time. An abundance of something good is never satisfying. If I remained an explorer and an adventurer, eventually, even that life would have stopped being meaningful. It was time to come home.

But now things are getting bad. As bad as I ever remember seeing things; worse, even. Zoldex, an eternal that I cannot even give the honor of calling a fiend or tyrant, has returned. I am not completely positive, but it appears that he has been manipulating events in the Seven Kingdoms for quite some time. Orcs and hobgoblins have been raiding the villages of elves and dwarves. Both Xylona and Vorstad—two proud and noble cities—have fallen. The humans have been experiencing uprisings, and now a fleet of mind-boggling magnitude has arrived to support Zoldex's rise to power.

Yes, things are bad. Karleena had been trying to change things. She, as the Empress, had seen the signs before they got too bad and moved to try and unite the races. An admirable goal, but one that was destined to fail. Back in the Race Wars, many of the races were united in a common goal. The humans betrayed the alliance and claimed the Seven Kingdoms for their own. Even with the threat of Zoldex, it is hard to fathom how generations of prejudice and resentment can be overcome.

Still, the Empress had been trying. Trying, and in a small way, succeeding. But then she was kidnapped, and now the Imperium has been plunged into war with Aezia. Master Askari assures me that Aezia is not behind the Empress's abduction, and I believe that he is right. Instead, Zoldex must have orchestrated it. He wants the unification to fail so that he can conquer the realm. That must not happen.

The one person who should be standing up to Zoldex is Pierce. The two were enemies before there even was a Mage's Council. At their final confrontation, Pierce won and Zoldex was banished. Now, the fool won't even let the Council get involved. He feels that the Mages are above the concerns of the realm. I hope he comes to his senses before Zoldex jabs him in the ass and shows him that we should have been involved all along.

Since Pierce isn't facing his nemesis, the fate of the realm has fallen onto my shoulders. Not that I am complaining. This will be a quest that would have made my mouth water when I was younger. Then her words come to me again like a dagger wedged in my side.

"It's been three centuries since your wild days."

Thanks, Cala. Is that what you really think of me? After all of this time? She is right, though. It has been three hundred years since I've last had the exhilaration of a true quest. Since the last time someone tried to kill me. Since the last time I leapt blindly off of a mountain and all that I could do was laugh at the absurdity of it as I plummeted to the water that I had not known was below.

Of course, those details I leave out when I tell my stories. I captivate audiences with retelling my adventures, but I never let them know the worst of the dangers, and the times when I thought I was going to die. No, I tell about the excitement, the glory, and the rewards. That's not how life really works, though. Not really. Life is full of pain, suffering, and hard work. I would spend years on one of my quests that could *be summed up into a short ten-minute tale that would raise the hair on the necks of listeners.*

I guess that makes me a good storyteller. This will take more than a story to save the day, however. It has the makings of a great tale. The realm in peril; a kidnapped damsel in distress; and the old adventurer coming out of retirement for one final quest to find an artifact that will reveal the location of the Empress, bring her back, confront Zoldex, and then usher in a new era of peace and prosperity for all races.

No pressure.

Three centuries of rust and dust. Cala and Herg were right to be concerned. They were right to have doubts. A lot has changed in three hundred years; not to mention my silken black hair has been replaced by this thinning whitish-gray. I'm older than any dwarf has a right to be, and I actually think that I still matter, that I can still make a difference.

Maybe I am deluding myself. Then again, maybe not. I may be old, but I still feel as young and as energetic as when I was a Paladin. The years have treated me well. I never gave in to the passage of time. I always worked hard to make sure that I was physically fit. Perhaps I may fall a step or two behind my younger self, but I will keep up.

Yes, I will keep up. I will not give in to the norms of society. I will not be an elder that others look at and brush aside as being frail and weak. I will not be a burden on those I care about. I am Ilfanti. I am a dwarf. I am a Mage. I am going to find the Orb of Prophecy, then the Empress, then see this war through to the end, and when I do, I am going to dance on top of Zoldex's grave.

CHAPTER 1

Of the Seven Kingdoms comprising the Imperium, Dartais was the wealthiest. Even the near-utopia of Danchul paled in comparison to the accumulated riches of the Dartais nobles and high lords. The fact that this affluence was grossly increased after Emperor Conrad forged the Imperium was not lost on people.

Prior to the formation of the Imperium, Dartais was a merchant kingdom that often lost its cargos to the stronger fleets of Frocomon. Though they were excellent merchants and fisherman, the people of Dartais could not withstand the powerful warships that preyed upon them.

Conrad and Morex—both from Dartais—decided to try and confront the Frocomon plunderers head-on. The two shared a vision and soon gained followers. They assembled a crew and acquired a ship. Though they began as only a single ship, they grew their fleet and fame as pirates, striking the Frocominians down and claiming the superior vessels for their own.

In time, the fleet of Frocomon was decimated, and the merchants of Dartais were able to prosper by increasing their trade routes and expanding their operations. As money continued to line the pockets of the nobles of Dartais, their ships and crews grew, making them the largest merchant fleet in the known world.

Today, those same nobles and their descendants had unimaginable wealth. Under the direction of Queen Dornela, they explored the Dartais Islands and soon claimed them as a retreat for the nobility of the realm. Only the rich and elite could hope to reside on these islands, and everyone who was anyone scrambled to prove their fortunes and relocate there.

The nobility that remained behind became the high lords of the two remaining coastal cities—Bellmore and Water Haven. Though other small towns and villages were scattered throughout Dartais, the workers and impoverished citizens populated these, and not a single member of the Dartais nobility would even acknowledge their existence.

As was often true in the realm, the rich got richer and the poor got poorer. The workers of Dartais are often underpaid and are forced to endure harsh working conditions, long hours, and life-threatening tasks. Many would claim that society was not fair, but with the nobles secluded and not even bothering to look at the workers that they employed, whom would they complain to?

Water Haven—the smaller of the two main Dartais cities—was a coastal harbor city. Its name was well known up and down the coast, for it was the central point of commerce for the eastern seabed. Not only did they dominate the eastern coasts with their trade routes and merchant fleets, but they also supported a bustling economy with tour ships that brought vacationers close to the Dartais Islands—the closest most people would ever come to nobility themselves.

This waterfaring city was the one that Ilfanti opted to visit to begin his journey. He was closest to the harbor ports of Trespias, but ever since the legions of Zoldex arrived, there was no way in or out of the harbor. Instead, he had to travel north to Dartais, and there was no better destination than Water Haven.

Stripped of his normal Mage's attire, Ilfanti was garbed in the wardrobe that had served him so well during his Paladin years. He wore a long sleeved cream-colored shirt with a pocket on each side of his chest. A light brown leather vest fastened on top of the shirt. His pants were of the same color and material, though he was shocked to admit that he had a little bit of trouble getting them to clasp—undoubtedly, they must have shrunk over the centuries because he certainly didn't feel as if he had gained weight since his Paladin years. He had dark brown leather boots and a belt that had a dagger and a Mage's satchel clasped to it. Too many people favored cloaks, especially Mages, but Ilfanti went with a dark brown koxlen-hide jacket—that appeared very worn—with the front left open to complete his ensemble.

Ilfanti walked down the cobblestone streets and studied the people that he passed. Many glared at him with spite, some in fear; all looked impoverished. Five children, all so thin that they looked as if they had not eaten in weeks, surrounded one woman who was dispensing small pieces of bread.

The Council of Elders member could not believe how bad things looked. Water Haven was supposed to be the most prosperous harbor city in the Seven Kingdoms. From what he saw though, it looked more as if the people were bonded in slavery and working for a few scraps of leftover food. It was not a sight he would soon forget.

Every turn he made was the same. There were definitely shop owners and street peddlers that did not look as destitute, but behind every corner, children that were little more than skin and bones held out their hands begging for scraps of food or money. Ilfanti only wished that he had brought more than just the Jewel of Amara to finance his passage to Egziard and back. If so, he would dispense all of his riches from his quests to these people so that they could afford a decent meal.

Spotting a tavern, Ilfanti decided to try and gain some information on the ships that were in the harbor. At any given time Water Haven had well over a hundred schooners and smaller vessels docked, and he needed to know which would be the most suitable for his purposes. The journey to Egziard would be a long and harsh one, and he had to be careful to select a ship that could actually handle the voyage.

As he stepped inside the doorway, the loud chatter and laughter slowly faded as every eye turned toward him. One man was still laughing until the person next to him hit him on the shoulder and beckoned him to look toward the door. Ilfanti scanned the room and held the gaze of each man present.

The prejudice of humans ever since the Race Wars ended never ceased to amaze him. They were the ones who had betrayed their allies from the Wars, and yet they had the audacity to act as if they were the ones wronged. Incorrigible. Refusing to be intimidated, Ilfanti strode over to the bar and sat down on an open stool.

"No dwarves allowed," the bartender barked as he glared at Ilfanti.

"You get a lot around these parts?" Ilfanti asked.

"What?" the bartender asked in amazement that the dwarf was

bothering to talk to him.

"Dwarves," Ilfanti clarified. "Do you get a lot of dwarves around these parts?"

"Of course not!" the bartender shouted as if offended.

"Then why would you ever make such a policy?" Ilfanti asked.

"It covers anything that isn't human," he said proudly.

"Oh," Ilfanti replied, mocking the man by acting that this was a great revelation he never considered. "I see."

"Good, then get out!" the bartender screamed, his patience lost.

Two men walked over and stood behind Ilfanti as if to persuade him that he should leave.

"Since you don't get a lot of dwarves around these parts, allow me to explain a few things," Ilfanti said. "If I was a normal dwarf, this conversation would have ended the moment you told me that no dwarves were allowed. If I was a normal dwarf, I would have pulled an axe or some other heavy-set weapon and attacked anything and anyone who dared to stand between me and my ale. *If* I was a normal dwarf."

The bartender glanced at the two men, his features showing the slightest hint of worry on his brow. "If you were a normal dwarf," he repeated slowly. "If you're not, then what in Tanorus are you?"

"Oh, I am a dwarf," Ilfanti admitted. "But I am also a Mage."

"A Mage?" the bartender laughed. "Where's your robes and cloak?"

Always the cloak, he thought, rolling his eyes before responding. "I am on a quest and seek a fast ship. It is of vital importance to the survival of the realm. Due to this, I opted to wear this ensemble instead of my normal Mage's attire."

"You're no Mage," the bartender snorted. "Vital importance to the realm? Bah! Not a single ship in this port would take on a dwarf as a passenger."

"I hope that you are mistaken with your claim," Ilfanti said, wondering if the prejudice of humans would extend so far as to cause him difficulties with securing a suitable ship.

"Find out for yourself," the bartender growled. "Boys, get this creature out of here!"

The two men reached out and placed their hands on Ilfanti's shoulders. "Come on, runt."

"You know, when on these little adventures of mine, I typically do not like to use magic," Ilfanti sighed. "Be grateful for my restraint."

"Yeah, sure," the bartender laughed.

As the two men began to lift Ilfanti out of his seat, Ilfanti twisted in the air, twirling over and kicking his feet toward the heads of those holding him. They dropped him as they brought their arms up to shield their faces.

"How the hell did he do that?"

Ilfanti dropped and landed on his feet. He then shot a leg out and kicked one of the men in the shin. As the man reached to grab hold of his leg, Ilfanti punched him in the chin with a violent uppercut and dropped him to the ground, unconscious.

The second man grabbed a barstool and slammed it down where Ilfanti had been standing, shattering the wooden legs. Ilfanti dodged out of the way, jumped up onto a second barstool, and then leapt on top of the man, his legs wrapped around his throat. Bringing his fists slamming down on the man's head, he kept punching until they fell to the ground and his second attacker was unconscious.

Ilfanti rolled off of the man and crouched, looking at the bartender. He raised his hand and began waggling his fingers. The bartender started to feel cold and began to shiver. He turned to look at the bottles of ale and grew infuriated as he saw them frostbitten and encased in ice. As he began to breathe heavier, he could see his own breath coming from his mouth like a white mist.

"What madness is this? I thought you said you didn't use magic?" he protested.

"Actually, I said that I typically do not like to use magic," Ilfanti corrected. "I find myself making an exception with narrow-minded imbeciles that feed on hatred, fear, and prejudice."

"Stop!" the bartender cried as icicles began forming on his nose. "Please stop."

"Only under two conditions," Ilfanti said.

"N-n-name th-th-them," the bartender struggled to say, his teeth now chattering.

"First is information," Ilfanti said. "Is what you said true? No ship will take on a dwarf?"

"N-n-no," the bartender said. "One sh-sh-ship may."

"What ship?" Ilfanti pressed, his fingers still waggling with his spell.

"The *Soaring Mist.* It's f-f-full of f-f-freaks like you."

Raising his other hand, Ilfanti waved it and a gust of wind toppled all of the bottles of ale, shattering them as they fell to the ground. "That wasn't very nice," Ilfanti said. "As for the second thing, there are children starving in the streets. You will offer free food and drink to them for the rest of the evening."

"Imp-p-possible!" the man protested. "I w-w-won't do it!"

"Oh really?" Ilfanti asked with a lopsided grin. Raising the hand he just used to send a gust of magical wind, he clutched his fist and it began to glow, emitting a bright illuminating light. "With this spell, I could leave this tavern as little more than a crater in the ground."

All of the patrons that had still been watching the exchange made a desperate dash for the door with the threat. Ilfanti glanced to the door and blinked his eyes. The first person that reached the opening crashed headlong into an invisible barrier as strong as any stone wall.

"Can't have people leaving the party," Ilfanti said. "You have five seconds to make up your mind."

"Do it!" one of the patrons pleaded.

"Don't be a fool!" another protested.

"Fine," the bartender sobbed in defeat. "Fine, just don't do anything else."

Ilfanti stopped waggling his fingers and stood up. His other hand was still glowing, though—the brightness continuing to increase. "In the future, will you serve members of other races?"

The man glared at Ilfanti with pure disdain in his eyes. Ilfanti could see that this man was not going to change his views for anything, much less a threat. "I will serve them," he sneered.

"Excellent," Ilfanti beamed, accepting what he was certain was a lie, as he unclenched his fist and the light vanished. "I'd hate to see you have to go through this again."

"You destroyed my stock!" the man cried. "I'm ruined!"

"Look again," Ilfanti beckoned.

The bartender turned and looked at his shelves behind the bar. All of the bottles remained as they were before Ilfanti's attack. "I don't understand."

"Like I said, I'm not a normal dwarf," Ilfanti claimed. "It's simplicity in itself to project an illusion into your mind. After all, not only am I a Mage, but I am a Council of Elders member."

"Trickery," the man growled derisively.

"Perhaps, but your inventory is fine," Ilfanti shrugged. Closing his eyes, he concentrated for a moment and then smiled. "I have just sent a message to the starving and poor. They will be arriving shortly. If I hear that you went back on your word, I will be back, and next time..."

"I understand," the bartender moaned in frustration.

"I'm glad we understand each other," Ilfanti grinned. "And by the way, thanks for the information on the *Soaring Mist*. I'll go look them up right now."

As he walked outside of the tavern, he had to grin as he saw hundreds of children lining up for food. It looked like he had what it took to help them out after all. He watched as they started inside, and though the bartender was not being very polite, he was handing each of them a plate of food.

Satisfied that his work was done, Ilfanti headed toward the docks. Though the bartender said that the *Soaring Mist* would work with a dwarf, he wondered if it would be capable of handling the demands of the trip he needed to make. The voyage to Egziard was not an easy one—the journey would be long and fraught with peril. Whoever accepted his commission would need to be aware of that and feel that they had a chance for success.

As he reached the docks, he was shocked to see a large gathering milling around a pair of individuals. The group did not seem violent by any means, but he was curious to see what was going on. Grabbing a lamppost, Ilfanti hoisted himself up so that he could peer over the people in the street. Two men, an adlesian and one who looked as if he was a barbarian, were handing out gold coins from several chests.

Ilfanti shrugged at the peculiar scene, but moved on further down the docks. Whoever they were, at least they were helping those less fortunate. Ship after ship was moored to the docks. Ilfanti was impressed by how large and sturdy the vessels looked compared to the one he had used when he first went to Egziard three hundred and fifty years ago. Back then, the ship was lined with one hundred able-bodied men with oars rowing the boat whenever the wind was not strong enough to keep them on course. Now, he saw very few boats with oars.

He spotted a heavily tanned barefoot man who had a scruffy face—as if he had not shaved in several days—and the overall look and feel of a sailor. The man was lying on the dock with one leg dangling over the edge.

"Excuse me, sir," Ilfanti said. "I was hoping you could point me in the direction of the *Soaring Mist.*"

The man looked up, squinting in the glare of the sun over Ilfanti's back. "Everyone knows the *Soaring Mist,*" he said. "What do you want with her?"

"I wish to charter her services," he said.

"My own ship may be available," the sailor said. "Where are you heading?"

"Egziard," Ilfanti replied.

"Egziard?" the man said as he scratched his chin. "That's a bit out of my normal shipping lanes."

"That is why I asked for the *Soaring Mist,*" Ilfanti clarified.

"Sure, sure," the man said. "Just keep going down to the end of the dock. You can't miss her."

"Thank you," Ilfanti said.

He continued down the dock, a little excitement and anticipation in his step. The sailor said that everyone knew of the *Soaring Mist.* That must mean that she was not a small, broken-down wreck that was willing to take on any passenger foolish enough to pay. At least he hoped that was what it meant.

Reaching the end of the dock, the wooden supports went off to the left and he turned. At the very end he paused in admiration. If this was the *Soaring Mist,* it was breathtaking. Never before had he seen such a magnificent ship.

The *Soaring Mist* was larger than any other ship he had passed thus far. It stretched two hundred and twenty-seven feet long and almost forty-five feet wide. A thirty-foot bowsprit extended from the bow of the ship. He easily recognized the finely crafted figurehead in intricate detail of Artriema, a legendary aquatican princess rising from the waves with a trident held forward. If what the bartender said was true, and this ship would accept non-human passengers, Ilfanti felt that the symbol of Artriema was a significant one. She was a young aquatican princess that paved the way to peace with the humans hundreds of years ago, ending a deep-set prejudice and conflict between the two civilizations.

There were three masts towering into the sky, the largest of which, the mainmast, was eighty-five feet tall. The flag of Dartais, the purple flag with a golden border and a scepter in the middle, was flapping in the wind at the top of the mainmast. As he studied the ship in awe, he realized that there would be no substitute for this one. Somehow he needed to convince the Captain of the *Soaring Mist* to take him on his quest. Grinning, he was ready for the challenge of persuading the Captain that Egziard was exactly where the *Soaring Mist* was always meant to go—with him along for the ride, naturally.

CHAPTER 2

Hearing somebody whistling a tune behind him, Ilfanti turned and spotted a most peculiar sight—though he was not one to comment since he was a beardless dwarf. A beardless gnome was skipping along the dock joyously. In addition to having no beard on his face, the gnome was mostly bald, with only a thin strip of gray hair around the back of his scalp. He did, however, have a long gray mustache that hung down from his upper lip to the bottom of his chin.

The gnome, who was no taller than three feet and three inches, was wearing a suit as if he were part of the Dartais nobility. His suit was a shade of pine green and consisted of a double-breasted jacket, a vest, and pants. Beneath his vest he wore a ruffled long-sleeve white shirt with a pine-green bowtie. He also had a plumed green hat with a white feather arching backwards. A black belt, buckled shoes, and white socks completed his wardrobe.

"Well, good day to you, sir," he smiled as he saw Ilfanti.

"Good day to you," Ilfanti replied, offering a grin of his own.

"I couldn't help but notice you admiring my ship," the gnome said.

"Your ship?" Ilfanti asked, taken aback by the statement.

"She's a beauty, isn't she?" the gnome beamed proudly.

"Most definitely," Ilfanti concurred.

"She's the largest, fastest, strongest, and most technologically advanced ship to ever sail the Terran oceans."

Ilfanti liked the description. Very much so. This was indeed exactly what he needed. This gnome also seemed friendly enough. If this truly was his ship, then there should be no trouble chartering the *Soaring Mist*. "Very impressive," Ilfanti said.

"I know," the gnome smiled smugly. "The name's Fasbender."

"Ilfanti," Ilfanti said as he reached out and shook hands with the gnome.

"What brings you to these parts?" Fasbender asked.

"I need to charter a ship," Ilfanti said.

"Destination and cargo?" Fasbender asked.

"The destination is Egziard," Ilfanti indicated. "As for cargo, that would be me alone."

"Egziard is pretty far," Fasbender said as he reached a finger up and twirled his mustache. "We would need additional provisions and have to make at least one stop. Of course, with no cargo but yourself, we would be able to sail faster and also have more hold space for provisions."

Ilfanti listened as the gnome analyzed the situation and began rumbling on with little facts and details. Ilfanti was pleased to hear Fasbender mention several of the perils that the voyage could present to them as well. If the *Soaring Mist* were to agree to take him to Egziard, at least they would do so knowing what to expect.

"We've never been there before," Fasbender added after he finished his analysis. "We can make it, though."

"Great," Ilfanti said. "What do we need to do to get started?"

"Well, first thing's first," Fasbender said, "you need to run this by the Captain."

Ilfanti frowned. He thought that Fasbender was the decision maker for the vessel. Even still, the ship was more than capable of meeting his requirements. "Can I speak to the Captain now?"

"Captain Augustus and the boys are with High Lord Dharien," Fasbender explained. "They are dining."

"I see," Ilfanti said. "Do you know when they shall return?"

"Before the night is done," Fasbender confirmed. "Come, let me show you around. The *Soaring Mist* is truly beautiful."

"You said that she was yours?" Ilfanti asked, trying to gain some insight.

"Oh yes, the Captain, Kemocay and I designed and built her ourselves."

"I see," Ilfanti replied. "Then let the tour begin."

"Splendid," Fasbender beamed. "Right this way. We can begin with the stern!"

"Designer's discretion," Ilfanti said, grinning at how excited and proud Fasbender was.

"When I was working on the designs for her, there was one thing that always bothered me. In both the normal Schooners and the Gallies we had designed for the Imperium, when in a heavy sea, the ships bring up the aft with a tremendous splash that winds up making everything crack both fore and aft when they are trying to move swiftly. That is because the ships have hollow counters and they settle down almost to the taffrails."

"I see," Ilfanti politely said, already lost. Mages had the greatest education in the realm, but he had to admit, something such as the water cracking along the side of a ship's hull was something they had never been taught about. "I presume you managed to overcome this problem?"

"Oh yes," Fasbender nodded triumphantly. "I designed the stern to be semi-elliptical in form with a planksheer molding for its base. The run is very long and clean, but it is much fuller than the bow, and under the stern it is rounded, so that means that it has no hollow counter for the sea to strike against when the ship settles aft."

As Ilfanti's eyes started to gloss over at the technical details, Fasbender began chuckling with delight as if his design schematics had been ingenious.

"You see, the *Soaring Mist* will move far more easily in a heavy sea. When she is going at her highest speed, the after-vacuum in the water will be filled by the run so as to enable her to sail upon the same lines forward and aft. Basically, I made the design to eliminate the defects of the other ships, like Schooners and Gallies, making her faster and more maneuverable."

"A grand accomplishment," Ilfanti said. "You must be very proud."

"Oh yes," Fasbender said, blushing slightly. "She is my pride and joy."

"I can see that," Ilfanti nodded.

"Now, I had another problem to overcome. What material do I use for the boat? So many choices! I wanted something that was sturdy and could survive the rigorous demands of our task, but also something that would not slow down our acceleration."

"Very astute concern. Most people fail to explore the little nuances that could impact the final outcome."

"Precisely!" Fasbender cheered. "So I decided not to use just one material, but two! I used a white oak for the keel, and a hard pine for the rest of the ship. I thought that..."

"Fasbender, I was asked to find you," a woman called from the deck above.

"What is it, Palisha?" Fasbender yelled back loud enough for her to hear.

"They need you in the engine room," she said.

Fasbender bit his lip. "Yes, yes, very well. It looks like we'll have to delay this tour, and I was so looking forward to showing you all of the intricate details that I had designed and explaining why."

"That's all right," Ilfanti said. "If your crew needs you, the ship must come first."

"Of course, of course," Fasbender said. "Well, might as well come on board. Perhaps Palisha can continue the tour."

"I'd like that," Ilfanti said. "Lead the way."

Fasbender led them over to a boarding ramp and onto the second level of the ship, which was only a slight incline from the dock. Palisha stepped down a flight of stairs and smiled warmly to meet their guest. "Can you show him around?"

"I'd be delighted to," Palisha replied pleasantly.

If this day was one for surprises, Ilfanti had to admit that he was a little shocked by the appearance of Palisha. It was not her looks, for she was five feet and ten inches with long blonde hair flowing freely. Hey eyes were a light grayish-blue that sparkled beneath her apparent bright personality. Her smile was warm and endearing. The thing he found odd was not how she looked or acted, but how she was dressed.

Palisha was wearing a tight fitting leopard skin top that covered her arms completely but had a v-section down the middle from her neck to her bellybutton. The shorts she was wearing were a light brown deer-skin, leaving her legs and feet bare. Upon her right ankle, she had a small anklet that was wound with several ropes and contained a variety of small stones, gems, and beads. Three strands of the rope with two gems attached to each trailed down her foot toward her toes.

"Well Ilfanti, we shall talk more later," Fasbender said. "I must change now and get down to the engine room."

"Until then," Ilfanti said pleasantly. After he was certain that Fasbender was gone, he glanced at Palisha and let out a sigh of relief. He looked forward to a tour and seeing more of the ship, but identifying the type of wood used and why was a bit more thorough an explanation than he really desired.

"I figured that you would need a way out of that discussion," she said. "I'm Palisha."

"Ilfanti," Ilfanti introduced, "and thank you."

"You're welcome," she said. "Are you looking to charter the ship?"

"Yes," Ilfanti replied. "I am on a vital quest to Egziard."

"Vital?" Palisha repeated with her head bowed to look him more closely in the eyes.

"There is a mystical artifact there that can help us to determine the true whereabouts of the Empress," Ilfanti explained.

"I see," she said as she tensed a bit.

"What's wrong?" Ilfanti asked, observing her body language.

"Will this quest be dangerous?"

"There are potential perils in every quest, but most of them will be after I arrive at Egziard. At least, that is what I believe. The last time I sailed there, I found a route that avoided some pretty nasty waters. Of course, it has been quite some time since I have been there, and the voyage may present some obstacles today that never troubled me in the past," explained Ilfanti. "I do not think you would need to worry about your safety, though I of course can not guarantee anything."

"Oh, it's not my safety I'm concerned with," Palisha sighed.

"No?" Ilfanti asked, hoping for clarification.

"It's my husband, Brondolfr," she said. "I'm afraid that the potential for a vital quest full of danger and peril will be quite alluring for him."

"And you think he would be hurt?" Ilfanti asked.

"No, I know better," Palisha laughed. "It's just that we had been discussing starting a family of our own. We agreed that we would begin trying after we arrived back here and had some time off. Now, with a vital quest, he'll want to push that off again."

"I am sorry," Ilfanti said. "Family is very important."

"Do you have any children?"

Ilfanti glanced down, a brief moment of regret. "No, I serve on the Council of Elders at the Mage's Council and fear that I have missed my opportunity to have a family of my own."

"Now I am the one that is sorry," Palisha said.

"No need," Ilfanti brushed off the sympathy. "I have led a full and exciting life, I assure you. I would not trade in a moment of it. Besides, in a way, all of the Mages I have trained and guided over the years are like children."

"Well, in that case, how about something to eat?" Palisha asked, still looking sorry for him even though he did not want her sympathy. "I myself am famished."

"That sounds wonderful," Ilfanti grinned. He paused as he saw a pair of adlesians walking past him and up to the top deck. "Forgive me for my nosiness, but Fasbender is a gnome, those were adlesians, and your husband, with the name Brondolfr, sounds as if he is a barbarian. This ship seems quite willing to accept various races without scorn or prejudice."

"That is true," Palisha confirmed. "We also have an aquatican and a pair of both aezians and rasplers on board."

"Amazing," Ilfanti said. "Empress Karleena had come to us to request assistance in uniting the races. I myself supported her, but many of the Council members felt that trying to reunite the races was an attempt at lunacy. Seeing it be successful here warms my heart."

"This crew has been through a lot together. I assure you, we do not look at each other with hidden attitudes or perspectives. Here, we all work together for the good of the ship. In fact, many of us consider each other to be part of our family. Very similar to how you see those you've trained and worked with."

Ilfanti nodded, grinning widely. Perhaps one day the entire realm could be as reasonably minded as those that served aboard this ship. Remembering the barbarian and adlesian he saw dispensing gold, he snickered to himself.

"What is it?" Palisha asked.

"By any chance, is your husband about six foot eleven with long, silky black hair?"

"Yes," Palisha said with an impressed look on her face. "How did you know that?"

"I saw a barbarian and an adlesian handing out gold to the masses," Ilfanti explained.

"Yes," Palisha smiled fondly. "The Captain has a decree that we will destroy any pirate ship we find. If we gain their loot, the money will first be used to pay for any repairs to the ship, and then all excess will be donated to those in need."

"Very admirable," Ilfanti said, growing more and more impressed with Captain Augustus and the crew of the *Soaring Mist.*

Palisha led him up to the top deck and then back to the after cabin. There, Ilfanti could spot several large and luxurious staterooms. The size and plush furniture was far superior to even some of the accomodations that a noble would be accustomed to. The hallway led directly into the dining saloon.

Ilfanti paused in the doorway and glanced around. The entire room—which stretched close to fifty feet long and fifteen feet wide—was wainscotted with mahogany and painted a pure white, like enamel. The saloon was also tastefully designed with floral gilded moldings. A large rectangular mahogany table stretched the length of the room. One woman was sitting there, eating soup, and her eyes watching him unblinkingly.

She was one of the aezians with pure white skin, silken black hair and a mixture of confident and charming features about her disposition. Even sitting and eating, she was heavily garbed in what he assumed were her family colors and markings. She had armored shoulder pads that were painted green with a design that resembled the flames of a dragon, with a long green cape fastened to it. Identical armored protectors were on her upper arms with green vambraces that had the image of a golden dragon upon each of them. Upon her chest was a golden breastplate with two dragons of intricately crafted design facing each other. Her belt had a buckle in the shape of a dragon's head with its mouth open. It secured a green cloth with golden dragon's flames that was clasped to her breastplate and hung down between her legs. A pair of greaves with identical designs as her vambraces encircled her lower legs, and she had armored boots. Underneath her armor she was adorned in a thick white shirt and pants.

On the table next to her soup was the helmet of an aezian noble. The front portrayed a golden dragon with its wings spread atop of a green armored helm. Golden flames streaked down the back and around the sides of the helmet and led to white tassels that dangled from the ends of each side.

"Good day," Ilfanti greeted the aezian.

The woman did not remove her eyes from him, nor did she say a word. Slowly she raised the spoon to her lips and slurped another mouthful of soup.

"This is Shimada," Palisha introduced. "Shimada, this is Ilfanti, he is looking to charter our ship."

Shimada flicked her glance to Palisha and then stood up. Placing her helmet on her head, she picked up a tray with soup and a sandwich on it. "I must bring this to Grandfather."

"Wish Jin Fe well for me," Palisha smiled.

"I shall do so," Shimada bowed before she turned and left.

"Was it something I said?" Ilfanti asked.

"No," Palisha replied. "Shimada was betrayed when she was younger. With the exception of herself and her grandfather, her entire family was slain while they were under the banner of truce. Ever since, she has been very reluctant to trust anyone."

"Does she trust you?" Ilfanti asked.

"Yes," Palisha nodded. "I am sure she will come to trust you in time as well. She will watch you like a hawk for any sign of deception and will also make you prove your trustworthiness by your actions first, though."

"Sounds like I have to be on my best behavior," Ilfanti shrugged.

"It is not as bad as it sounds. Once you have earned her trust, she will go to the ends of Terra and back for you."

"I'll have to keep that in mind," Ilfanti said. "Now, didn't you say something about food?"

❀ ❀ ❀ ❀ ❀

Several hours and many stories later, Palisha and Ilfanti began to hear voices from beyond the dining saloon. Palisha closed her eyes to concentrate on listening, and then smiled pleasantly. "They're back."

"Shall we go and make my introduction?" Ilfanti asked.

"But of course," Palisha said. "Come on."

Palisha led him to the main deck where Ilfanti watched her run and jump into the arms of the barbarian he had seen on the street giving away gold. Like Palisha, he was wearing deer hide pants, but he also had boots and a sapphire blue sash trimmed with a golden fringe on both ends wrapped around his waist. He had no shirt on, revealing his extraordinarily muscular physique. A single leather strap crossed his chest and fastened his battleaxe along his back. He also had a golden bracer on each arm and a sapphire blue bandana wrapped around his head, his silken black hair flowing from beneath it. As he spun Palisha around in a giant bear hug, Ilfanti also spotted a pair of daggers that were sheathed into the back of his sash.

"Palisha, my love," he practically sang as he greeted her.

"Brondolfr, my heart," she returned.

The adlesian walked up beside them and raised his chin with a silent question as to who the dwarf was. He was almost as tall as Brondolfr, standing at six feet and eight inches, and though he did not appear nearly as bulky and muscular he was still quite an intimidating individual. His hair was black and closely cropped to his head. His eyes, like those of all adlesians, were a vibrant red. As he stared at Ilfanti a red mist smoked from them.

He was wearing a long-sleeve black shirt, pants, boots, and bandana. The only hints of color in his ensemble were his light brown vest and matching gloves. He had a cutlass sheathed at his waist, and a bow and arrows strung across his back.

"Kemocay, Brondolfr, let me introduce you to Ilfanti," Palisha said. "He is looking to secure passage to Egziard."

"Egziard is pretty far," Kemocay said in a deep baritone voice. "Why do you need to go there?"

"I am on a quest," Ilfanti replied.

"Will it endanger the crew?" Kemocay pressed.

"I hope not," Ilfanti said. "But I can not be certain."

"At least you are not making false promises," Kemocay replied, the mist rising from his eyes ceasing, satisfied by the answer.

A woman stepped forward and pushed the adlesian and barbarian apart. Two rasplers stood behind her and peered down at Ilfanti. The woman had an air of authority and the hardened features of one who has experienced a lot in her life. She stood at five feet eight and looked as if she weighed about one hundred and fifty pounds. Her hair was a vibrant fiery red that hung in curls down to the mid-section of her back. Like Kemocay, she was wearing black pants and shirt, but she had a light gray vest and knee-high gray boots. She also was wearing a black naval officer's jacket with gray shoulder pads and a gray belt clasped at her waist. She too had a cutlass clasped to her belt and a pair of daggers sheathed along her back.

"I am Captain Augustus," she introduced. "This is my ship."

"You're the Captain?" Ilfanti asked, his jaw dropping open in shock.

"Do you have a problem with that?" Augustus challenged.

"I'm sorry, I always heard that women and the sea were taboo," Ilfanti shrugged. "I guess I was just expecting a male Captain."

"And here I was expecting a dwarf with a beard," Augustus retorted. "Things are not always as anticipated."

"I agree completely," Ilfanti said.

"So you wish to secure passage to Egziard, is that right?" Augustus asked.

"I do," Ilfanti confirmed.

"That is a long way to go," Augustus pondered. "How do you plan on financing the expedition?"

Ilfanti opened his Mage's satchel, reaching in and thinking of one of his prized items from a former quest—the Jewel of Amara. The jewel materialized in his hand and he pulled it out of the satchel—the diamond was so large that he had to hold it in both hands to present it properly—holding it out for the Captain to see. "With this."

Augustus nodded. "That will do," she said. "It is late now, though. We will discuss specifics in the morning."

"As you wish," Ilfanti said, grateful that the Captain seemed open to taking him to his destination.

"Beige," she called out.

One of the rasplers stepped forward. His reptilian hide was almost beige in color, which undoubtedly was the origin of his name. "Yesss, mother?"

Ilfanti's eyebrow lifted at the greeting: *Mother?*

"Please show Ilfanti to one of our staterooms," she instructed.

"Yesss, mother," Beige replied.

"Beige is our Quartermaster and will see to your every need while on this journey," Augustus explained. "Until morning."

"Until then," Ilfanti bowed.

"Come thisss way," Beige prompted.

Ilfanti followed the raspler to his stateroom. If nothing else, this would be a most memorable journey. It was already becoming a fascinating story.

CHAPTER 3

The dead of the night was dark and silent. Not a sound could be heard in the small harbor town of Brigdin, but the town was very much alive with activity. The predators were about, watching closely and listening for any indication that they would find unsuspecting prey that night.

Brigdin was a town that would not be found on any map. It was a murky desolate location that attracted citizens who were either less than reputable or too poverty-stricken to find a way out of their personal torment.

The rules of Brigdin were simple—anything goes as long as it did not interfere with lining the overseer's pockets with gold. The overseer was the only man in the entire town who appeared to maintain some station of stability. All shopkeepers, merchants, tavern owners, and the shipyard workers paid a substantial percentage of any proceeds they earned in their trade. A private army of ruffians was employed by the overseer to insure compliance by the businesses, and as a marshalling unit if a visitor disrupted the flow of money.

Of course, that did not deter murder, thievery, bar fights, and numerous other ways that the citizens exploited each other. In fact, the enforcers would turn a blind eye to such activities as long as they did not drive business away. As the rules said: anything goes in Brigdin.

It was a town that Kabilian could understand. Most of his life he had existed beneath the eyes of the law. Though he would never reveal his true age—and with the Ring of Eternity on his finger it was impossible to guess—he had always taken great pleasure in finding ways around the law. Not only did he consider himself an assassin extraordinaire, but also an adventurer who liked to live his life on the edge.

Yes, he could understand Brigdin. He even knew that as soon as he and his hobgoblin companion—Crick—entered the town, the predators would emerge from their lairs and try to overwhelm them. He was a newcomer, and one dressed in garb far more exquisite than anything these street dwellers would ever hope to wear. Of course, Crick's full suit of illistrium armor was worth more than this entire town could ever hope to make in a century. Oh yes, the predators would emerge. They would emerge and learn to fear the shadows all the more.

"Are you sure we have to do this?" Crick asked, for the hundredth time since Kabilian had made his decision.

"Yes," Kabilian replied, his attention still on the darkness of the alleyways where eyes were following their every move.

"But why?" Crick asked. "We're free now."

"Free indeed," Kabilian snorted. "But not free of destiny."

Until recently, Kabilian had sworn allegiance to Lady Salaman and the Hidden Empire. The criminal organization had been destroyed, at least for a while, by a group of adventurers who had caught Kabilian's eye more than once over the past few months. Without Lady Salaman's instructions, the two companions were free to do what they wished, until a mysterious creature by the name of Archer appeared and told them that they had a role to play in the changes of the realm. Kabilian despised thinking that his future was already written for him, and hated that he was unaware of this destiny even more.

"There are no mystral in Egziard," Crick whined. "I want to go back to Dragon's Myst."

For any other creature of the realm, especially other hobgoblins, Dragon's Myst—the home of the legendary mystral—would be the last place they wanted to go. The mystral, since abandoning their precepts of safeguarding the realm with their dragon companions, had chosen a life of solitude and isolation. Kabilian did not know of any other who even knew where the location of Dragon's Myst was, but his companion had seen it firsthand when a small group of mystral slaughtered a hunting party of hobgoblins that had dared to venture too close to their home. Crick had been oddly fixated on the maiden warriors ever since, desiring to acquire their weapons and learn more about them.

"Soon," Kabilian said. "For now, there is something overseas we need. After we have that, we'll return and kill the first mystral we find."

Crick's eyes narrowed into slits as he turned and grabbed Kabilian by the collar of his deep brown brigandine and lifted him up. "No killing mystral!"

"A slip of the tongue," Kabilian shrugged. "Better than a slip of a knife."

"No killing," Crick repeated forcefully. "Only take their weapons."

"Can we kill *them*?" Kabilian asked.

"Who?" Crick asked as he followed his partner's gaze. The hobgoblin's eyes widened immediately as he saw half a dozen mud-encrusted people emerging from the shadows and walking toward them. Their clothing was in tatters, and their weapons—if you could even call them weapons—appeared to be little more than splintered wood and the legs of bar stools.

"Are you going to let me down?" Kabilian asked.

Crick dropped him and turned to face the oncoming men. Their eyes were ravenous as they approached. To him, they appeared even worse off than the hobgoblin tribe he had been aligned with before becoming Kabilian's traveling companion. These men were pathetic.

"Gentlemen," Kabilian said with a wry smile as he stepped forward, no weapons or signs of defense apparent. "I am hoping to charter a ship. Could you please point me in the direction of the docks?"

"All you found was trouble," one of the men sneered back. "We'll be taking those fancy clothes and armor."

"And those daggers," another added in, pointing toward the two jewel-hilted daggers sheathed in Kabilian's belt.

"Now that's not very hospitable of you," Kabilian frowned. "We'll find the docks on our own. Thanks anyway."

"I don't think you heard me!" the first man shouted angrily.

Kabilian flicked his wrist, releasing a drug-tipped arrow from one of his mystical bracers. The small dart impacted the man in the throat. As it did so, his eyes widened, his body began convulsing, and then he dropped to the ground.

"I heard you just fine," Kabilian said calmly and coolly.

"There are only two of them!"

"Get them!"

"If you insist," Kabilian grinned as he flicked both of his wrists two more times. The small darts hit four more of the men with the same deadly accuracy and with the same results as the first man.

The last man standing glanced back and forth at his companions and timidly began to back away. He dropped the wooden stool leg and raised his hands pleadingly.

"You liked my daggers?" Kabilian asked as he stepped forward. "Let me give you a better look at them."

"No," the man cried. "Please."

"You must learn not to challenge those who are superior to you," Kabilian said as his eyes narrowed at the man. Twirling his two daggers, he whispered a short incantation and the blades mystically grew into full-length swords.

"May the gods have mercy," the man prayed.

"They better, for I certainly won't," Kabilian said as he slashed both swords down, cleaving a cross in the man's chest. The assassin looked at the tips of his swords and scowled. "Their clothing disgusts me. If I tried to clean the blood off on those, they would get even dirtier."

Crick reached out and grabbed Kabilian by the collar again, lifting him up and bringing their faces close together. "No killing mystral."

"Fine, fine," Kabilian agreed. "I didn't know you felt so strongly about it."

Satisfied, the hobgoblin let Kabilian down. The assassin shrank his two weapons back down to their dagger size, wiped them off on his pants and scowled at the potential stain as he sheathed them.

As Crick turned to look around, Kabilian studied him from behind. With a few rare exceptions—like when he fought alongside King Worren in the Troll Wars, or worked for Lady Salaman in the Hidden Empire—he had been a loner for millennia. His had been a solitude and loneliness that he thought had finally come to an end the day he found Crick, a creature who seemed to have a similar affinity for collecting rare artifacts. For Kabilian, it had always been mystical and enchanted items. For Crick, it was mystral armaments. He thought that it was a good pairing, but if Crick continued to assert himself in such a way,

Kabilian feared that his newfound partnership might come to an end as one of his blades slit the hobgoblin's throat. He hoped that it would not have to come to that.

Further into the town, a board creaked. Kabilian tensed and peered into the darkness, immediately alert and leaving his thoughts of Crick's eventual demise behind. He could not see anything. Fortunately, for a collector like him, that was not a problem. Reaching into his Mage satchel—a gift from a Mage he had met during his youth—he removed a wooden mask that had two glossy red eyes, white paint displaying a mouth with fangs, and vines with thorns protruding from them coming from its head like hair.

As he placed the mask over his face, the wood blended into his features and became darkened brown skin. His hair was as thorny as the vines that were hanging from the mask. His mouth hissed with large fangs. The feature he was after was the glossy red eyes, which allowed him to see as clearly at night as if the sun was shining. Though the effect made the entire environment a light red hue, all warm-blooded creatures and heat sources were easily uncovered and outlined with a glowing yellow radiance.

"What is it?" Crick asked.

"Shh," Kabilian exclaimed as he placed a single finger in front of his fanged mouth. He could see a figure clearly. A woman. Though she was dressed differently than the last time he had seen her, and the effects of the mask slightly distorted her features, who she was was unmistakable.

He had first seen the handmaiden in Trespias. He was there to deliver a message to Winton for Lady Salaman. What he stumbled across infuriated him. Though he may be an assassin and his ethical values were often questionable, certain boundaries were never to be crossed. One such boundary Winton had ignored with the handmaiden, Shiel. It was a violation that Kabilian had made certain that Winton would regret.

Seeing Shiel again was a bit of a shock. He did not know why she was here, of all places. Even if she had left the palace to escape the whims of the new Emperor, certainly one such as she would find a place other than Brigdin. Even her wardrobe was out of place. She had on a long single-piece gown with a shawl over her shoulders. A finely crafted necklace hung around her bare throat. Though she had a sword and a dagger strapped to her waist, Kabilian was shocked that she would come here—especially dressed like that. It was as if she was looking for trouble.

"What is it?" Crick asked again.

Kabilian watched as Shiel moved along the side of a tavern and glanced out toward the overseer's house. What was she doing? Was she planning on robbing the overseer? Or worse, trying to be an assassin like him? The possibility left him cold and somber.

Three other glowing yellow figures came into view. They were following Shiel, moving slowly behind her. Whatever she was doing here, he was not about to let her be attacked from behind. Reaching into his satchel, he pulled the scepter Inferno out, and then dropped it back in with a frown. He would prefer the flame powers, but to do so would decrease the effectiveness of his mask. Instead, he settled for Blizzard, his only other scepter.

"What is it?" Crick asked impatiently again, straining to see in the darkness.

"Remain here," Kabilian ordered.

"But-"

"No buts," Kabilian said. "Stay here."

The three men moved closer to Shiel. He watched as she turned and saw them. The games were over. The men lunged for her and managed to reach her as she was fumbling with her sword.

Kabilian ran toward them. As he approached, he raised his highly ornamented silver scepter—the scepter was crafted to resemble the effect of ice as it wrapped around a diamond tip—and unleashed a succession of jagged ice shards at the attackers.

One man spun around with a rather large icicle jutting out of his eyesocket. He dropped to the ground dead before his two companions could even react. The shards continued to burst from the scepter, pelting one of the men in his back and chest. He too dropped to the ground, blood oozing from his frosted wounds.

The third man was the one who had physically pinned Shiel down. Kabilian dropped the scepter back into the mystical satchel and unsheathed Pandring, his Xylona honor blade. "Try picking on someone who can fight back."

The man grabbed Shiel's sword, which resembled a mystral drantana but lacked the markings and craftsmanship of the maiden warriors. He charged Kabilian and swung the sword down at the assassin's shoulder. Kabilian easily deflected the blow and rammed his knee up into the man's groin.

The man stumbled backwards coughing and moaning. His face was turning red and his sword fell as both hands dropped between his legs. Kabilian twirled his blade and then slashed it straight across the man's neck, severing his head.

Bending down, he picked up the modified drantana and held it, hilt-first, to Shiel. "I believe this is yours?"

Shiel stared at him as if studying him. "What are you?" she asked, her features a blend of gratitude and terror.

"What?" Kabilian asked, almost forgetting about his mask. "Oh, the mask." He then pulled it from his face revealing his true features.

"I recognized the voice," Shiel said. "You're the one who stopped Winton when he was raping me."

"Guilty as charged," Kabilian said.

"Who are you?" Shiel asked.

"A friend," Kabilian replied. "I do not like to see women being taken advantage of."

"Does this friend have a name?" Shiel pressed.

Kabilian leaned over and bowed with a wave of his hand. "My name is Kabilian."

"Thank you, Kabilian," Shiel said. "For then, and for now."

"You should not be in Brigdin," Kabilian said. "It is dangerous for a lady to be alone."

"Who said I was alone?" Shiel asked with a wry grin.

Kabilian felt the tip of a sword on the back of his neck and closed his eyes in disbelief. How long had it been since someone had managed to sneak up on him? Five hundred years? Six hundred, maybe?

"Well, well, well," a female voice said from behind him. "Is he for me?"

"No," Shiel said. "He just saved me."

"Shame," the voice said. "He's kind of cute."

Kabilian felt the sword lower from his neck and turned around to see a very attractive woman in an extremely enticing outfit. "Perhaps I'll let you play with me a bit," he grinned seductively.

"As if, big boy," the woman replied.

"Angel, this is Kabilian. Kabilian, Angel," Shiel introduced.

"A pleasure," Angel said.

"The pleasure is all mine," Kabilian bowed a second time. "To think, I thought that I was here merely to charter a boat, and instead I find two of the loveliest women I have ever met."

"Charmer," Angel said. Turning to face Shiel, she raised an eyebrow.

"No," Shiel said. "We can still do it."

"Good," Angel replied. "Nice meeting you, Kabilian, but we have business to attend to."

"As do I, I assure you," Kabilian said.

"Thank you again," Shiel said. "You're like my own personal guardian angel."

"I'm afraid I cannot always be there for you," Kabilian said. "But if I am, my sword is in your service."

"We've got to go," Angel said a little more sternly. "No offense, Cabbie."

"Cabbie?" Kabilian asked with an eyebrow raised.

"She does that to most people," Shiel said with a shrug.

"Cabbie," Kabilian said again and shrugged himself. "Good luck, ladies."

He was not certain why they were there, but he placed his mask back on to watch them. They both crept to the overseer's house, and then around the back. They stopped and began to work on something on the ground. Kabilian could not make out what it was from his vantage point, but he did see several sparks flying as they hit something with the pommels of their swords.

The two then backed up and lifted a large barred door. Kabilian thought that he understood. The overseer had captured someone they knew, and they were here to rescue them. That made much more sense than them being thieves or assassins. He watched as they both helped pull a third woman out from the ground. Satisfied by his observations, he removed his mask and returned to where he had left Crick— who was sitting on the ground and scowling.

"What is wrong, my friend?" Kabilian asked.

"You don't trust me," he whined.

"What gives you that idea?" Kabilian asked, his mind drifting back to the thoughts he had of the possibility of killing Crick one day. If Crick had picked up on that, he was quite intuitive. Kabilian would have to guard his thoughts and demeanor much more closely.

"You left me behind again," Crick complained. "I could have helped."

"Which is precisely why I am taking you with me to Egziard," Kabilian grinned, grateful that Crick was unaware of the doubts he had been having. "Come, we must find a ship and a Captain willing to take us."

The two made their way to the docks and woke the harbormaster. He indicated a smaller ship that was the sturdiest in the harbor, and said that if any of the currently moored vessels could make the trip, it was that one. Kabilian woke up the Captain and convinced him that the trip would be most profitable.

As the morning sun pierced the horizon, Kabilian and Crick were preparing to set sail. Neither knew how long they would be gone, nor whether they would even find what they were looking for. But that was all part of the adventure.

❁ ❁ ❁ ❁ ❁

Unnoticed by Kabilian and Crick, a pair of glimmering yellow eyes watched them sail away from Brigdin. Rhyne's true features were hidden in the shadows and darkness of the black cloak he wore, but the wraith was not one to remain in the shadows for long.

He had found them weeks ago in Tenalong and had been following them ever since, studying them and their relationship with each other. The fight with the street rats was not very revealing, but he had noted the mystical weapons that Kabilian kept relying upon.

After Kabilian's ship vanished on the horizon, Rhyne visited the harbormaster. The man was quite willing to talk as soon as the wraith pinned him to the wall with small needles that dug through each of his fingers. The blades would not do permanent damage, but the gratifying part of Rhyne's job was terrorizing those who had information and using their greatest fears to make them talk.

The harbormaster told him all that he needed to know. Kabilian and Crick had secured passage to Egziard, a treacherous desert terrain. Rhyne smiled at the news, revealing his fanged mouth. He had never been to Egziard before, but with the bounty that Lady Salaman had put on Kabilian's head, he would follow the assassin into the depths of Tanorus itself if need be. The hunt was on.

ILFANTI'S LOG

Time just seems to be flying by. It seemed like just yesterday I was sitting in the Mage's Council talking to Cala, Herg, Askari, Cicero, and Centain about what we needed to do to help find and save the Empress. I had Askari and Cicero disobey Pierce's orders and go to Aquatica where Askari's sister reigns. Captain Centain I told to go to Faylinn, home of the Elandeeril, and though he doesn't openly admit it, the home of his great-grandmother. I stand by those decisions. The Imperium is at war, even if very few people would agree with that assessment.

For what else could you call this direct attack to our realm? What else could it be when the Empress was kidnapped; a King was murdered; the army's Warlord was hunted down and slain; the navy's Admiral was lost at sea and presumed dead himself; Xylona and Vorstad had both fallen under siege and been decimated; armies positioned themselves throughout the realm; and a massive fleet had moved into the harbor? Yes, we are definitely at war.

Everything seems to hinge on the return of the Empress. Such a young girl with so much riding on her shoulders. Her return would signal the return of the Imperial armies sent to Aezia, as well as the resurrection of the unification talks. I think both of those endeavors need to be successful for us to survive this plague of darkness that is sweeping the land.

Of course, my role is crucial. That knowledge is particularly damning when I watch the sun come and go every day. It took me over a fortnight just to arrive in Water Haven from Trespias, and it has already been another week since I arrived. I must be patient though. Captain Augustus is right. We need the proper supplies to successfully complete the voyage to Egziard, and unfortunately, acquiring what we need has been an excruciatingly slow endeavor.

The preparations are sound ones, though. We have been contracting with all of the blacksmiths and weapon makers of Water Haven. They have been working non-stop on large wooden arrows with metal tips that are ten feet long at least; large hollow iron balls for the cata-pults; and a variety of other weapons that Kemocay has requested. We also picked up large deposits of an ore known as coal. Fasbender ex-plained the whole thing to me and gave me a five-hour tour of his in-ventions. The experience was draining, but I must say, the gnome knows his business. Not only is this a magnificent ship, it also has en-gines! No wind? No problem for the Soaring Mist! That's something that will come in quite handy when we're in the Vast Expanse.

It is not only Fasbender and Kemocay; I am very impressed with the Captain and her entire crew. I have had this entire week to observe them, talk to them, and see them going about their business. On board the ship, while working, the crew is highly efficient and competent. When they are not working, they are laughing, joking and having a good time. They may be the officers and crew of a ship, but their inter-personal relationships seem so closely knit together that I could easily mistake them all for members of the same family. That is, if I didn't look at the fact that they all come from such different and diverse spe-cies.

I still can't get over how Beige and Green call Captain Augustus "mother." The way she treats them when not working, perhaps I shouldn't be surprised at all. For a hardened woman who clearly has some skeletons or demons in her cabin, she is very maternal and loving to the two boys.

What I find even more surprising, and I must say, inspiring, is the way the crew is treated around town. From the day I first arrived here, people seemed to discriminate against me for being a dwarf. It is some-thing I have come to expect here in the Seven Kingdoms, and some-thing that I think could be this realm's downfall. But here, with this crew, all I see in the faces and actions of the people of Water Haven is respect and admiration. No matter how hard I studied the crowd, I could not spot a single sneer or look of disgust. Perhaps there is hope for the realm yet. That is why the Empress's return is pivotal: she is looking to make what I have observed in this town with this crew a real-ity for the entire realm!

It is late now and the sun has gone down long ago. I haven't written in this journal since I first left the Tower, so I wanted to take the opportunity before we set off for the open sea. Captain Augustus informed me tonight that we would be setting sail at first light tomorrow. The morning can not come soon enough for me.

The rest of the officers and crew are scattered, doing their own last-minute preparations before setting sail in the morning. Captain Augustus and the two rasplers are visiting High Lord Dharien again. When they left this time, they were dressed formally, as if attending a ball. Never in my wildest dreams did I ever think I would see a pair of rasplers dressed in the fashionable evening attire of nobles! Fasbender seems to be of the impression that the High Lord fancies Captain Augustus. Good for them.

Palisha and Brondolfr both went out as well. I am not certain where they are going, but Palisha had packed a basket of food and they walked away arm in arm. Since Palisha does not have a formal role on the ship, I have been able to spend the most time with her this week. It warms my heart at how happy the two of them are. I hope that she can soon have the child she craves and not have their family's happiness tainted by the schemes of Zoldex. She's just one more reason I am determined to find the Empress and make certain Zoldex fails in his machinations.

The First Officer of the ship and I have been spending a lot of time together lately. I did not meet him until my third day on the ship, but was pleasantly surprised when I did. Though I had not previously met him, he is a Paladin from the Mage's Council. Krimdor, an aquatican.

Krimdor told me all about his paladinship so far. After leaving the Mage's Council, he met the elves of Wild Wood, an interesting experience in itself! Then he moved on to Tregador where he spent some time with the dwarves. A short time later, he moved north where he met Brondolfr on his way to seek Palisha's hand in marriage. The two teamed up and journeyed together.

The story he told was quite intriguing and entertaining, though he has a lot to learn about telling stories before he could even hope to rival some of the tales I have woven over the years. Along the way, they faced a cyclops and almost lost their lives, but they thwarted the giant's plan to raid a passing caravan. When they arrived in Karsinport, the two separated, but Krimdor soon found his barbarian friend on trial for his life. Allegedly, Brondolfr had not sought permission to marry Palisha; instead he tried to kidnap her. Of course, that wasn't true, but the barbarian's life almost ended nonetheless.

Krimdor told me that he was pondering how he could best rescue Brondolfr when Captain Augustus appeared and offered to purchase the barbarian as a slave for her ship. She kept raising the offer until the magistrate finally sold him to her. After that, she set Brondolfr free and offered him a place on her crew if he desired. He agreed as long as Palisha would also be welcome, and the Captain accepted his terms.

Krimdor said that he was so taken by the exchange that he too offered his services to Captain Augustus. He told me that in the sixteen years since joining her, he has not once regretted the decision. Like I said, this group is close like a family, not a normal hierarchy of officers and crew.

Tomorrow they will be put to the test. Well, not tomorrow per se, but over the next few months. Green plotted the course to Egziard and we will be coming awfully close to the Island of No Return, a known haven for pirates. That would be bad enough, but with the Soaring Mist's fame for hunting down pirate ships, we all expect to be targeted as we continue through their waters. To avoid the Island of No Return, though, would add an extra month to the voyage, so we will risk the attacks.

I am confident that whether it be pirate, sea creature, storm, or even the sun baking down on us, this crew will find a way to persevere. I was quite fortunate to find them. I hope that when this is over, I will be able to count all of the Soaring Mist officers and crew amongst my friends, even Shimada who still stares at me as if she is trying to decide whether to slit my throat or not.

Giggling. I hear giggling. Brondolfr and Palisha are back. It is getting late, too late to continue writing. Though I am too excited to sleep, I must try to get some rest. This will be a long voyage wrought with untold dangers and unexpected twists and turns. I can't wait.

CHAPTER 4

Morning could not have come soon enough. Ilfanti slid his legs over the bed and dropped to his feet. Today was the day their journey truly began. He could hear voices on deck and knew that the ship was already bustling with activity.

Stepping over to the mirror, the dwarf rubbed his fingers over his chin. His face was a bit rough, but it was nothing that he couldn't handle. He placed both hands over his chin and the side of his face. He felt them gradually begin to warm and his face began crackling beneath his grip as he magically incinerated the growth. After several moments, he rubbed his hands over his upper lip and also anywhere he had hair growing that he did not want.

Glancing into the mirror to check how he had done, he turned his head from one side to the other. His face was perfectly shaven. He put some water from the basin in his hands and splashed it over his face. The sensation was soothing and cool. He did not like to use his magic to do such small mundane things like shaving, but he wanted to be above deck as soon as possible to watch the ship set off.

After relieving himself, Ilfanti returned to the bed and pulled his pants on. Sucking in his stomach, he fastened the belt with a grimace, they were still a little too small, but the strain was not as bad as it had been a few weeks earlier. He put his vest on and began to button the links on the front when someone knocked on the door to his cabin.

"Come in," he called out as he clasped the last button.

Palisha opened the door and peeked her head in. "I'm not disturbing you, am I?"

"Not at all," Ilfanti smiled pleasantly. "It sounds like the whole ship is already awake."

"The Captain wanted to get off to an early start before the channel starts to get crowded."

"A wise precaution," Ilfanti nodded his approval.

"Would you care to join me for breakfast?" Palisha asked.

"I would really like to observe us getting under way," Ilfanti said.

"You wouldn't miss much," Palisha shrugged. "Right now, Brondolfr is in a dinghy with six adlesians. They are strung to the stem and will lead us out of the harbor."

"They're rowing?" Ilfanti laughed. "I thought we had engines?"

"We do," Palisha confirmed. "The Captain doesn't like to use them this close to a harbor. It's sort of like our personal little secret and advantage. She'll only turn them on once we're further away from the channel."

"In that case, breakfast it is," Ilfanti said as he put his jacket on.

The two walked over to the dining saloon, and Ilfanti was a little surprised to see that quite a few people were still there. He spotted Fasbender and half a dozen gnomes all talking in unison while devouring a stack of pancakes. Jin Fe—the grandfather of Shimada—sat by himself further down the table as well. Several other members of the crew were also clustered and talking over their coffee.

"I'm surprised to see so many people here and not working," Ilfanti said.

"This isn't unusual," Palisha explained. "The gnomes aren't needed until we're ready for the engines. Hopefully we are not in need of a doctor this early, so Jin Fe has some free time. As for the others, they are part of Kemocay's artillery units. They all have some time to themselves now too."

Ilfanti nodded as he considered it. It made sense. If you didn't have to work, you might as well rest and relax for a bit.

"Shall we join Jin Fe?" Palisha asked.

"That would be fine," Ilfanti agreed, thankful that they were not about to try and join in on the gnomes' conversations about ship designs and engine schematics.

Jin Fe did not resemble his granddaughter very much at all. He was shorter than Shimada, at only five feet and three inches. His physique was less imposing as well. He was practically skin and bones. If he were wet, Ilfanti suspected that his weight still wouldn't reach one hundred pounds.

The elder aezian was very calm and reflective. He did not often speak, but his vibrant green eyes were always in motion, observing those around him. The man was completely bald and wore a small black skullcap that had a red and gold frilled design around the edges.

Jin Fe wore a complete set of aezian nobility garments. He had on a kimono in a rich mauve fabric with a series of yellow flames accented with gold, rising up from the hemline and across his shoulders. A six-inch wide satiny silk obi—a piece of fabric much like a sash—was elegantly crafted with an image of a white dragon hidden amongst a forest of patterned bamboo, pines and chrysanthemums. A deep red ceremonial silk robe with an intricately designed yellow dragon embroidered into the satiny lining was worn over his kimono. His feet were wrapped in white lace and rested in a pair of black slippers.

As Ilfanti and Palisha sat down, the dwarf noticed that each of Jin Fe's fingers had at least one highly ornamented ring. He did not have to be a member of the Council of Elders to feel the mystical energies emanating from the jewelry.

"Good morning, Jin Fe," Palisha smiled pleasantly. "Do you mind if we join you?"

"Not at all," Jin Fe replied with a smile as warm. "Your presence always brightens my day, Palisha."

"Why, thank you," Palisha said, blushing slightly. "Have you met our passenger yet?"

"No," Jin Fe replied. "I have not had the honor."

"Ilfanti," Ilfanti said with an aezian ceremonial bow of respect. "Are you part of the Yutaka Clan?"

Jin Fe studied the dwarf for a moment with a skeptical gaze. "There is no more Yutaka Clan."

"I did not mean to offend," Ilfanti said. "I was told that Shimada is your granddaughter."

"She is," Jin Fe confirmed.

"Her armor, the golden chest plate with the two green dragons facing each other, if my memory serves, is the symbol of the Yutaka Clan."

"How do you know of the Yutaka Clan?" Jin Fe asked.

"Many years ago I was in Aezia, and while there, the Yutaka were counted amongst my allies in a war I was fighting," Ilfanti explained.

"What war would that be?" Jin Fe asked, most curious.

"I'm not sure what historians refer to it as, but it was when the Yanokura, Taira, and Sun Clans joined forces to challenge the rule of the emperor. I was in Aezia at the time and joined forces with the Takashi, Yutaka, and Wu Clans to help defend the Emperor and the state of the nation at the time."

Jin Fe glanced at Palisha with a look of doubt and then studied Ilfanti again. "That war took place over four hundred years ago."

Ilfanti bobbed his head in agreement.

"And you fought in the war?" Jin Fe asked.

"Though they are long since dead now, Le-Binh named me the godfather of all seven of his children."

"Le-Binh?" Jin Fe asked, his eyes widening slightly, sounding now more like an excitable child than the wise elder he was. "*The* Le-Binh of the Takashi Clan?"

"One and the same," Ilfanti confirmed. "We remained friendly for some time after that, but eventually my adventures took me elsewhere."

"Why were you there at the time?" Palisha asked.

"I had heard legends of a lost city that was paved in gold," Ilfanti shrugged. "I was spending my Paladin years searching for one treasure after another. Figured that a golden city was as good as any other quest I could go on."

"Otarima," Jin Fe clarified.

"Otarima," Ilfanti confirmed.

"Did you ever find it?" Palisha asked.

Ilfanti winked. "That's a tale for another time. What would you like for breakfast?"

"I can get it," Palisha offered.

"No trouble," Ilfanti replied as he stood up. "Coffee and pancakes?"

"I'd prefer milk," Palisha said. "I never developed a taste for coffee."

"Milk it is," Ilfanti grinned.

Palisha turned back to Jin Fe. "Was Otarima ever discovered?"

"If it was, I am unaware of it," Jin Fe said. "According to the legends, Otarima was lost many millennia ago when a greedy warlord defied the gods. He besieged the land and claimed all wealth for himself, paving the streets in gold as your dwarf-friend pointed out. The gods demanded that he cease his hostile ways and give the gold back to the people, but he refused to listen."

"What happened?" Palisha asked.

"The gods opened the ground and dragged Otarima down. Any that tried to flee were scorched alive as the blood of Terra spat forth and burned the very skies."

Setting the plate down in front of Palisha, Ilfanti smiled knowingly. "A very interesting description of a volcano."

"A volcano?" Palisha asked.

"That was where I found it," Ilfanti said. "An earthquake buried the city, and a volcano erupted, destroying all traces that anyone ever lived near Otarima."

"How did you find it?" Palisha asked, impressed.

"Like I said, that is a tale for another day."

Jin Fe studied Ilfanti for a moment as he drank his tea. He then reached beneath the fabric of his clothes at his neckline and pulled a medallion out. It was rounded in gold with frayed edges like flames. The middle had two green dragons facing each other.

"So you are from the Yutaka Clan?" Ilfanti grinned.

"The Yutaka no longer exist," Jin Fe solemnly repeated. "Though Shimada and I were once of that noble house, yes."

"Tell me the tale," Ilfanti requested, "so I may know what happened to the descendants of an old ally and mourn appropriately."

"Very well," Jin Fe said. "I will tell you the tale as I know it."

"That is all I ask."

"I had once been the leader of the Yutaka Clan, but as I grew older, I gave that privilege to my eldest son, Sakuaki. He ruled well and proved a wise and capable successor to the Clan. He had five sons, all as powerful as their father, and a single daughter."

"Shimada," Ilfanti guessed.

"Yes," Jin Fe confirmed. "Shimada. At the time, the Yutaka Clan had been growing its territory and influence considerably throughout Aezia. All five sons of Sakuaki had wed with other lesser Clans and brought their entire family into our own. Shimada was the last to be wed by treaty.

"Sakuaki selected the Koga Clan. They were very powerful and strong, but the only heir was a son that was weak and would never be able to handle the burdens of leadership. Sakuaki saw an opportunity to almost double the strength of the Yutaka Clan through the union, and Shimada, a very strong-willed girl, would never willingly allow her husband to gain the upper hand. It was a perfect union.

"On her fifteenth birthday, I escorted Shimada to the Koga Clan where she met Khoi for the first time. He was exactly as we had expected. He was small and feeble. His speech was stuttered and he could not even look Shimada in the eyes. A marriage with Khoi may weaken the bloodline with his heirs, but Shimada was not expected to carry on the family name anyway, so that point seemed insignificant.

"Upon our return, the ancestral home of the Yutaka Clan lay in ruins. The bodies of all of the guards and members of the family were scattered about. We soon learned that all members of the family had been slain, including all of my grandsons' wives and their families as well. Shimada and I were alone in the world."

Ilfanti listened intently. With such a tragedy in her background, he could understand why Shimada refused to trust anyone.

"Shimada was outraged. Though a woman and forbidden by our customs, she had always trained and fought with her brothers. When she learned that the Koga Clan was behind the attack, she donned the family's ceremonial armor and weapons and summoned all remaining soldiers of the Yutaka Clan.

"She then led her forces against the Koga. Shimada's army was insignificant compared to the vast numbers and power that the Koga held. However, her ferocity and relentless attacks soon showed that the Yutaka still lived. Her actions were so brutal and swift that word quickly spread of her vengeance. As her fame grew, so too did the number of her supporters as defectors fled the Koga and joined Shimada.

"She reached the home of her intended and his family and killed them all, one by one, only then allowing her own thirst for vengeance to be satiated. Before leaving, she declared that all Koga land now belonged to the Yutaka, and any soldier that wished to live could do so by continuing in her servitude. The lack of family members was devastating, but our armies grew larger than ever before.

"Stories of Shimada's actions spread throughout aezian culture. This was not a welcome development, for in our culture, there are very specific gender roles, and there was little room to allow a woman to run the family. The Yutaka soon came under siege of the combined clans of Aezia."

Ilfanti lowered his eyes. He had seen three clans in combat with each other. Combining all of the clans against a single enemy, there would be no hope for survival.

"The attacks were constant and our armies dwindled," Jin Fe explained. "I could see that the Yutaka would ultimately fall. There was no hope. I then took Shimada and fled in search of a sanctuary. A sanctuary, that I found here, thanks to the generosity of Captain Augustus."

"That's quite a tale," Ilfanti said. "Thank you for sharing it. I think it helps me to understand Shimada quite a bit more now."

"She is a good girl," Jin Fe said. "She just has her own demons that she must overcome before she'll be willing to trust anyone again."

"I can imagine."

"If she does trust you, though, and you are more open-minded than my people, she is a great warrior to have fight by your side."

"I can vouch for that," Palisha smiled.

"Well, I hope she finds that she can trust me, then," Ilfanti said. Drinking the last of his coffee, he stood up. "If you'll both excuse me, I'd like to head up on deck."

Palisha hurriedly drank the rest of her milk and stood up as well. "Jin Fe."

"A pleasant day to you both," Jin Fe said.

As the two walked toward the stairs, Ilfanti glanced back and watched as the elder aezian sipped his tea once more. "You could have stayed with him, you know?"

"And miss a chance to see my husband in action?" Palisha snickered. "Perish the thought!"

The two stepped on deck and Ilfanti glanced around. The ship was bustling with activity. Sailors were running around and finishing up last minute details as they were slowly making their way through the channel. He saw Captain Augustus, Krimdor, and Green all standing on the bridge close to the helm and instructing the crew. Shimada was standing on the bow with her arms crossed as she stared out at the world they were approaching.

"What is she doing?" Ilfanti asked.

"She always stands there when we leave the harbor," Palisha explained. "It's her own personal little ritual."

Beyond Shimada were ropes fastened to the stem of the ship and being dragged by a smaller boat. Brondolfr was standing in the boat and systematically was barking the word "Row!" every seven seconds.

"If you'll excuse me," Palisha said as she joined Shimada and watched her husband working.

Ilfanti made his way up onto the bridge.

"Good morning, Ilfanti," Captain Augustus said. "We are fortunate today, the wind is by the lee."

"By the lee?" Ilfanti asked.

"The wind is coming from behind us on the side of the sails," Krimdor explained. "Once we clear the channel, we will be able to let the wind propel us until we reach the islands."

Though a Mage, Krimdor was wearing an outfit that was far more fitting of his post as first officer aboard the *Soaring Mist* than that of a Paladin. He wore a red naval officer's jacket that stretched to his knees. It had golden laces across its chest and on the shoulders with tassels hanging down from each end. A black belt with a golden clasp was fastened at his waist and separated the jacket as if it were two pieces. His shirt underneath was white with a jabot—an ornamental cascade of ruffles down the front of his shirt—and frilled cuffs. A red vest that matched the tinge of both his jacket and his pants was clasped across his chest. His black boots extended past his knees and folded over at the top. His outfit was completed with a cutlass sheathed to his waist and a black officer's hat upon his brow.

The man himself was a striking image of an aquatican. His blue skin was deep and vibrant. His eyes were a lighter blue that made him look as if he was one of the gentlest men that Ilfanti had ever met. His face was never found in a scowl or a frown, making him appear eternally joyous and happy. His hair and beard were a dark green, almost like the shade one would find on the leaves in a forest. He kept both neatly trimmed and short. Standing at five feet ten inches, Krimdor held himself well; he was strong and commanding, demanding the respect from those around him, but also innocent, caring and compassionate. He was a good man, and Ilfanti was glad to get to know the Paladin.

"Thank you," Ilfanti said. "Will that reduce the time estimates you gave me?"

Green glanced at a compass and then raised his hand to feel the wind. "You are certain we can not travel in the normal ssshipping lane?"

Captain Augustus raised an eyebrow expectantly to hear the reply. Ilfanti had cautioned them that an entire fleet was in the channel near Trespias. The normal shipping lanes would have them travel close to the coast down Dartais all the way to Trespias and further down. Though the maps make it look like this would take longer than reaching the open sea, the currents were quite favorable to ships bearing a southerly direction. With the potential danger, they decided to plot a course through the Dartais islands and then to the open sea. Green's projections were quite conservative, but he still estimated that it would take slightly over ninety-four hours before they completely cleared the islands and could sail at their top speeds.

"I stand by what I said," Ilfanti replied.

"Then ssso do I," Green replied.

"Very good," Augustus said. "Feel free to enjoy the scenery, Ilfanti. Once we reach the islands, they are quite breathtaking, as are the luxurious houses the Dartais nobility built there, and the immaculate gardens. You shall certainly see some interesting sights."

"Thank you," Ilfanti said.

He stayed a while longer listening as the Captain issued some commands to her people, but when Brondolfr reboarded the ship and they unfurled the main sail, he found a spot to lean back and relax. With only the main sail open, the ship remained at a pace of about five nautical miles per hour. He closed his eyes and relaxed as the breeze blew through his hair, visualizing what this would be like when all of the sails were full with the wind blowing. Though he did not want to, he soon nodded off.

CHAPTER 5

"Please, I'm telling you the truth!"

Rhyne twisted the knife around, forcing a scream of agony from the Captain. "You better be."

"I am," he sobbed in pain. "Please believe me."

Rhyne stepped back, pulling his knife from the man and wiping the blood off on the Captain's shirt. "If you are able to acquire a ship, I trust that you will let me know?"

"Yes," the man panted. "I will, I promise."

"Good," Rhyne said as he bared his fangs, his lips creasing into a terrorizing smile. "That is precisely what I wanted to hear."

As he stepped off the dock, he clenched his fist in frustration. His bounty was getting further and further away from him, and he could find no Captain with a ship sturdy enough to make the trip to Egziard. He knew that none of them had turned him down because of the extent and perils of the trip, for he was quite persuasive. No, these ships were run-down and only were good enough for short merchant trips from port to port.

What he needed was a Gallie, or a Schooner. Either would do quite nicely, in his opinion. Of course, to acquire one of those, he would have to venture to the eastern coast, a journey that would take far too long for him ever to catch up to Kabilian again.

"Excuse me."

Rhyne glanced down and glared at a barefoot boy with dirt on his face and a tooth missing. "What do you want?" he said in almost a whisper.

"I heard you were looking for a ship?"

Intrigued, Rhyne kneeled down and looked the child directly in the eye. "You heard correctly."

"I know of someone that may be able to get you on the ship that you need."

"Oh, really?" Rhyne said as he stood back up. He should have known, in a small decrepit town like this, even the children were rats looking to swindle a quick coin. "How is it that you would know of a ship when I have been unsuccessful?"

"I have connections," the boy grinned as he raised his empty palm out.

Rhyne swept both arms out to their full extension, knocking his cloak back and revealing his outfit underneath. From neck to toe he was garbed in black studded leather. Encircling his chest and stomach were leather straps that fastened hundreds of throwing knives to his body. Smaller rings circled both of his legs with blades as well. Fastened to his belt were over a dozen Aezian throwing stars. The inside of his cloak was laced almost completely with tiny dart-like throwing needles.

With his arsenal revealed, Rhyne was impressed that the child still kept his hand extended as he awaited payment. The wraith pulled three needles and in one throw sent them darting between the boy's fingers and into the ground. "If I learn that you are deceiving me, those, and many more will strike their mark."

The boy grinned confidently. "Threaten me all you want, the price for the information will be the same."

Rhyne waited several moments, his glimmering yellow eyes boring into the child. When he saw that the boy was not backing down, he decided that the information must be legitimate, and if not, it would be worth the few coins that it would take to make this child content.

Reaching into a pouch fastened behind his back, Rhyne removed several silver coins and tossed them into the boy's hand. "Now speak up."

The boy bit one of the coins and grinned again. "This will do," he said. "There's a man at Pikel's that has information about a boat."

"Pray that he does," Rhyne said as his eyes narrowed to slits in warning. "Pray that he does."

The boy shrugged as if he couldn't care less and then ran away.

Rhyne watched him leave and then walked straight to Pikel's; yet another tavern with even more drunkards telling tales of how they had swindled someone or conquered a damsel's virginity. The scene disgusted him. He would only remain as long as he needed to, and then he would be on his way. How these fools could ever allow their lives to turn so poorly was beyond him. Even a criminal should live by certain standards. He certainly did.

As Rhyne stepped inside the tavern, he glanced around searching for someone who might seem out of place. In a table at the back, he found one such person. As a wraith, the darkness and shadows did not disturb him. He could see as clearly in them as a human could see on a bright and sunny day. The man in the corner was garbed in an attempt to disguise his features, but Rhyne could see that he was at least part tigrel, though he seemed larger and stronger than any tigrel he had ever seen. Interesting to see one so far from Dartie.

Sitting down in front of the man, Rhyne stared directly into his eyes. "I hear that you have information about a ship?"

"You heard correctly," the tigrel said quietly.

"Will it be sufficient to take me to Egziard?" Rhyne asked.

"It is already going to Egziard."

Rhyne leaned back. If this were true, then this information could well be worth the price. "Is it a good ship?"

"The fastest to sail the high seas."

"How much will this information cost me?" Rhyne asked, suspicious, for this information seemed too good to be true.

"Not a thing," the man replied.

"Nothing in this world is free," Rhyne pressed. "I will not take information without knowing the cost."

"Let's just say, Lady Salaman will not be around much longer."

"What?" Rhyne spat as he reached beneath the table and removed a pair of his throwing knives. "What are you trying to say?"

"Lady Salaman has become weak and vulnerable," he said. "Her time as a crime lord will soon be coming to an end. My employer will do you this favor now in hopes that you will remember that when Lady Salaman is no more."

"Are you threatening Lady Salaman?" Rhyne demanded.

"No," the tigrel replied. "There is no need. Lady Salaman's days are numbered."

"And your employer wishes to gain my services?" Rhyne asked to clarify.

"Only your favor," the tigrel smiled disarmingly.

"I will not act against Lady Salaman in any way," Rhyne sternly promised.

"We understand that, and would never ask you to violate your current oath. Do we have an understanding?"

Rhyne considered the proposition for a moment. If Lady Salaman did falter, it might be good to have another crime lord to support him. There was one thing that was certain in this business: loyalties shift. "Who is your employer?"

"Someone who shall remain anonymous."

"Not acceptable!" Rhyne snarled as he pulled his arm up above the table and flung his two throwing knives.

The tigrel hardly seemed to move at all, but a staff suddenly appeared above the table and twirled like quicksilver, intercepting both projectiles and deflecting them so that they dug into the wall rather than the tigrel. "There is no need for that."

"I will not vow my services to an unknown master!" Rhyne growled as he removed several more knives.

"No vow is necessary," the tigrel replied. "We only ask that you remember our assistance. If we approach you in the future, the decision will be yours as to whether you will return the favor or not."

"And if I refuse?" Rhyne asked; certain that a refusal would mean that he would wind up with a bounty on his head.

"If you refuse, then we underestimated your values."

Rhyne still was not convinced, but he felt confident in his own abilities if he suddenly found an enemy of this elusive employer. He also needed a ship very badly. "Very well," Rhyne conceded. "Tell me about this ship."

"It is known as the *Soaring Mist.* It has just set sail from Water Haven."

"Water Haven?" Rhyne growled. "That is in Dartais!"

"Yes," the tigrel confirmed. "Our sources confirm that the *Soaring Mist* will reach the Island of No Return in approximately twenty-two or twenty-three days."

"No ship can travel that fast," Rhyne said.

"The *Soaring Mist* can," the tigrel replied confidently. "In fact, if it reaches its top velocity throughout the voyage, it could even beat our estimates by a week. However, I would say that twenty-two or twenty-three days is an are accurate projection."

"Even still, that means that my prey has a five- or six-week head start," Rhyne winced in frustration. "That is unacceptable!"

"The ship that Kabilian is on is not nearly as fast. Even with the late start, you will beat him to Egziard unless other factors intervene."

Picking up another knife, Rhyne glared at the tigrel. "How did you know I was going after Kabilian?"

"These things are well-known to us."

"I don't like it," Rhyne sneered.

"Noted," the tigrel replied. "I would recommend that you find some way to get on board the *Soaring Mist* as it sails past the Island of No Return. It will not be making a stop until it gets well past pirate waters and through the Vast Expanse, so you will have to find a way to convince them to take on a passenger."

"How do I suppose to do that?" Rhyne asked.

"I trust that you will find a way."

"If I learn that this information is not true, that perhaps you were telling me this to give Kabilian more time to flee, I assure you, no place on Terra will keep you, or your myserious employer, safe from me."

"I expect no less."

"I am glad that we understand each other," Rhyne said with a slight bow. He then stood up and walked away from Pikel's, leaving the stench of smoke and booze behind. He might not find a ship that would get him all the way to Egziard, but he certainly could get one to take him to the Island of No Return.

❋ ❋ ❋ ❋ ❋

Archer waited until Rhyne was gone and then departed himself. He tossed several coins onto the bar to settle his tab and then walked around the back of the building. There, he spotted a female elf and nodded. "It is done."

The elf's skin was a deep pink tinge, marking her as a member of the Madrew who had seen at least five centuries come and go. Her eyes were aglow, a faint bluish-green glisten that revealed her presence far more than the candlelight from a nearby window. Her sparkling-silver hair waved from beneath her black cloak with purple lining and extended down to the middle of her back.

Beneath her cloak, she was garbed in exquisite silver-plated armor that had an ornamental pattern consisting of a golden line down the middle and a web of violet, like the branches of a tree, intersecting it and spreading out towards the edges of her armor. The armor rested atop purple garments that had similar designs, only with silver vines swirling through them. A single scimitar, a dagger, and a whip were fastened to her belt.

"Then it is only a matter of time," the elf said. "Things are proceeding as anticipated."

"Rhiannon, your mother may be pushing a little too far with this one," Archer said.

"Explain," Rhiannon commanded.

"Our dealings thus far have all been with, shall we say, more reputable individuals. First we approached Kabilian because your mother was certain that he has a pivotal role to play in things. Now Rhyne? I fear the line we are walking is a narrow one. We may fall."

"Do not doubt the wisdom of my mother," Rhiannon replied. "Besides, is this Rhyne any more disreputable that Rawthorne? With mother's guidance we turned a knight into a tyrant to serve our needs."

Archer snorted at the memory. Rawthorne obviously had been a man who could be tempted and corrupted, and they had pulled his strings, destroying not only him but nearly an entire Kingdom just because it would serve the needs of the Eye.

"Rhyne will help to convince Kabilian that it would be in his best interests to join us," Rhiannon continued. "We do not expect him to succeed."

Archer turned and watched the bounty hunter as he walked to the docks. The wraith was one of the deadliest individuals he had ever had to deal with. He hoped that they were not making a mistake. Rhyne was far too dangerous an individual to cross.

CHAPTER 6

Standing two-thirds of the way up the mainmast, Ilfanti closed his eyes, extended his arms and leaned his head back. The feeling was exhilarating. It was as if he were soaring through the sky like a bird. He could feel the patterns of the wind around him and the gentle shifts along the landscape. So calm and peaceful, he knew that if he ever had the power to truly fly, he would probably never wish to return to the ground.

They soon reached the islands and began making frequent turns to avoid outcroppings and areas where the seabed would not allow the nearly thirty-foot draft of the keel to pass without running aground. He looked forward to being on the open ocean so he could feel the exhilaration of soaring once more. Below he could hear Brondolfr shouting out the Captain's orders to the crew. They always responded quickly and efficiently.

To help provide the *Soaring Mist* with more maneuverability, the sails were brought down again and Ilfanti got his first glimpse of Fasbender's engines. They were quite impressive. The gnomes had a variety of gears connected to an illistrium furnace. The illistrium itself was a wise investment since the metal is almost indestructible and will not become malleable unless the temperature can be raised to a degree equivalent to the heat of the raging lifeblood of the planet's molten lava. The dwarves of Tregador had mastered this ability and could sell their wares at almost limitless prices.

The furnace was fed the coal that the crew had picked up before leaving, and kept burning as long as the engines were needed. This was all connected to other levers and gears that were constantly in motion if you were in the engine room, but ultimately it was connected to two large propellers at the stern of the ship beneath sea level. These would spin at a speed dictated by the engineering crew and allow the *Soaring Mist* to travel up to ten nautical miles per hour even on the calmest day, with no wind present.

One downside of the engine was the refuse it created. The gnomes were constantly covered in blackened soot that seemed to take them hours to remove when their shifts were over. Several pipes for ventilation extended backwards through the ship from the engine room and emitted a dense billow of grayish-black smoke that remained behind the ship in its wake and slowly drifted into the sky.

He could feel the ship slowing down slightly and opened his eyes. There was a small outcropping jutting from the water. The course that they plotted appeared to be full of areas that threatened to rip the hull and shorten their voyage. Glancing down, he spotted Green holding a compass and counting. He raised his hand with three fingers extended, and then slowly lowered them. As soon as all of his fingers were down, Captain Augustus called out a command, one that Krimdor repeated down to Brondolfr, who shouted it for all to hear.

The ship veered to the starboard side and Ilfanti watched as they easily evaded the shallow waters. This crew was highly efficient; he had to give them that. Over the past couple of days, he had seen a pattern emerging. The ship ran in three primary rotations of the crew to keep everyone fresh and ready for whatever obstacles they may face. The officers also maintained separate duty watches, but even so, Captain Augustus and Green seemed to always manage to make an appearance on the bridge whenever a slight course alteration needed to be made.

They were sailing very close to one of the smaller islands. Ilfanti studied the landscape and had to admit that the homes built there were exquisite. If he had not seen the starving people of Water Haven, he would have appreciated this more, but as he saw rows and rows of gardens, sculptures that were probably the culmination of a lifetime's work for their sculptors, and buildings that were so large and immaculate that one could mistake them for small palaces, all he could think of was how badly these nobles were exploiting the workers of their kingdom.

The thought troubled him. He was trying to find the Empress in hopes to unite the races—how could the races unite though if humans discriminate and segregate, even amongst themselves? Perhaps he should not judge all humans by what he had seen since arriving in Water Haven, but never before had he heard of elves or dwarves or centaurs or aquaticans or nearly any other race forcing members of their own race into poverty and despair just to see their own lifestyles improve.

Grabbing a line from the rigging, Ilfanti wrapped his arms around it and slowly slid back down to the deck. He needed some way to get his mind off of his current thoughts. Adventures always sound grand and exciting, but he vividly recalled the waiting, the traveling, and the times that his mind waged a virtual war with itself over what he was doing and why.

Not sure exactly what to do, Ilfanti decided that he would take some time to reflect on his thoughts and write another journal entry. It was a way for him to keep a record, as well as a way to balance his thoughts. His concern about the success of the unification was something that he might one day wish to look back upon. He would either laugh at the absurdity of his doubts, or cringe at how accurate his instincts had been. He sincerely hoped that it would be the former.

He walked down the stairs to the mid level and started to approach his cabin. As he did so, he heard grunting and paused. Following the sound, which seemed systematic and repetitive, Ilfanti walked into a small room that had padded walls, floors, and numerous items for training within.

Kemocay was lying on a bench and lifting a bar that held steel weights upon each side of it. He slowly lowered the bar to his chest, and then raised it back up again, extending his arms fully. Ilfanti watched a he did this several more times, and then the Adlesian placed the bar on a stand that was directly over his head.

"I've never seen that done before," Ilfanti grinned.

"How do you train, then?" Kemocay asked.

"At the Mage's Council, we have entire wings filled with magical equipment that constantly pushes us to our limits. When I'm not in the Tower, I typically do a lot of jogging, push-ups, sit-ups and things like that. When I was younger, I would do that with packs full of sand on my back, arms, and legs to make it more strenuous."

"Well, have a seat," Kemocay said as he stood up and lowered his arm indicating the bench.

Ilfanti walked over and set himself as Kemocay had been.

"Let me adjust this for you slightly," Kemocay said as he lowered the two supports that held the bar. "Can you reach the dumbbell easily?"

"Dumbbell?" Ilfanti asked. "You mean the bar?"

"Yes," Kemocay confirmed. "It is called a dumbbell."

Ilfanti reached up and wrapped his fingers around the bar. "Yes."

"Excellent," Kemocay said. "How much weight would you like?"

Ilfanti glanced from side to side. This was certainly an interesting invention. It was far different from the mystical training methods employed at the Council. There, weight really had no meaning. It was force and pressure that was applied and modulated by the enchanted machines. "I'll trust your judgment."

Kemocay unscrewed a small support that held the weight in place and then removed four of the large metal rings from each side of the dumbbell. When he was satisfied, he screwed the supports back into place. "Try that."

Ilfanti lifted the bar up and did the same thing that Kemocay had done. He lowered the bar to his chest and raised it back up again. The entire time, Kemocay stood behind him, his hands slightly below the dumbbell. "What are you doing?"

"It's called spotting," Kemocay said. "In case the weight is too much and you need help."

"You did not have someone doing that for you," Ilfanti pointed out.

"Unless Brondolfr is with me, I do not work out at my full potential."

"A wise precaution," Ilfanti said. "This is too easy, though. I need more weight."

Kemocay waited until Ilfanti returned the bar to its original position and then added two more weights to each side. "Try that."

Ilfanti lowered the bar and raised it again. It was decidedly heavier, but still did not strain the dwarf. "More."

"I'll set you up with what I was doing," Kemocay said.

After he was finished, Ilfanti lifted the weights again. This time they were much heavier. Unlike the tools he was used to working with, though, this pressure was constant. The actual workout involved more repetition and increasing weights, rather than having your muscles properly stimulated and developed. Different, but not necessarily better or worse.

When he finished five sets, Ilfanti sat up and felt his arms. It was as if they were burning. "Will I always have this burning sensation?"

"No," Kemocay said. "It is a good sign, though. It means that the weights were pushing you. You did well on that exercise."

Ilfanti scanned the rest of the equipment in the room. There were smaller bars that looked as if you could hold them with a single hand, rows upon rows of the metal weights, and a variety of wooden swords. "Do you come here often?"

"I am here at least three hours a day for myself. If there are new crew members or another member of the crew requires assistance, that time extends considerably."

"Would you mind if I joined you for these exercises?" Ilfanti asked.

Kemocay nodded his approval. "Just so you know, when I work with others, I push them to their limits and back. You will know that you have been training."

Thinking of his pants and how they still seemed a little too snug, he grinned in anticipation. This would be great. He could spend the months traveling to Egziard preparing himself. He had sat on the Council of Elders for too long. It made him slower, and as much as he hated to admit it, fatter. Kemocay's offer appeared too good to be true. It was just what he needed to get himself ready for his quest.

20ᵗʰ day of Esbai, 7951 AM

We have finally cleared the islands and set the course south. As soon as we did so, Captain Augustus ordered Fasbender to shut the engines off and then had all of the sails unfurled. I couldn't believe how many sails there were. I never knew that a ship could have that many! 17,838 square feet worth of sails!

I probably am forgetting some of what Krimdor was telling me about them, but there are two jibs, two courses, a spanker, three top-sails and three topgallant sails. These are arranged throughout the fore-mast, mainmast, and mizzenmast. These also include the jig headsail, the jumbo headsail, the foresail, the main sail, the main top sail and the queen top sail.

Whatever each and every one of those is, I can sum it up with this: there are a lot of sails on this boat! The wind has been accommodating too, bringing us up to a speed of twenty-two nautical miles per hour. Green seems quite pleased with this, claiming that we are at the ship's peak speed, two nautical miles faster than his projections had antici-pated. We'll take them. The faster we can get to Egziard, the faster I can find the Orb of Prophecy.

Of course, we won't always have the wind at our back. It's just luck right now that we do, so I won't hold my breath thinking that we'll maintain this pace the entire journey. Undoubtedly, there will be times when we're stuck on the engines alone with no wind at all. Even so, unless that becomes the norm of our trip, we should reach our destina-tion somewhere within the vicinity of four months. If we can arrive at the harbor port of Zaman by the 15ᵗʰ of Cytrellis, I'll be overjoyed.

Then again, I hope I'm still alive to see Zaman! Kemocay was true to his word when he said that he would push me to my endurance. I always thought that the Mage's Council had the best training in the realm. Our physical stamina is something that is really focused on from an early age. Of course, I'm not as young as I used to be, but these workouts with Kemocay are quite strenuous.

I have found more aches and pains in places that I never knew could cause aches and pains than I ever dreamed possible! Kemocay assures me that he isn't torturing me, and that the pain is a good thing. Easy for him to say, he doesn't appear to be in pain at all!

He told me that we would be working on a rotation. He said that the muscles will need time to heal and that I can't push them. So we do a variety of exercises every day, but focus on either the arms, chest, or legs in a three-day rotation. I started with the chest, did the arms today and tomorrow will be legs. I wonder if I'll still be able to walk the following morning?

I'm not complaining, though. He's a magnificent teacher and he really knows what he is talking about. Perhaps after the realm has been saved and the legions of Zoldex are naught but a memory, I'll hire Kemocay to introduce this variation of physical training to the Mage's Council. We boast the best education in the world; that might as well include the most strenuous workouts as well!

This entry I am cutting short, though. This may only be my second day working out, but I find myself extremely fatigued and craving my bunk. Kemocay promises that this, too, is a good sign. Well, good sign or not, I'm going to sleep.

CHAPTER 7

"So what do you think of our ship so far?" Captain Augustus asked as she cut a piece of chicken.

"I am very impressed," Ilfanti nodded. "The ship is magnificent, but it pales in comparison to the efficiency and closeness of the crew."

"Thank you," Augustus said as she placed the chicken in her mouth.

Beige stepped over with a pitcher of ale. "More, mother?"

"Yes, please," she smiled compassionately.

"I must say, seeing you dine with the crew is a bit unusual compared to many of the Captains I have known over the years," Ilfanti commented. "I find it refreshing."

"This is more than just my crew and I am more than just their Captain," Augustus explained. "I see no reason for preferential treatment."

"The Captain has always done things to make sure we all felt welcome," Palisha added. "To make us feel like equals."

"We are equals," Augustus said. "I may command this ship, but when we are not on duty, I am no better or worse than anyone else on board."

"As I said, refreshing."

"Are you going to eat that?" Brondolfr asked Ilfanti.

Ilfanti glanced down at his plate. He had been talking so much that he had neglected his meal. "I'm sorry, I'll eat more and talk less."

The barbarian's brow furled in disappointment.

"Here, you can have the rest of mine," Palisha said as she dropped three ribs of pork onto his plate.

His eyes widened appreciatively and then he reached over and hugged her. "Many thanks."

"What are wives for?" she teased.

"There's a few things I can think of," Fasbender said with a wink to Palisha.

"What?" Brondolfr growled, the juice from the rib dripping down his chin.

Fasbender giggled and began nodding. "You know!"

"*What?*" Brondolfr demanded, slamming the bone on his dish.

"Calm down, Brondolfr," Kemocay cautioned him. "I believe Fasbender is just trying to point out that it might be nice to have some children around here."

Brondolfr leapt up and lunged across the table at Fasbender. He grabbed the gnome by the collar and lifted him from his chair. "How dare you! She is my wife!"

Kemocay grabbed Brondolfr by the arms and tried to pry his grip away. "Let him go, what's wrong?"

"There will be no little gnomes running around this ship!"

Everyone at the table began laughing, including Beige whose laugh sounded more like a wheezing hiss.

Brondolfr glanced around in confusion from face to face. "What is it?"

Palisha gently rubbed her pinkie over his bicep in a circular motion. "He meant barbarian children running around."

Brondolfr turned a bright shade of red, his eyes widening as he gently lowered Fasbender back into his seat.

"Dolt," Kemocay said as he slapped Brondolfr on the top of his head.

"My apologies," Brondolfr offered sincerely.

Fasbender looked from side to side and shrugged. "Nothing wrong with a little excitement!"

"I don't know if this ship is ready for more barbarians," Augustus said with a laugh.

Brondolfr blushed again and kept his gaze intently on his plate. After a moment, he picked up another rib and began devouring it.

Fasbender picked up a roll and threw it at Brondolfr, hitting him in the head.

"What?" Brondolfr snapped back. "What did I do this time?"

"It's not what you did, but what you did not do," Fasbender said. "So when do I become Uncle Fasbie?"

Everyone at the table burst out laughing as Brondolfr glared at the gnome.

"Captain!"

Augustus glanced up as Shimada hurriedly made her way into the dining saloon. "What is it, Shimada?"

"Krimdor would like to see you on the deck."

Captain Augustus wiped her mouth with her napkin and squeezed Beige's hand. "Dinner was delicious."

"Thank you, mother," Beige said.

Kemocay watched Shimada for a moment, seeing that she appeared agitated. "What is wrong?"

"There is an unknown ship coming this way," Shimada explained.

Brondolfr shot up from his chair. "All hands, battle stations!"

Those still in the saloon began to scurry about to their positions, leaving Palisha, Ilfanti, and Beige alone. Ilfanti studied his plate for a moment and shrugged. "What little I ate was quite good."

"Thank you," Beige bowed.

"If you'll excuse me, I'd like to see this myself," he said.

"Certainly," Palisha replied.

Before Ilfanti left, he stopped and turned to face her. "You seem so calm. If we're really about to enter battle, should you not be someplace safe?"

"We enter battle quite a bit. Captain Augustus has her own personal vendetta against pirates. It is not very often that we set off and not have at least one skirmish or two. This crew is quite adept and capable. I have every confidence."

Ilfanti nodded his approval. He had chosen well in selecting the *Soaring Mist.*

❋ ❋ ❋ ❋ ❋

Captain Augustus stepped onto the deck and glanced up at the bridge. Krimdor was standing by the wheel looking through an optical enhancer at an oncoming vessel. Green was standing behind him with a compass in hand.

With Brondolfr, Kemocay, Fasbender, and Shimada directly behind her, Augustus led the way up to the bridge. "Report."

"A ship of unknown origin and design has plotted an intercept course and is coming this way," Krimdor explained.

He handed her the optical enhancer and pointed off of the port bow. Augustus raised it to her eye and turned the knob slightly to make the image a little clearer. The boat was of a design she had never seen either. The entire front of the ship looked as if it was the skull of a horned dragon. The hull was wooden and curved at the stern like the tail of a scorpion. One large sail was drawn on the mainmast, the only one that it looked like it could support.

She studied both the boat and the occupants onboard. The crew was heavily armed with a variety of weapons, including spears, tridents, swords, and daggers. Their heads, at least those that were not covered by helms, were a shade of moss-green, with a single fin that looked like that of a shark protruding from their skulls and extending down their backs. One of the crew jumped up onto the mainmast and she could clearly see that he also had a long tail, covered in armor, but with what appeared to be a double fin at the end.

Taking her eyes away from the ship she glanced back at Krimdor for answers. "Do you know what they are?"

"I've never seen anything like them before, Captain," Krimdor replied.

Augustus frowned, but spotted Ilfanti stepping up onto the deck and tossed him the optical enhancers. "Let me know what you make of those."

Ilfanti used the mechanical instrument and then lowered it with a shrug. "I traveled much of the world in my younger days, but I have never come across anything that looks like that."

"Captain, look!" Brondolfr shouted.

Augustus watched the ship and could see the eyes of the skull begin to glow an eerie red color. "Could it be magic?"

"I don't want to wait to find out," Krimdor said. "They look hostile."

"I agree," Augustus said. "All right everyone, you know what to do."

Brondolfr stepped forward. "Fasbender, to the engine room; Kemocay, prepare your men; non-essential personnel, clear the bridge!"

Ilfanti watched as the crew scrambled to carry out their orders without hesitation. Kemocay stopped by the forward catapult and spoke with three men stationed there. They pulled the large arm down and tied it in place, a large hollow steel ball placed in the netting. He then walked to the aft of the ship and the crew did the same thing. When satisfied, Ilfanti watched as the Weapons Master went below decks.

Augustus stood sternly on the bridge facing the oncoming vessel. She shouted out an order to the helm, which was promptly repeated by Krimdor and then by the helmsman. The ship turned and began heading directly toward the other ship.

"Krimdor," she called out. "If that is a mystical attack, I want you on the foremast preparing some kind of defense."

"Aye, Captain," he said as he grabbed the railing and leapt over to the deck. He then ran to the foremast and climbed the rigging until he was standing along the second support beam. He arrived just in time to see the two glowing red eyes send a projectile beam lancing out at the *Soaring Mist*.

Krimdor raised his hands and created a mystical barrier in front of the ship. When the red beam impacted, he felt the blast rip through his defenses and strike him like a battering ram. He strained to keep his shield in place as the beam continued to pour surging energy at them. A trail of blood began to leak from his nose.

As the power ray stopped, Krimdor dropped and barely managed to hold onto the rigging. The blast was too powerful. He had barely managed to deflect the first one. A second such attack would surely be his undoing.

"Ilfanti!" Augustus called out.

Ilfanti jogged over to the bridge. "Yes, Captain?"

"We can not withstand a blast like that. Krimdor looks like he will be unable to deflect an additional attack. I need you to do it!"

"Yes, Captain," he said somberly. He did so hate to use magic on these adventures of his, but he could feel the power behind that blast. Krimdor was in no shape to withstand another one, and unless he used his powers, this quest would be over before it even truly began.

Sprinting over to the mainmast, Ilfanti climbed up and grabbed onto Krimdor. The Paladin was bleeding from more than just his nose. A stream of blood was dripping from each eye as well. "Damn," he said. "We need to get you down."

"Must protect the ship," Krimdor wheezed.

"I'll do it, you need to get to Jin Fe," Ilfanti said as he lifted the aquatican over his shoulder, held him with one hand, and began to climb down with the other. Krimdor weighed about one hundred and eighty pounds, but Ilfanti hardly even noticed the extra weight in the heat of the moment.

When he reached the deck, Shimada was there to take Krimdor. Ilfanti watched her as she led the trembling Paladin below to her grandfather. He then climbed back up and peered at the oncoming ship. The red glow in the eyes of the skull was not as vibrant as it had been before the blast. Perhaps it needed time to recharge before it could strike again.

Augustus glanced back at Green who was counting to himself. He held up three fingers, then two, then one. "Now."

Augustus turned around and cried out: "Fire!"

Brondolfr, standing below her on the deck repeated in a loud roar: "Fire!"

The forward catapult snapped and launched the first round projectile towards the enemy ship. It crashed in the water inches from their starboard hull. The armory crew quickly lowered the catapult arm, placed another projectile on it, made some minor adjustments and fired a second round. This one slammed into the white skull and bounced off.

"Archers on deck!" Augustus ordered.

"Archers on deck!" Brondolfr shouted out, and a dozen archers ran up from beneath the deck and positioned themselves along the side of the boat, waiting until they were in range to attack.

Ilfanti could see that the red glow was intensifying. If his hunch was right, they would soon be able to fire. He watched as another steel ball slammed into the skeleton head, cracking it slightly. "Heh!" he cheered triumphantly.

Raising his hand, he extended his fingers, balled them into a fist and then opened them by thrusting his arm forward. A large ball of flame burst from his palm and bore down on the oncoming boat. It impacted the front of the enemy vessel where the mouth of the skeleton was and erupted.

Ilfanti squinted as he tried to see through the flames, but was dismayed to see that the enemy ship was only blackened, and that the red glow was still intensifying. Frowning at the lack of success, he decided to try a lightning attack instead. Extending his arm again, blue bolts of energy lanced out from his fingertips and kept striking the front of the oncoming vessel. The skull cracked further and large pieces of it shattered and fell into the sea.

"Keep up the barrage!" Augustus called out.

The catapult launched another steel ball, this one slamming into one of the green-skinned warriors and dropping him into the sea. A second ball crashed into the mainmast, splintering it and dropping the sail. The crew aboard the *Soaring Mist* all cheered.

"What is that?"

Augustus ran to the side of the bridge and peered over. Several objects directly beneath the water's surface were soaring toward them like torpedoes. As soon as they reached the boat, they sprang from the water and landed on the deck. They were, in fact, armored fighters from the other ship.

Brondolfr reached over his back and pulled his double-bladed battleaxe down to defend himself. "Attack!"

Several of the archers lowered their bows and pulled cutlasses that were strapped to their belts. They followed Brondolfr as he led the charge against the boarders. The first one began crying in a high-pitched sound that resembled the speech of a dolphin. He then swiped a trident at the barbarian.

Brondolfr deflected the blow and raised the pommel of his axe, impacting the amphibious creature in the head. He floundered back a step, shaking its head, and soon found Brondolfr bringing his axe directly down at him.

The green-skinned creature tried to deflect the blow with his arm, and screamed in agony as it was severed. He then lashed its tail out and knocked Brondolfr clear across the deck.

Brondolfr stood back up, turned his neck from side to side and cracked it. "You won't be able to use the same trick twice." Charging with his axe above his head, he cried out to the barbarian god of earth, wind, and fire, "Xeorn!" The raging barbarian rushed back toward the invader and leapt over the tail as the creature tried to strike him again. As he came back down to the deck, he swung his mighty axe and ripped into the creature's chest, dropping him to the ground.

A second creature grabbed him from behind and he dropped his axe. Growling with the thunderous roar of a grizzly bear, Brondolfr extended his arms and forced the creature from his back. Turning to face him, he pulled two daggers from behind his back and jumped on top of him, thrusting the daggers down again and again until he was no longer moving.

Shimada returned to the deck and saw three of the creatures still fighting. Several sailors and archers were dead by their feet. She bowed to the foes without taking her eyes from them, and then lunged for them, several throwing stars preceding her. Before she reached the creatures, two Aezian blades were in her hands, one a full-length sword and the other half its size.

The creatures tried to deflect or avoid the throwing stars, but one fell dead, the star jutting from his cheek. Shimada slashed down with her blades, disarming a second one. She then turned both swords and brought them thrusting up, slashing both blades across the creature's unprotected throat leaving two deep lines that looked like claw marks.

The final creature rushed for the bridge and leapt over Brondolfr as he tried to swing at him. He landed on the bridge and snarled at Captain Augustus.

"Mother!" Green cried out as he lashed his tail around and struck the creature in the chest, the blow so powerful that the armor showed creases.

Augustus unsheathed her cutlass and followed her reptilian son into battle. She brought the cutlass down and dug it into the creature's forehead. "Get this thing off of my bridge," she called out as she pulled her sword back out of the lifeless body.

A sailor on the bridge nodded and dragged the armored creature from the command deck.

Augustus ran to the edge of the bridge again and nodded as she watched the two ships running parallel. "Fire!"

Brondolfr, who was now standing by his post again, repeated the order and shouted into a cylinder that allowed him to communicate below decks. "Fire!"

Kemocay heard the order and lowered his arm. Six wooden windows snapped open and large ballista—these in the form of massive crossbows with projectiles that could tear through the hull of a ship—were rolled forward with the arrowheads sticking through the opening. "Fire!" he called out and watched as the giant crossbows launched arrows directly into the hull of the opposing ship.

"Reload!" he called out in command.

Captain Augustus clenched her fist when the arrows hit. The smaller ship moved back with the arrows jutting from its hull. "Archers!"

"Archers!" Brondolfr repeated.

The archers who still lived rushed to the port side, where the other ship was, and began launching arrows at it. The creatures in the other boat were defenseless as the wooden shafts kept raining down upon them.

From the foremast, Ilfanti dropped back to the deck and rushed over to the side where he continued to barrage the boat with blasts of lightning. Within minutes, the opposing ship was taking on water and sinking, all hands were dead.

CHAPTER 8

"What were those things?" Augustus asked. "Anyone?"

"Their blood," Brondolfr said as he wiped some from his chest with a towel. "It's blue."

Ilfanti kneeled down and examined one of the bodies. They had gills, so they could breathe underwater, but also appeared more than capable of breathing air as well, just as the aquaticans could.

"Bring one down to Jin Fe to study," Augustus ordered. "Get the rest of them off of my ship."

"Aye, Captain," Brondolfr said. "You heard the Captain, get them out of here."

"Damage report?" Augustus asked.

"Minimal damage," Green reported. "We were fortunate that Krimdor deflected the firssst blassst."

"Yes," she said glancing at Ilfanti. "What effect did your magic have?"

"Very little," he admitted. "The fireball had no effect, and the lightning only worked after the head of the ship had been chipped by one of the catapult balls."

"Was that one of the ships you saw in Trespias?" Augustus asked.

"That design, yes."

"We do not want to have to fight many more like that without knowing more," she said. "Brondolfr."

"Aye, Captain?"

"Before that ship sinks, get me a sample of that skull for Fasbender to analyze."

"Aye, Captain," he said. He walked over to the rigging, unfastened a line and swung to the other ship.

Kemocay stepped onto the bridge. "At least their hull was susceptible to our arrows."

"A minor victory," Augustus said. "Other than their mystical blast, they appeared to have no offensive weapons."

"I wouldn't be so quick to call that blast mystical," Ilfanti cautioned.

"We'll need to learn more about them," Augustus surmised. "Whatever they are."

"It would be advisable to face them from the side, then," Kemocay concluded. "Avoiding the blast, and focusing on the portions of the ship without offensive weaponry."

"Head-on is definitely a mistake," Augustus agreed. "Ilfanti, why did they not fire a second time?"

"I suspect they needed to recharge," he hypothesized, convinced that something non-magical was responsible. Whatever it was, the sheer amount of power that red blast had was uncanny.

"Is there any way to prove your theory?" she asked.

"I will join Brondolfr and see if there are any clues before the ship sinks."

"Excellent," she said. "Kemocay, you go as well. I want to know their weapons capabilities."

"Aye, Captain," he said. "Come."

The two walked over to where Brondolfr had swung across and did the same. Ilfanti dropped down onto the deck and was knee-deep in water. "Wonderful." Kemocay landed next to him and water splashed all over Ilfanti, soaking him. "Thanks."

"Let us move to the front and see if there is a power source," Kemocay advised.

"Agreed," Ilfanti said. The two stepped forward until they reached the large white bony head of the ship. Brondolfr was there chipping part of it off with his knife. "Did you get some?"

"Only where it was already broken," he admitted.

"At least you have some," Ilfanti said.

"Over here," Kemocay called out. "Look."

Ilfanti studied the small lever and panel Kemocay was indicating. He opened it and saw a small round container glowing in a vibrant red hue. "I can feel the power pulsating through that. It is most unstable."

"It looks like this lever is attached to the top of this container," Kemocay said. "As if pulling it would open part of it."

"The power source must be inside this container then," Ilfanti speculated. "Perhaps when they wish to fire, they need to pull the lever."

"There is one over here as well," Brondolfr pointed out.

"Is the same thing inside?" Kemocay asked.

Brondolfr carefully opened the panel and nodded.

"Then it is some kind of power source, not a magical weapon," Kemocay concluded, nodding to Ilfanti with respect for the dwarf's hypothesis. "I am taking them."

"Do you think that's wise?" Ilfanti asked.

"If we can adapt these for the *Soaring Mist*, it will give us a formidable weapon," Kemocay said.

"I hope you don't blow us out of the water trying to adapt it to our needs, though," Ilfanti warned.

"I'm sure Fasbender and I will rise to the challenge," he said. "Brondolfr, carefully remove the one near you."

Brondolfr reached in and gently removed the small clasp that was attached to the lever. He then lifted the glowing cylinder. "I have it."

"Excellent," Kemocay said. "I have this one as well."

"Don't look now, boys, but we have more company," Ilfanti said.

The two followed his finger and spotted two ships identical to the one they had just fought.

"Let's get back to the *Mist*," Brondolfr ordered. "We have all that we need here."

The three moved back to the side of the ship and grabbed onto a rope that was lowered for them from the *Soaring Mist*. They each climbed back up and rushed to the bridge.

"Captain, more ships," Brondolfr warned her.

"Do you have what I sent you for?" she asked.

"We do," Brondolfr confirmed.

"And more," Kemocay added.

"Very well, we'll get underway. They have only one sail. We should be able to stay ahead of them with ease."

"You heard the Captain, let's get us moving!" Brondolfr shouted out as he leapt into action, directing the sailors and shouting orders.

"Ilfanti," Augustus called out.

"Yes, Captain?"

"Is there any way for you to try and find out some information on our foes?" she asked.

"I could contact the Mage's Council," he said. "Have them conduct some research. We may not get an answer right away, though."

"That's all right," she said. "Conduct the inquiry. I wish to learn as much as we can before we face these creatures again."

"I will contact them immediately," Ilfanti promised.

"Excellent," she said. As she glanced back at the two ships, she clenched her fists. They would meet again soon enough. The next time, though, she wanted to have more information about who they were fighting and why.

CHAPTER 9

Returning to his cabin, Ilfanti reached into his satchel and removed a corryby. He held the small crystalline orb before him and thought of his former apprentice Cala. The orb began to glow and hum as the image of Cala appeared above it.

"Ilfanti!" she smiled in greeting.

"Hello, Cala," he said.

"Boy, is Pierce upset that you left," she said.

"Let me talk," a deeper voice said through the corryby. The large hairy form of the lupan, Herg, appeared above the corryby directly behind Cala.

"Hello, Herg," Ilfanti smiled. "You're both there, good."

"Don't be too hasty," Herg said. "Pierce is more than upset."

"Oh?" Ilfanti asked.

"He sent Master Zane and his dozen avarians after you."

Ilfanti began laughing.

"What's so funny?" Cala asked.

"All they'll find is an ass," Ilfanti said.

"What?" Cala asked.

"Never mind," he said to brush off the discussion. "Thanks for the information. I need some more of it, though."

"What's wrong?" Cala asked.

"We were attacked by some greenish mariners with incredible power. I need to know as much about them as I can."

"Amphibiers," Herg said.

"What?" Ilfanti asked. "I've never heard of them."

"Master Askari got to give us the scoop when he and Cicero landed right in the middle of their fleet. They are moving to Aquatica to invade it."

"They're invading Aquatica?" Ilfanti asked. "Is Askari okay?"

"He made it, but these amphibiers are quite powerful. Aquatica has their work cut out for them," Herg explained.

"So do we," Ilfanti said. "Do you know where they came from?"

"No," Cala said. "They are just one of the seven new races we have identified coming into Trespias's harbor."

"Zoldex has been busy," Ilfanti said.

"Yes, but not only here," Cala said.

"Who knows how vast his legions truly are," Herg added.

"Wonderful," Ilfanti said. "Thanks for the update."

"How about you?" Cala asked.

"I'm fine. I found a good ship known as the *Soaring Mist.* We're heading south, which unfortunately means we'll probably see more of these amphibiers before too long."

"Be careful," Cala said.

"Who? Me?" Ilfanti grinned.

"Yes, you!" Herg roared. "Don't tease her."

"I will," Ilfanti said. "I promise."

"Wow," Cala said. "You gave in."

"Wouldn't want to worry you," Ilfanti winked. "Thanks again for the information. I'll check in later."

The corryby stopped glowing and Ilfanti stared at it for several minutes before returning to report to the Captain. Zoldex was moving quickly, very quickly. The invasion had begun. He only hoped that by the time they got back and found the Empress, they had something to come back to.

❀ ❀ ❀ ❀ ❀

The griffin soared through the air as Zane followed the trackbar to his prey. Six of his golden-clad avarian Gatherers flew along each side of him in an angled v-pattern. They had been tracking Master Ilfanti for close to three weeks, and he was confident that they were closing in on him.

Ilfanti was a well-known and respected member of the Council of

Elders, but even he was not above the rules of the Council. To go against the orders of Pierce and just leave of his own accord was unacceptable.

The circular sphere in his hand began glowing more brightly. They had found him! Below, they saw a small wagon being pulled by a mule. He did not see Ilfanti, but the trackbar did not lie. The Mage Master was somewhere below.

His griffin swung into a landing directly in front of the small cart. Zane stepped down and barred the merchant's path. As always when on a mission, Zane was completely encased in his durable golden armor. A white cape with golden designs hung from his shoulders blowing wildly in the wind, as was his long lime green hair.

"Stop," he ordered. "We are investigating the disappearance of a Mage Master."

"I don't know anythin'," the man said. He was an elderly man with a lisp in his speech. "I'm only tryin' to make me a livin'."

The twelve avarians all swooped down to a landing and encircled the wagon. Each of them was garbed in golden armor, including helms upon their brows, with white tunics wrapped around their chests and fastened at their waists by a golden belt.

Zane stepped forward with the trackbar and paused directly in front of the mule. "You thought you could disguise yourself from me?"

"Why are you talkin' to old Bessie?" the merchant asked. "I've had her almost as long as I've been alive."

"I'm sure," Zane sneered. "Come on, Ilfanti, you cannot hide from us."

The avarians stepped closer to the mule. The mule looked back and forth and appeared to grow slightly agitated.

"I am growing impatient," Zane growled. "Transform back to your normal form."

"I'm tellin' you, this here is old Bessie," the merchant persisted.

Zane raised his hand and sent a jolt into the mule. The mule began pushing backwards and kicking with its hind legs.

"I don't understand," Zane said. "That should have forced him to transmute back into his normal form."

"I demand satisfaction!" the merchant cried out. "You have no right to land in front of us and hurt old Bessie!"

Zane glanced at his troops and stepped back. "My apologies, there must be some mistake."

"I'll say!" the merchant called out as he pushed his wagon past the avarians and continued along his route. "Damned stupid Mages!"

Zane picked up his corryby and contacted Master Pierce.

"Report," the image of Pierce demanded.

"Somehow we have been misled," Zane commented. "We followed the signal but only found a mule."

"Where are you now?" Pierce asked.

"We are on the road near the Dimmu Forest."

"Head south," Pierce ordered.

"South?" Zane asked.

"Yes, I have intercepted a transmission between Ilfanti and his supporters in the Council."

"Herg and Cala," Zane sneered.

"Yes," Pierce confirmed. "Ilfanti is sailing aboard a ship known as the *Soaring Mist* and is traveling south. They will be upon Aquatica soon."

"Then we are to head to Aquatica?"

"No. Go to the Carrion Mountains. You will have a better vantage point closer to land. Stop him there."

"Understood."

"Do not fail me again, Zane," Pierce said in a threatening tone as the corryby stopped humming and the image faded out.

Zane jumped on top of his griffin and called out to his troops: "To the Carrion Mountains! Let's fly!"

CHAPTER 10

As she watched the ships fall further and further behind them, Augustus finally unclenched her fists. "Green, the ship is yours."

"Yesss, mother," Green replied.

"Keep her straight and steady," Augustus added. "If you see more of those ships, sound the alarm at once."

"Yesss, mother."

"Brondolfr, you're with me," Augustus instructed as she stepped down from the bridge.

"Aye, Captain."

The two headed below decks and went straight to the infirmary where Jin Fe practiced his art. As they opened the cabin door and stepped inside, Augustus saw that the Aezian was still working relentlessly on the Paladin.

Jin Fe's right hand was above Krimdor's head. One of the rings on his finger glowed and cast a slight light down to his patient. Where the light touched Krimdor, his face was almost transparent, revealing the muscles and bone beneath the skin.

"How is he?" Augustus asked.

"He is bleeding internally," Jin Fe replied with a note of concern.

"What can you do?" Augustus asked.

"Shimada, get me my potions," Jin Fe instructed.

"Yes, grandfather," she bowed slightly.

Brondolfr peered over Augustus's shoulder and spotted a small rodent-like creature shaking slightly on Krimdor's hand. "Get away from him!" he shouted angrily.

Jin Fe glanced up and then down at the hand. "Do not fret, proud Brondolfr," he said. "The karonoul is helping him."

"What?" Brondolfr gasped. "How?"

"The karonoul drinks blood," Jin Fe said. "Krimdor is bleeding from his very pores. The karonoul is drinking the blood, but its saliva also has regenerative powers and the wounds are closing."

"It's some kind of rodent vampire?" Brondolfr asked in disgust.

"No, no, nothing like that," Jin Fe hastily replied. "Just one of my many pets."

"The potions, grandfather," Shimada said as she handed a small box to Jin Fe.

"Thank you, dear," he replied. He pulled several bottles out, read the labels and returned them again. Finally, he found one that he was happy with. "Ah, here we go."

Removing a needle attached to a small tube, he carefully inserted it into Krimdor's arm. "Shimada, I need something to tie this in."

Shimada stepped over with a ribbon that she wrapped taut around the arm.

"Thank you," Jin Fe said. "Could you fill this with water?"

"Yes, grandfather," Shimada said as she took a small squeezable container and left the room.

"What is the treatment?" Augustus asked.

"I am going to inject a potion into his system intravenously. It will flow through his veins and help to seal any wounds," he explained. Reaching into a small round can, he removed a brownish ooze and spread it over Krimdor's eyes and nose.

Brondolfr furled his nose in disgust. Whatever it was, it smelled like something that had died in the depths of a swamp.

Jin Fe glanced up and smiled. "It looks like our barbarian friend does not like the excrement of the hortabyl."

Augustus glanced back at Brondolfr who looked as if he was about to vomit, and had to admit that she could not blame him. The stench was quite pungent.

"The water, grandfather," Shimada said as she returned and handed it to Jin Fe.

Jin Fe took it and bowed his acknowledgement. "Thank you, dear." He then took a small eyedropper, carefully measured the amount of the potion he wished to use, and released five drops into the water. "That should do it."

He carefully fastened the squeezable container to the end of the tube that was fastened to Krimdor's arm and applied some pressure to force the liquid to start moving into Krimdor's veins. Once he saw that the diluted potion was flowing, he hung it on a small hook above Krimdor so that it would continue to drip and flow into his patient.

Augustus watched for several more moments and then nodded to Jin Fe. "Have Shimada report to me when there is any change."

"Of course, Captain," he bowed.

As she turned to leave, she spotted the body of one of their attackers. She wished to learn more, but Krimdor's health was more important right now. She would ask about the creature after Jin Fe was able to safely leave Krimdor's side.

The two stepped down another flight of stairs and approached the room that Fasbender and his gnomes had built for a lab. It truly was more of a tinker shop, but they had invented some amazing gadgets here. As she opened the door, she saw Fasbender, his staff of gnomes, and Kemocay all standing around a table talking. The two items that Kemocay had found on the enemy ship were perched in the middle of the table.

Fasbender was still wearing the suit that he wore to dinner. Augustus knew that the gnome did not like to work in his suit, but they had been attacked and he had needed to return to the engine room quickly. To help protect his garments, he had an oil-stained apron wrapped around his neck that hung down to his legs. He also had rubber gloves that extended to his elbows and boots that extended to his knees.

Atop his head was one of his more useful inventions. It was a small round helmet that had several jointed mechanical arms jutting from it. Each arm could bend and move as he needed it to and was attached to another tool—such as a magnifying glass, a light, a wrench, a screwdriver, and a towel.

"Any progress?" Augustus asked.

Fasbender stopped talking when he heard the Captain and ran to greet her. "Yes, yes, let us show you!" He led her over to a small oven and opened the door. "That is the fragment from the stem of their ship."

"What are you trying to show me?" Augustus asked.

"It won't melt!" he shouted as if it was an obvious answer.

"We saw that when Ilfanti released a fireball," Augustus said.

"You don't understand—we have this oven currently set at five hundred degrees rhelvin. Even illistrium begins to lose its pure form at such temperatures."

"Theories?" Augustus asked.

Kemocay stepped forward. "I'll tell you so you don't have to listen to a discussion about the molecular composition of the material."

"I would appreciate that," Augustus said.

"Everyone's a critic!" Fasbender protested.

"We concur that whatever this substance is, the fact that it doesn't melt means that it was designed to protect the ship from the weapon it used," Kemocay explained.

"Can it be destroyed?" Augustus asked.

"As you saw, a catapult ball did damage it, and in doing so, made the structure much weaker—so yes."

"It is just not susceptible to heat?"

"Correct," Kemocay said.

"At least not at temperatures we can get to," Fasbender clarified.

"What about the weapon itself?" Augustus asked. "Can we modify and use it?"

"Perhaps," Kemocay replied uncertainly.

"We think so," Fasbender said. "We can make a barrel to hold the power source, but we are not certain that it can handle the amount of energy channeled through it."

"What would that mean?" Augustus asked.

"It could melt the barrel," Kemocay said shaking his head. "Illistrium might work, but like we said, this substance might not be as strong as illistrium, but it also does not melt anywhere near as quickly."

"Keep me apprised of your progress," Augustus said.

"Aye, Captain," Kemocay returned with a salute.

"Where to now, Captain?" Brondolfr asked.

"To see Ilfanti," she replied.

The two climbed one flight of stairs and spotted Ilfanti climbing down a flight himself.

"I was looking for you," he said.

"You have learned something?" Augustus asked.

"Yes," Ilfanti confirmed. "We are fighting a race known as the amphibiers. There is little known about them, but they are part of the legions of Zoldex and are currently preparing to invade Aquatica."

"Aquatica?" Augustus asked, a look of horror in her eyes. "Our course will have us upon Aquatica by first light."

The crew is uneasy. It doesn't take a Mage Master to see that. Our first conflict with the amphibiers may have resulted in victory, but the weapon they used is terrifying. Krimdor remains in a coma, and if that blast can knock out a Mage, this ship may be defenseless after I return the first volley. That is something that everyone seems quite aware of.

The two ships following us have fallen further behind, but we can still see them in the moonlight on the horizon. It is like we are being herded directly for Aquatica, and who knows what we will find once we get there; a fleet lying in wait, or the aquaticans cheering triumphantly over their victory? I hope for the latter but fear that reality will bring us the former.

Zoldex is moving quickly. I had evidence that he was behind the fall of Xylona and Vorstad, as well as the attacks on the Dartian Plains and Arkham. It was foolish of us, naïve to think that this was all that he had done. Zoldex knows whom he is going up against, and has had almost eight thousand years to plot and plan his revenge on Pierce. We are definitely playing catch-up here, and so far, that is not working out particularly well for us.

If Aquatica falls, what significance would that play in the grand scheme of things? So far, Zoldex has picked his targets well. Xylona is not as big as Turning Leaf, but it has a deep heritage and history of being involved in the wars of the realms. Sure, Wild Wood is full of elven warriors, but Xylona was the embodiment of a true elven warrior city. Honorable, noble, just, and all of that with a touch of diplomacy. The fall of such a great city will be felt for generations. That was definitely a good target to go after first.

Then there was Vorstad. Neither as skilled as Tregador as craftsmen, nor as wealthy as Carnelian, but they were the "true sons of Vorstad." They were the warriors. The proud soldiers who would march to battle against overwhelming odds and somehow find a way to walk back out singing songs of glory and victory. Their whole existence centered around their skill in combat, and in all of the history of the realm, other than perhaps the Elandeeril, no army or race has ever come close to matching the ferocity, skill, determination, and honor of Vorstad.

What about the Elandeeril? They single-handedly managed to thwart the Zarlextix invasion. No small feat. But will they become involved in this war? The maiden unicorn riders are mystical and skilled, apparently gifted by the gods themselves. They are lovely, peaceful and alluring, but also swift, brutal and unyielding. Could that be a paradox? The Elandeeril, in fact, all of the elves of Faylinn, have sworn that they will no longer become involved with the matters of the land. I hope to change this. That is why I am arranging to have my meeting with the heroes of the realm there upon my return. Centain could be the key to the success of getting the Elandeeril involved. He'll have a year to persuade them and prove the necessity of our quest.

But I am getting ahead of myself. The future is still unwritten. What is happening in the present is of paramount import. Aquatica. Sovereign Arianna, due to her relationship with her brother Askari, was one of the first races to heed the Empress's call for unification. She is a strong supporter and holds a lot of weight in the realm. Where she goes, others will follow.

Not only that, but the aquaticans can rule the seas. Frocomon is a pale image of what it was merely sixty years ago. It was once the strongest fleet to sail the oceans blue. Now, they struggle to keep smaller fishing barges from sinking.

Dartais? I don't see much help from them either. This ship may be extraordinary, but it is a unique case due to the passion and drive of its creators. I still don't know what led Augustus to so boldly design this ship and hunt down pirates for a living, but something sinister had to have happened to her. Perhaps a pirate either murdered her family or raped her. Either way, I'm not about to ask and bring up somber memories. Other than this ship, though, Dartais has grown too fat for its own good. Their merchant ships will be useless, especially against foes like the amphibiers.

So the battle for the sea falls to the aquaticans. If the newly elected Emperor had not sent the Imperial forces to Aezia, at least the Imperial Navy could have offered some resistance, but they are gone as well. Yes. If Aquatica falls, it will have a severe impact on the realm.

Fifty years ago, a young idealist named Conrad created the Im-

perium. Prior to that, though, he gained his success by conquering the seas. Once he had done that, he could barricade coasts and block the shipping lanes. Frocomon and Dartais depended on the sea considerably. With the armies of Danchul, the conquest of the sea soon spread to the land and the Imperium was formed.

Could the same thing be happening now? If Zoldex conquered the sea, would he have a similar advantage over the realm? What is even more frightening, with the orc and goblin armies in the south that Ferceng reported, he has an army just as strong, if not stronger than, the army of Danchul so long ago. Zoldex is already a step ahead.

What other allies does he have? Cala mentioned seven unknown races arriving at the shores of Trespias. Seven! To be unknown to the Mage's Council is quite a feat. We boast the best education not only in the Seven Kingdoms, but the entire world. To not know of seven races is unthinkable!

But who else is working for him? Hobgoblins? Giants? Cyclopes? Slitharell? Trolls? All of these and more have fought against the races of the realm during the Race Wars. Could Zoldex have forged an alliance between these old comrades, settling their differences and moving to destroy all in their path?

Too many questions and not enough answers. All I have right now are doubts. Doubts about the chances the Seven Kingdoms and all the races within have of survival. Doubts about the true chances Empress Karleena has to unite the races. Even doubts about this mission I am on. Perhaps I would serve the resistance movement better by trying to persuade the rest of the Council of Elders of the severity of this situation. I may not have ever sought it, but I have always carried a lot of weight in the Council. Perhaps I should be using that to the advantage of the entire realm?

No. I cannot allow my thoughts to stray that way. The Council is as blind as Jeffa. I would not be able to convince people who are unwilling to listen. That is why there are only a small handful of us. The brave few that are willing to defy the Council and try to help save the realm. May the gods, whichever gods each of us pray to, look fondly upon us and protect us. Before this is over, the will of the gods may be all that can save us. If that is the case, then I fear we are already doomed.

CHAPTER 11

A storm. The lightning crackled, the skies grew dark, and the seas pelted the hull. The fog was so dense that Ilfanti felt like he was trying to walk through water. He raised his arm to shield his face as the rain hammered down on him. Straining to see, his worst fears came true: hundreds of the amphibiers' ships spread across the horizon, waiting for them. In his ear, he could almost hear the faint laughter of the sinister Zoldex.

"No," he cried out. "You will not beat me so easily!"

Then something unexpected happened. The ships sailed directly past the *Soaring Mist*. Ilfanti bit his lip as some came so close that they could reach right out and touch each other, but he refrained from saying anything, from even breathing, in hopes that they would go unnoticed.

The laughter of Zoldex passed by like an echo, further and further away. Ilfanti climbed up the mainmast and tried to see the ships below, but none could be seen. What happened to them? Where were they? Were they just lying in wait to destroy them?

No answers came to him. The laughter was gone, and so too were the ships. As quickly as the storm had descended upon them, it let up, and left the *Soaring Mist* alone on the open ocean with nothing more than calm waters and a clear sky.

Ilfanti studied the ship, but it appeared as it did on any other day. The crew was hard at work swabbing the deck, raising the sails, and plotting their course. The amphibiers' fleet was behind them, and sailing would be clear straight to Egziard.

Closing his eyes, Ilfanti took a deep and steadying breath. He could not believe the fortune that had shined down on them and the ease by which they had managed to elude their pursuers. It was a sign; an omen from the gods that they were watching and that fortune favored this expedition.

Opening his eyes again, the Mage Master was disoriented and confused. He lay on the bunk in his stateroom, not atop the mainmast. The room was still dark and as he peered through the window, he saw that the sun had not yet risen above the horizon. Beyond his door, he could hear voices speaking in the halls, and footsteps rushing about their duties.

Was it a dream? A vision? Either way, he knew what had to be done. He now possessed the knowledge of how to survive this day, and with some preparations, he was certain that he could put it to good use.

❖ ❖ ❖ ❖ ❖

Augustus stepped down into the room where Kemocay and Fasbender were still working on the weapons acquired from the destroyed ship. As she scanned their faces, she could see that they were quite frustrated. "Anything to report?"

Fasbender glanced up and rubbed his face, leaving black soot smeared from his forehead down to his mouth. "We can definitely make something to allow us to fire the weapon."

"That is excellent news," Augustus said with a sigh of relief.

Kemocay shook his head back and forth.

"What?" Augustus asked.

"The earliest we could have it ready is a week if we're lucky, but probably closer to two," Fasbender explained.

"Two weeks?" Augustus repeated, her shoulders slumping with the news.

"Even then, we are not certain how many shots we can fire before the illistrium would melt," Fasbender continued.

"We have enough illistrium to do what you need?" Augustus asked.

"We're pushing it a bit, but we can scrape together enough weapons and tools to make it happen," Fasbender shrugged.

"The gnomes have made some ingenious designs in a short period of time, but to pull this off properly, we really need a Tregador dwarf," Kemocay reported. "Some raw illistrium wouldn't hurt, either."

Fasbender frowned at the observation and folded his arms. "We can do it."

"But a Tregador dwarf would do it quicker," Kemocay said confidently.

"We don't have a Tregador dwarf," Augustus replied. "Let me make certain that I understand you completely—there is no possible way to use this weapon if we were to see battle today above Aquatica?"

"Correct," Kemocay replied.

"Then I see no reason to continue spending time on this now. The sun will be up soon and we will need to be prepared for battle. Fasbender, have your staff prepared in the engine room and ready for whatever may come."

"Aye, Captain," Fasbender said.

"Kemocay, I know your staff has been preparing throughout the night, but I need them to confirm that our defenses and weapons are truly ready. We could be upon the enemy on a moment's notice."

"Aye, Captain," Kemocay replied.

"That will be all, gentlemen," Captain Augustus said as she watched them bow slightly and go. Augustus remained for a moment looking at the amphibiers' weapon and wishing that they had enough time to add it to their own arsenal. No use worrying about things that could not be controlled, though.

Walking back up to the mid-deck, Augustus stepped into the infirmary and glanced over at Krimdor, who was heavily bandaged and still not awake. Jin Fe was sitting cross-legged before him and chanting softly.

Shimada stood up and quietly led Augustus back out of the room again. "Grandfather is still working on him."

"There is no sign of improvement?"

"Not yet," Shimada said.

Augustus clenched her fist. She was not pleased by the news her rounds were uncovering. "Shimada, you should arm yourself and prepare. We will most likely be in open combat soon."

"I understand," Shimada said with a bow.

As she started up the final set of stairs, she heard footsteps behind her and turned to look. Ilfanti jogged over to her and smiled. Augustus could not help but notice Shimada narrowing her eyes in an untrusting glare before she returned to her cabin to arm herself.

"I think I may have an idea that can help us."

"I would welcome such an idea," Augustus said.

"It came to me in a dream," Ilfanti said.

"I'm listening," Augustus prompted.

"In my dream, we were sailing through a storm. We could hardly see what was even directly in front of us, but we managed to sneak past the amphibiers' fleet."

"How will this storm help us? Can you control the weather?"

"Of course not," Ilfanti said. "However, a child in the Mage's Council by the name of Kyria told me that she had once come across a ship that seemed to be able to do just that. From what she said, the very water obeyed this ship, lightning cracked, and it was as if the ship could dictate the direction of the storm."

Augustus did not respond, but the *Soaring Mist* had been sailing long enough to know about the reports of the *White Squall*. Every mariner had heard the tales of the unyielding Captain Kor and his crew of humans and aquaticans. Though she and her crew had hunted pirates, the *Squall* was one ship they were probably fortunate to have not encountered thus far.

"I believe that this effect is being manipulated by a Mage," Ilfanti speculated.

"Krimdor has given us many advantages over the years. He has added wind to the sails when we needed speed; fireballs and lightning to strike our foes from afar; and protection spells to help defend our ship. Never, though, has he been able to affect the sea and storms themselves."

"What you say is true," Ilfanti agreed. "However, Mages can do things like creating shrouds to hide us. I can make a fog that will make us virtually undetectable. Lightning blasts could be perceived as lightning. Strong gusts of wind, also something I can do, could be why the waters appear to obey the will of this ship."

"And you can do this for us?" Augustus asked to confirm.

"I could, but I think that with just the fog, we may be able to slip past them without engaging the enemy."

"That would be ideal," Augustus agreed. "We will undoubtedly see much battle getting you to your destination, but any skirmishes we can avoid will help to increase the odds of your success."

"Captain," a deep voice called from above.

Augustus stepped all the way onto the deck and faced her second officer, Brondolfr. "Report."

"We can see torches in the distance."

Ilfanti joined them on the deck and strained to see. There were torches in the distance. Many torches.

Augustus held her hand out and Brondolfr handed her the optical enhancers. She held them up to her right eye and closed her left, studying the lights in the distance. What she saw was rather odd. There were hundreds of ships like the one they had already fought, but there were also dozens of flat platforms that these ships had strung up between them. Standing atop the platform was what could only be the invasion force against Aquatica.

"Have you had any signs that they have spotted us or know that we are here?"

"No, Captain," Brondolfr said.

"We are no match for a pair of those ships. There is no way that we would survive an encounter with hundreds of them. This is an invasion force. Even if Aquatica itself came to our aid right now, we still might not survive the day."

"I came to the same conclusion, Captain," Brondolfr said.

"Sound the alarm, quietly. I want everyone in position and ready in case we are uncovered. The sun will be up soon, and when it is, I have a strange suspicion that the amphibiers will learn that there will be a storm today."

Brondolfr looked up in the air in confusion. As a barbarian, he had lived in the elements all of his life. His people, though not gifted with any specific abilities, could accurately anticipate changing weather patterns. At this moment, he had no sense of any type of impending storm.

Augustus patted him on the shoulder as she walked past him to go to the bridge. "Do not worry, brave Brondolfr, our passenger will assure us a storm."

Brondolfr glanced at Ilfanti, who only winked in reply. If this dwarf could control the elements, then he was more powerful than any Mage the barbarian had ever met. By the will of Xeorn, he prayed that be true.

CHAPTER 12

The *Soaring Mist* slowly closed in on the fleet lying in wait on the waters of the Artrillis Ocean above Aquatica. The fog that Ilfanti mystically summoned had been a brilliant idea, leaving the air around them so thick that people could barely see two feet in front of them.

Captain Augustus had another idea, and instructed Ilfanti to create another illusion. To those that they passed close enough to, the *Soaring Mist* looked identical to one of the amphibier warships.

The dwarven Master had cautioned them, though, that in spite of the illusion, the *Mist* was far larger than their opponents' ships, and it was quite possible that this discrepancy could draw attention to them. Since they appeared identical, an onlooker would think that there was open air where there was really still part of the hull.

To help support the illusion, Augustus ordered all sails lowered with the exception of one. It would not be convincing if they soared through the enemy ranks far more quickly than any of the amphibier vessels. She also demanded silence. All weapons were primed and ready, but she was directing her crew with hand signals and messengers that would run and relay her orders. Undoubtedly, amphibiers would not speak in the common tongue when only with their own kind.

Those on board were tense. This tactic was extremely risky, and if their true identities were revealed, then odds were not in favor of surviving this morning. Thus far, however, they had slowly inched their way through almost half of the opposing armada and still seen no signs of discovery.

Ilfanti could hear splashing in the distance. It started with a few, but quickly escalated in frequency as if hundreds, or perhaps even thousands of amphibiers were leaping into the ocean. Ilfanti strained to see Augustus, and could see that the Captain was well aware of the dangers of the amphibiers taking to the water.

He heard cracking right behind him and turned to see Brondolfr. The barbarian was anxiously working on his knuckles as he anticipated the impending attack. If they were to fall this day, Xeorn would look proudly on this brave warrior for sending many to the hellish depths of Tanorus, a feat that would certainly guarantee Brondolfr an eternal home in Wolhollm, where he could share his tale with other slain heroes and warriors of honorable deeds.

As Ilfanti pondered what the barbarian must be thinking, he shuddered as something impacted the hull. First, it was a single bang, but it was quickly followed up with several more. From the waters below, they could hear the high-pitched chatter that served as the amphibier language.

"They hit the hull," Brondolfr clarified for everyone on the bridge. "We have been uncovered."

Augustus still did not move. There was definitely increased communication around them, but thus far, they had not been attacked. She would hate to reveal themselves prematurely. After all, perhaps the divers that hit their hull were still under the impression that this was an amphibier vessel.

Whispering so only those around her could hear, Augustus asked for a status update. "Green, how long before we clear the fleet?"

"At this pace, five more minutesss," Green replied.

"That will be a long five minutes if we are uncovered," Brondolfr observed.

"Indeed it would be," Augustus agreed. "Ilfanti, can you gain a better understanding of what is happening?"

"I do not understand the amphibier tongue," Ilfanti solemnly said. "However, the words appear to be growing in agitation. They must expect an answer that we are not providing."

"Damn," Augustus tensed. "Very well, raise the rest of the sails. Let's try to get out of here while there is still some confusion surrounding us."

"Aye, Captain," Brondolfr said. He stepped over to the side railing of the bridge and issued a series of hand signals to three individuals who all ran off to relay the orders.

"Once the sails are up, can you somehow help with the wind?" Augustus asked looking at Ilfanti. "You mentioned that you could control wind spells."

"I can," he said. "We shall have the wind at our backs, and perhaps right in the faces of any pursuers," Ilfanti grinned with the thought.

"I wish we had a better idea about what was going on," Augustus said in mild frustration as another amphibier slammed into the aft hull.

"Just a theory, but I would guess that the amphibiers are beginning their assault on Aquatica. The splashing we heard was the initial attack group taking to the water. They just don't expect to run into a ship that shouldn't be where we are," Ilfanti speculated.

"Sounds plausible," Augustus agreed. "Too bad for us they did not wait another five minutes."

"Captain!" a voice shouted out.

"Damn," Augustus cried as she gritted her teeth. "Doesn't whoever that is know we are trying to maintain silence?"

"I will find out, Captain," Brondolfr said.

"Captain!"

"Quiet, sailor," Brondolfr said through gritted teeth as he grabbed the man and covered his mouth. "Now, quietly, what is it?"

"The amphibier weapons! We spotted some of the glowing eyes ahead of us!"

Brondolfr glanced back at Augustus and could see her working through the problem.

"Ilfanti?" she asked.

"If it is a single ship, maybe I could take her, but you'd be losing me from the fight if the effort is anywhere like what happened to Krimdor."

"Brondolfr, you and Ilfanti go to the bow and check it out," Augustus ordered.

"Aye, Captain," Brondolfr returned.

Ilfanti followed the barbarian, keeping up with his massive strides. The two reached the mast and could clearly see the eerie glow of the amphibier weapons in the distance before them. Not just a single ship, but what looked like half a dozen ships lined up in wait for them.

"Go report, I'll see what I can do," Ilfanti said.

"May Xeorn look kindly upon you this day," Brondolfr said as he grasped Ilfanti's shoulder before turning to inform the captain.

"May he look kindly upon all of us," Ilfanti whispered in reply. As he finished his comment, he saw the glowing intensify. The ships were about to fire. There would be no way to deflect them all.

Then he had an idea. It certainly would be a strain, but all Mages learned from a young age how to move things. It could be something small like lifting a pen and bringing it to you from across the room, but in theory, the spell would work the same for a much larger object. If he could do that with the *Soaring Mist*, they would at least have a chance at survival.

* * * * *

Brondolfr rushed back to the bridge and stared up at Augustus. "Trouble!"

"How bad?" Augustus asked.

"At least six ships already powering up their weapons," Brondolfr replied.

"All hands, battle stations!" Augustus called out.

"All hands, battle stations!" Brondolfr shouted, repeating the order. There was no more need for silence—their presence had been detected.

The deck of the ship swirled into motion. Kemocay's men emerged from below decks and positioned themselves along the sides. Other men worked on the catapults at each end of the ship. Sailors were scurrying about too, working to make certain that the rigging was set and the ship as mobile as possible.

As Augustus watched, everyone on board began losing their balance and stumbling backwards. She grabbed hold of the railing and held on, but could see others falling all around the ship. "What is happening?"

Green wrapped his tail around the railing and leaned over the side. "Imposssible!"

"Report!"

As he watched, the ship continued to lift higher into the air, and several red blasts lanced below them.

"Are we hit?" Augustus shouted. "Report!"

"We're flying!" Green replied in shock.

Augustus tried to balance herself as she stumbled over to join Green and looked over the edge. They were indeed in the air and floating above the ships that had been barring their path. Straining to look back, she could see flames in the fog. The blasts of the amphibier ships had hit their own fleet.

Several moments after they cleared the amphibier fleet, the ship angled back down toward the water again. They were dropping too quickly. "All hands, brace for impact!"

Next to her, Green grabbed Augustus with both hands and tightened his grip on the ship with his tail. He refused to allow any harm come to his mother. They both held on tightly as the ship crashed back into the water below and the forward section of the ship continued to dive underwater with the thrust of the impact.

Augustus's eyes widened as she watched her entire ship submerging and being dragged under by the impact. Taking a deep breath, the water was quickly upon her and she too was lost to the chilling waters of the Artrillis Ocean.

The ship continued downwards and then slowly began to correct itself and angle back up again. Augustus's lungs were bursting in desperation for another breath, but she could feel the ship rising back to the surface again. With a loud crash as they pierced the surface, the front of the ship came up and then slammed down flat onto the water again.

Augustus took several deep breaths and was grateful to have survived, but saw the deck full of water. "All hands, quickly, we need to get the water off of the ship or we'll still sink!"

All around her, dazed crewmembers shook off their confusion and amazement and scurried about, grabbing pails and trying to remove all water from the ship. Augustus wondered what had happened. How had they flown? The only possible answer: Ilfanti.

Kemocay ran to the stern of the ship and looked back. "We still have trouble!"

Augustus glanced back at her weapons officer. "What is it?"

"They're following us!"

"How many ships?" Augustus asked.

"It looks like the six that had been blocking our path," Kemocay replied.

Augustus clenched her fists. How could they face six warships when they were taking on water and in danger of sinking?

※ ※ ※ ※ ※

Shimada rushed to the bow of the ship and spotted Ilfanti hanging unconscious, one of his arms wrapped around the rigging. She had seen the whole thing. He was responsible for this. He somehow lifted them into the air and also corrected the descent of the ship after they plunged into the water. He had saved them all.

Carefully removing his arm from where it was wrapped, the dwarf slumped to the ground. Shimada stared down at him and then slapped him across the face. No response. Frustrated, she slapped him a second time, a little harder.

This time, Ilfanti's eyes opened slightly, but the Mage Master was still groggy and struggled to remain conscious.

"You are still needed," Shimada said.

"Help me up," Ilfanti replied weakly.

Shimada pulled him to his feet and supported him by letting Ilfanti lean on her. "You saved us, but the ship has taken on water. We are sinking."

Ilfanti blinked several times as if trying to regain his focus. He was soaked and could see the water on the ship. They would sink unless something was done.

"We are also being pursued," Shimada informed him. "The Captain cannot fight the amphibiers and try to salvage the ship at the same time. You must do something!"

Ilfanti struggled to concentrate, but one thought kept crossing his mind—Mage's robes. The clothing that the Mages wore was highly mystical and prevented the garments from ever becoming dirty. If something spilled on them, they cleaned themselves. If they ripped, it would mend the fabric. If it got wet, the cloth would dry. That last fact was exactly what he needed.

Trying to concentrate on the task at hand, he closed his eyes and balled his fists.

"This is no time to pass out!" Shimada screeched at him.

Ilfanti opened one eye and glared at her. "I must concentrate. I assure you, I'll have the decency to wait to pass out until after I have saved us."

Closing his eyes again, he focused on the water on the ship. It wasn't just on the deck, but below decks as well. He could see the gnomes in the engine room struggling to get away from their shop as it filled with water. Jin Fe in the infirmary was waist-high in water and trying to move his pets and patients higher above the water for as long as he could. Palisha and Beige were still in the dining saloon, placing sacks of grain along the creases in the doors to try and stop the water from flowing in.

Calming himself, he concentrated on all of this, and then focused on the drying spell. The magnitude was far more intense than he had ever tried before, but just as with launching the ship in the air, he could not fail.

Shimada felt a burning warmth and glanced around. The entire deck was steaming around her. "You're doing it!"

Ilfanti could feel the water swirling on the boat. It was as if he had melded with it. Become one with it. He could see the chemical composition of the water. He knew exactly what temperature he needed to raise the water to in order to boil it off, and it was working, not only on the deck, but also throughout the entire ship.

He could see the gnomes ceasing their struggles and returning to the engine room, now dry. Jin Fe slumped down in a chair and breathed a sigh of relief. Palisha and Beige shared a hug of relief. He had done it. He had saved the ship.

Opening his eyes, he grinned at Shimada and winked. "Told you I wouldn't pass out until I was done."

With those words, he crumpled down before her and was unconscious once more. "Rest, noble dwarf," Shimada said. "You have earned my respect this day. I now promise you, by the sword of my ancestors, we will survive today so that when you awaken, you will be on your quest once more."

CHAPTER 13

"They're gaining, Captain," Brondolfr warned.

Augustus glanced back at the pursuing ships. Ilfanti had managed to stop them from sinking, but they had been dead in the water for too long. The amphibiers were almost upon them.

"Mother?" Green asked.

"Kemocay, get below decks and get the ballistae ready to fire," Augustus ordered. "Everyone else, arm yourselves. We'll see our share of fighting this day."

"Aye, Captain," Kemocay said as he rushed to the hatch and down to the mid-deck.

Green stepped back and reached into a small cabinet on the bridge, removing a mace. Unlike Beige, he never was fond of fighting with weapons. He preferred more educational and theoretical practices, which is why he had studied to be the ship's Navigator. Regardless, any intruders that dared set foot on his bridge would find him more than capable of defending his ship.

Augustus drew her cutlass and held it firmly above her head for all to see. Stepping forward, she called out to the sailors on the deck. "This ship and all of you have been trained in the tempest of a blazing inferno. We may not be facing pirates this day, but there is no better crew, and no possible way that I could have more faith than I do in all of you. We will fight! And we will triumph!"

"Victory!" Brondolfr shouted as he raised his axe over his head.

"Victory!" the crew repeated his call.

"Everyone, to arms!" Augustus ordered.

"To arms!" Brondolfr repeated.

The archers lined up along the sides of the deck, sailors vanished and returned with cutlasses and daggers. They were ready for whatever this day might bring.

"Helm, bring us about," Augustus ordered.

"Aye, Captain."

The ship slowly turned, and Augustus could clearly see the six advancing ships off of the port bow. Raising her sword in the air, she waited, watching the ships approaching them.

Brondolfr carefully watched for her signal, one hand clutching his battleaxe, the other the microphone to signal Kemocay below decks.

"Fire!" Augustus shouted as she slashed her sword down.

"Fire!" Brondolfr shouted into the mouthpiece.

The crew all watched as six wooden lances with steel tips launched from the mid-deck out toward the oncoming vessels. They impacted the ships, but did very little damage.

"Keep bringing us about," Augustus ordered.

"Aye, Captain."

"Catapults, begin the barrage," said Augustus, signaling Brondolfr.

"Catapults, fire!" Brondolfr shouted the order.

From the forward and aft of the ship, the catapults began launching one single hollow steel ball at a time toward the enemy vessels. Some hit, others landed in the water, but the artillery crew worked relentlessly to reload and release the next volley, making minor adjustments to strike their targets.

"Steer us between the two middle ships," Augustus commented.

"Are we ramming them, mother?" Green asked.

"No, I'm hoping to divide them," she explained. "Engines, full ahead!"

Brondolfr pulled the microphone to his mouth again and called down for Fasbender and the engineers. "Engines, full ahead!"

First there was only a single burst of blackish smoke emitted behind them, but the intensity increased as the engines fired to life and began propelling them closer to their foes.

"Archers, on my command," Augustus instructed.

"Archers, stand ready!" Brondolfr shouted. Along the sides, each of the archers strung and nocked an arrow, waiting to unleash a volley of their own.

Shimada and Beige stepped onto the main deck and approached the bridge.

"Report," Augustus demanded.

"Ilfanti has been brought to my grandfather," Shimada said. "I do not think he will be able to revive quickly enough to participate in this skirmish."

"What is the status of Krimdor?" Augustus asked.

"Still unconscious," Shimada relayed.

"Understood," Augustus replied, showing no sign of distress at the dismal news.

"My grandfather has news that may be beneficial," Shimada began.

"Go ahead," Augustus prompted.

"The amphibiers have healing and regenerative abilities," she explained. "Not super fast, but quick enough. Grandfather was conducting an autopsy overnight, and he found this morning that one of the severed limbs was reforming. This ability does not seem hindered by the fact that the amphibier is deceased."

"Continue," Augustus said.

"They also have redundant organs to help keep them alive longer if say, one's first heart was pierced," Shimada concluded.

"Sever its head and it will still die," Brondolfr confidently replied as he spun his axe in his hands.

"Anything else?" Augustus asked.

"Nothing else that we have learned from a dead one—yet, at least," Shimada replied.

"Very well," Augustus said. "Spread the word that just because you think one is down, it doesn't necessarily mean that it is."

"Aye, Captain," Brondolfr said.

"Do not worry, mother," Beige placated as he slammed his staff on the deck. The staff—a traditional raspler weapon known as the raspler warpike—resembled a large spear with three blades, two arching down and a single longer blade stretching up. Unlike Green, Beige had studied the use of weapons frequently, and this particular one he had crafted himself in the style of his people's dreaded warpike, with the assistance of Kemocay. "We ssshall protect you."

Augustus reached down and caressed his head for a moment. "I will see you soon," she commented, full of confidence.

With that, Beige darted toward the stem of the ship, his warpike firmly clasped in both hands waiting for an enemy to dare set foot on the ship. Shimada followed him, her swords still sheathed, but her bow in her hand.

"Mother," Green prompted.

Augustus followed his gaze and smirked devilishly when she saw the amphibier ships arch slightly apart to allow them to sail through. They must be assuming that they could trap the *Soaring Mist* between them and the rest of the fleet. They would soon learn the folly of their decision, she thought.

As they sailed directly through the six ships, so close that they could practically touch them, Augustus slashed her cutlass down again. "Now!"

"Fire!" Brondolfr shouted.

The archers on the deck began unleashing arrows down at the amphibiers on the ships below. At the same time, six large arrows were released by the ballistae on each side and dug into the hulls of the two ships closest to them. Both began taking on water almost immediately.

The *Soaring Mist* continued through the pursuing ships and then began to turn a second time. As they were running perpendicular to their opponents, Augustus sent the order again and six more ballistae arrows lanced out at the ships, impacting the stern of two more ships, causing them too to begin taking on water.

"We did it, Captain!" Brondolfr cheered. "Took them by surprise!"

"Don't get too excited," Augustus cautioned. "Those crews can swim and we still have two more ships to deal with."

The other two ships seemed to learn from the mistakes of their comrades. They tried to turn along with the *Soaring Mist* and not allow their vessels to fall in sight of the ballistae. The distance they left, however, allowed the catapult gunners to continue their own attack, and one ball was successful as it impacted the mast and splintered it in two, leaving the ship stranded in the water.

"Captain! They're swimming toward us!"

"Archers, try to take out as many of them as you can," Augustus called in reply.

"Archers, take them down!" Brondolfr commanded.

The archers leaned over the sides and continued to unleash arrow after arrow into the water at the amphibious creatures. Many arrows hit armor with little effect, but some managed to dig into the amphibiers' heads or tails and halt their progress or leave them presumably dead.

"Brondolfr, with only one ship left, get us out of here," Augustus commanded.

"Full speed ahead!" Brondolfr called out.

The *Soaring Mist* accelerated to try and leave the wreckage of the amphibiers behind. Five of the ships might be disabled, but there were far too many of the creatures in the water trying to board them. They needed to escape before they were overwhelmed. Then the first one leapt onto the deck.

"Swords!" Augustus bellowed.

"Swords!" Brondolfr repeated as he brandished his axe and rushed toward the intruder.

Augustus glanced back at Green. "Keep us going, no matter what."

"Yesss, mother," Green replied.

She then grabbed the railing and leapt over it onto the deck. This was her ship, and she would be damned if she was going to watch as these slimy-green-skinned cold-blooded creatures invaded her.

The first amphibier on the deck held a trident. He twirled it once, but his whole body began convulsing as a volley of arrows from the archers hit him. Dark blue blood trailed from his wounds as he slumped to the ground.

Several more amphibiers crawled over the side of the ship and onto the deck. Brondolfr charged directly at them and brought his axe swinging down at the first head that he saw. The amphibier dodged down and then sprung toward the barbarian, hammering into his chest and sending them both hurtling backwards.

Brondolfr, who dropped his axe with the thrust of the impact, began punching the amphibier in the head with both of his hands, one on each side. The creature jolted with the impact but kept trying to strangle the barbarian.

"Xeorn!" Brondolfr defiantly cried as he slammed both fists one last time into the amphibier's head and rejoiced as the blue blood spurted from the impact. The creature dropped on top of him, but Brondolfr just pushed it aside and wiped as much of the blood as he could from his face.

Another amphibier charged him. With a demonic smile, Brondolfr removed the two daggers from his sash and lunged for his new attacker. With three jabs to the creature's stomach with his blades, followed by a double slash to its throat, he screamed triumphantly again, "Xeorn!"

As more of the creatures leapt onto the deck, Shimada lowered her bow and removed two of her swords. The blade of the longer one was two and a half feet, whereas the second one was not quite two feet in length. The smaller of the two she held backwards to slash upwards at a foe, with the larger in front of her in a defensive posture.

The first amphibier raised a dagger and lunged at her. Shimada deflected the dagger with her larger sword, and then brought the second one slashing up, ripping into the creature's jaw and leaving a trail of blue blood past its nose and right eye. The creature dropped back, but Shimada then rammed her larger sword up, digging in below its chin and impaling its head. As she pulled her blade back out again, the green-skinned opponent slumped to the ground.

By her side, Beige twirled his warpike above his head and then brought it slicing down, digging into one amphibier. He then forced it forward, ripping through the amphibier's skin, and dug the forward blade into the chest of another. The force of the blow was so powerful that it sliced right through the creature's armor.

Kemocay returned to the main deck and saw the skirmishes. Brondolfr was in a rage as he sent foe after foe to meet their makers. Shimada and Beige had managed to overcome the enemies at the front of the ship, and Augustus and a few crewmen were battling the remaining amphibiers on the middle of the deck.

Glancing backwards, he could see that they were leaving the sinking ships behind them. The strategy was sound. This way they were only forced to deal with a handful of the amphibiers rather than the crews of all six ships.

One amphibier closed in on the captain from behind. Raising his spear, Kemocay sent the weapon hurtling through the air, into the back of the foe. As it slumped to the ground, Augustus turned and saw it. She nodded briefly to Kemocay as she then spun around and brought her cutlass slashing down to slit the throat of the final living amphibier on her ship.

As it fell to the deck, its blue blood oozing out, she surveyed the damage and saw that several of her own sailors were down, but the invaders were gone. "Get these carcasses off of my ship!" she ordered, remembering what Shimada said about redundant organs. She'd hate to think that they were dead and then find them lunging at her and the crew again.

"Kemocay, I want you to see to the wounded. Get them to Jin Fe," Augustus instructed.

"Aye, Captain," he said as he rushed to the first group of fallen men and began issuing orders to those around them.

Augustus returned to the bridge and glanced at the one remaining amphibier ship. Just as they had done the night before, they were out-distancing it. Soon, the ship would fall too far behind them and would no longer even be a concern.

"Keep us moving," she said to Green. "Top speed."

"Yesss, mother," Green replied. "Top ssspeed."

CHAPTER 14

Many hours after the fighting ceased, Jin Fe finished his work on the last of the wounded and sighed a long breath of relief. They had only suffered five fatalities. Though that was more than they would have liked, it was truly remarkable that they had managed to pass through an entire fleet as almost completely unscathed as they had. Five would be mourned, but it certainly was an acceptable loss considering the circumstances.

Glancing over at Shimada with weary eyes, Jin Fe was amazed to see his granddaughter still keeping a constant vigil over the unconscious Mage. "You should get some rest."

"I am fine, Grandfather," Shimada said.

"He will still be there in the morning," Jin Fe smiled pleasantly.

"He saved us all," Shimada replied quietly.

"He did, but he would not then want you to sacrifice your own well-being by being too fatigued to continue. Rest now."

Shimada rubbed her forehead and then stared at her grandfather. Jin Fe held her gaze and she could see that there would be no reasoning with her hardened ancestor. "Very well."

"Excellent," Jin Fe bowed slightly. "We shall see you in the morning."

As she turned to leave, she paused and looked over at the slain amphibier. "What about that? Captain Augustus ordered all of them removed from the ship."

"I wish to continue studying it," Jin Fe said. "Everything I did to it last night has already healed. It is as if I never even touched it. If I can study it further, perhaps I will be able to uncover some new medical remedy. The possibility is far too alluring to pass up."

Shimada nodded. "Just be careful."

"Of what?" Jin Fe asked. "It is dead." To prove his point, he lifted a small scalpel and slashed the creature's cheek. "Even that mark will be gone by morning."

"I will make certain I check it when I return, then."

"Come, I shall walk you to your cabin," Jin Fe said.

"You just want to make sure that I actually go to sleep," Shimada said with a snicker.

"Ah, granddaughter, you know me so well."

As the two walked out of the infirmary, neither noticed the body of the amphibier. If they had, they would have seen its eyes open and the creature watching them as they walked away.

❂ ❂ ❂ ❂ ❂

As Jin Fe left Shimada's cabin, he smiled to himself. She was so much like her father, Sakuaki, that it was unbelievable. Both were vibrant, alive, determined, and both were extremely stubborn. He actually had to use one of his mystical rings to make sure she went to sleep, something he had done more than once when Sakuaki was her age.

Youth always seemed so focused on the moment. They saw exactly what was happening right then and felt that the most recent obstacle, incident or tragedy was the pinnacle of their being. Both Shimada and Sakuaki before her would become so focused on the current problem that they would lose sight of the grander scheme. Not that he thought they were negligent of their duties, for both had been quite efficient and gifted, but sometimes they needed to take a step back and do some actual planning and thinking ahead rather than living in the moment.

That was a lesson that age would teach. They were on a long and perilous voyage. What would be the consequences of staying awake and forcing herself to ignore fatigue? Would she fall a few steps behind when they encountered the next threat? Be a little slower against a drelenkin or a pirate? That was why one could not lose sight of the big picture. That was why he insisted that she sleep. The thought of Shimada being the next patient in the infirmary because she was fatigued and became overpowered by a lesser foe was terrifying.

As he stepped back into the infirmary, he tensed and paused immediately. Something was wrong. Normally, he could hear his creatures when he was in the room. They always communicated in their own way. A hoot, a growl, a purr, a bark or whatever they did. Now though, complete silence.

He could see the eyes of his pets looking back at him, so he knew that they were still alive. Why, then, were they so quiet? The sound of a footstep startled him, but the Aezian swiftly sprung away.

At the age of eighty-three, Jin Fe was in the twilight of his life. His wars had long since passed. However, he had still been the ruler of the Yutaka Clan in his youth. He had been trained, as all Aezians were, in martial arts. He may not be as practiced and refined as he had been even a decade before, but he was far from being defenseless. In Aezia, even an unarmed man was a deadly weapon.

Focusing on where he heard the footstep, Jin Fe's jaw dropped in amazement. It was the amphibier, the same one that he had been examining for the Captain. It was somehow alive, and clearly held resentment about the work he had been conducting on it.

The amphibier did not speak; it just closed in on him, moving slowly to make certain that he could not dodge away a second time. Jin Fe steadied his breathing and prepared to relax himself. He started to consider what he had learned about this creature and tried to formulate a strategy.

The tail of the creature shot out, just like that of a raspler attacking. It was something Jin Fe could anticipate, for he had seen Green and Beige training with Kemocay and Brondolfr since they were hatchlings.

Leaping over the tail, Jin Fe narrowed his hands into flat surfaces and jabbed straight ahead. His right hand hit the amphibier in the throat as his left jabbed into its unarmored ribcage.

The amphibier stumbled back, and then emitted a snarl as it lunged forward again. Jin Fe waited for the right moment and then grabbed its arm, using it to twirl his body around and land behind the amphibier. As he did so, he felt something in his back pop and knew that he was beginning to weaken.

As the amphibier turned to face him again, Jin Fe jutted both thumbs towards its eyes and dug into them, blinding the creature. The amphibier knocked him backwards with a fist and began screaming in its high-pitched voice.

Jin Fe lay on the ground, hurting more now. He had landed awkwardly and knew that a leg had broken. The amphibier might be blinded, but he too was out of this little skirmish. Unless someone had heard the amphibier's cry, these might very well be his last moments on Terra. If so, he regretted not telling Shimada one last time how proud of her he was and how much he loved her. Despite his regret, he knew that she understood that.

The amphibier stopped screaming, stood defensively, and began listening. Its head turned several times, concentrating, trying to find him. It must have heard the beating of his heart, because suddenly its head snapped directly toward him and it started to slowly walk towards the fallen Aezian.

Jin Fe raised his chin defiantly. He would not give this creature any kind of satisfaction. He would stare at it and defy it to end his exiled existence. As he watched the amphibier reach out for him, its head began glowing, and then, miraculously, combusted into flame.

Jin Fe watched as the body of the entire creature began burning as if it had been doused in oil and then ignited. The creature thrashed for several moments but ultimately slumped to the ground, presumably dead, hopefully this time for good.

Glancing around the infirmary, Jin Fe spotted Ilfanti, still lying on his bed with his arm outstretched at the amphibier.

"Hope you didn't mind me cutting in," he whispered, his voice still weak.

"I was tired of that dance anyway," Jin Fe replied, thankfully.

Ilfanti closed his fist and the flames doused. He watched the creature for a few more moments and then passed out once more.

Jin Fe remained on the ground, his broken leg preventing him from standing. He would not have to wait long. Brondolfr and Palisha ran in to see what was wrong. They had heard the screaming, and together, they helped Jin Fe bind his leg and then removed the body and tossed it into the sea. No use taking any more chances.

CHAPTER 15

The following morning—with the exception of Krimdor, who was still too badly injured to leave the infirmary—every officer and member of the crew stood on the deck of the *Soaring Mist*. The five sailors who had perished in the skirmish with the amphibiers were wrapped in a shroud and lying before them.

Captain Augustus stepped forward and bowed her head at them and then looked at the crew. "These five men have died valiantly, defending this ship and all of us. Already, they are sharing the tales of their honorable deeds in Wolhollm."

"May we all be so fortunate," Kemocay added.

"We shall remember them, and their sacrifice for us, and honor them always," Augustus said. "Fasbender?"

The gnome stepped forward and nodded briefly. "As is our tradition, any money we claim from salvaging pirates' plunder will be split. A sizeable amount will be presented to any family members of our slain comrades. The remainder will be donated in their names to charitable organizations in Water Haven."

Augustus watched the faces of the crew and then nodded to Brondolfr.

The barbarian stepped forward and beckoned four sailors per slain body to lift them and drop them into the sea. After the last body was gone, the entire crew stared at the flag of Water Haven in a moment of silence, and then Brondolfr dismissed them.

Ilfanti watched the entire ceremony and was thankful that many more had not perished helping him to pursue this quest. Though undoubtedly many thousands would die in the upcoming years, he hated to see lives needlessly thrown away.

Augustus and Green walked over to Ilfanti and beckoned for him to join them in the officer's stateroom. Ilfanti nodded to Jin Fe, who was being helped by Shimada and walking with a cane to help support his broken leg.

Following the two into the stateroom, Brondolfr walked in behind him and closed the door.

"We have run a little behind schedule," Augustus began.

"That is understandable," Ilfanti said.

"We are naturally hoping to pick up the pace," Augustus said. "The further away from the amphibiers we are, the better off we will be."

"I agree," Ilfanti said.

"Also, your quest is of vital importance, so delays would not be fortuitous."

"You have a suggestion?" Ilfanti asked.

"While we were preparing for combat, you commented that you could put the wind at our backs and leave all other ships in irons?"

"That is correct," Ilfanti said.

"You could still put the wind at our backs?" Augustus asked. "Even in your condition?"

"I am fine," Ilfanti said. "I was just a little strained from lifting the ship, but sleep does wonders."

"Then you can do it?"

"I don't see why not," Ilfanti said.

"Excellent," Augustus replied. "We are in drelenkin waters. They have plagued the fisherman of Frocomon for years. I'd prefer not to stick around here long enough to let one grow curious enough to check us out."

Ilfanti nodded his agreement. Drelenkins were massive sea creatures that were extremely destructive.

"Green will instruct you as to exactly how much wind the sails can handle and will direct you from that point on," Augustus said. "At our normal pace, we would have few obstacles for the next fifteen days, but then we'd enter pirate waters. I wish to cut that transit time down to ten days and get the crew prepared for the next conflict."

"Agreed," Ilfanti said.

"Excellent, then why don't you two begin."

"Thisss way," Green prompted.

Brondolfr opened the door to let them both out.

"Oh, and by the way," Augustus called out. "Thank you for saving the ship and Jin Fe yesterday."

Ilfanti met her eyes, nodded, and then walked out. He only wished that he could have done even more.

ILFANTI'S LOG

Things finally seem to be getting back to normal. Well, as normal as things can get for this crew. We are a week removed from the amphibiers, and leaving them behind has been like putting down a huge burden. The spirits of the crew have returned, and the ship has gone on like the invading armada was just another day at work.

Fasbender, his gnomes, and Kemocay have been working relentlessly. They have finished a prototype barrel that they hope can harness and direct the amphibier weapon. They call it a cannon. It is still untested, but they feel that it is a good design, though they all agree that the iron they used, even laced with illistrium, will melt and become unstable, so we might only get a single shot or two out of each one. Not a very efficient weapon, but we can't deny the potency of the amphibier abilities if we can find a way to properly harness the raw plasma and use it to our own advantage. This is a good working model. I have every confidence that Fasbender will not rest until he finds some way to keep the barrel of the cannon from melting.

Krimdor has finally awakened. He is still very weak and Jin Fe refuses to let him leave the infirmary, but the fact that he is awake again has relieved everyone. I spoke to him a bit, but he still doesn't even remember the encounter with the amphibiers. That's one tough weapon to knock a Mage out of commission and leave gaps in the memory like that!

The past week has been good, though. All repairs on the ship have been made and now we're cruising. Green has explained that the wind pressure from my magic might be a bit of a strain on the sails and masts, so we are limiting my mystical contributions to two-hour intervals. But it's good to be doing something productive.

We just reached the peninsula in southern Frocomon. I can see the Carrion Mountains from here. From this point until after we bypass the pirate waters, we'll be hugging the coast much closer than we have thus far. There's something soothing about seeing land right off of the starboard bow. You just don't feel as overwhelmed by the open ocean when land is in sight.

Kemocay has increased our little workout sessions as well. Beige has recently joined us. It seems like ever since the battle, he is determined to master his skills with weapons, and Kemocay has been quite willing to work with him. Who knows, maybe one day Beige will be the new Weapons Master on board this ship!

Well, that's all the time I have for now. I'm meeting Palisha and Shimada for lunch and then have a two-hour shift on the bridge filling the sails with wind. Maybe I'll write some more later if I have a chance.

CHAPTER 16

Zane was kneeling atop of a ledge on the Carrion Mountains that overlooked the ocean, watching and waiting for his quarry to arrive. They had reached this point a couple of days before, and only now was his prey in sight. The *Soaring Mist* finally was sailing below. The confrontation with Ilfanti was so close that Zane could almost taste it.

"Do we attack now, sir?"

Zane stood up and glanced at the avarian speaking to him. "No, we will wait until the ship is right on top of us, and then we will strike."

"Very good, sir."

Zane knelt back down, licking his lips in anticipation. Mages like Ilfanti always thought that they were above the rules of the Council. Today would send a message to everyone in the Council—nobody was above the law. If Ilfanti, one of the most famous and influential members of the Council could be brought to justice, then what hope did any other lawbreaker have? None, while he was around.

❊ ❊ ❊ ❊ ❊

"Well, ladies, lunch was delicious, but I must get up to the bridge for my shift," Ilfanti grinned appreciatively to Shimada and Palisha.

"Of course," Palisha pleasantly returned. "We'll see you for dinner."

"I am looking forward to it," Ilfanti replied.

As he walked up the stairs whistling a tune he had picked up centuries ago from a band of traveling satyrs, the dwarf burst out in laughter as the memories of his youth flooded into him again. This quest was doing more than just helping him to locate the Empress; it was reminding him of the person he once had been, and also letting him know that gray hair did not automatically preclude him from partaking in adventures like he had in his youth.

Reaching the main deck, the hairs on the back of his neck stiffened and Ilfanti sensed that they were in danger. Some might not even recognize a response like that, but he had learned to trust his instincts during his two-century long paladinship. Searching for any sign of something out of the ordinary, he saw Captain Augustus, Brondolfr, and Kemocay standing on the bridge and studying something with the optical enhancers.

As he approached the trio, he could see the scowl on Brondolfr's face. Kemocay also seemed concerned, but his look was more calculated as if he was trying to derive the solution to a problem. Augustus, as always, was calm and professional.

"What's wrong?" Ilfanti asked as he stepped up to join them.

Augustus handed him the optical enhancers and pointed towards the Carrion Mountains. Ilfanti adjusted the instrument slightly and looked through. With perfect clarity, he saw Master Zane and his twelve avarians.

"Damn."

"You know them?" Brondolfr asked with a hardness to his voice.

"They are Gatherers," Ilfanti answered. "The eternal riding the griffin is Master Zane. He is the leader. The twelve avarians are his own private air force."

"I see a lot of gold on them," Kemocay added. "The more gold the Mage wears, the more powerful he is, right?"

"Correct," Ilfanti said.

"So we're up against thirteen powerful Mages," Kemocay observed, confirming his fears.

"It would appear so," Ilfanti said.

"Recommendations?" Augustus asked.

"The amphibier weapons," Kemocay replied. "We can put the cannons to the test."

"That would most likely kill them," Ilfanti shook his head at the prospect.

"I agree, we're not declaring war on the Mage's Council," Augustus said. "Other ideas?"

"This is nothing you need to become involved in," Ilfanti said. "Zane is here for me. I will be the only one involved."

"What of your mission?" Augustus asked.

"Don't worry," Ilfanti said. "It will continue as planned."

"You know how to beat them?" Brondolfr asked.

"I'll think of something," Ilfanti shrugged.

❀ ❀ ❀ ❀ ❀

"We have him now," Zane said as the *Soaring Mist* sailed almost directly beneath the ledge the Gatherers were perched on. Standing on the bridge, he could see the renegade Ilfanti. The dwarf wasn't even wearing his robes; he was a disgrace to the entire Council.

As he hopped on top of his griffin and pulled out his sword, he heard the humming of his corryby in his satchel. Gritting his teeth at the interruption, he reached down and picked up the small orb. It immediately began to glow and the image of Pierce appeared above it.

"Master Pierce, Ilfanti is about to be ours."

"You will abort," Pierce declared.

"What?" Zane shouted, unable to comprehend what he was hearing.

"You heard me, Zane, abort your mission."

"But sir, he is right below us, I can see him!"

"Other matters of more import require your attention," Pierce cryptically stated.

"What could be more important than returning a rogue member of the Council of Elders?" Zane spat in disdain.

"The child has left again," Pierce said.

"Her?" Zane asked.

"Yes," Pierce confirmed. "Only you and yours can hope to bring her back."

Zane bit his lip so hard that a single stream of blood began flowing down his chin. The girl that Pierce was referring too could only be Kyria, a child with more power than anyone her age should ever have.

Unlike most Mages, though, her powers had not manifested and presented themselves until she was already twelve years old. Zane was the Gatherer who finally managed to bring her back to the Council after another platoon was unsuccessful. But ever since she had been at the Council, she had been finding ways to bend the rules, cause problems, and become a major nuisance; at least, that was how Zane saw her.

"What of Ilfanti?" he growled with irritation.

"He wishes so badly to go on a fool's quest, then let him," Pierce said. "The child is more important to the Council."

"Very well," Zane conceded.

"Excellent," Pierce said. "Return to the Council for a new trackbar. You will then begin the hunt immediately."

"Yes sir," Zane begrudgingly said as the corryby stopped glowing and the image of Pierce faded.

"Are we really letting Master Ilfanti get away, sir?"

Zane glared down at the *Soaring Mist* in hatred and spite. So close, but he had his orders. "There will be another time."

"But sir, he is right there!"

"Then he is fortunate that, unlike him, some members of the Council still know how to follow orders," Zane sneered. "Everyone, back to Trespias."

Zane watched as the avarians took to the sky and began to fly away in formation. Taking a last glance to see his quarry below, Zane gritted his teeth as he saw Ilfanti drop his pants and wave his bare bottom at him. Turning away in disgust, he dug his heels into his griffin and took to the skies. There would indeed be a reckoning, just not this day.

❋ ❋ ❋ ❋ ❋

"They're leaving?" Brondolfr asked. "What happened?"

"Beats me," Ilfanti shrugged after pulling his pants back up and buckling his belt. "Permission to go to my cabin and contact my sources in the Council? Maybe I'll get some information."

"Agreed," Augustus said. As she watched Ilfanti walking away, she let out a long breath of relief. If the Mages had fought, her ship would be one thing that definitely would have suffered.

Ilfanti stepped into his cabin and pulled out his corryby. As he thought of Cala, the crystalline orb began to glow and hum as the image of the elf appeared above it.

"Ilfanti," she whispered.

"Why the whisper?" he asked.

"Hold on," she said.

Ilfanti sat and watched the image for a moment. It appeared as if Cala was sneaking around and trying not to be discovered. What could have happened that would make it so that a member of the Council of Elders needed to sneak around?

The image of Cala flattened as if she was against a wall, and after several moments, she nodded. "We're fine now."

"What was that all about?" he asked.

"Pierce is becoming more and more secretive about what he is doing," she explained. "He's even doing things behind the Council's back."

"Does he finally accept Zoldex's return?" Ilfanti asked. "Is he doing anything about it?"

"That's just it," she said. "He's not doing anything about that. Instead, he seems to be on this maniacal tirade of controlling all of us here. Perhaps he is still on edge about Kruskall."

"If Kruskall taught us anything, it was that Zoldex truly is back," Ilfanti shook his head in frustration. Kruskall was a fourteen-year-old boy who had somehow become influenced by Zoldex. He considered himself the Apprentice of Zoldex, and even assisted in releasing the Renegade Mages—criminals of the Mage Order—from the dungeons of the Mage's Council. Not only that, but he caused quite a bit of a distraction that left the entire Academy in turmoil during this year's Founding Celebration.

"What was he doing this time?" Ilfanti asked, getting back to finding out what was going on with Pierce.

"Ordering Zane to leave you alone."

"Oh, really?" Ilfanti grinned. "So that's why Zane flew away."

"What do you mean?" Cala asked.

"He was here," Ilfanti explained. "Right above us, waiting to swoop down and attack. Then they just all flew away. Do you know why?"

"Unfortunately, I do," Cala said.

"I don't like the sound of that," Ilfanti braced himself for bad news.

"It's Kyria."

"Kyria?" Ilfanti asked, shocked that it was something to do with her. "What happened to Kyria?"

"Nothing, yet," Cala said. "But she is gone."

"What do you mean, gone?"

"Kyria and a few of her friends are nowhere to be found," Cala explained. "Pierce went down to the Seers and demanded an explanation. They gave him a trackbar with her whereabouts."

"What was going on there?" Ilfanti asked.

"Apparently, the Seers had not reported Kyria's absence like they normally would if someone left the Council."

"So Pierce is seeing conspiracies everywhere," Ilfanti surmised.

"Something like that," Cala agreed.

"You need to make sure that she doesn't get hurt," Ilfanti advised. "She is a very special child."

"No need to worry," Cala promised. "Herg and I are on top of it."

"Good," Ilfanti nodded with relief.

"Convenient timing, though," she laughed. "At least you will no longer be hindered by the Council. Until you try to return."

"I'll face that problem when I come to it. For now, I'm just relieved that we've managed to overcome the challenges this quest has already presented us."

"What's next?" Cala asked.

"Pirates."

ILFANTI'S LOG

I just came down from the bridge. Tonight is an eerie night—dark, foreboding. I think every member of the crew is on edge tonight. We've been in pirate waters for the past couple of days with no incidents, but that isn't what's bothering people. No, I think it's Grool.

Of course, no one else on this ship even knows what Grool is or that it exists, but I have learned that these sailors have fine instincts. They know that evil lurks around them. It's too dark and foggy to see, but off to our right is the coast of Tenalong, home of places with names like Forbidden Peaks, Nekros Lake, and the Bloody River. Aptly named for what I know is there.

Grool. I had heard rumors of an orc city for years. A city that had one hundred thousand orcs, the home of the Murky Death Clan. Master Ferceng had put a name to go with those rumors, though, and found something even more terrifying. Grool doesn't have one hundred thousand orcs; it contains closer to three times that many. They also have slaves of different races forging them weapons of craftsmanship that most in the realm would pay a fortune to hold. Even that gets worse—the orcs of Grool are bigger, stronger, smarter, and live longer than any orc has a right to.

Don't get me wrong; I'm not prejudiced. We have orcs in the Mage's Council. I have seen them develop and grow into fine Mages, but they have been granted the education that we provide, the structure we offer, and the values of decency that we pass along. I have never met an orc outside of the Council that would not try to attack me when a handshake could get them what they want. The orcs of Worren's Faith may be an exception, but I have never met one from there, so I'll stick with my instincts and what I know.

With Grool, where orcs take bloodthirst to extremes, Zoldex has somehow engineered a powerful army indeed. One of these days I'll have to go myself. I believe what Master Ferceng told me, but at some point I feel that the slaves of Grool will be calling to me. Summoning me to liberate them. Begging me to set them free. One day, I will go.

One day, I will fight as many orcs as it takes to set those poor unfortunate souls free.

But that is another day. For this night, I will just be glad when we are further away from Grool and what it represents. There will be no sleeping tonight. It doesn't matter who is scheduled to work the night shift. Every officer is onboard the main deck right now. Everyone else, myself included, will anxiously wait for the sun to rise in the morning and hopefully reduce this veil of foreboding that has dropped down upon us.

I only hope that in the morning, this crew is not too fatigued to fight pirates if we come across any! Green has informed me that we'll be able to see the Island of No Return before the sun goes down tomorrow. We may be deep into pirate waters now, but the Island of No Return is where they are rumored to reside. We will most likely see them tomorrow. How many and how hard it will be to bypass them is the question, but this crew certainly knows how to fight pirates. Krimdor is back on the bridge now too, so we'll be at full strength.

The Soaring Mist is coming, Pirates everywhere, beware!

CHAPTER 17

Ilfanti waited in the dining saloon for thirty minutes, but Palisha did not join him that morning as she normally did. In the back of his mind, Ilfanti wondered if something was wrong. Not only had there been a dark and foreboding atmosphere the night before; not only were they close to Grool, but they also were under constant threat of raid from a pirate ship.

Ilfanti brushed his concerns aside. He knew that if they had been attacked, the ship would be in an uproar and he would certainly know about it. Finishing his drink, Ilfanti thanked Beige for the meal, then headed for the stairwell to the main deck.

As he stepped onto it, he had to stifle a laugh. Was Palisha in trouble? No, she was sunbathing. Walking over to where she lazily was resting and taking in the morning sun, he knelt down. "Morning."

"Oh, good morning, Ilfanti," Palisha said. "I hope you will forgive me for missing our breakfast, this sun was just beckoning me to do this."

"Already forgiven," Ilfanti said. "Things seem very calm today."

"They are," she agreed. "After the night we had, this morning is very welcome."

"Aren't we a bit close to the Island of No Return to just be lounging around, though?"

"Not at all," Captain Augustus said from behind Ilfanti.

Ilfanti turned and his mouth dropped open as he saw the Captain. She had always been so formal and professional, but like Palisha, she was wearing only a pair of garments that kept her modest. She then lay down next to Palisha and closed her eyes.

He definitely was not accustomed to seeing her like this. He had fought by her side and seen her fiery spirit and indomitable will, but now she looked so tiny and frail.

Augustus opened one eye and peered at him. "Are you going to kneel there gawking all day or join us?"

"You want me to join you?" Ilfanti asked; his head tilted to one side.

"Why not?" Palisha asked. "This is wonderful."

"It really is," Augustus agreed. "We've been rushing too much to truly enjoy days like this."

"What about the pirates?"

"Krimdor has the bridge," Augustus shrugged. "If there is any sign of pirates, he will sound the alarm."

"Well, you talked me into it," Ilfanti said.

"Good," Palisha grinned. "Because you were blocking my sunlight."

"Captain!" a crewman shouted out.

Augustus sighed and looked slightly frustrated by the interruption, but she sat up and held the gaze of one of her men. "What is it?"

"There is something off of the port bow."

"Something?" Augustus repeated, a slight edge of annoyance in her tone.

"It looks like a humanoid, Captain."

"Very well," Augustus said. "We'll investigate."

"So much for sunbathing?" Ilfanti asked.

"That's the way fate works, I'm afraid," Augustus shrugged. "Duty calls." She stood up and went over to the bridge.

"I think I'll join her until we find out what this is," Ilfanti said. "Perhaps I'll be back soon."

"You know what they say about all work and no play," Palisha winked.

Ilfanti joined the Captain and tried his best not to smirk. If Augustus looked odd lying on the deck without her uniform, the image paled to seeing her in the same state on the bridge next to the completely uniformed Krimdor.

Augustus lifted her optical enhancers and studied the figure for a moment. Lowering the tool, she appeared confused and glanced at Krimdor for confirmation. "A wraith?"

"It would appear so," Krimdor agreed.

"I haven't heard of any wraiths on pirate crews," Augustus speculated. "What do you think?"

"We are in pirate waters," Krimdor said. "He is either from a pirate ship, or perhaps from a ship that was destroyed by pirates."

"Well, bring him on board and we'll find out," Augustus ordered. "Make sure Kemocay has his guards armed and ready, I don't want any surprises."

"Aye, Captain," Krimdor nodded as he issued her orders and directed several men.

Ilfanti glanced overboard and watched as they closed in on the wraith. He was lying across a single board; perhaps part of the hull of his ship had broken loose. His head and arms were above water, his body and legs beneath the surface.

Kemocay directed his men to the port side. Two of them held onto ropes and crawled down the side of the *Soaring Mist* to reach out and help the wraith up. The rest stood with weapons ready in case there was any need to defend the ship.

Ilfanti watched as the two men pulled the wraith from the water. The shadowy-black creature seemed very frail and weak, as if he had been adrift for days. As he reached the main deck, he called out for water in a scratchy and parched voice. A sailor brought him a flask and helped him to drink.

Augustus walked over and glanced down at the wraith. She noted the projectile weapons he had strapped all along his body. "Is he coherent enough to speak?"

The wraith moved his jaw up and down gasping for air, but did not make any other indication that he knew what was happening around him. "More water," he weakly pleaded.

"Take him to Jin Fe," Augustus ordered. "Kemocay, remove his weapons and make sure that he is guarded at all times."

"Aye, Captain," Kemocay bowed.

Augustus watched as two men hoisted the wraith up by the shoulders and then helped him below decks. She would be unnerved until she learned who this creature was. She certainly was willing to accept a wraith on her ship, but she wanted to know more about him before continuing.

"Let me know as soon as he seems able to speak," Augustus called out to Kemocay as he descended the stairwell. Shaking her head, she silently said to herself, "So much for sunbathing."

❁ ❁ ❁ ❁ ❁

As Rhyne was being dragged below, he had to commend himself on his act thus far. The hard part was over. He was on board the *Soaring Mist*, and headed to Egziard after Kabilian. The Captain had accepted him without knowing anything about him, and the crew even seemed a bit sympathetic to his condition. Manipulating these people would be mere child's play.

He was dragged into a room that was full of animals, potions, and an elderly Aezian who was walking slowly with a noticeable limp. It could only be the infirmary. He was not happy as the Adlesian ordered all of his weapons removed, but he made certain that he saw exactly who was taking his armaments. If he needed them, undoubtedly he could find that man and torture the information out of him.

"Jin Fe," the one identified as Kemocay said. "The Captain would like to be made aware as soon as your patient is coherent enough to tell us what happened to him."

"I understand," the elderly Aezian said.

Rhyne was placed on a bed and watched as all but two of the Adlesians left the room. Those two were evidently his own personal guards. Not that he would, but how easy would it be to slaughter them both right here and now? That was not the plan, though. Deception. He would reveal his true intentions all in good time.

❁ ❁ ❁ ❁ ❁

Kemocay walked out of the infirmary and led his two men who were carrying the wraith's weapons to the storage facility for armaments. He unlocked a cabinet door and beckoned them to place the weapons inside. As they did so, he made a mental note of the types of weapons the wraith had been found with. Apparently, this creature preferred weapons he could throw. He would need to remember that and prepare for it in case their guest turned out to be a threat to the crew and ship.

"All set, sir."

"Thank you," Kemocay said as he locked the cabinet. "Have the men join me in the training room. I want to devise defenses against projectile weapons."

"Yes, sir," the man replied.

Kemocay headed straight to the weight room and began moving the bench and other physical training equipment to the side of the room. They would need an open floor to do this properly. His men were trained to repel boarders, to utilize a variety of weapons that could be beneficial on the high seas, and a variety of other tactics, but never had he trained them to defend against knives and throwing stars. How often were those weapons used in sea battles?

After he set up the room, he decided that the best individual to help with this training session would be Shimada. Her heritage presented her with an excellent grasp of projectile weapons use. She would be the perfect one to help instruct his men. With the decision made, he left to find the Aezian and begin the training.

CHAPTER 18

Captain Augustus stood on the bridge, back in her normal attire, thoughts of sunbathing now hours old. She had just received a report from Kemocay that the training with Shimada to help defend against projectile weapons was going slowly. Their grasp of theory on how to deflect a throwing weapon was sound, but the men missed just as often as they succeeded. She hoped that their passenger would not be a threat, because as of right now, the odds that many of her crew would be injured if he turned out to be a foe were pretty high.

As for the passenger, Jin Fe reported that the wraith was in perfect health and just needed sleep and water, both of which he was being provided with. Hopefully by nightfall or the following day she would have the answers that she craved.

Over the next hour, however, her concerns about her new passenger would be forgotten as the sight of pirate ships crept up on the horizon. Augustus watched them through her optical enhancers. There were three schooners, all bearing the black flag with a skull and crossbones.

Lowering her optical enhancers, she glanced at Krimdor and Brondolfr. "This is what we have all been trained for."

"After the amphibier fleet, what are three pirate ships?" Krimdor joked, though everyone could see him wince as he mentioned the prior battle.

Augustus looked at him for a moment and then smiled. "That's it exactly."

"What?" Krimdor asked.

"Brondolfr, could you ask Fasbender and Kemocay to join us?"

"Aye, Captain," Brondolfr said. He stepped over to speak to a crewman, and they then ran off below decks to summon the two officers.

"What do you have planned?" Krimdor asked.

"The amphibier weapon," Augustus answered as she looked through the optical enhancers again.

"Are you sure that is wise?" Krimdor asked. "Look what it did to me. Those things could do more damage to us than we do to them if it is not used properly."

"Agreed," Augustus said. "Still, three ships will be formidable, and the closer we get to the Island of No Return, who knows just how many ships we really will be up against. I think it is worth the risk."

"Life is a risk, yes it is. Risky," Fasbender said as he joined them on the bridge. Kemocay stood behind him.

"Can we use the amphibier weapon?" Augustus asked.

"The cannon is ready," Fasbender nodded. "Just remember, no guarantees on how many shots before the barrel melts."

"Understood," Augustus said. "Bring them up and position them on the forward bow. They will be the first thing to greet the pirates."

"Aye, Captain," Kemocay said as he rushed back down below decks to prepare the cannons.

Fasbender started to rub his hands together in excitement. "This should be good."

Krimdor glanced down at the gnome. "For all of our sakes, that barrel better not blow up on us."

"A minor concern," Fasbender said, though everyone on the bridge noticed he stopped rubbing his hands together and began rubbing his chin in thought. "Minor. Yes, minor."

❂ ❂ ❂ ❂ ❂

It took almost an hour to set the weapons up on the forward bow. Fasbender stood beside the cannons along with several other gnomes and some of Kemocay's artillerymen. Augustus walked to the front of the ship and stood with them. The pirates were closing in quickly and were now in range of the amphibier weapon.

She glanced at Fasbender for confirmation. "If you are not positive that this will work, now is the time to tell me. We can still use our normal defensive capabilities."

"It will work," Fasbender said.

Ilfanti walked up and stood next to Augustus. For all of their sakes, he certainly hoped so. He intended to create a mystical shield between the cannons and the crew so that if the weapons did explode, at least he could protect some of them.

"Very well, Fasbender, fire when ready," Augustus commanded.

Fasbender rubbed his hands again and then nodded to two gnomes and the artillerymen positioned by each weapon. The artillerymen pulled the levers that opened the power source container, and two lances of pulsating red energy shot from the barrels and surged at the oncoming pirates.

Each blast hit a ship and immediately the vessels were engulfed in flames. The masts crumbled and the ships tore themselves apart. The power blasts were so efficient that not a single survivor managed to flee from either of the two doomed vessels before all that remained was a smoldering ruin sinking in the ocean.

"The last ship is turning to flee," Kemocay observed.

"What is the status of the weapons?" Augustus asked.

Fasbender watched his two gnomes, but both shook their heads. "The barrels melted. One shot from each is all that we'll get."

"They don't know that, though," Augustus said. "Let them flee and warn their other ships of what they saw this day. Perhaps they will avoid us from now on."

"Perhaps," Kemocay said, but he was hardly convinced that the pirates would follow conventional wisdom.

"Since they fled so quickly, they also must not be aware that the weapon must recharge," Ilfanti pointed out.

"Bad for them, good for us," Augustus replied. "I think this was a success, gentlemen. Any chance we can build two more barrels?"

Fasbender shook his head. "No. We could melt this down and use it again, but it may be more unstable the second time around. I would not recommend it."

"Very well," Augustus said. "Then add the acquisition of enough metal to create more barrels or stronger barrels to our list of things to do."

"I know someone in Egziard that may be able to help out with that," Ilfanti said. "It's been awhile, but if he's still alive, we might get some assistance at our destination."

"Good," Augustus said. "Everyone back to your positions. Stay on the lookout for additional ships. If they come back, it will probably be with even more force. We need to be ready for that."

How humiliating would that be? The pirates thought that the *Soaring Mist* had an unstoppable weapon and might come after her with everything they had. Without the weapon, though, the ship would be at a great disadvantage. Of course, with Ilfanti and Krimdor on board, they would fight valiantly, but hopefully the pirates would give the *Mist* a wide berth and leave it at that. The next couple of days would decide.

CHAPTER 19

"Ah, finally awake, I see," Jin Fe smiled pleasantly at his patient.

Rhyne smiled back appreciatively, making sure that the deception was in place. "Where am I?"

"You are on board the *Soaring Mist*," Jin Fe explained. "The Captain will answer the rest of your questions."

"Thank you," Rhyne replied.

Jin Fe stepped over to one of the guards. "Could you please inform the Captain that our patient is awake?"

"Yes, sir," the guard said as he rushed off.

"You helped me?" Rhyne asked. Now that he was no longer pretending to be nearly unconscious, he studied the elderly Aezian. He had his left leg in a splint and was using a cane with a dragon's head handle. His movement, though there was a slight limp, was almost natural. Rhyne suspected that the doctor was nearly recovered from a broken leg. At his age, perhaps he had fallen.

"You were merely dehydrated," Jin Fe answered. "I did not need to do much to help you."

"What happened to my weapons?" Rhyne asked.

"We put them in a safe place," Jin Fe answered. "Lean back now and rest until the Captain gets here."

The wait was not long. Captain Augustus, who was fully dressed, much to Rhyne's dismay, arrived along with the one named Kemocay, a barbarian, and an aquatican.

"Hello, my name is Captain Augustus," Augustus said in greeting.

"Alaran," Rhyne lied. He would usually use his own name, even in deception, but ever since the assassination of Emperor Conrad, he had found that this name was becoming much more widely known.

"Welcome Alaran, this is the *Soaring Mist*," Augustus said. "These are some of my officers. Krimdor is my first mate, Brondolfr is my second mate, and Kemocay is my weapons master."

Rhyne glanced at each in turn.

"I believe you have already met the ship's doctor, Jin Fe?"

"Yes," Rhyne said.

"Could you tell us why we found you like we did?" Augustus asked.

"There was a battle," Rhyne said. "We were betrayed."

"What was the ship?" Augustus asked. "We saw no wreckage."

"You wouldn't have," Rhyne said. "We were betrayed by a pair of passengers. A man named Kabilian and his companion, Crick. They assassinated the Captain and commandeered the ship."

"What ship?" Brondolfr demanded.

"The *Falestian Pride*," Rhyne said.

"The *Falestian Pride*?" Augustus gasped. "I know that ship. You say the Captain is dead?"

"Yes," Rhyne said. "Captain Pondaven was stabbed in the back by Kabilian."

"What was the *Falestian Pride* doing all the way out here?" Augustus asked.

"The Captain was trying to establish a trade route with Vohlmuth."

"Vohlmuth?" Brondolfr repeated, growing very skeptical of this story. The *Falestian Pride* hailed from Karsinport, the same location where he was almost sentenced to death, and the home of his beloved Palisha. He had never heard of any Karsinport ship taking on wraiths as passengers, nor did he believe that one of their ships would attempt to forge a trade route with dwarves. It was not their way.

"Yes, Vohlmuth," Rhyne repeated.

"What is Vohlmuth?" Augustus asked.

"A dwarven city located in the Mourning Mountains," Brondolfr explained.

"I have never heard of it. How do you know if it?" Augustus asked.

"I am a barbarian from Falestia," Brondolfr said defensively. "That does not mean I believe his story, though."

Rhyne watched the exchange. The barbarian might have to be dealt with.

"He has a point," Augustus said. "Let's say for the sake of argument that I believe that Captain Pondaven is willing to have a wraith on board and is trying to forge a trade route with dwarves. That still does not explain why he would risk his own ship by sailing through pirate waters. The *Falestian Pride* is not known as a warship."

"Which is exactly why I was contracted," Rhyne said. "Along with twenty others, I was chartered to defend the *Falestian Pride* against any and all threats as the trade route was forged."

"A knife thrower against a pirate ship?" Kemocay asked, skeptical.

"We were very skilled," Rhyne grinned.

"Mercenaries," Krimdor sneered.

"We all must make a living," Rhyne shrugged.

"So what happened?" Augustus asked. "Who is this Kabilian?"

"Kabilian and his companion Crick were found in Falestia after we left Vohlmuth. They said that they were fleeing the Hidden Empire and needed safe passage. Captain Pondaven was not convinced, but with my colleagues and I aboard, he allowed Kabilian and Crick to join us. For a hefty fee, of course.

"As we were returning back to Karsinport, Kabilian started to talk to the crew and claimed that he had urgent business in Egziard. Something about ascertaining his true destiny. He offered money, much more than we were being paid, to join him."

"So the crew mutinied?" Augustus asked.

"Not everyone," Rhyne pointed out. "The Captain refused to go to Egziard and several of his officers, along with myself, tried to calm the crew down. Kabilian was swift, though, and carried many mystical items. He killed them all, and when I refused to go along with him, he tossed me overboard as if I was not important enough to kill right away."

"Why did you not join him?" Augustus asked.

"I live by the code of honor. I do not turn my back on my word," Rhyne testily replied.

"What do you intend to do now?" Augustus pressed.

"Find Kabilian, and kill him," Rhyne sternly said without hesitation.

Augustus glanced at her officers for a moment and then returned her gaze to Rhyne. "Very well, Alaran. We are going to Egziard ourselves. We will take you that far, but you will have to find Kabilian on your own."

"Really?" Rhyne asked in a convincing display of shock. "That is more than I could have hoped for. The fates must be looking kindly upon me."

"Captain Pondaven was a friend," Augustus said. "But do not think that if I learn that you have lied or deceived me in any way that I will not then give you a fate far worse than the one Kabilian left you to."

"I promise," Rhyne said. "No deception. I just wish to avenge the Captain."

"Very well," Augustus said. "Welcome then to the *Soaring Mist.* I will send Beige over to see to your accommodations."

"Thank you," Rhyne replied again.

As Augustus walked out, she spotted Ilfanti leaning against the doorway. He was pale as if he had just seen a ghost. She would have to ask him about it later, for he certainly did not seem ready to speak about what was bothering him now.

"Kemocay, I still want him under surveillance," Augustus ordered.

"Aye, Captain," Kemocay said as he motioned for the two guards to remain behind.

She would believe his story for now, but deep down, she felt that something was out of place. Until she knew what that was, she would not let Alaran have free access to her ship.

ILFANTI'S LOG

Kabilian. Talk about a blast from the past. This can't possibly be the same man. How old was I at the time? Twenty-six? Twenty-seven perhaps? I was young, idealistic, and had only been a Paladin for a few years. It was my first real adventure and quest, one that was built more on folly and fool's dreams than reality, but hey, I was young.

Every student of the Mage's Council has heard of the legend of the Zecarath. According to the story, Pierce and his band of eternals discovered the mystical spring and spread magical abilities around the realm. But the true origin of the power isn't really known. The legend of the Zecarath is enough to satisfy most people's curiosity.

I don't want to bore myself with the details of the folklore, but basically, there were nine orbs of power, the true orbs, known as the Zecarath. Apparently, these fell from the sky as if a gift from the gods, and where they hit Terra, mystical springs were formed. Those who drank from the springs were granted amazing mystical powers, but those who wielded the Zecarath became immortal and gained enough power to rival the gods themselves.

Not one to believe in gods, I only am willing to believe this legend so much, but there is a possibility that there is a grain of truth to the legends. It was that possibility which got me into one of my first true quests. The legends also state that the bearers of the nine Zecarath became corrupt with power and near-immortality, and became ruthless tyrants. Apparently, this all happened long before the Age of the Dragon, so we're talking almost sixty thousand years ago.

These nine tyrants were struck down, though. A race of creatures that were not affected or influenced by magic challenged these supposedly all-powerful beings, and somehow managed to win. After the nine were killed in a most gruesome fashion—for the Zecarath can only be removed by tearing out the bearer's heart—these creatures dispersed around the world and built temples where they would guard and protect the Zecarath for all eternity.

I had a theory when I was younger. There was a temple of a race of minotaurs in the Seven Kingdoms—were they the creatures that had overthrown the bearers of the Zecarath? Who knows, but at the time, no minotaur was in the Mage's Council and I felt that it was a plausible theory. Looking back, no minotaur had ever displayed mystical abilities and joined our ranks. Of course, the minotaurs have all been slaughtered now, but my theory was plausible.

I researched the temple and eventually found it on an expedition in Dartie. It was magnificent and ageless. It most definitely could have been standing from the time of the Zecarath. The minotaurs were everywhere, on guard and aware of their surroundings. It was more like a vault or fortress than a temple, but I was determined to find out whether the Zecarath was there or not.

Heh, even if it was, what would I have done with it? The nine Mages who bore the Zecarath were all ultimately corrupted by its power. I was little more than a kid. I am not so naïve to think that I could have controlled the power when the former bearers failed to do so.

I remember that adventure like it was yesterday. I had purchased a map of the temple, and it was a good thing that I did, for as soon as I set foot inside the inner labyrinth, all of my mystical powers diminished and I could not sense any of the creatures that could be lying in wait around each corner.

I sneaked through the temple and right to a wall that my map said would move. Behind that wall was supposed to be the treasure of the minotaurs. Whether I found the Zecarath or something else didn't seem to matter, it was a grand adventure regardless.

I wasn't prepared for what was there, though. The wall was open and five minotaurs lay dead by the entrance. I carefully crept around to investigate and spotted a human. A human! How could a human overpower a quintet of minotaurs?

He was taking items from the treasure room and putting them into a Mage's satchel. I was shocked and speechless. Was this a Mage from the Council? If so, I had never seen him before, but that didn't necessarily mean much. I called out to him, and he turned around and lifted his wrist at me. Several darts shot out and struck me. I was so confused *that there was nothing I could do but slump to the ground and watch as this man finished pillaging the treasure room.*

I could still talk, but my speech was slurred. I asked if he was a Mage, and he just laughed at me. He told me that his name was Kabilian, the assassin extraordinaire. I will never forget the arrogance, the cockiness, and the ease with which he moved and looted the minotaurs.

Before he left he leaned down and patted me on the head. Said that maybe I would have better luck next time, and that the drugs from his darts would wear off in a few minutes. We could both hear minotaurs coming toward us, and with a laugh, he actually vanished right before me.

I struggled as best I could. My toe was the first thing to move, and it felt like the greatest accomplishment of my life. I was desperate to get away before the minotaurs found me with their slain kin. I did regain all of my mobility right as they walked in. They were outraged, and with good reason. I managed to get away in a heart-pounding escape, but I was never able to find out more about Kabilian. Who was he? Where did he disappear to? What had he stolen?

I eventually gave up on my quest to find the Zecarath. If it was real, I was sure that after Kabilian had stolen it that I would have heard about it, and I had not heard a thing, so I went looking for my next adventure and never looked back. Until now.

Could Kabilian be the same man? Or is this just a freak coincidence? If it is the same man, then the legend of the Zecarath must be true. The orb-bearers are granted immortality as long as they do not have either their hearts or the Zecarath removed from their bodies. Kabilian must have the Zecarath; it was the only way a human could still be alive more than five hundred years later.

Or it could just be another man with the same name. Either way, I will need to learn the answer. If this is the same Kabilian that I met so long ago, then that means the Zecarath are real. If that is the case, then I must try to get it. The power of the Zecarath could help to sway this war in our favor. But which is the priority? The Zecarath, or the Orb of Prophecy?

Just thinking that the Zecarath is real makes my heart race. It is in-

toxicating. I want it. I want it more than I ever wanted anything before in my life. Perhaps in that desire lays the danger. I cannot pin the hopes of the entire realm on the possibility that the Zecarath truly exists. No, the Orb of Prophecy is my priority. It has to be. I must find the Empress. After she is returned, then, and only then, can I entertain the possibility that the Zecarath is more than a fairy tale.

And if Kabilian just happens to find me, and if he is the same man that I met so long ago, then perhaps fate is indeed playing a role and dropping the most powerful weapon we could hope for in my lap. If that is so, then I will answer the call and use the power of the Zecarath to help support the Empress and bring down the forces of Zoldex.

CHAPTER 20

"Faster!"

The boy bit his lip, frustrated by the instruction. How much faster could he go? His father had already blindfolded him. If he tried to increase his pace, then he would lose his balance and falter. "I can't!"

"Have faith in yourself," the man said. "You are nothing more than a human. Do you think that a sorcerer will slow down for you to strike him down? Do you think they will be easy prey? If you are to become a Sorcerer Slayer, then you must learn to overcome your weaknesses."

"How?" the boy pleaded.

"Become familiar with your surroundings. Learn the land. A sorcerer may steal your sight, but if you know the terrain, it will really be he who has the disadvantage."

"What if I don't know the land?"

"Never leave the land you know," the man advised. "Trust me on this. We choose our own battles, and we choose to fight the sorcerers who seek to harm others. In their arrogance, they come to us, and fight in our territory. We have the advantage."

"But father, what if we need to go to them?"

"Then be prepared. Research. Study. Be vigilant and thorough. Learn the layout of where you are going. Seek allies who may assist you, but beware those who will betray you as well."

"Yes, father."

"Now, faster!"

The boy took a deep breath to steady himself. He tightened his grip on his staff and stepped forward, hesitantly at first, to make certain he would not fall. The hesitation was enough to anger his father, who swiped his legs out from beneath him.

He felt the air swirling around him and then struck the hay piled below. Removing his blindfold, the boy looked up at his father, who was standing atop a wooden plank that was attached to several trees. There were dozens of planks, all of different heights and widths, designed to hone their skills and balance. The boy had thought that he had been doing well, but then his father had added the blindfold.

"Again," his father said.

The boy looked up at his father and studied the man, whose reputation he wondered if he could ever live up to. His father was none other than Sabourin, the Sorcerer Slayer. In a time when sorcerers either were mad tyrants or employed by them, Sabourin was a lone figure willing to defend the common man and help put an end to the tyranny. His name was known throughout the Seven Kingdoms, loved by the people, and hated by sorcerers.

He stood six feet and three inches tall, but even taller people who saw him always felt like they had to look up, as if he were a giant trapped in a man's body. He had long auburn hair, tied back into a ponytail, with light brown eyes that were at some times loving, and at others harsh and demanding. His garments were simple, little more than a red vest and pants, but he wore them well.

The boy stood up and climbed one of the vines that would bring him back up to the planks. "Do I need the blindfold?"

"Yes," Sabourin said.

The boy set his staff down and tied the blindfold over his eyes again. He did not want to disappoint his father, or become a burden to him. His father had often been gone lately, fighting sorcerers and spending his life defending the towns and villages nearby. He was not home the day one of his foes decided to seek retribution. Only the youngest child of nine survived, losing his siblings and mother on a night that should have been his last. But he had survived, and a grieving father returned and vowed that his youngest son would be prepared to defend himself if ever attacked again.

The boy was not quick to learn, though. His dreams were haunted by images of his slain family, and rather than driving him, they made him second-guess everything. Sabourin worked long and hard to break the boy of his fears, but there was always a pause, no matter how slight, that would be fatal if it were a real fight.

"Begin," Sabourin said.

The boy stepped onto the plank without hesitation this time. He twirled his staff and turned his head from side to side, listening for his father. He knew where Sabourin had been, but he was certain that his father had silently moved to another plank by now.

"Listen to your surroundings. Find my heart beat," Sabourin said.

"What if a sorcerer somehow masks sound?"

"Then smell your enemy. Let his sweat give him away," offered Sabourin. "Or if all else fails, feel the gentle changes in the patterns of the air. The currents will warn you. Trust your instincts and go with them."

The boy absorbed his father's words, but wondered if he could ever actually master the skills. It was so difficult.

"Trust yourself."

Taking a breath, the boy gave in to his instincts. His father's voice was before him, but he felt that there was someone behind him. Twirling his staff again, he shifted position and lunged back, striking another staff.

"Excellent!" Sabourin beamed. "Well done."

The boy's lips creased to a grin. It was the first time he had ever connected while blindfolded. Perhaps he could learn these skills after all.

"Sabourin! Sabourin, come quickly!"

"That's enough for now," Sabourin whispered. "What is it, Tamael?"

"Algammiel is coming!"

The boy watched his father nod, and then glance down at him. "It is time for you to face an enemy of your own."

"You think I am ready?"

"I know you are," Sabourin said. "Remember, trust your instincts, but also know your enemy. What do you know of Algammiel?"

Information was one thing the boy was confident about. He had always been good at researching things and learning things. He also had a talent for persuading others to part with information that they did not really know that they were revealing. His father had always told him to know an enemy. Not just who they were, but where they had come from and what motivated them.

"Algammiel is a goblin from the Kreblahn Mountains," the boy said. "He was trained in the mystical arts by Grallcarn, a sabrenoh of tremendous power and influence. You killed Grallcarn, and Algammiel has sworn vengeance."

"Is he as powerful as Grallcarn?" Sabourin asked.

"Not that we know of. His training is incomplete. But he has had access to Grallcarn's library and spellbooks, so he could have learned more than we think. Of course, without a master, he may not be doing the spells entirely correctly."

Sabourin took the next few minutes to quiz his son on goblins and their abilities. He then asked dozens of questions about spells and mystical items that Algammiel was rumored to be in possession of. After his son had satisfactorily answered all questions, Sabourin back-flipped off of the planks and landed on his feet on the ground below. He walked over to where his weapons were, and selected a pair of jewel-hilted daggers. He studied them for a moment as he waited for his son to climb down and join him.

"These are for you," Sabourin said.

The boy looked questioningly at his father as he took the two daggers.

"You've heard me speak the incantation?"

"I have," the boy said.

"Then it is time for you to take your training to the next level. We must develop your confidence. We cannot do that by practicing, only by doing. Algammiel is yours."

"Mine?" the boy gasped.

"I have faith," Sabourin said. "Make me proud."

"You're sending him?" gasped Tamael.

"He will kill Algammiel," Sabourin said, his tone leaving no doubt that he believed what he was saying.

"What are you to do, father?"

"I shall wait here for you to return and continue your training,"

Sabourin said.

"You are not coming?"

"If I did, then it would not be a true test. You would think that I could come to your aid and help you. I shall not. Algammiel is for you alone. I know you can do this."

The boy tightened his grip on his father's daggers. He would not disappoint his father. He might not be as big, as swift, or as strong as some of his siblings had been, but he was the son of Sabourin, and he would prove that he deserved the honor of that name.

Tamael walked with him as they returned to the village. Tamael was trembling, his teeth chattering. He clearly did not share Sabourin's faith. The boy would not let that sway him. His father believed in him, and that was good enough for him.

"He's over there," Tamael pointed.

The boy did not wish to face Algammiel head-on. He was, after all, only human. He needed a plan. "Thank you, Tamael. I shall handle it from here."

As he ran around one of the small huts, he heard Tamael yell after him, saying that he was going the wrong way. The shriek had also caught the attention of Algammiel, who spoke an incantation and sent a gust of hurricane-force winds blowing the huts away.

"Where is Sabourin?" Algammiel shouted.

Tamael was crouching down, hysterical.

"Speak, *human*, or die!"

"You will be the one dying on this day, Algammiel!" the boy shouted, placing as much scorn and intimidation as he could muster into the words.

Algammiel spun around, paused, and began laughing. "You? You are to kill me? A mere boy?"

There was truth to what Algammiel was saying. He had only just reached his twelfth year less than a month ago, but he had been working with his father for nearly two years now. He was ready, and Algammiel's underestimating him would be his downfall.

"I am glad that your last moments on Terra will be of laughter," the boy said. "It will give you something to think about when you rot in

Tanorus."

Algammiel's lemon-yellow eyes narrowed to slits. "If I must make an example of you to get to Sabourin, then so be it." He raised his hand, began waggling his fingers, and whispered something beneath his breath. Small globules of flame sparkled and danced towards the boy, cracking and igniting with anything that they touched.

The boy leapt aside, diving behind the debris of one of the huts. He could feel the flames singe his leg, but he had successfully evaded the strike.

"Had enough, *boy*?" Algammiel spat. "Bring me Sabourin!"

The boy was no longer where he had been. After dodging aside, he had rolled and lunged away, using the flames and smoke as cover, just as he was sure his father would have done. He watched as Algammiel studied the location he had leapt from, and grinned with the satisfaction of knowing that he could sneak up on the sorcerer.

Clutching his father's twin daggers, he walked toward Algammiel, hoping to slit his neck from behind. The goblin was laughing, confident that he was untouchable. He would soon learn the folly of such beliefs. Only a few more steps and he would end this. His father would be so proud.

Crack. The boy glanced down, horrified. He had stepped on the debris of one of the huts, and the sound was so loud that even the laughing goblin had heard it. Raising the two daggers, all that he could do now was lunge. Algammiel spun around and tossed sparkling dust in the boy's eyes. His eyesight first blurred, and then his vision faded into white.

"No," the boy gasped. In that moment, he felt so hopeless. So vulnerable. He heard Algammiel whispering another incantation, and then he felt his feet sinking into the ground as if he were trapped in quicksand. He had failed. He was blind and trapped. There was nothing he could do. He had failed his father.

"Pathetic," Algammiel said.

The boy had to agree; how could he ever hope to become what his father was? Then he remembered the daggers he was holding. They were enchanted. To fight a sorcerer, one must also use the tools of a sorcerer. It was another of his father's lessons. Recalling that, he managed to steady his breathing and calm down. If he could remember all that his father had taught him, then he had a chance.

He listened to Algammiel's breathing. It was erratic, almost a wheezing or hissing. The goblin was stepping closer, but not close enough. "If I am so pathetic, then why don't you strike me down as my father did your master?"

"You?" the goblin gasped. "You are the son of Sabourin? I shall take you from him as he took my master from me!"

The boy waited. Algammiel was enraged now, stepping forward without thinking. To the sorcerer, he had already won. He was merely coming in for the kill. That would be his last mistake.

The boy grinned as he heard the breathing close by.

"What are you grinning about?" demanded Algammiel.

"This," the boy said. He raised the two jewel hilted daggers, pointed the blades at Algammiel, and uttered the incantation he had heard his father speak so many times. The two blades extended into full-length swords, piercing the shocked goblin in the chest.

The boy rotated the blades, trying to do as much damage as he could. He felt the weight of the goblin as the body slumped down, lifeless. The earth binding him around his legs crumbled and he climbed free. His eyesight still had not returned, though.

He had done it. It had not been easy, but he had managed to overcome his fear and defeat the sorcerer. For the first time since the death of his family, he actually felt like the son of Sabourin. The future was an open book. He would be an adventurer just like his father, saving the realm from those who preyed upon it. Everything was so clear to him, even if he could not see.

"Kabilian, well done."

Kabilian turned at the sound of his father's voice. "Thank you, father."

"I am proud of you," Sabourin said. "You used your surroundings, you trusted your instincts, and you were able to manipulate and goad your enemy. You have done well."

"Thank you, father," was all that Kabilian could say. He wanted to say so much more, but nothing else would come to his mind at the moment. He was just overjoyed with his accomplishment. Today was the beginning of the rest of his life.

His eyes flickering open, Kabilian glanced around, momentarily disoriented. He was not in a small village that had long been lost to the ages, but was on board a ship heading toward Egziard on a quest to find his destiny. He could not remember the last time he had dreamed of his father, and wondered if there was some significance to his doing so now.

Kabilian had lived longer than any human had a right to live. Aided by mystical artifacts and enchanted items that he had claimed over the millennia, he looked the same today as he did the day he had found the Ring of Eternity. In all of those years, though, he had never left the borders of the Seven Kingdoms. His father's lesson about knowing the land was something he had lived by, while increasing his fame in the realm as a collector of rare items and as a self-proclaimed assassin extraordinaire.

Now, however, he was turning his back on that teaching, and voyaging to a foreign land in search of yet another mystical item. Kabilian was determined to succeed, and knew that the reward was well worth the risk, but this little adventure of his had seemed much more enticing before being stuck on a boat for two and a half months.

Where they were now would make even the most practical man question his sanity. The wind had abandoned them weeks ago, not a single island or outcropping of land had been seen in all of that time, and the water was dead calm. If not for oars, the boat would have done little more than drift aimlessly. Even still, Kabilian began to question the wisdom of enduring such a maddening trip. If nothing else, this was a good reminder as to why he had never before journeyed beyond the borders of the Seven Kingdoms.

Crick did not help much on these long days. With the sun baking down on them, the hobgoblin was even more surly than usual, brooding and ignoring everyone. Crick had not agreed with going on this quest, and Kabilian decided to give him a wide berth until they reached their destination.

That left him with little to do other than to think, and to remember. The dream had been an interesting one. He could barely recall ever being that child who was so full of fear and doubt. Now, everything was a game to him. Life, death, it did not matter. When you had seen and done as much as he had, perspectives began to change.

Kabilian did wonder what exactly his father would think if he saw him today. Would he be pleased that Kabilian had become a gifted fighter who had used his training to become the most highly-demanded assassin in all of the Seven Kingdoms? Or would he be disappointed that Kabilian had turned his back on helping those in need by taking money from individuals who Sabourin probably would not have even been willing to talk to?

Being an assassin was not Kabilian's entire identity, though. He may be good at what he did, but he always liked to think that he had a strong moral code as well. He carefully selected the jobs that he was willing to do, and also tried to help people whenever he could. The handmaiden Shiel, for instance—he had helped her twice already, all for no gain whatsoever.

Of course, helping Shiel was probably the only thing he had done recently that Sabourin would have approved of. There were other occasions when his father might have been proud—like when he had joined King Worren in the Trolls Wars—but more often than not, he focused on his pursuit of enchanted artifacts more than charitable causes. Maybe that was one of the things he would change when he finally found the Orb of Prophecy. Maybe he would learn that it was time to give up his ways and become more like his father.

But what had that life given his father, other than the torment of a slain family and an early grave? Kabilian stood up and headed above deck, not bothering to stop and speak to Crick. Perhaps some fresh air would do him some good. Too much time to think would only bring back old self-doubts and hesitation, and Kabilian was glad to have those aspects of his personality dead and buried.

As on every other day since entering The Vast Expanse, the sun baked down on their ship, the wind was non-existent, and the water remained calm and flat for as far as the eye could see. There was no way to escape the doldrums. There was nothing to do but lose yourself to your thoughts, and in some instances, let them torment you. Kabilian had never realized how tormented he really was.

CHAPTER 21

Ilfanti placed the journal on top of the stack that he had been searching through. The log entry could not be denied. On the 16th of Glannath, 7446 AM, he had an entry that referenced the assassin and thief—Kabilian. He stared at the log, as if unable to believe what he had read. He had hoped that he had just confused the names, or that there was some mistake, but it was in his own handwriting—Kabilian was the man he met all those years ago. Too many years ago for a human to still be alive.

Leaning back, Ilfanti thought of the complications that Kabilian might add to his quest. If he could trust Alaran's story—and for some reason Ilfanti could not bring himself to trust the wraith—Kabilian was searching for a mystical artifact through which he could ascertain his destiny. That could only mean that he too was after the Orb of Prophecy.

At their last meeting, Kabilian had wished Ilfanti "better luck next time." Well, this was the next time. Even if his quest had not already been vital and urgent, having a competitor seeking the same prize certainly made it so. Ilfanti trusted that the *Soaring Mist* was a magnificent ship, with a capable crew. Kabilian, even with a head start, might beat him to Egziard, but not by much. Then it would come down to a race to Ramahatra.

Ilfanti had hoped that his old friend Osorkon could help him, but with Kabilian also seeking the treasure, could he even take the time to seek out his old friend? The answer had to be yes. Without the assistance of Osorkon, Ilfanti doubted very much that he could accomplish what he had to do quickly. The time it would take to find Osorkon, presuming he was still alive, would be a wise investment.

A knock broke Ilfanti's concentration. He glanced at the door to his cabin, and when he heard a second knock, he stood up, walked over, and opened the door to find Captain Augustus standing there.

"May I come in?" she asked.

"Of course," Ilfanti replied. He stretched his arm out to beckon her to go first. As she walked past him, he closed the door and then rushed back to his stack of journals. "My apologies for the mess. Let me clean this up."

Augustus took a seat and watched as Ilfanti placed each of the journals, one at a time, into his Mage's satchel. As each journal went in, the satchel remained the same size, showing no sign that it was being filled. "Remarkable," Augustus said.

"Huh?" Ilfanti asked, pausing long enough to glance up and see Augustus watching him work. "Oh, the satchel. It's like a void. I can put anything I want in here, as much as I want, and then retrieve it simply by thinking about it as I reach into it."

"No wonder you had no bags," Augustus reasoned. "I have to admit, I was wondering where all of these books had come from."

"These are my journals," Ilfanti said. "During my Paladin years I used to keep detailed logs of my adventures. Figured I might want to look back at my thoughts sometimes. Turns out, they come in handy."

"I'm sure," Augustus said, no stranger to log entries herself as the Captain of a seafaring vessel.

Ilfanti left out the journal out that referenced Kabilian. He would read more from that one after the Captain left. With the others all put away, he fastened the satchel back to his belt and then sat down. "Sorry about that," he said. "What can I do for you?"

"When Alaran mentioned the name Kabilian, you seemed to recognize it. If we come across him, I want the crew to be as prepared as possible. What can you tell me?"

"Very little, I'm afraid," sighed Ilfanti. "I'm not even sure if I'm right. If I am, Kabilian is well over five hundred years old."

"An eternal, maybe?" asked Augustus.

"Perhaps," shrugged Ilfanti. "I definitely remember thinking he was human, though."

"Tell me about the encounter," Augustus instructed.

"The short version is that I was seeking a mystical artifact in a minotaur temple. Kabilian beat me to it. He had some kind of drug that he launched at me by flicking his wrists. I have faint memories of seeing him and thinking that perhaps he was a Mage, but little more than that. I know his name. I know he claimed to be the assassin extraordinaire. I know he was looting the minotaurs. Anything more than that, I cannot say."

"Did he get the mystical artifact you were after?" Augustus asked.

"I'm not even convinced that what I was after existed," said Ilfanti with a shrug. "If it does, though, he probably has it."

"What were you after?"

"The source of magic," Ilfanti explained. "An orb known as the Zecarath. Every Academy student has heard of it, but none have ever seen one. Through my travels, I found evidence that may support the existence of the Zecarath, but I've never managed to get closer to proving it than I did that day with Kabilian."

"What evidence?" asked Augustus, curious.

"The best way I can explain it is by citing an example," began Ilfanti. "At the Council, we have Seers that identify all Mages and Mage potentials. When a newborn Mage is found, the Gatherers go out to bring them back to the Council."

"I know this," Augustus said.

"Well, I have come across other Mages in the Seven Kingdoms, but ones who are not identified by Seers as Mages," explained Ilfanti.

"Curious," Augustus said.

"My theory is that they are Mages who gained their power through a *different* Zecarath, and that a Seer can only perceive others from their own mystical origins."

"Possible," Augustus said. "How many of these discrepancies did you come across?"

"In two hundred years of adventuring, I have come across three others," Ilfanti said. "The Frost elves of the Mourning Mountains, the Aezians, and Egziardians. If the legends are true, and my theory is right, then the source of their powers come from a different Zecarath. That means that at least four had at one time been in the Seven Kingdoms, Aezia, and Egziard. Five others are most likely elsewhere in the world."

Augustus nodded. Ilfanti's theory was indeed plausible. Of course, magical artifacts and the nature of their existence was something she normally would leave to her first officer, as a Paladin from the Mage's Council. "Getting back to Kabilian, do you think that this is the same man?"

"He could be," shrugged Ilfanti. "Or it could be a coincidence and someone else has the same name and claim. If he does have a Zecarath, though, legend states that it provides the bearer with immortality. So he could definitely be the same man."

"I do not think it is a coincidence that he too is going to Egziard," Augustus said.

"Nor do I," agreed Ilfanti. "He is after the Orb of Prophecy."

"Then it is a race," concluded Augustus. "One that we must win. Not only to get you to Egziard, but also to avenge Captain Pondaven, and to see that you are able to go on your quest for the Orb uninterrupted."

"That would be nice," Ilfanti said, his eyes drifting back to the journal entry of his first encounter with Kabilian. "That would be nice, indeed."

CHAPTER 22

All officers of the *Soaring Mist* stood on the bridge and deck as the last sign of land faded behind them on the horizon. They were moving away from the coast, and into an area that was described as the Vast Expanse. The name might be crude, but it was accurate. These waters were very calm, with little to no wind to help propel a ship over it. With no land around them for what could be months at a time, the only thing that sailors could do to keep their sanity was watch the stars gradually shift at night.

Ilfanti studied the flag at the top of the mainmast. There was still a gentle breeze coming from behind them, but the flag was no longer flapping in the wind. Before long, it stopped moving completely. The sails also began to sag, unable to capture the nonexistent wind.

"Well, this is it," Augustus said. "The Vast Expanse. Fasbender, fire the engines up."

"Aye, Captain," Fasbender replied. He bent over the bridge and yelled to one of the gnomes to start the engines. The gnome ran below decks, and within a matter of minutes, the thunderous roar of the gnomish invention could be heard, followed by the trail of billowing smoke behind them.

"Engines are running, Captain," Fasbender reported.

"Excellent," Augustus said. "I want projections. Based upon fuel and operating efficiency, how long can we use the engines?"

Fasbender scratched his head and then began twirling his mustache. "To be on the safe side, I would not recommend using them for more than seven or eight hours a day."

"Should we break up usage?" Augustus asked. "Maybe a couple of hours at a time?"

"No, no," Fasbender quickly retorted. "The consumption of fuel is highest during ignition. We'd be better off running for the full time each day, and then stopping."

"Very well," Augustus said. "Krimdor, Ilfanti, can we count upon both of you to split up into two shifts of eight hours to use your magic to fill the sails?"

"Only for short periods!" Fasbender quickly reminded. "The strain on the masts. Remember the strain!"

"Of course," Augustus said.

Ilfanti nodded. "I'm at your disposal."

"You know you can count on me, Captain," Krimdor confirmed.

"Excellent," Augustus said. "Between the engines and both of you, we should cut our time in the Vast Expanse considerably."

"A month, maybe more," Green agreed.

Rhyne, who was climbing up on the bridge, grinned at the estimate. He quickly tried to hide his reaction as some of the officers turned to look at him. Ilfanti had caught it, though. He hoped that Alaran was just pleased that they would catch up to the *Falestian Pride*, but his instincts were screaming that it was more than that. One didn't survive two hundred years as an adventurer without trusting his instincts.

Krimdor stepped over to the map and glanced down at it over Green's shoulder. "We should take this opportunity to begin thinking about the rest of our course."

"We have nothing but time," Augustus agreed. "Proceed."

Green pointed to a lone island in the vastness of the open ocean. "Our next ssstop is the Amahani Islandsss," he said. "That is where we ssshall sssupply and provisssion the ssship."

"Don't forget maintenance!" Fasbender added. "The engines should make it, but I want my team to completely overhaul them once we reach the harbor."

"Understood," Augustus said. "How long would that take?"

"If you could give me a month, I'd take a month, but at a minimum, we'll need a week," Fasbender said.

Rhyne gritted his teeth at the news. Ilfanti watched his reaction closely. The wraith definitely was determined to catch the *Falestian Pride*. Delays would not be tolerated.

"What are the security risks involved with going to the Amahani Islands?" Kemocay asked.

"Minimal," Ilfanti said. "The islands are populated with felines. The last time I was there, they openly welcomed ships traveling by, and even were willing to trade if you chose. I found them to be gracious hosts."

"Felines are predators," Kemocay said. "We should be prepared just in case anything has changed since the last time you were there."

"A wise precaution," Ilfanti admitted.

"See to the training," Augustus said. "We'll have plenty of time while in the Vast Expanse to do so. It will keep the crew active."

"Aye, Captain," Kemocay said.

"Brondolfr, work with Kemocay to create a revised crew rotation while in the Vast Expanse. We still need to man the ship, but not as much as usual. Have the extra shifts begin training and preparing for the worst."

"Aye, Captain," Brondolfr said. "It shall be done."

"Beige, how are our provisions?" Augustus asked. "Will we make it to the Amahani Islands?"

"Yesss, mother," Beige said. "And a bit further, too."

"Good work," Augustus said. Seeing Krimdor unfold another chart, she motioned for him to continue.

"Once we leave the Amahani Islands, we will have a choice to make. There are five ways to get to Egziard, some more dangerous than others," Krimdor indicated.

"Explain," Augustus prompted.

"The safest route, unfortunately, is the longest," Krimdor began.

"Then we shall risk the dangerous routes," Rhyne growled, then looked angry with himself for speaking what was on his mind.

"Alaran, that is for the Captain to decide," warned Brondolfr, rising to his full height and trying to sound as intimidating and imposing as possible.

"My mistake," Rhyne humbly replied. "I spoke only what was on my mind. My apologies for the intrusion."

"No need to apologize, Alaran," the Captain added. "Krimdor, please continue."

"The route I am referring to will circumvent most of the obstacles, but add a considerable amount of time onto our journey," Krimdor said.

"That may not be in our best interests," Augustus said, glancing sidelong at Ilfanti. "What are the other routes?"

"One is through a chain of islands where it is rumored that beasts of such size and magnitude live that they would be many times the size of our ship," Krimdor said.

"That's not a rumor," Ilfanti added. "I went that way once. Only once."

The officers remained quite for several moments, absorbing the news that Ilfanti had given them. The island pass was certainly not the way to go.

"Another is a stretch of the ocean that is highly unstable," Krimdor continued.

"What do you mean by unsssstable?" Green asked.

"Trust me, you don't want to know," Ilfanti said. "At least, you don't want to experience it. The water can be as calm as it is now, and then without warning, dozens of whirlpools begin raging all around you. You can look down and see the wreckage of ships from the ages that have not survived the journey through those waters."

"Not recommended," Krimdor clarified. "The next way we could go is through something called the Gates of Tanorus."

"Sounds ominous," Kemocay added.

"Ilfanti?" Krimdor beckoned.

"I haven't gone this way," Ilfanti shrugged. What I heard, though, was that it was a passage that has cursed sailors roaming about. Those who are trapped between this world and the next."

"Xeorn!" Brondolfr gasped. "How do you kill something that is already dead?"

"Your guess is as good as mine," replied Ilfanti. "I personally would recommend the final route that Krimdor is about to announce."

"Which is that?" Augustus asked.

"We head to the Taelific Ocean and sail the waters there," Krimdor said.

"I'm waiting for the catch," Kemocay said.

"Beneath the Taelific is a series of underwater cities that span at least five times the size of the Imperium," Krimdor said.

Fasbender whistled in awe at the announcement. "No fishing, then!"

"You recommend this route?" Augustus asked Ilfanti.

"I do," Ilfanti said. "The first city we sail above is Pantalica, the largest and most influential of them all. Sovereign Eorynth considers me a valued friend and promised safe passage on the Taelific whenever I need it."

"What if that, too, has changed?" Kemocay asked.

"Unlike the Imperium, where the races are at war, those in the Taelific live in peace and harmony. I'm sure we'll be fine," said Ilfanti.

"Then we shall go with your recommendation," Augustus said. "Green, plot the best course to the Amahani Islands, then from there to Egziard via the Taelific Ocean."

"Asss you wisssh, mother," Green said.

"Are there any other questions?" Augustus asked. She glanced at each of her officers in turn, and when she saw no questions, she nodded. "Very well, dismissed."

Ilfanti nodded his agreement with the Captain's decision and stepped down from the bridge. Palisha was waiting below, and along with Brondolfr, the three went to have lunch.

CHAPTER 23

Regardless of what the Captain might say, Rhyne knew that he was not as free as Ilfanti was on this ship. He stood just out of sight, daring to glance around the corner, trusting that the darkness of his body would blend with the shadows as he studied the two adlesians that were guarding the weapons. His blades were in there, he knew it. If he really wanted them, the guards would be little deterrent, but he instead hoped to gain the crew's trust enough to have his weapons returned to him.

To gain that trust, he needed to be more careful. His Alaran persona was believable enough for him to be invited to join the journey to Egziard, but his demeanor put this crew on edge. He knew that the Mage Ilfanti and the barbarian Brondolfr already distrusted him. He could sense it.

He was so used to killing people alone. He never had a partner, nor had he ever before felt the need to fabricate some elaborate deception when he had to interact with others. If he spoke to anyone, it typically was to threaten and intimidate them into doing what it was he wanted. He could not run this ship by himself, though, so he needed this crew to take him, putting him in a most uncomfortable position.

That meant leaving his weapons where they were for now, and doing his best to become friendly with other members of the crew. Leaving the area, he heard voices and grunting down the hall. Stopping by an open cabin door, he saw a vast array of physical training equipment, the dwarf mage, Kemocay, and one of the rasplers.

"This looks interesting," Rhyne said. In an instant, he scanned the room and found at least a dozen ways he could kill the three occupants. The Mage would need to be first. He would have to catch Ilfanti with his guard down. As he held the dwarf's gaze he began to wonder if that would be possible. Ilfanti looked as if he could see right through

Rhyne's deception.

"Greetings, Alaran," Kemocay said. "This is where I train members of the crew. We all have to remain physically fit, after all."

"I thought the Captain ordered the crew to do more training?" Rhyne asked, doing his best to sound interested.

"She did, but the three of us have been regularly having our own training sessions and decided to continue them without interruption," Kemocay explained.

"My apologies, then," Rhyne said, feeling as if he would choke on the word 'apologies.' "I shall not disturb you further."

"You may join us if you would like," Kemocay offered.

"I do still feel a little weak," Rhyne said. "Perhaps a slight workout."

"It is best to begin gradually and then allow your sessions to increase over time," advised Kemocay.

Rhyne entered and decided to use some of the hand weights. As he did so, he watched as Kemocay and the raspler went back to working together. Kemocay was walking the raspler through a variety of defensive combat techniques. Rhyne would consider the raspler a weak link if he had to kill the crew. It was strong and powerful, but untrained. He would have little trouble with it.

The dwarf must not have been as open to allowing Rhyne into the room. He stood up from the bench he was lifting weights at, grabbed a towel to wipe off some sweat, and then thanked Kemocay for the workout. He said he was going to jog around the ship a bit before returning to his cabin to clean up. Rhyne was not convinced that that was the real reason.

Normally, if he had such suspicions about someone, he would see to it that they had a fatal accident. On a ship such as this, however, he wondered if he would be able to get away with it. An "accident" for a Mage would have to be pretty severe to be effective. That would make his involvement far more transparent. He could not risk it. If Ilfanti became a threat, he would act then, but in doing so, he suspected that he would have to kill the officers and crew too. He hoped that it did not come to that.

ILFANTI'S LOG

I never thought that it would be possible, but after only six weeks, Green predicts that we will almost be out of the Vast Expanse. Maybe a few days more, but that is it. That will be a substantial timesaving on both ends of the voyage. If the rest of the journey is as efficient as it has been thus far, then this will be the quickest trip to Egziard I have ever been on. Since my quest is so vital to finding the Empress and directing the efforts of the war against Zoldex in the right place, I can definitely live with the speed.

It will be good to reach the Amahani Islands. I may be in a rush, but I definitely would not mind having my feet on dry land again for a few days. Fasbender will probably be the most grateful for the break. Not necessarily from sailing, but from the strain on the engines. The last few days, he has been shutting them down several times per shift because he says they are overheating. Krimdor and I have been extending our shifts using magic to fill the sails, but Fasbender would rather not have to rely upon Mages to make the ship go. Funny, I'd rather not have to rely upon some kind of gnomish contraption, myself. Although I can't deny the efficiency of the engines. The speed at which we got through the Expanse was almost enough to sell me on the concept.

One person who may not be too anxious to reach the islands is Palisha. With little to do, the Captain has allowed Brondolfr to spend more time with his wife. It warms my heart to see the two of them spending time together and looking so happy. Once we reach the islands, though, Brondolfr will be resuming his duties. Palisha understands that. She is very understanding and accepting, but I still think she'll be a little sad by the shifted focus.

The Captain will be pleased to see her crew have a break, but she seems anxious to reach Egziard and to get me there as quickly as possible. I don't think she'll dally too long with the felines. Only long enough to secure the provisions that we'll need for the rest of the voyage. I can't argue with her determination—after all, she's pushing to help me!

Her "children," Beige and Green, are as different as different can be. Beige tends to his duties as the Quartermaster, and then spends every other waking moment practicing with weapons or defensive tactics. He so desperately wants to do more than he does, and he seems to fear his mother being hurt unless he is around to protect her. Admirable. Green, on the other hand, seems to care less whether he ever learns how to fight. I've seen him do it, so he is capable, but he spends his nights studying the stars, and his days reviewing maps and logs. He has not yet made a single calculation or course correction that has been wrong. He would easily put a seasoned navigator to shame, and he is so young!

Just in case there are problems once we reach the Amahani Islands, Kemocay has really been pushing the crew lately. He's even stopped our morning workout sessions so that he has added time to work on tactics and defenses with his men. Not that I mind, I can finally fit into my outfit without having to hold my breath!

He has asked Shimada to help him with the training. Not that she fights anything like a feline would, but her instincts are sharp, and she moves more quickly than anyone else on the ship. He hopes that with her help, the crew will learn to fight and defend themselves better than they normally could. Shimada also seems pleased to be doing this, and feeling useful.

Jin Fe's leg has healed quite nicely. He no longer has a limp, but sometimes I still catch him walking with his cane. I think he likes it! Shimada is after him to lose the cane, but he seems as stubborn as his ancestors. Some things never change.

I've been spending a bit of time with Krimdor lately. When I leave the Council on a quest, the last thing I typically want is to be bothered by another Mage, but I see quite a bit of myself in Krimdor. He may not seek buried treasures, lost cities, and priceless artifacts, but he is quite passionate about his position on the Soaring Mist. I remember when I had that kind of passion about what I was doing. Until I saw it in him, I never really realized that I had lost it. Kind of puts things into perspective for me.

Lastly, there is Alaran. I still can't really figure him out, and the more that I watch him, the more I am convinced that he is not to be trusted. At times he seems pleasant and at ease, but at others, he seems tense and alert. It is almost as if he is trying to act at ease, but really is not. Why?

He acts like a ranger at times. He walks into a room and I can tell that he captures everything in an instant. I can do that, and I can recognize it in him. Is it because of what happened on his old ship? Is he just cautious and trying to be careful in case there is another mutiny? Or is it something more?

He's been on board for almost two months now, and other than my lingering doubts, I know little about him. He hasn't done anything that would stand out as out-of-place or malicious. But there is just something about him. I'll be quite glad when we're rid of him for good. I hope he returns to the Imperium with the Falestian Pride, and not the Soaring Mist.

Then again, maybe this is just an old dwarf's imagination running away with him. Losing my passion, and gaining paranoia. Oy.

CHAPTER 24

Kemocay charged Rhyne, his hands outstretched. Rhyne timed his move and leapt over the rushing Adlesian, and grabbing one of the rafters, spun around and brought his feet slamming into Kemocay's back. The weapons master tumbled to the floor with the blow and rolled back to his feet, kneeling and ready to strike.

"Impressive," Kemocay said.

Rhyne dropped back to the ground and stood facing the man. "Really, Kemocay, we have been doing this for what? Almost two months now? When will you face reality? You will never beat me."

"That attitude will be your downfall, Alaran," Kemocay grinned. "During each of our daily contests I have watched you. Learned from you. Never is an awfully long time, and one of these days, I will find a way past your defenses."

He lunged forward and raised his fist in what would have been a battle-ending uppercut if it had connected. Rhyne moved in a blur and dodged the blow, then moved to the offensive as he brought his knee up and rammed it into Kemocay's stomach. The Adlesian dropped to the floor again, coughing and wheezing.

"Perhaps, but not this day," Rhyne said.

Beige walked onto the mat and helped Kemocay to his feet. The Adlesian rubbed his stomach and shook his head.

"Thanks, Beige," he said.

Beige nodded, his tongue slithering as he glared at the wraith. "Let me ssstrike him."

"Yes, let the pet raspler attack me," Rhyne laughed with delight.

"If you insist," Kemocay replied. "He's all yours, Beige. Remember, he's fast."

"He'sss mine," Beige grinned as he helped Kemocay into a chair next to Ilfanti, whose eyes remained on Rhyne the entire time.

"Anytime you are ready," Rhyne grinned, baring his fangs.

Beige made no move to attack, but then suddenly his tail darted out and struck Rhyne on the lower calf. The wraith fell to the ground, but quickly back-flipped up into a standing position again.

"Wasssn't expecting that, were you?" Beige laughed, hissing as usual.

"Each opponent brings on new surprises," Rhyne grinned. "That trick won't work again."

"We ssshall sssee," Beige said as he reached out, grabbed a chair and flung it at his opponent. Rhyne started to dodge the projectile and then realized his mistake a moment too late. After he was committed, Beige sprang at him and pounded both fists into his chest.

Rhyne hurtled through the room and slammed into the container holding the weights, all of which toppled and fell on top of him, pinning him to the ground. "It appears I may have underestimated you."

"You won't make that mistake again," Kemocay said. "Beige may be big, but he certainly isn't slow."

Beige walked over and reached his hand down to help Rhyne up. "No hard feelingsss?"

"I am in no position to argue," Rhyne said, making a mental note of at least five weaknesses that he could exploit if he ever had to fight the raspler for real. It was so hard to hold back and not fight with his normal prowess, but just as he was helping the crew with their skills, he did not want them to become familiar with his. He could gauge them, study them, learn their weaknesses, and still fight at a mere fraction of his abilities.

"I think that will be all for today," Kemocay announced. "Everyone get your rest and we'll do this again tomorrow."

Shimada crossed her arms in frustration and glared at Kemocay. "I was supposed to be next!"

"Fortunate for me, then, that we are calling it a day," Rhyne said. His words were sincere; he was not trying to flatter her at all. Of all the members of the Soaring Mist crew that he had sparred with, Shimada was the hardest for him to defeat. She was quick, always altering her strategy as if she fought with her instincts instead of a formulated plan, and she was quite skilled. If he ever had to truly fight this crew, she would need to be the first one he killed, for she was the most dangerous. Her, and the two Mages, of course.

"There is always tomorrow, Shimada," Kemocay grinned. "You can take my place and fight twice." Everyone had a good laugh at this.

"Land ho!" an announcement echoed through the ship.

"Land?" Ilfanti asked.

"At lassst," Beige said. "I wasss running out of food."

"Hopefully we will be able to re-provision here," Kemocay said. "Green has been telling us to keep an eye out for these islands for the last few days."

"It will be good to set foot on dry land again," Ilfanti agreed.

"Yes," Kemocay said. "We've never been this way before, though. I hope that what you and the port master in Water Haven told us is true."

"What was that? That the felines will welcome us and provide us with provisions?" Ilfanti asked as the two began walking up the stairwell to the main deck.

"I'll settle for the inhabitants being friendly and peaceful," Kemocay said.

"That would be a welcome change from the way our voyage began," Ilfanti laughed at the truth of the words. They had somehow managed to survive a fleet of amphibiers, bypass the wrath of Master Zane and the Council's wishes, and travel through pirate waters with only one incident. Not bad, but still more than most ships would ever have to deal with on an expedition.

As they reached the main deck, Ilfanti squinted to see in the distance a series of mountainous islands. "How long before we get there?"

"A few hours, perhaps," Kemocay said. "More than enough time to get washed up."

"It will be good to see felines thriving again. Especially since they were mostly wiped out in our own land after the Race Wars in the Seven Kingdoms."

"There should be many of them," Kemocay said. "From what we

were told, they are the only sentient race on this island chain, and each island has a different tribe of felines on it."

"I've only stopped here once," Ilfanti said. "But when I did, the felines sure were inviting."

"Let's hope that remains true today," Kemocay said. "I, for one, hope to enjoy the new experiences as they come. The unknown is intriguing. Enticing. As long as they aren't hostile, we should all enjoy it, my friend."

"Yes," Ilfanti said as he considered the words. Not knowing what to expect or what he would find was quite appealing. He felt like he had during his Paladin years again. He felt more like the dwarf he once had been. This entire journey had started to erase who he had become due to the passage of time. The doubts of advancing age were overwhelming and had stifled the true rebel that he had been for so many years. That was something that he was now determined to change. He had a renewed purpose, and though it had been lacking at first, he was regaining his passion for adventure.

"Yes," he repeated. "I think I will enjoy this."

CHAPTER 25

The sense of excitement and anticipation flowed over the officers and crew of the *Soaring Mist* as the morning sun revealed land on the far horizon. The relief of reaching the Amahani Islands was infectious, and soon, every member of the crew was on the main deck, anxiously staring at the islands as they sailed closer to them.

Green was especially proud that morning, and with good reason. Even some of the most seasoned sea captains could stray slightly off-course through the Vast Expanse, but he had efficiently plotted their course, getting them safely there sooner than anticipated.

Captain Augustus used her optical enhancers, watching as the several feline natives upon the golden sand of the beach quickly grew to dozens, and then hundreds. She did not see weapons, but was wise enough to know that a feline could be a weapon without need for a physical instrument like a sword or spear. They were garbed in skirts of leaves or bamboo, and most wore headdresses and necklaces of flowers. Some also had leaves wrapped around their wrists or ankles, but carried nothing that appeared hostile.

Dozens of canoes were carried from the trees, down the beach, and into the water. The canoes varied in size, some small, perhaps three- or four-person canoes, whereas others were substantially larger, with sails that looked like they were made of leaves, and enough room to fit perhaps one hundred felines.

"What do you make of that?" Augustus asked, handing the optical enhancers to Krimdor.

Krimdor studied the beach, moving from side to side and adjusting the lens. He watched as felines began to fill the canoes and paddle out toward the *Soaring Mist*. "If I had to guess, I would say that they are welcoming us."

Augustus took the optical enhancers back and glanced at Kemocay, who appeared slightly on edge. "Do you concur?"

"We should be ready for anything," Kemocay said.

"I don't want to appear hostile," Augustus said. "Ilfanti, did they do this when you were here?"

"No," admitted Ilfanti. "But many cultures I have come across would come to greet you and make you feel invited when you arrive. I do not feel that their intentions are hostile."

"I agree," Augustus said. "Kemocay, have your troops stand down, but be ready just in case. I want the first thing the islanders see to be a symbol of friendship, not a bow."

"Aye, Captain," Kemocay said. He stepped down from the bridge and went to relay orders to his men.

"Drop anchor," Augustus said.

"Drop anchor!" Brondolfr shouted. Several crewmembers rushed over to the anchor and began lowering it. As it reached the bottom, the ship began to slow and come to a halt.

The feline were swift, and the canoes were soon upon the *Soaring Mist*. Many were waving at the crew aboard the ship. If there had been any doubts about their intentions, the laughter and smiles of the natives dispelled them.

Several felines grabbed hold of the rigging and climbed aboard. They hugged crewmembers as they reached them, moving through the crew. The feeling of warmth was infectious and many of the crew began laughing and smiling as well. Captain Augustus was quite pleased by what she was witnessing.

By her side, Fasbender began mumbling under his breath.

"What is it, old friend?" Augustus asked.

"I thought felines were supposed to be afraid of the water."

"Perhaps when they live on an island, they overcome that fear," Augustus suggested.

"Perhaps," he mumbled under his breath.

"What is it?" Augustus asked again.

"Nothing worth mentioning," Fasbender said.

"Fasbender, tell me," Augustus replied. "Don't make me turn that into an order."

"Well, Captain, it's just that I'm, well, I'm allergic to cats," Fasbender admitted.

"You're allergic to cats?" Augustus repeated, one eyebrow rising as she regarded him.

"Yup," Fasbender sighed. "So when I was staying behind to work on the engines, it also kept me away from the felines."

"I see," Augustus said.

"But now they are on the ship," he groaned. "I'll have to have the entire deck scrubbed just to keep me from sneezing every three seconds!"

"You're not sneezing now," Augustus pointed out.

"Oh, just you wait," Fasbender moaned. "Once a single hair gets near me, I can't control myself."

"Well, then, we'll just have to head to the island so that they don't linger on board too much," said Augustus.

"That sure would be appreciated," Fasbender said. "It really would be."

"Brondolfr, lower the barges, we're going to shore," Augustus ordered.

"Aye, Captain," Brondolfr said. "Lower the barges!"

Four barges, two on each side of the Soaring Mist, were lowered into the water. Twenty members of the crew made their way down into each barge, lifting oars and preparing to row. The officers, Ilfanti, and Alaran made their way onto the different barges as well, leaving the gnomes and a skeleton crew behind on the *Soaring Mist.*

As soon, as the officers were situated, the barges cast off and the crew began rowing toward the shore. The felines in canoes reversed course and rowed alongside them, escorting the crew to shore. Augustus could see that even more felines were strewn out along the beach now. They too were waving and calling out to the approaching visitors.

Glancing over the side of the boat, Augustus marveled at how clean and pure the water was. It was pure blue, crystal clear, allowing her to see all the way to the sand at the bottom. She could not image the waters around the Imperium ever being so clear.

As their barge hit the beach, felines crowded around, touching each member of the crew as they came off. They backed away from Augustus, though, as if recognizing her as the leader.

An opening in the crowd appeared, creating a path that Augustus followed. Krimdor and Brondolfr stood directly behind her, with Kemocay, Beige, Green, Ilfanti, Jin Fe, Shimada, Palisha, and Alaran following closely behind. The opening led them up the beach and into a thicket of bushes and palm trees. They made their way through small openings, where the felines held the branches back, and emerged behind the trees where there was a vast clearing with houses.

The houses were large residential buildings. The base and walls were made from the trunks of coconut trees, and the roofs were vegetal tiles made from coconut leaves. Several families could easily reside in each one.

The crowd led Augustus to a waiting group. One feline sat on a wooden throne with feathers jutting out from the top. The feline was garbed as the others, but also wore a belt made of red feathers, and had an exquisite headdress that easily contained hundreds of feathers.

Before the feline was a wooden log, creating a divider between himself and the visitors. Augustus assumed he was the king. She kneeled down before the log, and bowed gracefully to the feline. As she glanced up, she studied him more closely. His fur was mostly a light gray, with darker gray and even some black markings throughout his coat. His whiskers were long and hung down to his portly belly. It looked as if he valued the length of his whiskers almost above anything else.

Captain Augustus remained on her knee, waiting for the King to reply. He raised his clawed hand and waved her forward. Augustus stood up, stepped around the log, and approached the King.

Kemocay tensed, worried that he would not be able to defend his Captain if there was a problem. Ilfanti eased forward and clutched his arm. He shook his head from side to side, and Kemocay nodded. The Captain was not in any danger, and he needed to be a little less on edge.

Augustus reached the feline King, who stood up and stared into her eyes. He bent over and smelled her hair, then pulled back and purred.

All of the felines then erupted into cheers. Augustus was not certain exactly what it was she was supposed to do. The King must have realized that, as he beckoned her to take the log. Following his signal, Augustus stepped over to it and sat down.

As the crowd quieted down and the King sat again, Augustus glanced at Krimdor. "Could you translate for me?"

"No need," the King said. "Many visitors have come to us over the years. We have learned each of their languages to make them feel more welcome."

Augustus nodded her understanding. "That is most gracious and kind of you. I am Captain Augustus, of the *Soaring Mist.*"

"Welcome to Amahani," the King said. "I am Al'ashi, King of the largest of the Amahani Islands. What brings you before me this day?"

"We are traveling far and hope that you would be so kind as to permit us to seek provisions on the outer islands," Augustus said.

"No," Al'ashi growled. "Whatever you need, you will get here."

"That would be most gracious," Augustus said. "We would be very grateful."

"I can offer you in abundance fresh pig and fish, vegetables from our harvest, and exotic fruits that you will not find anywhere but here," Al'ashi said.

"That is more than we could have hoped for," Augustus said, pleasantly surprised. "In return, we could offer you clothing, tools, gemstones, and even some inventions that will boggle your senses."

"We have no need for such things," scoffed Al'ashi. "Every ship offers us their baubles. Entertaining for a time, but disruptive to the young."

"I understand," Augustus said. "What is it then that would interest you, and I shall do my best to accommodate?"

"We shall feed you, and treat you as if you were the very children of the gods, in exchange for something more precious than your gemstones and fancy inventions."

"What is that?" asked Augustus, almost afraid of the answer.

"We wish to hear stories," Al'ashi said. "Your tales will be scribed and saved for all to hear. Do you have stories of interest?"

"I'm sure we will not disappoint," Augustus said, turning and glancing at Ilfanti, winking at the dwarven Master who had entertained many crewmembers with tales of his Paladin adventures.

"Then we are agreed," Al'ashi said. "How long shall you be with us?"

"If possible, we would like to stay until repairs are completed on our ship. Perhaps a week? Maybe a little longer, if that would be all right?" Augustus said.

Al'ashi twirled his whiskers with one stubby finger. "Many stories I hope that shall bring."

"Many indeed," Augustus agreed. "Thank you again for your hospitality."

As Augustus stood up, Rhyne pushed his way past the officers and glared at Al'ashi. "Have there been other ships here recently?"

"Alaran, don't," Krimdor said as he grabbed Rhyne's arm.

Al'ashi looked back and forth between Rhyne and Augustus. "Does this one speak for you?"

"No, he does not. My sincerest apologies," Augustus said with a bow. "His Captain was slain and he is hoping to find the murderer. I'm afraid Alaran is not very patient."

"The folly of youth," Al'ashi said. "You may go."

"What about other ships?" Rhyne asked again, his tone more sinister and demanding.

"Alaran, now is not the time," Augustus said, a finality to her words. With another bow to King Al'ashi, Augustus turned and led her officers back the way they had come.

Rhyne clenched his fists. He was trying to act the way a concerned enforcer would act. After the sun vanished over the horizon, these felines would see how a bounty hunter acted. They would give him the information that he craved.

CHAPTER 26

The remainder of the day, for Rhyne, seemed to take an eternity. The felines had led the crew to several of their houses and told them that they could remain there. A feast and celebration were then prepared in honor of the guests. After the feast, several felines prepared scrolls and quills and Al'ashi requested that the tales begin. Ilfanti spoke eloquently before the bonfire, the felines mesmerized by the talented orator.

Rhyne did not care about the tales. He did not care about relations with these people either, though he did note that more than one female had approached him and tried to make him comfortable. He was not sure whether he was imagining it or not, but he felt that the felines were inviting him to do more than just take advantage of their comfort. Perhaps he would do so before leaving, but for now, he needed information.

The feast was barbequed pig, fish, rice, and vegetables. Containers of a sweet nectar were located every few feet for people to drink from. Rhyne avoided the drink, but observed the diminished capacities of those around him. Words were being slurred, and people were acting quite intoxicated.

He spotted a pair of felines wandering off. One was stumbling and the other was helping him walk. Silently, without disturbing anyone around him, Rhyne stood and made his way into the darkness to follow the pair. One thing he had learned from a young age was that the ability to move silently and use the shadows allowed you to get closer to your quarry than anyone would ever expect. The felines did not know he was there until they felt the warmth of his breath on the back of their necks.

One feline spun around, startled and alarmed. Rhyne attempted a pleasant grin. "Need a hand?"

The feline laughed, as if the laugh would wash away the sudden dread he was feeling. "Pala'ti had a bit too much to drink," the feline said. "I was bringing him home."

"I'll help," Rhyne offered. He lifted one of Pala'ti's arms and began walking in stride with the feline. "Do you have these parties often?"

As soon as he asked the question, he wondered whether he was becoming soft. Even now, in the darkness, away from prying eyes, he was acting more like the persona of Alaran than that of Rhyne. He should kill the drunkard and threaten to do the same to the friend. Then he would learn what it was that he needed to know. Deception and manipulation were tricks more for Kabilian than for him, but a pair of dead felines could arouse suspicion. Of course, he could eliminate the bodies, but the missing duo could still cause problems.

"We have many celebrations," the feline admitted.

"For what occasions?" Rhyne asked.

"Weddings, births, funerals, good harvests, and welcoming visitors."

"When was the last celebration?" Rhyne asked, deciding that if the answer did not come soon, he would become a bit more persuasive and forceful.

"About a week ago," the feline admitted.

"A week?" Rhyne asked. "What was the occasion?"

"Another ship," the feline said.

Rhyne could not contain his joy at the news. Kabilian was here merely a week ago. They were close. Very close. Soon, he would catch Kabilian, and then he would end this little chase, once and for all.

CHAPTER 27

After a week's time, Ilfanti was anxious to return to the *Soaring Mist* and be on his way. Many of the crew were enjoying themselves, and Ilfanti feared that they would be reluctant to leave. Even Jin Fe was practically dancing with joy, exploring new forms of alternative medicine. In his hut were dozens of plants that he had gathered, all of which he claimed had strong medicinal value. He also was practicing a variety of techniques that allowed positions and varying pressures to alleviate pain. If finding the Orb of Prophecy was not so vital, Ilfanti would love to spend more time here with Jin Fe learning about all of this too, but he could not.

Shimada did not share her grandfather's optimism. She had had enough of the felines after the first night and had returned to the *Soaring Mist*, where she refused to even consider returning to the island. Ilfanti could not figure out why she was so adamant about staying on board, but at least she was ready to go.

Fasbender and the gnomes never left the ship either, though whenever Ilfanti glanced at the *Soaring Mist*, he was a little surprised to see that they were not working, but rather lying on deck and sunbathing. He trusted that the gnomes would have all of their maintenance completed and ready to go on time, though.

Brondolfr and Palisha had opted to take the week to themselves. Al'ashi had sent an escort with them and brought them to a secluded part of the island. They had not returned yet, but Ilfanti heard some of the felines talking about it. It was a small lagoon with emerald water and breathtaking flowers. There was even a warm-water waterfall that bubbled and steamed at the base. Ilfanti could imagine how hard it would be for the couple to leave such peace and tranquility and return to their stations.

Kemocay's suspicions faded, and he soon found new sparring partners. The felines were quite willing to fight with him, and Kemocay even seemed to be moving a little quicker than he had been when they first arrived. Ilfanti wondered if Kemocay could defeat Alaran now.

Alaran certainly was ready to leave. He seemed almost desperate. He begged and pleaded the Captain whenever he saw her. Perhaps that was why Captain Augustus and the two rasplers spent less and less time with the crew as the week went on.

The crew also seemed quite content to stay. The *Soaring Mist* was often at sea for months at a time. Some of the men had not seen their wives for quite some time. Others had never even been with a woman before. Here, though, the feline women were seductive and suggestive. Ilfanti saw quite a few claw marks and bites on members of the crew, and overheard them talking with their friends about what happened.

Ilfanti spotted Krimdor talking to a pair of felines. If anyone knew what the Captain was planning, it would be her first officer. He waited patiently as Krimdor finished his discussion, and then approached the aquatican.

"Ilfanti, how goes it?"

"The day is pleasant enough," Ilfanti said. "How are preparations to return to the *Soaring Mist* progressing?"

"Not very well," Krimdor shrugged.

"Are we being delayed?" Ilfanti asked, certain that he knew the answer.

"We will be leaving at first light," Krimdor said.

"First light?" confirmed Ilfanti.

"Yes, I spoke with the Captain earlier today. She informs me that King Al'ashi is preparing another feast and celebration before our departure. That will be tonight."

If there was another party tonight, Ilfanti sincerely doubted that they would be leaving on time in the morning. The nectar that they drank at the first celebration left the crew of the *Soaring Mist* sleepy well into the following afternoon. At least the plan to depart was in place.

"When will provisions be brought on board?" Ilfanti asked.

"Beige is already seeing to it," Krimdor said. "The felines are helping him bring it all to the *Mist*."

Ilfanti chuckled at that. Poor Fasbender. Just when he thought that the ship was clean and ready to go, more felines were coming aboard—his allergies would really begin to bother him.

"If you don't mind, I think I'll return now. I'd like to take care of a few things in my cabin before leaving in the morning," Ilfanti said.

"As you wish," Krimdor said. "We'll see you in the morning."

Ilfanti still doubted they would be leaving then, but when the sun appeared on the horizon, he dressed and went to the main deck, where the barges were being fastened into place and the Captain was standing on the bridge, instructing the crew. Within the hour, they were on their way again.

ILFANTI'S LOG

The closer that we get to Pantalica, the more anxious I become. We'll soon be at the Taelific Ocean, where the children of old friends will greet us, and then Egziard is just beyond. This mission is so vital, but sometimes, it is wise to lean back and reflect upon things.

The Seven Kingdoms is a land that has been plagued by wars for millennia. If the siege of Zoldex brings forth the end of the Imperium, then the Age of the Imperium will not even last fifty-five years. Such a short period of time, but one that has been relatively peaceful. Well, at least for the humans.

The Imperium certainly is not the model civilization. Any non-human race has been in seclusion, and the amount of prejudice around the realm is stifling. But the wars had ended. Perhaps some discontent and ill thoughts, but no physical combat. Not until recently. Not until Zoldex began pulling strings and whispering into the ears of those that are easily swayed.

Before the formation of the Imperium, the realm was little better. The races were still in seclusion, and the humans were at war with each other. The "Great Wars." What makes them so great? Kingdoms fighting with kingdoms? In the case of Dartie and Dartais, it was like brothers fighting against each other. For what? Land? Power? Such a waste.

The Great Wars began as The Race Wars ended. A five thousand-year war, finally concluded as the aligned forces of what many considered good were victorious, only to have the human allies betray them all and claim the land as their own. After five thousand years of fighting, who could blame the individual races for harboring resentments toward their allies and wanting nothing more to do with them?

That makes things much more difficult today. The resentments and mistrust linger, and at a time when the races should be united against a common foe, they would rather fight amongst themselves. This land is ripe for Zoldex's conquest. I find it amazing that nobody else has tried before now.

The realm was not always at war. Or, at least, that is what the history books claim. The Age of the Dragon lasted for more than fifty thousand years. The dragon and mystral united as peacekeepers and defenders, and for that period, the realm was at peace. Fifty thousand years is a long time. I wish we could somehow forge a peaceful new era that would be as lasting.

But nothing lasts forever. The Dark Ages came when tyrants and warlords began their reign. First there was the persecution of the dragons, and then the dragons left the land. Those left behind had little idea as to how to govern themselves, and the strongest began to rule through conquest, subjugating those weaker than them. Certainly not an ideal lifestyle. Everything that had been accomplished in The Age of the Dragon was lost during the Dark Ages. Most literature and artifacts from the prior era were also burned and destroyed, removing all vestiges of a utopian society.

In response to The Dark Ages, a group of eternals led by Pierce and—I hate to admit it—Zoldex went in search of a mythical spring that would grant the drinker uncanny abilities. It was the dawn of the era of the Mages. Pierce summoned representatives from every race to drink from the spring, as long as they agreed to abide by the laws he established. With all of the new Mages in the realm, the Dark Ages soon came to an end, and like the mystral and dragons before us, the Mages became the new peacekeepers of the land.

Our attempt at harmony was nowhere near as successful, though. Perhaps it was because the desire for power is contagious. Perhaps not all warlords and tyrants had been defeated. Whatever the reason, nearly two thousand and five hundred years after peace had been restored to the land, it was plagued by wars again. The aforementioned Race Wars. The Mages tried to stop it from spreading, but failed. Many Mages perished, beginning the trend toward isolation that Pierce is so fond of.

War after war after war. Even if we defeat Zoldex, how long before another threat is on the horizon? How long before harmony is again overcome and the cry for war is heard again? Maybe the Seven Kingdoms are cursed, and war is our eternal damnation.

But that is not the way things are everywhere. The Amahani Islands *that we just left have never experienced war. It is a foreign concept to them. Even with vast tribes of felines throughout the islands, not even once has one tribe attempted to claim power by attacking another. If only their attitude and outlook could somehow be adopted. Instead, I'm afraid that if the attempt was made, it would be they who would be corrupted, and we would doom the felines to centuries of conflict.*

Pantalica is also peaceful. In the Seven Kingdoms, the only nearby submariner civilization is Aquatica, home of the aquaticans. Beneath the Taelific Ocean, though, there are aquaticans, aquanas, shorlachai, turtics, whalari, and the mer people. In the Seven Kingdoms, imagine a troll and a dwarf or elf in the same room? Chaos would likely ensue. Not here, though. Here, all races exist in complete harmony with each other and their environment. I admire that so.

The last time I was here, Sovereign Eorynth was kind enough to spend time with me. He introduced me to life in his city, Pantalica, and showed how everyone, regardless of their race, worked together for the common good of all. They even had sea creatures helping them without coercion. That, too, is a model that I would like to somehow adopt for the Imperium.

But again, in the land I am from, I have little confidence that such a union would work. Especially after the Race Wars. Centaurs will never trust humans. Elves will never trust trolls. It is sad, really. We fight a common foe, but then what? Those who fought together will become foes. Perhaps that is the way the Seven Kingdoms were meant to be. Perhaps it is fate that there will always be conflict. Whatever our destiny may be, it does not change the today's threat. Zoldex must be defeated, and I sincerely believe that Karleena is the person to usher in a better tomorrow, a bright future that few others can see.

CHAPTER 28

Ilfanti finished his workout with Kemocay and Beige and made his way to the main deck. The day was overcast and cool, but the waters were calm. The crew was moving quickly, preparing the ship and tying everything down in case a storm broke out. Ilfanti glanced at the sky and shrugged. He certainly would not presume to predict the weather, but he did not feel like a storm was coming.

At the bow of the ship were Palisha and Shimada. Ilfanti went to join them, making certain to avoid the crew so that he would not get in their way. The two women were sitting on the bow, looking out at the sea.

"Anything interesting?" asked Ilfanti.

Palisha turned around and smiled pleasantly. "Ilfanti, join us."

Shimada nodded her head in a slight bow. In matters of pleasantries, she was of few words.

"Don't mind if I do," Ilfanti said, sitting down next to Palisha. "What have I missed so far?"

"Be careful, you might not like the answer," said Palisha with a wink.

"Try me," said Ilfanti.

"We were discussing the future," said Palisha. "More specifically, the next generation."

"Why would that bother me? At the Council I watch the next generation of Mages all of the time. Perhaps they are a little more immature and prone to taking chances than I recall being at that age, but then again, I'm probably forgetting how I really was back then."

"She meant the next generation of our lineage," Shimada clarified. "I am the last Yutaka. Since I am not a man, and am unable to carry on the family name, hundreds of years of heritage and honor will be no more."

"Not necessarily," said Ilfanti. "Even if you do not carry on the clan's name, you still are passing on your values and beliefs to your children. Teach them, and they will remember."

"In Aezia, that would mean very little," said Shimada solemnly.

"You're not in Aezia anymore," reminded Ilfanti. "Make your history what you want."

"As you said, I am not in Aezia. Where am I to find a mate?"

Palisha leaned forward and put her hand comfortingly on Shimada's leg. "Shimada, you will find someone when you least expect it. Look at Brondolfr and me. Who ever would have thought that I would marry a barbarian? Certainly I didn't."

Ilfanti nodded encouragingly to try and cheer Shimada up, but he knew from the Aezians whom he had met during his Paladin years that they valued tradition and honor above anything else. For Shimada to marry someone who was not of Aezian descent would be traumatic for her. He wondered, since she already violated tradition so much by avenging the murder of her family, if she would be open to marrying outside of her race.

"What about you?" Palisha asked.

Ilfanti was momentarily startled, lost in his own thoughts. "What?"

"What about you?" Palisha asked again. "Ever have any children?"

"No," admitted Ilfanti. "When I was younger, I was always going from adventure to adventure, and thoughts of settling down, even for a short while, went against the lifestyle I was living. There may have been a dwarf here or there, but nothing that lasted long enough to make me think twice about leaving. Then when I got back to the Mage's Council, my name became so popular that I was not certain if people were interested in me for me, or for my reputation."

"So you gave up trying?" Shimada asked, frowning.

"It's not that, not really," said Ilfanti, trying to collect his thoughts and explain it properly. "Mages have children, but we don't get to keep them. The Gatherers take them to nursery at the Academy. The desire to have a child, guide them, and see them grow isn't really allowed for Mages."

"That is so sad," said Palisha. "I am glad that I am not a Mage. I cannot wait to have Brondolfr's child, and to help him or her become just like their father."

"Or like their mother," added Ilfanti.

"Or like me," agreed Palisha, grinning happily.

"You two were gone the entire week we were at the Amahani Islands. Any chance this crew will have a new addition before we get home?" asked Ilfanti.

Palisha grinned. "We're hoping," she said.

"That's wonderful, Palisha," Shimada said.

"I wish you the best," said Ilfanti. "I hope it works out."

"And for you," Palisha said.

"What do you mean?" asked Ilfanti.

"You may act like you don't want children of your own, but I can see it in your eyes and hear it in your voice. You do want children, and you regret not having them," said Palisha.

Ilfanti thought about it for a moment. He was not certain. He was too old now. If he had a chance along the way, he had missed it. No use harboring regrets about that now.

"You would make a wonderful father," Shimada said.

"Um, thanks," said Ilfanti, suddenly feeling an emptiness welling inside of him. Perhaps he should not have joined in on this particular conversation. He certainly did not need another regret to add to his list. There was enough on his mind already.

"You must!"

Ilfanti spun around at the sound of Alaran's shout. He saw the wraith on the bridge, arguing with Captain Augustus, who was looking through her optical enhancers. Ilfanti followed her line of sight and saw a small blurred image on the horizon, possibly a ship.

"If you ladies would excuse me," said Ilfanti. He stood up and made his way to the bridge. Krimdor, Brondolfr, and Kemocay were all on the bridge with Augustus and Alaran.

"That is the ship I am after," growled Rhyne. "We must pursue her!"

"You are mistaken. That is not the *Falestian Pride*," said Augustus.

"We will not alter course just because we see some random ship."

Ilfanti watched Alaran closely. The wraith's eyes glowed with such an intensity that they looked like they could ignite in flame. His jaw was clenched, his teeth grinding inside his mouth. Every muscle was tense.

"Apologies for my outburst," said Rhyne, in what clearly was an effort to speak politely. "I was mistaken. Merely anxious to find the mutineers."

"You will find them, Alaran," Augustus said. "In a time of the fates' choosing, not your own."

"Quite true," Rhyne said. He then spun around and walked away from the bridge. Ilfanti and the officers watched him until he climbed down beneath the main deck.

"I do not trust him," Brondolfr said.

"He is deceiving us," Kemocay agreed.

"Or at least he is not telling us the entire truth," added Krimdor.

"I agree," Augustus said. "We will have to watch Alaran very closely."

"We should just maroon him," suggested Krimdor.

"As we would any disruptive member of the crew," concurred Kemocay. "It is part of the code we all follow on this ship."

"I do not intend to offer him passage back to the Seven Kingdoms after we reach Egziard," Augustus explained. "We will leave him there. Doing so before then would be an act of cruelty. We're not even near any established shipping lanes."

"Let us hope that we can control him until we reach Egziard," Krimdor said.

Ilfanti listened to the officers' discussion. He had harbored many doubts about Alaran since he had arrived on the ship. He did not trust him, and also felt that Alaran was being deceptive. He was glad that the officers openly suspected him as well.

Glancing out to where the ship had been on the horizon, Ilfanti spotted movement in his peripheral vision. He turned to study it and smiled warmly. Submariners riding sea horses were approaching. They had reached the waters of the Taelific Ocean on the outskirts of Pantalica.

CHAPTER 29

The sea horses rose from the water, each with a rider, encircling the *Soaring Mist*. The riders were not all aquaticans as Ilfanti had assumed, but were of varying races. He spotted several that he recognized from other adventures—like the green-skinned aquannas, the vicious and deadly shorlachai, the wise turtics, and the massive whalari—as well as a few other creatures he did not recognize. One looked like some kind of hunched-over humanoid shark, another looked like an octopus with a humanoid face, and a final one looked like a jellyfish that also had a somewhat humanoid frame.

"All stop," Captain Augustus ordered.

"All stop!" Brondolfr shouted.

One of the sea horses with a shorlachai rode forward. The creature had coral over his shoulders, torso, and feet. His mouth barely contained his teeth that jaggedly grew everywhere. His head was ridged with spikes trailing back. In his hands, which were webbed with an opposable thumb, he held a trident.

"Passage on the Taelific Ocean is forbidden," he roared. "Leave. Now!"

Captain Augustus glanced at Ilfanti, questioningly. Ilfanti was at a loss. "We are traveling on a desperate mission to Egziard," Augustus explained. "Time, I am afraid, is critical."

"Surface dwellers will not be tolerated on our waters," the shorlachai explained, hostilely. "Leave. Now!"

Ilfanti stepped in front of Augustus and shouted out to the riders. "I have traveled these waters before without incident. Why are we not allowed to do so now?"

"Surface dwellers have no respect for their surroundings," the shorlachai growled. "You drop refuse in the oceans, polluting them for us.

This will no longer be tolerated. Leave. Now. I shall not warn you again."

"I demand to speak to the Sovereign of Pantalica!" Ilfanti shouted. "I had a longstanding relationship with Sovereign Eorynth! His descendents will know of me."

"The time of Eorynth is no more. Old arrangements will not be honored," the shorlachai said. "You have been warned."

The shorlachai raised his trident in the air. A pair of aquaticans blew horns into the water. Within seconds, the water around the *Soaring Mist* swirled to life. Mermaids and mermen appeared with harpoons ready to throw, drelenkins with riders rose directly behind the sea horses, and dozens of other creatures that were even larger than the whalari emerged from the water and surrounded the ship.

"You ignored our warning. Now your fate is sealed," the shorlachai said.

Krimdor rushed forward and raised his arms. "Wait!"

The shorlachai's eyes narrowed into slits. "What trickery is this? An aquatican in the midst of the topsiders?"

"My name is Krimdor. I serve as the first officer aboard this ship. These people are honorable and noble. I have never witnessed them polluting the oceans or harming anything that was not vile already. I plead with you to spare their lives and let us continue with our mission."

The shorlachai glared at Krimdor for a long moment. His mouth furled into a sneer. "You are a traitor to your own kind and are not welcome here. But if you leave immediately, we shall let you go."

Ilfanti hated the thought of leaving. The Taelific Ocean was the best and quickest route available. He thought it ludicrous that they could not pass. But as he looked out at the forces amassed against them he knew that even with the amphibier weapons working at their peak efficiency, and a pair of Mages on board, they would not stand a chance against the submariner forces.

Krimdor glanced at the Captain, who nodded her assent. "We graciously accept your generous offer and shall depart immediately."

The aquaticans blew their horns again, and the mounted creatures, mermaids, and mermen dropped beneath the water and vanished from sight, leaving only the original sea horses and mounts around the *Soaring Mist.* They too moved away, allowing the ship to turn and navigate.

Augustus stepped over to Green. "Get us out of here."

"What courssse, mother?"

"Any. Just get us out of here."

CHAPTER 30

After reversing course, the *Soaring Mist* sailed for an hour before Augustus issued the order to come to a stop. She then assembled all officers for a meeting to discuss their alternatives. Ilfanti was also invited to attend. Everyone there knew that the remaining options were not encouraging ones.

They had already had the discussion about the five routes that the *Soaring Mist* could take to travel to Egziard. Now, the best route was no longer open to them. The Captain had to choose the next best alternative, and she wanted feedback from her trusted officers and advisors.

"We all know the options we have. They are not good. But we have to choose the best one in light of what we have left," Augustus said.

Ilfanti shook his head. "There is no decision to be made. I will not jeopardize the lives of the crew merely to shave some time off of our voyage. We've already gotten this far sooner than expected, so if we need to add a month or so to our route, then so be it."

"It is the best alternative," Krimdor agreed. "At least, the safest."

"What would the delay mean to lives back home?" Kemocay asked. "You know I am cautious and adamant that we be prepared, but we *are* prepared. This ship and this crew are prepared to face the more difficult challenges."

"How do you prepare to fight the dead?" asked Brondolfr.

"I trust that mighty Brondolfr would find that his axe does just as much damage to a skeleton as it does to a flesh-and-blood foe," returned Kemocay.

"My mission is vital, and I do not know what delays could mean to those back home, but that risk was there from the day I first decided to leave. We have to have faith in those who were left behind. Those in the Imperium are responsible for holding Zoldex off long enough for the Empress to be found, and the races united. I understand it may be best if we go the long way. After all, what is the point if we chose a dangerous path and never make our destination?"

"Ilfanti's words are wise, and selfless," Jin Fe said. "He wishes to steer us to a safe passage when those we left behind may very likely be fighting for their very survival. Should we not risk the same?"

"I concur," Fasbender said. "I'd sure hate to think of Adlai or Underwood under siege if there was some way we could have avoided it by taking a few risks."

"Very well," Augustus said. "We will risk one of the dangerous routes. All three pose a challenge. All three could end our voyage. Which would be the shortest passage?"

"The way of the whirlpoolsss," Green said. "There are no islandsss in the way. Jussst a ssstraight route."

"With many course corrections," Krimdor pointed out. "What happens when one of the whirlpools forms directly beneath us without warning?"

"Could you and Ilfanti arrange a full-coverage rotation so that if that happens, one of you can lift the ship to safety?" asked Kemocay.

Krimdor glanced at Ilfanti with a worried look on his face. "I don't think I could do that at all."

"Even if he had the ability and control to do so, being able to do it more than once in a short period of time would be too much," Ilfanti said.

"Why would he need to do it more than once?" asked Brondolfr.

"The whirlpools are unpredictable," explained Ilfanti. "One may appear in a day's time, or one hundred in an hour. There is no way to plan for it, or anticipate when and where it'll happen."

"Xeorn," whistled Brondolfr. "It is like the very ocean conspires against us."

"Which is the next quickest route?" Augustus asked.

"The Gatesss of Tanorusss," Green said.

"Comments?" Augustus asked.

"I only know legend and rumor," reminded Ilfanti. "I have never gone this way."

"I wonder just how many cursed ships roam that passage?" Kemocay speculated.

"It could be a few, it could be many," shrugged Krimdor.

"Other than warningsss, there is little I found on that area," added Green.

"The unknown is often scarier than reality," Jin Fe pointed out. "We may find this route quite easygoing."

"Or we might not," growled Brondolfr. "This is the walking dead we're talking about."

"What about the final route?" Augustus asked.

"We would really be putting Green to the test," Ilfanti said. "I was traveling one time with five vessels heading to Egziard. We chose that route because it looked the easiest. As long as we didn't go near the islands, we thought that we'd be unharmed. But the seabed is jagged and shallow, and two ships ran aground in different locations. Some creatures came down and killed the crew. The other ships were forced to flee. Fortunately, we saved some of the crew.

"It doesn't end there, though," continued Ilfanti. "Some of the creatures were winged. They flew out and attacked us. We lost another ship to this strike. The fourth we lost to sea creatures that struck from beneath. The ship I was on only barely managed to survive."

"Not very promising," whispered Brondolfr. "So which do we choose?"

"The answer is obvious," Kemocay said. "We go to the Gates of Tanorus. It may be unknown, but at least the route itself is not part of the threat. We can sail. We see anything dead coming towards us, we can fight or we can flee."

"Yes," Brondolfr said. "I do not want to see cursed beings, but I would rather a threat I may be able to fight."

"Even the dead have weaknesses," Jin Fe said.

"Krimdor?" Augustus asked.

"It sounds like this is our best choice amongst less-than-desirable options," Krimdor said. "We should risk the Gates of Tanorus."

"Agreed," Augustus said. "Green, plot a course."

"Yes, mother."

"Brondolfr, arrange a minimal rotation. I want everyone properly rested before we reach the Gates of Tanorus," Augustus continued.

"Aye, Captain. I shall see to it."

"Jin Fe, any of your Aezian wisdom and insight will be appreciated. Spend some time with Krimdor, Kemocay, and Ilfanti to try and design some kind of defense against whatever we may face.

"Of course," Jin Fe bowed.

"Prepare for the worst, gentleman, and hope for the best," Augustus said. "How long before we reach there?"

"No more than three daysss," Green said.

"We have three days," Augustus said. "Let's use them wisely. Dismissed."

ILFANTI'S LOG

Death. Most people fear it. Some embrace it. Some think nothing of it. Others challenge it. What we are doing now is taking that to an extreme. We're not facing our own mortality, but actually going to fight creatures of the dead. Or, perhaps, the undead? Take your pick of what to call them. As far as I'm concerned, the day they were cursed and stopped breathing was the day they died. The spirit that makes an individual who they are is gone, leaving only a shell behind. But it's those shells that we will be facing soon.

I feel compelled to write by candlelight this night, two days away from the Gates of Tanorus. Not that I feel we are about to knock on the doors of the mythical underworld, but there is something on this route that has terrified sailors in this area. There is a reason they refuse to even consider this route, and we probably would have been wise to heed that warning.

Perhaps Jin Fe is right. Maybe, way back when, the Gates of Tanorus were nothing more than a fable to scare people away from the passage. Maybe there are islands with vast riches hidden here. Maybe there is a utopian society where the food is plentiful and your every whim and desire is fulfilled. Maybe I should stop fantasizing and start going over what I know.

What I know is that this passage is rumored to be cursed. What I know is that sailors fear it. What I know is that it is rumored to have the dead sailing the area looking for victims. Well, this ship hunts pirates, so the crew are used to what they will face. Of course, their foes are typically alive, but that's just a detail.

If we do not make it and the decision to go through the Gates of Tanorus is our last, then hopefully at least this log will somehow survive and provide a testament to the bravery and nobility of the officers and crew of the Soaring Mist. I could not have chosen a better ship, and there are none that I would rather be on this quest with than Captain Augustus and her crew.

But hopefully we will survive, and instead of being remembered for their sacrifices here, may their names live on to become the giants that I know they shall all be. Augustus, Krimdor, Brondolfr, Kemocay, Jin Fe, Fasbender, Green, Beige, and even the non-officers—Shimada and Palisha. These are names that should become recognized and admired. If we make it home, I shall begin immortalizing this group by telling tales so grand that generations of Mages will anxiously want to hear the story again and again.

That, is the least I can do.

CHAPTER 31

The *Soaring Mist* slowed as it reached the Gates of Tanorus. None of them had expected the name to be so literal, but the officers and crew stood on deck and watched as they approached a towering arch constructed entirely of skulls of various creatures. The bones of the rest of the bodies were piled to construct a wall that extended from both sides of the arch as far as the eye could see.

On the side of the gate where the *Soaring Mist* was, the sun was shining and there was hardly a cloud in the sky. Glancing through the gate, all that they could see was a dark, dismal, reddish haze.

"Xeorn! How does it do that?" whispered Brondolfr.

Ilfanti glanced at the barbarian, checking to see what Brondolfr was referring to. Brondolfr's gaze was set on the bone-construct resting on the ocean surface.

Augustus ignored the question. Nobody on their ship could possibly explain what they were looking at. Instead of focusing on useless banter, she preferred action. "Brondolfr, take a dinghy out and see how deep the gateway is."

Brondolfr took a moment before he acknowledged that the Captain had given him an order. He pulled his eyes away from the wall and nodded. "Aye, Captain." Walking down the steps of the bridge, Brondolfr beckoned four crewmen to join him. He could see that they too were nervous, and knew that they would look to him for leadership. His own fears and doubts would have to be pushed aside for the sake of his men.

The dinghy was lowered, and Brondolfr watched the opening as the four men rowed closer to the gate of skulls. The nearer he got, the more he began to hear a definite pattern to the blowing winds. It was not just a gentle breeze, but a moan, with voices of the damned carried to him. Brondolfr felt a chill shudder down his spine, but forced himself to remain straight and stern.

"Row!" he barked as the four sailors began to slow down, all of them hearing and sensing the closeness of the gateway.

"But, sir," one of the men gasped. "That is death in there."

"And that is precisely where we are going," said Brondolfr, relaying a confidence he did not truly feel. "This ship has looked into the face of death before, and we're still alive to tell the tale. This time will be no different."

The men did not seem convinced, but they did begin to row again, reaching the opening between the skulls. Brondolfr studied the orifice and was amazed at how deep the skull gateway was. It descended at least fifty feet.

"We'll have to measure the depth straight through the opening to make sure we don't run aground," Brondolfr said.

One of the men lowered the cable into the water and kept lowering it—the end in the water was weighted down so that it would reach the bottom and provide a good estimate for them to go by. Brondolfr was pleased when he noted that the depth was further than the twenty-nine feet and six inch draft of the *Soaring Mist.*

The five of them worked carefully for well over an hour, trying desperately to ignore the moans and wailing around them, checking and rechecking their measurements to make certain that there were no flaws in their estimates. After Brondolfr finally decided that they were done, he noticed that the crewmen rowed quite a bit more quickly to return to the ship.

As they approached, Brondolfr saw that all of the sails were down. They would be using their engines to enter the Gates of Tanorus. Several members of the crew helped them secure the dinghy and board the ship. Brondolfr headed directly to the bridge where he handed a listing of the measurements to Green.

Green scanned the list, making a few notations here and there, and then nodded in satisfaction. "Mother, we may proceed."

"Thank you, Green, Brondolfr. Engines, ahead minimal speed."

"Ahead minimal ssspeed," Green nodded his acknowledgement.

Brondolfr went to his station and yelled into the microphone to the gnomes belowdeck. "Ahead minimal speed!"

"I should head down to the engine room," Fasbender said.

"I want an engine status update after we pass through the Gates of Tanorus," Augustus said. "We may not have wind in there, and I'd like to try to rely on the engines for the bulk of our passage, like the Vast Expanse, but slower."

"Aye, Captain, I'll get her working just the way you need her to," Fasbender promised.

Augustus hoped that by traveling at a reduced speed, they could rely upon the engines more. She was hesitant to use the sails or to travel at top speeds until they learned exactly what they would be facing throughout this passage.

As the *Soaring Mist* approached the gate, everyone on board heard the moaning and wails that Brondolfr had experienced. The sound was terrifying and would haunt many of them in their dreams that night. That did not deter them or hinder their course.

Ilfanti was impressed by the spirit and determination of the crew. They faced the unknown with such bravery and certainty. He hoped that the next few days would not prove that they had faced the unknown in folly.

The *Soaring Mist* entered the gate of skulls and was encompassed by it. Only Green seemed unfazed as he kept his focus on his compass and charts, counting off and making subtle shifts to their course. The gate may only have been fifty feet, but for the crew, it seemed like an eternity before they were through and clear.

Passing through did not improve their situation, though. The red mist had a strong sulfuric stench that made many members of the crew cover their mouths, and some lean overboard and vomit. The mist was thick and hot. Ilfanti could feel the sweat beginning to pour off of him. His eyes were also itchy and scratchy, and felt like they were burning. Giving in to the sensation and scratching only irritated them more.

"Mother, problem," said Green, still the only crewman on the deck that was not hindered by the conditions.

"What is it?" Augustus asked.

"Compasss," he said, holding it up for her to see. The needle was spinning freely, completely out of control.

"You'll have to trust your senses," Augustus said. "I know you can do it."

"Yesss, mother," Green said. "I will make you proud."

"You always do," Augustus said.

Krimdor stepped over to Augustus and leaned over so that only she would hear. "Might I suggest having only essential personnel on deck at once? We should try to rotate both officers and crew out of this as much as possible."

"Agreed," Augustus said. "Separate the crew into four shifts. Have Brondolfr and Kemocay both command a shift, as well as the two of us. I don't want anyone exposed to this for more than an hour."

"Green does not seem affected. May I suggest Beige being given a shift as well?" suggested Krimdor.

Augustus glanced at Green. "Do the elements bother you?"

"No, mother," Green said. "I am fine."

"Have Beige assume second-in-command for all shifts," Augustus said. "We'll get him rest every few shifts."

"Understood. I'm sure he'll be pleased."

Augustus had to agree. Beige definitely wanted to take on more responsibility. This would be the perfect opportunity. As Krimdor left to begin issuing instructions to the crew, Augustus beckoned Ilfanti to her. "Is there anything you can do? Some kind of protective bubble?"

Ilfanti closed his eyes to concentrate, but shook his head. "I wish there was something I could do, but it is like the mist somehow negates the power of a Mage. I can feel the power deep within me, but I can't summon it."

"Then could you see if Jin Fe and the gnomes could design some kind of mask that will help us?"

"I'll go right now," Ilfanti said, glad to be of service to the crew.

As he left, he did not notice Rhyne, squatting beneath the stairs to the bridge, listening to everything that was said. If he had, perhaps he would have been able to somehow determine the pure malice that Rhyne was plotting.

CHAPTER 32

Rhyne waited for Ilfanti to go below deck before he stepped out from behind the stairs. He found it quite interesting that the red mist had the unpredicted side effect of suppressing the powers of a Mage. That could be very useful indeed.

Rushing to the dining hall, Rhyne paused as he saw Krimdor talking to Beige. The raspler was practically jumping up and down in excitement over his new responsibilities. Rhyne found the creature pathetic. Beige existed to pick up scraps that Augustus gave him, and when she did, he got so excited that he did not even know he was being used. Rhyne knew creatures like that well. He had exploited quite a few of them.

After the two left, Rhyne made his way into the galley and found a few extra canteens. They would work quite nicely. He did not want to be seen collecting the mist, because then there would be questions. Instead, he made his way to one of the officer's cabins where a porthole could be opened. The officers were all preoccupied. He would not be disturbed.

Rhyne held the first canteen out the porthole and grinned deviously as the red mist flowed into it. He carefully twisted the lid on to make certain that he did not lose the precious vapor, and then began to fill the others he had brought with him.

Killing Mages was not his current mission, and Kabilian was certainly no Mage, but Rhyne knew that Ilfanti suspected him, and there was nothing wrong with taking a few precautions to help ensure that the Mage Master could not get in his way. With this mist in his possession, there was nobody on this ship who could possibly keep him from his mission.

CHAPTER 33

Far from the Gates of Tanorus, another ship sailed the ocean, opting for the long, yet safe path. Kabilian was not pleased with the route that the Captain had selected, but he and Crick could not run a ship by themselves, so they were at the mercy of the crew. At least until they reached Egziard, where Kabilian knew that it would be his own cunning, skill, and prowess that they would rely upon.

Kabilian knew that he could manipulate the crew mystically. The Ring of Euphoria would have been quite effective. When he wore it, anyone within a ten-foot radius would be caught under its spell, and feel trusting and happy. There was only one person he had ever met, a dwarf from Tregador, who had not become instantly blissful and exceptionally happy. These sailors were certainly not as strong-willed as that dwarf.

Under the influence of the ring, they would do anything that Kabilian suggested, just to keep him happy. But how long would he need to keep up the charade? Usually those affected believed that they had done whatever he asked of them under their own power, but if they had to face giant sea monsters, he figured that the crew might begin to second-guess their decision, and that could lead back to him.

Of course, if it did, he could just use the ring again, or even just kill the crew. But that brought him back to his and Crick's inability to run the ship by themselves. All in all, he had to accept the longer route. After all, he was going to learn about his future. It would still be there whether he learned it today or in a couple of months. Perhaps the travel time would do him good. It seemed unlikely, but it had been quite a long time since he had the chance to relax. There was always an artifact to go after, a mystical item to find, a contract to fulfill, or some random individual that merely deserved to die.

Thinking of contracts and his profession, Kabilian wondered what was happening back in the Seven Kingdoms. He had felt a sense of freedom since the lair of Lady Salaman had been destroyed. In his mind, the Hidden Empire had fallen, and his obligations to the crime lord were fulfilled. Deep down, he doubted that was actually the case. Even now, he suspected that Lady Salaman was rebuilding her criminal organization one way or the other.

If she managed to reclaim the criminal underworld, what would that mean for him and Crick? She had called to him, asking for his assistance when her lair was burning and collapsing around her. Kabilian had chosen to ignore that plea and instead had tried to claim the mystical weapons of Arifos, Ashwin, Mylvannan, and Baldock. Even though he failed, he did not regret his decision, but he had been around long enough to know that if Lady Salaman returned to power she would not be so forgiving of his indiscretion.

Kabilian had never been one to ignore a threat or a challenge. Rather than hiding from one, he normally would seek it out, and face whoever was after him. If Lady Salaman was coming after him, then perhaps he had to do what she least expected, and go after her. It would be dangerous, and perhaps even the last thing he did, but he would not live his life waiting for some hired hand of the Hidden Empire to show up. That was not the way Kabilian lived.

He decided to give Lady Salaman the benefit of the doubt. He would not plan to go after her unless she came after him first. Although he would be prepared and begin to accumulate information, in the event that he did indeed have to go after her. If she made the mistake of trying to hunt him down, then no matter how powerful her new Hidden Empire became, he would show her why he was the assassin extraordinaire who had proved to be so useful to her on the most dangerous of missions.

It would take time. Kabilian rarely went into a job without learning as much as he could. For example, he had gone all the way to Tregador to learn more about the dwarf Baldock. When he met Baldock the next time, he knew who he was, and knew exactly which strings to pull. He dangled the murder of the king in front of Baldock's eyes, and the dwarf lost all reason. Of course, when Baldock returned home, he would realize that Kabilian had lied to him, and that King Kendall lived, but it was satisfying enough to know that he could get to Baldock and harm him if he needed to.

Lady Salaman would not be the same. She was a gorn, which meant that using family ties would reveal little to him. Even if he could find her family, they would probably just as soon kill her themselves than wish her well. The gorn were a strange race in that regard. They considered everyone, even their own kind, to be adversaries.

But Lady Salaman had weaknesses. She, too, relied on information. She had invested much time in her rise to power to design an information network she could use to learn what she needed to. It would not take Kabilian long to find those same sources and silence them forever. It would not be a direct strike, but it would be enough to infuriate his former employer.

Her trusted lieutenants and enforcers would be next. Without them, she would be forced to act on her own. One thing he had learned about crime lords over the centuries: they dirtied their hands rising to power, but once they were there, they rarely risked jeopardizing their position by doing things personally. They had others do things for them. Those others who worked for Lady Salaman would begin to vanish.

Kabilian chuckled at the thought. He could visualize Lady Salaman lost and disoriented. Without her information network, she would be clueless about how to respond and where. Without her enforcers, she would be lashing out blindly. He was not naive enough to think that this would make her an easy mark. The ultimate downfall of Lady Salaman would have to be well-plotted, carefully constructed, and expertly executed. The slightest misstep might very well be his own undoing.

If he were forced to kill Lady Salaman, he wondered what that would mean for his future. Would any crime lord ever be willing to trust him with a job again? Would this act of survival be the one incident that would force him to change his methods and lifestyle? This, too, was something that he hoped the Orb of Prophecy could reveal to him.

Perhaps the Orb would tell him that it was time to become a hero again. After living so long, shifting lifestyles so often, he could go from assassin to champion without too much effort. He had made the shift before, and back again, keeping his life from growing dull. The one common theme, no matter his disposition, was his perpetual craving for mystical artifacts. If he needed to be a hero, a warrior for the greater good, he would do so with an eye on the artifacts to be claimed from fallen fiends.

"Kabilian, look."

Kabilian glanced at his companion, Crick, glad that the hobgoblin had spoken to him. Crick had been brooding most of the trip, and the silence was beginning to get on Kabilian's nerves.

Following Crick's gaze, he saw what looked like immense cages in the water. There were hundreds of them, constructs that extended for miles. Standing up, Kabilian made his way over to the Captain. "What are they?"

"I've never seen anything like it," the Captain shrugged.

"Move in closer," Kabilian said, his curiosity demanding to be satiated.

"Not wise," the Captain said. "Could be dangerous."

"Then we'll know that better after exploring them, won't we?" Kabilian said.

"I won't take the ship any closer, but you can take a dinghy and row over to it," decided the Captain.

Kabilian frowned. This Captain definitely did not fear him nearly as much as he should. But he would not argue the point. "Crick, prepare the dinghy. We're going to see what those are."

Crick lowered the dinghy into the water, unassisted, and then climbed in. Kabilian jumped down and joined him. Crick pushed away from the ship and began rowing for the cages. Kabilian studied them as they got closer to see if there were any kind of booby traps, but he saw none.

As they reached the first cage, Kabilian climbed up and looked in. The cage held kelp, packed very densely together. "Interesting," said Kabilian. There was a walkway atop the cage, and Kabilian followed a small connector bridge to the next one, where he saw thousands of fish trapped within.

He examined a dozen of the cages, and found similar things in each. Different types of fish and marine life, or different forms of vegetation, including fruits and vegetables, which he was shocked to discover on the ocean. Each cage contained a vast quantity of identical things.

Kabilian was at a loss for why the cages were out here. This certainly wasn't a processing center being used by the sea creatures who had deterred them from sailing directly to Egziard. The maps and charts that they were using did not show any islands or continents nearby, so who could have constructed these? Trying to figure out the mystery, Kabilian began to make his way back to where he had first climbed onto the cages.

Crick had remained at the first cage, with the dinghy. As Kabilian was returning to his companion, he froze as he heard a humming that sounded strangely familiar. He tensed and tried to find the source of the humming, which was growing louder, and then he remembered what it reminded him of—Wind Soarers!

The avarians of Estonis had a vast fleet of ships that were called Wind Soarers. They used the flying vessels to travel great distances, and whenever they actually became involved in wars. Kabilian had not heard the sound of a Wind Soarer since the early years of the Race Wars, before the avarians had decided that they had no place becoming involved in the wars of the creatures that roamed the lands below them. The sound was unmistakable.

Glancing up and studying the sky, Kabilian spotted a shadow approaching the cages. Even though he could not make out the vessel with the sun glaring in his eyes, he knew exactly what was coming his way. Avarians. That answered a lot of questions. These cages were designed by the avarians as a food processing and storage center. Even if their floating cities were far from here, with their Wind Soarers, they could easily come to cultivate and collect whatever they needed.

After the way the aquaticans had treated the Captain, Kabilian was pretty confident that these avarians would also see them as invaders and threats. Even if not, they would at least consider them to be trespassers on their property. Potentially even thieves, though Kabilian had not taken anything.

Kabilian was not nervous, though. This was an opportunity. An opportunity to hasten his journey. Perhaps he had just spent his last day sailing aimlessly on a ship that was forced to ride the sea and rely upon either wind or the backs of her crew. A Wind Soarer needed none of that. It could take him to Egziard in a fraction of the time it would take the ship he now sailed upon.

Reaching into his satchel, Kabilian thought of a pair of items that may come in handy. The first was the very same ring he had considered using on the crew of his ship to persuade them to choose a quicker route. The second looked like nothing more than a pearl, but it was so much more.

"Crick, to me, at once!" Kabilian shouted.

Crick climbed onto the cages. Kabilian winced when he saw that Crick had chosen not to bring his armor with him. Nevertheless, he would make this work. "What is it?" Crick asked.

"Trust me," Kabilian said. Without waiting for a reply, he struck Crick several times in the face. The hobgoblin dropped to his knees, growling angrily.

"Why?"

"Trust me," Kabilian repeated as he kneed Crick in the stomach.

Crick growled in anger, but did not retaliate.

Kabilian placed the pearl on his forehead, and four small legs dug into his skin. Kabilian watched as wings sprouted from his back and began to flap. His attire began to change as well, shifting to the light blue and silver armor of the Aeronel. Neither the armor nor the wings were real, but even under close scrutiny, they would appear to be authentic.

Crick had seen this transformation before. Kabilian had used the pearl to look like King Echalas of Xylon in his attempt to deceive Ashwin into thinking her father was a prisoner of the Hidden Empire. This time, though, Kabilian's features did not change, nor why should they? He did not have to look like anyone in particular. Crick was not surprised to see the clothing begin to fray and tatter, rope burns appear around his wrists and ankles, and bruises form around his eyes and on his cheeks.

"How do I look?" Kabilian asked.

"Like a beaten avarian," said Crick.

"That's exactly what I want," Kabilian grinned. He held the Ring of Euphoria in his open palm, ready to use it if need be. "Go get the good Captain's attention. Tell him we need him."

Crick nodded and ran back to where the dinghy was. He waved his arms and shouted out: "Help! We need help!" Crick was not sure that the Captain would respond. After all, he had not wanted to explore the cages in the first place. But a pair of dinghies was lowered, and eight men were quickly rowing to help them.

Crick returned to Kabilian, who now pointed to his wings and winked. "What is it?" Crick asked.

"Those savages cut my feathers," Kabilian sighed. "Alas, I can no longer fly!"

"They are coming," Crick said, not sure why it mattered that Kabilian could not fly. He was not truly an avarian, after all.

"Now, take me by the arm and help me," Kabilian said. "We are to flee from our crew."

"Why?" Crick asked.

"The deception must be complete," Kabilian said. "They may be close enough to see us with their avarian eyes."

Crick stared at the shadow that was approaching. So they were avarians, and Kabilian was up to something, as usual.

"Let's go," Kabilian said as Crick took his arm. The two moved at a limp, Crick dragging Kabilian.

The Wind Soarer flew directly overhead. Kabilian could see the distinctive light blue glow of every crease of the ship as it soared past them. A pair of avarians swooped over and flew down to where Kabilian and Crick were. They were armed with only harpoons. These clearly were not warriors.

They were wearing fishnet garments that looked almost as primitive as those of the felines of the Amahani Islands. After seeing the avarians of Estonis, Kabilian was not impressed. One raised the harpoon and pointed it directly at Kabilian and Crick. "What goes on here?"

Kabilian lightly brushed several hoop earrings that were on his right ear. He had heard the avarian language before, but this dialect was somewhat thicker than he was used to. The earrings would mystically translate the language for him, and allow him to speak it fluently as well. After only a short pause, he answered: "Slavers," he wheezed, in the exact dialect used by the avarian who spoke to him. "Help. Please."

Kabilian did not dare look back, but his lip slightly creased when he saw the avarian glance over his shoulder at the eight crewmembers now running at them. The poor fools thought they were coming to help. Instead, they were only sealing their own fates.

"Where are you from?" the avarian asked, still not convinced that Kabilian was being entirely truthful.

"Estonis," he said.

"Estonis?" the avarian asked, glancing at his companion. "There is no Estonis near here."

"Seven Kingdoms," Kabilian said. "They were bringing us to Egziard in trade."

The second avarian nodded as if to confirm that what Kabilian said was probable. The two then swooped into the air and soared at the eight crewmembers. They circled around them, diving and stabbing with their harpoons. Kabilian watched as the men screamed in agony, their lives torn from them by these fishermen.

Kabilian saw the ship raising its sails. The fools, he thought. To think that they had any chance of evading or outrunning a Wind Soarer. The two avarians returned, lifting both Kabilian and Crick and flying them up to their ship.

Once on board, a more distinguished-looking avarian stepped over. He had a long gray beard and hair. His skin was tanned and weathered, but he had an aura of authority about him. He was carrying a scepter that Kabilian recognized as the control device for the ship. This was the Captain.

"What is going on?" the Captain asked.

"Slavers," one of the avarians said.

"Not on my watch," the Captain growled angrily.

"Wait," Kabilian wheezed. "My companion is a hero of the Imperium. They confiscated weapons and armor that are priceless."

"We'll salvage them if we can," the Captain promised. "Prepare the gannolins."

Kabilian cringed at the order. Gannolins were large spheres that were heavy and very destructive when dropped from above. One would splinter his former ship in two. If they dropped one, the odds of recovering Crick's armor would be negligible. "The armor," Kabilian protested.

The Captain ignored Kabilian as he lowered his scepter and touched an orb, altering the ship's course. As they flew toward the fleeing ship, he shouted: "Fire!"

Kabilian rushed to look over the side. The gannolin soared through the air at an angle, striking the main mast and shattering it. Kabilian breathed a sigh of relief to see that the hull had not been damaged. Kabilian glanced at the Captain and noticed that he was being observed. Kabilian nodded his thanks.

"Prepare a boarding party," the Captain said.

"I want to go," Kabilian said.

"Can you fly?" the Captain asked.

"No, but I should be the one to go," Kabilian pleaded.

"My crew will take care of this. These slavers will not bother you again," the Captain replied.

"At least let my companion go," Kabilian said.

The Captain paused for a moment, then nodded. "Very well."

Kabilian looked at Crick, trying to communicate without actually saying anything. He knew that Crick might not understand, but appearances were everything. Crick was a hero, and the crew that helped them get this far were now ruthless slavers who needed to be silenced. Crick looked solemn, but he prepared to go, lifting a harpoon. Kabilian was proud of him.

Two avarians, the same two who had first spoken to Kabilian, grabbed Crick by the arms and flew down to the ship. Kabilian wished that he could be down there – it had been too long since he had the pleasure of sinking his blade into somebody. He listened as the crew screamed and protested, but Crick and the avarians soon silenced those screams. Within moments, it was over.

Crick returned, his armor carrried by a pair of avarians. He glanced at Kabilian: "They will not profit from people's suffering any longer."

"In the end, we all get what we deserve," Kabilian said.

The Captain walked over and kneeled down beside Kabilian. "My men tell me you are from Estonis? That is a long way from here."

"It is," Kabilian said. "The name is Kabilian. I am a member of the Aeronel. Slavers kidnapped the Avistar's granddaughter. I was running an investigation when I ran into Crick, a well-known hero of the realm. He was also tracking the slavers. We found that they were sailing to Egziard, and selling the children there. Not only the avistar's grand-daughter, but also princes and princesses from all around the Seven Kingdoms.

"Unfortunately, rather than finding the slave traders and bring them to justice, we were caught unawares and were to be sold as slaves our-selves. This is most embarrassing," concluded Kabilian.

"What do you intend to do now?" the Captain asked. "The ship is destroyed, and you are a long way from anywhere."

"We hope to continue our investigation," Kabilian said. "We must reach Egziard and find the heirs to the thrones."

"Perhaps a Wind Soarer at Vysellius will take you there. If not, I am sure in one of the Fifteen Cities you can charter a ship," the Cap-tain said. "It is a long way, though."

"Not too long for a Wind Soarer," Kabilian said.

"Perhaps not, but too long for us," the Captain concluded. "We're here to pick up supplies and bring them home. Not to help stop the slave trade."

Kabilian slipped his ring onto his finger. "I understand. You have already done more than I could possibly have hoped for. I just hope that the children are all right, and that the delay does not prove, dare I say it, fatal."

The Captain frowned at the comment. "The children could be in danger. That is true. All royalty, you say?"

"The avistar of Estonis would be willing to reward whoever helps us quite handsomely, I would imagine," Kabilian said.

"I'm not in it for the reward," the Captain said. "But perhaps we could go a little out of our way to help the children."

"Really?" asked Kabilian, a tear welling up in his eye. "That is more than I could have hoped for."

"Then it is settled," the Captain said. "Full speed to Egziard."

Kabilian tightened his hand into a fist. People were so easily manipulated when you had a mystical edge over them. This was almost too easy. Perhaps he should have gone to the avarian city and tried to charter a ship without using the ring, but that would mean more people to deceive, and no guarantees. This ship and this crew had already helped them without the ring's influence. They were good people. He even suspected that he could remove the ring, and they would still be willing to help.

As the ship increased speed and headed on its course, Kabilian felt the wind through his hair. In minutes, they were already further than their former ship could have sailed in hours. At this rate, they would be at Egziard soon, and then, his fate would be revealed at last.

CHAPTER 34

The days traveling through the Gates of Tanorus were uneventful, but certainly not restful. The crew was constantly alert and on edge. The shift rotations were becoming more frequent as prolonged exposure to the red mist began to make people's lungs burn and their bodies tremble. The incessant moaning and wails from all around them plagued the crew both as they worked, and as they tried to sleep.

There had not been any sign of ghosts, phantoms, or undead creatures lashing out at them, but more than one crew member reported sensations of something touching them when nothing was there. Some crewmembers even were shaken so badly that they would arrive at locations on the ship that they did not remember going to. Whispers of crewmembers being possessed began spreading.

Navigation of the ship became nearly impossible as well. Without the compass, Green had to rely upon other seafaring methods, such as landmarks and the stars. There were no landmarks that any could see, and none could see through the red mist to find the stars.

He thought that he was remaining on course, but if there were a slight miscalculation, none of them would ever know it. Without their power, Ilfanti and Krimdor were also helpless. Usually, they could sense the way to go, as if their destination was beckoning them. Now, there was nothing.

Every now and then, one of the lookouts would think that they saw something. Thus far, they called out claiming that there was a ship trailing them, that the water was red and aflame, and that there were creatures flying around the ship. With every instance, the alarm was sounded and the crew sprang to action, but not once was the report verified.

The crew began to wonder if they were going mad. The curse of the

Gates of Tanorus might not be to wander aimlessly as undead spirits, but to do so until you lost your sanity and chaos ensued. It was as if the sea was taunting them, fooling them, and daring them to even try and push onward.

There was no turning back, though. Even if they wanted to go back, Green was not certain that he could find the opening to the Gates of Tanorus. They were trapped within this mindless, haunting void. All they could hope to do was move forward, and hope for the best. In time, even hope was lost.

ILFANTI'S LOG

Time. So precious. So fleeting. It has lost meaning. There is no rising and setting sun. Have we been traveling through the Gates of Tanorus for days, weeks, or dare I even suggest, months?

The engines have failed us. We were pushing them too far, hoping to get out of this damnable place sooner. Fasbender has been working around the clock, at least we think it is around the clock, trying to fix them. Even his patience and good spirits are beginning to wane the longer we remain here.

Without the engines, without magic, and without wind, we are drifting aimlessly. Kemocay has converted his artillery hatches into rowing stations, but the crew is drained and is weakening steadily. They collapse even while trying to row. None of us are the way we were when we first entered the Gates.

I look into a mirror, and I no longer recognize myself. I was worried about fitting into my old outfit? Now, it is actually a bit loose. Even trying to work out daily, my muscles are leaving me, as if the mist is dissolving them from within. The biggest change I see, though, is on my face. My hair has been growing in disarray, hanging over in front of my eyes. My eyebrows are big and bushy. My once clean-shaven chin is now sporting a full mustache and beard. I look horrid.

None of us look good. If we don't find a way out of here soon, we never shall leave.

Date Unknown, 7951 AM

Provisions have been stolen. Kemocay and Brondolfr are looking into it, but nobody is talking. Everyone is watching each other with suspicion. I even saw Brondolfr and Palisha screaming at each other. Tensions are high.

The only two on board who seem unaffected are Green and Beige. They look the same as always, and act it as well. Green has become a bit frantic with trying to get us out of here, I pray that he is successful.

Too tired to write any more. My strength fails me. I don't have the energy to lift my quill. Yet I cannot fall asleep. I am at a loss for what to do.

Date Unknown, 7951 AM

They're after me. I know it. They are all after me. I see it in their eyes. They all blame me for being here. It started with a slight bump by Krimdor as he walked by. He said that he stumbled, but I could see it in his eyes. He did it on purpose. They are all doing it on purpose now.

Palisha and Shimada were sent to try and kill me. They keep knocking on my door, but I know better. I know better than to let them in. I will die before I let them in to do what they plan to do to me.

It is not just me. The Captain has locked herself in her cabin too. She knows that there is a conspiracy on board the ship. Krimdor must be leading it. He is the logical choice. He wishes to be both a Mage Master and a Captain. The roles of Paladin and First Mate must be wearing on him.

I wonder who remains loyal to the Captain. Green and Beige, I am sure. But who else? If Palisha is after me, then Brondolfr most likely has sided with Krimdor. What about the gnomes and the adlesians? They always were loyal to Augustus. Will they come to her aid now, stand aside and do nothing, or join those that look to take over the ship?

What was that? I thought I heard something. Noises. There are always noises. Why do I constantly hear noises? I just want to be left alone! Leave me alone!

Ilfanti Day, 7951 AM

Holidays. I love holidays. There are not enough holidays. Let's say the word again and again: holiday, holiday, holiday, holiday! I can shout it if I want to. I hear people yelling to be quiet, but who cares what others think? It's Ilfanti Day! My day! Let me be loud!

Founder's Celebration? Bah! Ilfanti Day will be the best day of the whole year. Wait a minute...why can't EVERY day be Ilfanti Day? I'll have Ilfanti Day 1, then Ilfanti Day 2, then Ilfanti Day 3, then Ilfanti Day 4, then Ilfanti Day 5, then Ilfanti Day 6...

CHAPTER 35

Green and Beige stood alone on the bridge of the *Soaring Mist*. The officers and crew had gone mad. They were delusional, and living in their own minds. None of them had been able to sleep, and without it, the rasplers feared for the crew's safety and wellbeing.

It was not easy locking the crew and officers up. They had to seal them into their rooms, and then use part of the storage bay containers to board up the doors so that there would be no escape. Wandering around unattended would make the crew dangerous to themselves and to each other.

Only a few were not affected by the lack of sleep and the constant pressure of the Gates of Tanorus. Green and Beige were now the commanding officers of the ship. Jin Fe and Shimada were also unaffected, claiming that their periods of meditation were just as restful as sleep. The gnomes, thankfully, were also unaffected. Fasbender had been working on the engines and had actually managed to get them working for short periods of time.

The problem, he had found, was in the ventilation. The red mist was somehow clogging the engines, jamming them and shutting them down. Fasbender allowed the rasplers to use the engines for several hours at a time, and then had his gnomes completely pull the engines apart to clean them. The process was quite extensive, but it was working.

Green never left the bridge, always trying to find some way to determine how to exit the Gates of Tanorus. Beige remained with him most of the time to handle any repairs or maintenance that Green requested. Every hour, though, he would be joined by Shimada and they would make their rounds through the ship, making certain that everyone was still locked in their rooms and that there were no problems. He also went to the galley twice a day, and prepared meals for the entire crew. The gnomes distributed the food for him, Shimada with them to make certain that the crew did not strike out at the gnomes when they were sliding the food into slits they had cut in the doors.

Everything was becoming routine, though everyone on board who maintained their faculties hoped that they would soon be out of this passage and things would return to normal. Jin Fe had assured Green, Beige, and Fasbender that once the crew was able to sleep for an extended period of time, they would gradually settle down and return to normal. They all hoped that day would be soon.

Shimada stepped onto the deck and made her way to the bridge. "It is time."

"I am ready," Beige said. "I'll be back sssoon."

"Take care of them," Green said.

"I will," Beige replied.

He and Shimada then made their way below deck and began walking around the ship, carefully checking each door to make certain that it had not been damaged or tampered with. As he checked Ilfanti's door, Beige heard the dwarf giggling happily within. He could not understand how the aezians and gnomes had managed to combat this nightmarish part of the voyage when a disciplined Mage Master could not.

Leaving Ilfanti's door, they checked on the Captain next, followed by Krimdor, and then headed to the crew quarters. The cabins for Palisha and Brondolfr, and Kemocay were in the same section of the ship. Beige wondered if they should have separated Palisha and Brondolfr since they had been screaming at each other for days now. As he reached their door, he was worried when he heard nothing within. Did something happen?

"We ssshould check," he said.

"Very well," agreed Shimada.

Beige lifted a dagger that he had brought with him and slid it between the nailed board and the door, separating the two. With the extra lock removed, he reached for the knob and slowly began to open the door. The door swung open and Brondolfr's muscular arm grabbed

Beige by the throat. Beige was dragged backwards, the door opened completely as he was pulled through it.

Brondolfr looked like a madman. His long silky black hair was frayed and in disarray. Food and dirt could be seen scattered throughout. He, too, had grown a beard, which grew on his cheeks and neck as well as his chin. His sky-blue eyes, normally so peaceful, glared almost demonically as he tightened his grip on Beige's throat. From his lips escaped no words, only growls.

Palisha, walking and acting more like a simian than a human, charged Shimada, who did not notice her friend as she was trying to pry Brondolfr off of Beige. Palisha struck from behind and knocked Shimada over, toppling her outside of the cabin.

Shimada rolled into the hallway with the impact and was back on her feet without pause. She saw Palisha exiting the room and her heart nearly broke. "I am sorry, my friend," she said as she swung her leg and kicked Palisha across the jaw. Palisha spun around and fell to the ground by the doorway, unconscious from the blow.

Glancing at Beige and Brondolfr, Shimada saw that the raspler had managed to break the barbarian's grasp. Brondolfr was still pressing the attack, but Beige would be able to hold his attacker off for a few moments longer. Shimada dragged Palisha back into the room, and left her lying on her mattress, which had been knocked off of the bed.

As Shimada stepped back out, she saw Beige swat Brondolfr in the stomach with his tail. The barbarian dropped to the ground, the wind knocked out of him. Beige grabbed him from behind and headed for the room. Brondolfr saw what Beige was attempting to do and began kicking and punching wildly. Reaching the door, he spread his legs too wide for the entrance, making it impossible for Beige to push him inside.

"I need help!" Beige shouted.

Shimada brought her elbow down and struck Brondolfr on his thigh. The barbarian cried out but did not loosen his position. She then took a small fighting stick and swung it up, striking Brondolfr beneath the knee. His leg gave and Beige managed to push him into the room.

"Shut it, quick!" Shimada cried.

The two swung the door closed. Brondolfr was already back on his feet and charging it. Beige tried to brace the door as the barbarian kept slamming into it. "Get the board," Beige ordered.

Shimada grabbed the board and raced back to Beige, where she placed it in front of the door. "No hammer," she said.

"I'm the hammer," Beige said, punching each nail and driving it into the door and frame. Brondolfr kept slamming into the door and screaming, but it did not budge.

Beige stepped back, watching the door closely to see if the support would hold. It did.

Shimada took his hands in hers. "You're bleeding."

"It'sss nothing," Beige said.

"Let my grandfather determine that," Shimada said. "No arguments. We can't afford to lose you, too."

Beige frowned, but accepted the truth of her words. "We go."

As they made their way to the infirmary, neither noticed that one of the doors had a pair of boards missing from the bottom. Neither noticed that the armory had been broken into and confiscated weapons had been recovered. Neither noticed that the deadliest man on the ship was now free.

CHAPTER 36

He was free at last. Rhyne did not like being caged. He had been caged once before, captured by Imperial forces after he had assassinated Emperor Conrad. He refused to ever be caged again.

It was easy escaping from his room. He had used his knife from dinner to pry two boards from his door. Now he was free, and without the guards monitoring his weapons, he was finally able to reclaim them.

Something was happening. He was not certain what. This ship had been overrun. At every turn, he saw what looked like people who were somewhere between the living and dead. There was a variety of types of creatures, but all were mostly skeletal with their flesh rotting and hanging from their bodies.

Their movements were silent, and they spoke very little, but around every corner, he saw several of them. He had to move up and down several decks to avoid them before he had been able to reclaim his weapons, but now he had them and no skeletal creature would dare get in his way.

Rhyne felt more confident. His blades had that effect on him. He was calm, soothed, and ready to face these cursed beings. He approached a corner, and rather than peering around as he had been doing, he boldly walked around it. Three of the creatures were there. They turned and glared at him as he came for them.

Rhyne reached into his tunic and grabbed three throwing knives. He grinned with satisfaction as he sent them hurtling at the creatures before him. The blades passed right through them and dug into the wall behind.

"Impossible," gasped Rhyne, as he grabbed more throwing blades and sent them at his foes. These too went directly through them and into the wall.

The creatures began laughing with a near-hiss while reaching for Rhyne. Rhyne threw several more blades, but still with no effect.

Realizing that he could not harm these creatures, he turned and began to run. They must be ghosts, and not solid, he realized. Every now and then, he still paused long enough to throw some blades, but he did so more to try and slow them down than with any hope that he would be successful. Of course, the blades sailed through them, and they did not slow at all. It was Rhyne who was being delayed.

As he ran around another corner, and struck something very solid, and fell backwards, landing on his backside. He glanced up to see what he hit, and shrieked when he saw a demon with burning eyes and smoke coming from its mouth. It was with a smaller demon, a female with red skin and fangs in her mouth.

Rhyne growled in frustration, grabbing several blades and throwing them. The larger demon moaned in agony, and then growled. The female charged at him, drawing a sword that burned with hellfire itself. Rhyne threw several blades at her, but she deflected each one.

At least, he thought, these creatures he could strike. Dodging the flaming sword, he rolled on the ground and kicked out, striking the demon behind the legs and tripping her. He then pulled a dagger to slit her throat, but the tail of the larger demon batted it away. As he reached for more daggers, he heard the hissing of the ghosts, and realized that he had been delayed too long. He must get away. Standing up, Rhyne ran for his life.

❁ ❁ ❁ ❁ ❁

"Are you alright?" Beige asked as he reached out and helped Shimada up.

"Alaran is free," she said, stating the obvious.

"And he hasss hisss weaponsss," Beige groaned as he held up his arm and began pulling daggers from his reptilian hide. "Thessse hurt."

Shimada grimaced. "Grandfather will bandage you up, then we'll go after Alaran."

"What wasss he running from?" Beige asked.

Shimada glanced down the corridor as she picked up her dropped sword and shrugged. "He is clearly seeing things, as are most of the crew. Whatever he is seeing is haunting him."

"Thisss place isss good at hauntsss," Beige said.

"It is, indeed," Shimada agreed. "Come, let's get you bandaged."

"No," Beige said. "Alaran firssst."

Shimada began to object, but then she stopped herself—Alaran was too dangerous to leave wandering freely. They would try to stop him first.

CHAPTER 37

Green squinted as he looked ahead. He hoped that he was not beginning to suffer from the same delusions that the crew were. If not, then he may have just found the way out of the Gates of Tanorus. Ahead of them, though it was not entirely clear, the red mist was lighter, as if illuminated by sunlight.

It was only a minor course correction to head for the light. This endless nightmare may soon be over. Green was too good of an officer to allow his hopes and excitement to cloud his duties, but he prayed that this would be the exit from the passage, and that soon, the crew would return to normal.

"Die, demon!"

Green barely had time to move as a trio of daggers came soaring at his chest. He raised his arm in defense and hissed as the blades sunk into his arm hilt-deep. Lowering his arm, he glared at the wraith, who even now was pulling more blades to throw.

❁ ❁ ❁ ❁ ❁

The demons were everywhere! Just when he managed to evade the ghosts, he found another demon. Rhyne would not be deterred, though. The demons, he remembered, he could hurt. Lifting another trio of blades, he hurled them at the demon. It was fast, and leapt out of the way. But he could see its blood, burning like acid through the hull of the ship where it landed. He had wounded it, and soon, he would kill it.

He heard the latch of the hatch open, and Rhyne knew that he was no longer alone with the demon. Daring to take his attention away from his foe, he watched as the other demons he had fought joined them on the main deck. Three-to-one were odds he could live with.

Spinning around, he hurled a trio of blades at each of the demons. The female demon deflected them with her flaming sword again. The other pulled the hatch from its latches and used it as a shield. They were learning. That would make this that much more interesting.

❈ ❈ ❈ ❈ ❈

"Be careful, Alaran isss crazed!" Green shouted to warn his brother and companion. "He mussst have essscaped."

"We fought him below," Shimada replied. "Be careful of his daggers."

"I know," said Green as he held his arm up. He glanced back at the unattended bridge and saw that the wheel was turning slightly. The ship was moving away from the light. If he lost sight of it, he may never find it again.

Jumping from his perch, Green leapt to the bridge and tried to grab the wheel. Three blades dug into his side as he was in motion. He gasped in pain, but refused to let the blades hinder him. He needed to get them out of the Gates of Tanorus. That was all that mattered. The safety and well-being of the crew came before any single life, and he was more than willing to sacrifice himself for those he served with.

They had drifted to the right. Green adjusted the heading to the left, and could see the brighter mist. His eyes began to blur, but he clenched his fists and stayed at his post. Three more blades struck him in the back, forcing Green to his knees.

"Get him away from me," he wheezed, calling for help. He was on course for the light. He just had to hold it.

Shimada threw an aezian throwing-star, which Alaran flipped out of the way of. If nothing else, the act managed to get him to leave Green alone. As Alaran landed, he already had a trio of blades between his fingers, and tossed them at Shimada. Shimada spun her sword, but only managed to deflect two of the three blades. The third one sliced her forehead, grazing her.

"Die demon, die!"

"You die!" Shimada cried as she lunged at Alaran and knocked him to the ground, sitting on top of him. She punched him several times, and felt his body soften beneath her. "I think he's unconscious."

"Finally," Beige said as he walked over to see.

Alaran slammed his open palm up and struck Shimada in the chin, snapping her neck to the side. Shimada slumped to the ground, unconscious.

"You were tricking usss," Beige hissed angrily. He raised his tail and swung it at Alaran, but Alaran leapt over the tail and dug his elbow into Beige's neck. Beige shrieked in pain, dropping to his knees. "You won't get me ssso easssily," he promised, every word a strain.

"Die demon, die!"

Beige tightened his hands into fists, extending the claws on the back of them. He stood up, hoping to connect and end this. He did not wish to kill Alaran, but he had little choice left. He swung, and the wraith grabbed his arm, swung around, and poked Beige in the eyes. Beige stumbled backwards, momentarily blinded.

"Die demon, die!"

Beige tried to use his other senses, listening for Alaran, turning in the direction of the wraith's words, but he quickly lost track. He was completely defenseless. All he could hear was the incessant moaning and whining of the red mist. Was this his time to die? Were they all doomed because he had failed to properly keep Alaran locked up?

He heard the battle cry as Alaran was pressing the attack, but no blow came. Instead, he heard a thump on the ground, and then the gentle voice of Jin Fe.

"It is over now. Let me tend to your wounds."

"Green firssst," Beige said, adamant that his brother be tended to.

"Of course," Jin Fe replied.

Beige was disoriented. Without his eyesight, he could not know where anyone was, or what was happening. The moaning and whining began to lessen, and Beige wondered if he were losing his hearing as well. He felt a warmth upon him, and he cringed at the thought that perhaps he had died, and if so, what a terrible fate it was to be going to the ever-after blind.

Refusing to accept that, Beige forced his eyes open. There was a glare so intense and bright, a blinding white light. It was true. He was dead. He had to be. But if he was, then why was his body still in so much pain from his fight with Alaran? Then he heard a bird, like the seagulls that were in the harbor of Water Haven. Surely now he was delusional like the rest of the crew.

His eyesight slowly began to regain focus, and if rasplers had tear ducts, Beige would have been in tears. They had made it through the Gates of Tanorus. There was a clear blue sky with only a few clouds and the sun shining down on them.

Beige turned to see to his brother, and trembled when he saw that Green was not conscious. "Green!"

"His wounds are deep, but he will live," Jin Fe promised.

Beige turned to see Shimada, and saw that she was leaning against the mast, a small piece of fabric torn from her shirt used to stop the blood flowing from the wound on her forehead. Her chin was also swollen, but Beige felt confident that she would heal in time.

"We made it," Beige whispered. "We made it."

Jin Fe glanced up and smiled encouragingly. "The ship is all yours."

"Mine?" Beige asked, shocked by the statement.

"Until your brother recovers, you are in command," Jin Fe reminded him.

"What about mother?" Beige asked, hopeful that Augustus would be up and about soon.

"I would not expect anyone who has been affected to be back to normal for at least a week, maybe more," said Jin Fe.

"My ssship," Beige said, hesitant to even think it. He had wanted more responsibility, but not to take command and be responsible for the lives of everyone. It was more than he ever expected.

Shimada struggled a bit to stand up, but made her way over to the wheel. "What course, Captain?"

Beige glared at the skull-arched gateway shrinking in the distance behind him. "Away from that," he said. "Anywhere that isss away from that."

CHAPTER 38

Standing at the bow, Ilfanti watched as the *Soaring Mist* made its final approach to Zaman. The first part of his journey was coming to an end. Now, he would be on his own in one of the most tumultuous and deadliest locales on all of Terra. He would be done sailing on seas of water, replacing them with endless seas of sand.

Zaman looked larger than Ilfanti remembered. The last time he was here, the harbor port had been slightly smaller than Water Haven, and nowhere near as developed. Now, he saw towering stone buildings, walls that surrounded the city—very similar in design to the ones at Trespias—and hundreds of small ships moving in and out of the harbor. A lot had changed.

He could understand why Zaman had grown over the centuries. It served as the sole entrance to Egziard. Not only that, but any Egziardian city that wished to trade by sea would need to do so by going through Zaman. It was only logical that as Egziard became more advanced, Zaman would grow to accommodate that expansion.

Ilfanti wondered briefly what other changes he would be in for. He had already experienced things on this voyage that were a result of changes since last he had come this way. Going mad was amongst them. It was something he wished to forget.

Reaching into his satchel, Ilfanti removed his logbook. This journal and many like it had served him well over the years, allowing him to reflect upon what he was doing and also to provide a record of his many adventures. Flipping open the log, he thumbed through thirty pages of entries, all filled with the same thing:

...then Ilfanti Day 321, then Ilfanti Day 322, then Ilfanti Day 323, then Ilfanti Day 324, then Ilfanti Day 325, then Ilfanti Day 326, then Ilfanti Day 327, then Ilfanti Day 328, then Ilfanti Day 329, then Ilfanti Day 330...

Had he really been so lost that he had written that non-stop for thirty pages? Ilfanti rolled his eyes as he thumbed through the entries. He even had gone beyond the three hundred-and-sixty-five days in a calendar year. *If Herg and Cala could see that, they would never let me live it down,* Ilfanti thought.

He debated tearing the pages out, but as he went to do so, something deep in the back of his mind made him stop. He may not want to remember being the drooling, shaggy-bearded imbecile that he had turned into while in the Gates of Tanorus, but it was still part of this adventure, and cutting it out would not be fair to the *Soaring Mist* crew who had managed to overcome the insanity and see them safely through to the other side.

Taking his hand off of the pages, Ilfanti closed his log and slid it back into his satchel. He would have to write something soon, just to show that he was cable of writing a coherent thought again. But that was something to do after his disgust over the thirty pages withered a bit.

Once they were settled at Zaman, things would begin to happen quickly. Ilfanti would have to secure passage to Memtorren, the dwarven city where Osorkon hopefully still resided, and then he would need to acquire supplies and provisions for the trip through the desert to Ramahatra. "Simple," Ilfanti chuckled to himself.

"Uh-oh, talking to yourself," Augustus said as she walked up behind him, accompanied by Palisha and Shimada. "Perhaps you are not fully recovered from our ordeal?"

"I'm fine," said Ilfanti. "Just going over what I need to do once we reach Zaman."

"Yes, you will be leaving us soon," said Augustus.

"I will," confirmed Ilfanti.

Palisha looked concerned—the way a daughter would be for a father that was going off and doing something foolhardy. Ilfanti could not help but grin at the expression. Had she come to regard him so fondly?

"How long will you be gone?" Palisha asked.

"If I'm lucky, and the desert is accommodating, which it rarely is, I could be back in as early as two months," said Ilfanti.

"And if the desert is not accommodating?" asked Shimada.

"Probably closer to four to six months in all," shrugged Ilfanti. "Odds are, though, that if I can find my old friend Osorkon sooner rather than later, I'll make it back here in two to four months."

"If he still lives," reminded Shimada.

"Always the optimist," grunted Ilfanti. "Osorkon was too stubborn and feisty to die early. I'll find him."

"Ilfanti, just be careful," pleaded Palisha. "Please, promise me."

"I always am," winked Ilfanti. He saw right away that Palisha was not in the mood for his humor as she glared at him angrily. "I will. I promise."

"I will have Green plot our return course, taking into account the changing weather patterns for each month that you may return," said Augustus. "I want to be ready to leave the moment you return."

"As do I," agreed Ilfanti.

"We cannot remain here forever, though," cautioned Augustus.

"I understand," Ilfanti said.

"We'll spend some time in the first couple of months acquiring charts and navigational information. We'll also try to charter our services for small tasks. After two months, though, we will remain at Zaman awaiting your return."

"I appreciate that," said Ilfanti.

"It will be the first of Amorlytar in a couple of days. We will wait until the first of Esbai before leaving Zaman for home. If you are not back by then, then we shall assume that your quest has ended in failure," explained Augustus.

Ilfanti nodded that he understood. That gave him six full months for his quest. He could not be late. It would not only leave him stranded here, but also would mean even more time for Karleena to be lost. Time was of the essence.

CHAPTER 39

The *Soaring Mist* docked in the harbor port of Zaman in the late afternoon on the 28th of Homsymbith, 7951 AM. Ilfanti had stepped out of the Mage's Council and begun his quest six months and seven days before. He had originally projected a four-month voyage with a fast ship. The *Soaring Mist* far exceeded his expectations, and they had made it through the Vast Expanse in record time, but the setback with the amphibiers and again when they had reached the waters near Pantalica had slowed them down considerably.

That was all behind him now, though. As he stepped down the plank to the dock, Ilfanti left the familiarity of his ship and the Seven Kingdoms behind him, and for the first time in over two hundred years, set foot on Egziard. Technically, the wooden dock was not on the soil of Egziard, but it was an extension of Zaman, so as far as he was concerned, he had arrived.

Captain Augustus, Krimdor, Brondolfr, Kemocay, Fasbender, and Green were also disembarking along with him. The remaining officers and crew would stay on board until Augustus could arrange for an extended docking arrangement. Alaran would be leaving shortly behind this group as well, but he had to reclaim his weapons, which was taking time. After the incident in the Gates of Tanorus, all of his blades had been confiscated again, and this time they were even more securely guarded.

Palisha, Shimada, and Jin Fe stood at the top of the deck and waved goodbye to Ilfanti, wishing him luck on the remainder of his journey. Ilfanti had the distinct feeling that Shimada wished to join him, but Jin Fe was adamant that she not leave the ship for any reason. Ilfanti would not ask, but he wondered if Jin Fe feared that Shimada might be deported to Aezia if she were apprehended.

"Well, this is it," Ilfanti said, turning back and holding his hand out to Captain Augustus to shake it.

"May you find much success on your journey," Augustus said.

"Thank you," Ilfanti replied. "And thank you all for everything you did to help me get here. I will not forget everything that you all went through and sacrificed for me."

Kemocay rubbed his hand through Ilfanti's hair—which was now back to normal and no longer in disarray, to match his clean-shaved chin—and grinned. "We shall resume our workouts soon."

"I would enjoy that," Ilfanti said, pulling at his pants to show that he was thinner and in far better physical shape now than when his journey had first begun. Ilfanti glanced at Fasbender. "I'll talk to my friend Osorkon about trying to get you some better metals for your cannons. Maybe with his help, we'll get more than a shot or two out of those amphibier weapons on the way home."

Fasbender grinned excitedly and began rubbing his hands together in anticipation.

"Any help would be appreciated," Augustus said.

Ilfanti nodded. If anyone in Egziard could help them with the cannons, it would be Osorkon—or, if not Osorkon, then one of Osorkon's contacts.

"Master Ilfanti, it was an honor fighting alongside you and living one of your legendary adventures with you," Krimdor said. "I only wish that my part in this journey were not coming to an end."

"Don't worry," Ilfanti winked. "Your part will pick up again as soon as I'm back. The dashing Paladin first mate will have more adventures to come, I assure you."

"You honor me," Krimdor said.

"It is I who am honored," Ilfanti replied. "But now I must take my leave. If I don't get started, it will be nightfall, and I'd hate to try and find my way at night."

Fasbender chuckled at the comment. He knew that Ilfanti's eyesight, as a dwarf, was just as good at night as it was during the day, perhaps even better.

"Oh," paused Ilfanti, "don't drink the water."

"No?" Augustus asked.

"Not without Jin Fe having a look at it first," said Ilfanti with a devious little laugh. "The last time I was here, the water made me so sick that I had stomach cramps for a week!"

"We'll keep that in mind, thank you," Augustus said.

"See you soon," Ilfanti replied, trying to force himself away from the companions and friends that he had made, but not truly wishing to leave them behind. His duty was too pressing, however, and finally Ilfanti departed the docks and made his way onto the sandy roads of Zaman.

The roads were packed with people everywhere he looked. There were people selling things, people buying things, people patrolling and trying to maintain order, people stealing things, and people lying on the streets begging for scraps from passersby. Ilfanti also noted the slave traders advertising their recent catches. Ilfanti wondered how many of these slaves had been free just days before.

Everywhere he looked, people were vying for his attention. Ilfanti felt somewhat overwhelmed by the market, and wondered if this style of commerce was actually successful enough to support one's lifestyle.

"Look, good fabrics, you buy!"

"Ah, a dwarf such as yourself, clearly you have trouble growing hair! Try my tonic and you will have a beard as if by magic! Wait, wait, I have wigs, too! Come back!"

"Are you hungry? I have the best fruit in all of Zaman!"

"No, I have the best fruit! You can trust me on that!"

"Genies! Male genies, female genies, genies of all types! You want a slave? Why settle for one without magic? Get a genie! Genies!"

"Weapons! We have weapons! Axes, swords, clubs, spears, daggers! If it cuts or stabs, we have it! Weapons! We have weapons!"

"Rugs! Beautiful and exotic rugs! Beautiful for the ladies, yes?"

"Look at these sarnals. Big, strong, and fit. You will not find rotting teeth and disease here. Oh no. All you will find are quality sarnals who will carry your burdens for you!"

Ilfanti tried to push his way through the crowd, but he could not drown out the noise of the merchants. The peddlers were everywhere.

They were of a wide array of creatures, but they all spoke as if they were gnomes, as if they needed to squeeze a ten-minute conversation into a matter of seconds.

"Hey dwarf, you need a guide?"

Ilfanti glanced down at the hand tugging on his jacket. A tanned bare-chested small boy in rags, sandals, and a turban was looking up expectantly at him. Ilfanti was pleased that the boy was trying to offer his services rather than picking pockets, something Ilfanti had already seen several young hands doing in the short time he had been here.

"Perhaps," Ilfanti said. "What would this guide have to offer?"

"Anything you need," the boy said. "You want a tour of Zaman? Then I'm your man. You hungry? I know all the best places to go. You need transportation? No problem. You want a map? I can get you a real one. You want to stay away from thieves? I can steer you clear. Or," he said, glancing around and lowering his voice, "if you want to find some trouble, I can point the way."

"Impressive credentials," Ilfanti said. "What's your name?"

"My father named me Abaraphas. My friends call me Abar," Abar said.

"Pleased to meet you, Abar," Ilfanti said. "I'm Ilfanti, and I can use some of that transportation you were talking about."

"Where are you headed?" Abar asked.

"Memtorren," answered Ilfanti.

"Memtorren," Abar repeated. "That is far. Pretty far indeed. You'll need good transportation. Expensive transportation."

"Will I?" asked Ilfanti. "If I recall, Memtorren is a thirteen-day journey by camel."

"It is, but you need a good, strong, healthy camel to make the journey! You wouldn't want one that was sickly and only get you halfway, would you?"

"I see your point," Ilfanti said. "Where can I find such a camel?"

"There are places I know," Abar said. "I would be glad to show you, and to negotiate a better deal for you."

Ilfanti reached into his satchel, thought of gold coins—the standard form of currency in Memtorren—and pulled five out. "I am willing to spend five gold coins on my camel. Not a coin more. But if it is less, then you can keep the difference."

"I know just where to go!" Abar shouted joyously. "I'll get a real good rate, and a good camel, too!"

"After that, I will need enough food and water to last the journey. Not the water with the parasites in it, but good, distilled water."

"It takes times to clean the water," Abar said, rubbing his chin as if in deep thought. "That may cost almost as much as the camel."

"Then it is a good thing I have you to negotiate for me, isn't it?" Ilfanti asked, reaching into his satchel and pulling out five more gold coins. "You take these. Get me everything I need, and keep the change."

Abar's eyes widened when Ilfanti handed him the coins. He had sure chosen wisely with this dwarf. He would make more money in an evening with him than he would in a month with the locals. Visitors, he thought, sure were foolish sometimes.

CHAPTER 40

Without a single word to anyone, Rhyne walked down the plank and onto the dock for Zaman. He knew eyes were upon him. Beige had been trailing him since they had arrived in the harbor port. Rhyne briefly considered killing the raspler as a parting gift, but decided against it. He doubted that anyone on the crew of the *Soaring Mist* would cause him setbacks, but why risk having them interfere with his hunt for Kabilian?

The first thing he had to do was find a reputable source of information. If Kabilian's ship had reached Zaman already, then he had to know. Rhyne paused as he was about to step off the wooden docks and enter the sandy roads of Zaman. A small stone building rested at the end of a pier further down. Perhaps a harbormaster was stationed there.

Rhyne made his way to the small building, grinning deviously as he saw Captain Augustus and Krimdor walking away from the building. They must have had to check in, Rhyne decided. He waited until the two entered Zaman, where they were practically swallowed by a swarm of people. The roads were so noisy; Rhyne knew that nobody would even hear the harbormaster scream.

He stepped inside the doorway—which was covered only by a piece of cloth—and scanned the small building for any sign of danger. There was a portly man, balding, who was sitting on a small carpet and writing something. He glanced up and smiled pleasantly, welcoming Rhyne to Zaman.

"Ah, welcome, welcome," the man said. "Please, come in, come in."

Rhyne stepped all the way in and let the cloth flow back in place behind him. "Ships check in here?"

"They do," the man said. "Did you just arrive?" He stood up, sluggishly, his smile never leaving his face.

"I am looking for a ship," Rhyne said. "A specific ship."

"I'm sure I could help you," the man said. "When would it have arrived?"

"Recently," Rhyne said. "Within the past fortnight."

The man glanced at a woven basket and pulled the lid. Inside were a dozen or so scrolls. "Are you looking to charter the ship?"

"Perhaps," Rhyne lied. "It comes from my homeland."

"Oh?" the man asked. "Where would that be?"

"Far from here," Rhyne said.

The man lifted one eyebrow at Rhyne. "I do need information if you want me to help you."

"The Seven Kingdoms," Rhyne said.

"Ah, yes. The *Soaring Mist* is from there. Someplace called Water Haven," the man said excitedly. Perhaps this is the ship you are looking for?"

"I came aboard that ship," Rhyne said. "The vessel I am looking for has a pair of passengers on it. A human, and a hobgoblin. You could not have missed them."

The man hesitated. Not long, but Rhyne saw it in his eyes.

"You are looking for these two?" the man asked.

"I am," Rhyne said.

"Are you a representative of your government's security force?"

Rhyne grinned at the comment. "No. These are old friends. I came in pursuit of them as a favor to Kabilian's mother. His father had an accident and she needs him to come home to help with the family business."

The man's eyes wandered down to the many blades that Rhyne had wrapped around him. Rhyne could see that his deception was not working.

"I'm sorry," the man said. "I wish I could help, but I have not seen a human and hobgoblin traveling together."

"What about another ship from the Seven Kingdoms?" pressed Rhyne.

"None," the man said, placing the lid back on the basket without looking at the scrolls.

"I see," Rhyne said. "Unfortunate."

"Yes, I am sorry," the man said.

"Unfortunate for you," growled Rhyne as he extended his arms, pushing back his cloak and revealing his full arsenal of projectile weapons.

"What are you doing?" the man gasped, watching in horror as Rhyne lifted a dagger in each hand. "Please, I know nothing."

"We shall see," sneered Rhyne.

"I beg of you, I have three wives and nine children that depend on me. Please!"

Rhyne stepped closer, touching the blade to the man's face and slowly dragging it down. The slightest trickle of blood appeared on his cheek where the tip dug in. "I am looking for a human and a hobgoblin," he said, his tone leaving little room for argument.

"I told you, I know nothing," the man cried.

Rhyne grimaced at the sudden stench that filled the small room. The man had wet himself. Pushing the man down, Rhyne knocked him into the basket he had been looking in before. "Show me who arrived in the last two weeks."

"Of course, of course," the man said, desperately trying to please the wraith. He pulled out the scrolls and began unfolding them, reading off the names of the ships, their origins, and their cargo manifests.

Rhyne kept his eyes directly on the man, his blades slowly turning in his hands as he listened, but not a single report was about another ship from the Seven Kingdoms. "Where are the other reports?"

"There are no other reports from the past two weeks," the man groaned, his eyes pleading for his life. "Please, I beg of you, I am telling you the truth. *Please*, let me live."

If there was no report of a ship, then Kabilian either had not yet arrived, or he had arrived and managed to mask his presence. Rhyne would not put it past Kabilian to sneak into Zaman, or to deceive the officials, but why would he? Kabilian was cocky and arrogant. He would most likely walk into Zaman boldly, refusing to even consider that he might be in jeopardy. That meant he was most likely not here yet.

"If you see a human and hobgoblin, I trust you will find a way to inform me?" asked Rhyne.

"I will find a way, I promise," the man said, his head bobbing quickly to show his willingness.

"Good, because if I find out that Kabilian and Crick arrived and you did not let me know, I shall be back. Not for you. I shall be back for your three wives and nine children. I will let you live knowing that the butchery of your loved ones was your fault."

"No," the man gasped. "Please, do not harm them."

"Then do not fail me," said Rhyne, his voice low and sinister.

"I won't," the man said, crying again.

Rhyne left him that way, crying and sitting in his own refuse. If he had known anything, he would have talked. This made it a waiting game. He had beaten Kabilian to Egziard. Now, he simply had to wait for Kabilian to arrive, and then, when Kabilian least expected it, he would act.

❊ ❊ ❊ ❊ ❊

As Rhyne was stepping out of the harbormaster's outpost, Kabilian was flying over Zaman with the avarians in their Wind Soarer. He still had the wings of an avarian, but he had taken the ring of persuasion off of his finger. These avarians were noble souls, and though they had not originally wanted to go on a quest to save the Avistar's granddaughter, now that they were flying over Egziard they were anxious to help.

Kabilian had come to know the Captain and crew much better. The Captain, Glynn, had been the only son in his family in seven generations not to become a member of the Avistinel, the highly trained defenders of the Avistar. Though Glynn had been trained to become an Avistinel, almost since birth, he had felt a passion for sailing through both the sea and the clouds. He defied his family's wishes and signed onto a fishing Wind Soarer the day he reached the age of maturity.

He spent years signing on with various ships, trying to absorb and learn as much as he could. Then he found an old military ship for sale, one that was mostly broken down and in disrepair, and purchased it, spending three years' salary in one afternoon. It took him five more years before he had the finances and ability to completely renovate the ship and make her almost as good as new, complete with the necessary additions to assist in a fishing career. He dubbed her *Passion*, named for his love and excitement for the air and sea.

He assembled his crew gradually over the next fifteen years, five others—including his wife's brother, Buoen, their uncle, Wien, and his eldest son, Stavn, who was now fourteen. Of the remaining two, Falch was a long-time friend that Glynn had met when he first began soaring, and the other, Rossis, was a hired hand who had been with them for several years now, and, Kabilian had discovered, had a few secrets that he was trying to hide.

Kabilian suspected that Rossis was not his real name, but rather one he adopted to hide his identity. Too often, his name was called and he did not react. It was not overly apparent, and Kabilian didn't think that Crick suspected anything, but he knew how to be observant, and Rossis definitely was someone to watch. Kabilian did not know what Rossis's secrets were, but with the ease with which he had killed the other ship's crewmembers, Kabilian could see a killer trying to hide. A killer could rarely disguise himself from another killer, however.

Shortly before reaching Egziard, Glynn had been the one to recommend landing in the desert, about an hour out from Zaman. He suggested that word of avarians arriving might tip off the slave traders. Kabilian found the added delay somewhat tedious, but he hoped that as long as the avarians felt that they were helping, he could still have access to their ship.

As the Captain brought the *Passion* down to a landing—which was really the ship hovering slightly off the ground with several weighted anchors thrown overboard to keep it down—he turned and faced Kabilian. "We are here. May we find the children swiftly."

"That would be ideal," Kabilian said.

"Let us be off, then," the Captain said.

"Wait," Kabilian said, holding up his hand. "You were wise to have us land outside of the city so that the sight of avarians would not make the slavers weary. Let us now be equally cautious."

"What are you suggesting?" Glynn asked.

Kabilian hated to waste a potion for nothing, especially since the pearl on his head would allow him to alter his appearance with little more than a thought, but he had to make the deception seem real. He reached into his satchel and pulled out a vial of Chill. This potion's effect would allow his body to remain cool regardless of the heat. Of all of his potions, this one would at least be somewhat useful on a hot open desert.

"The Mages of the Avistar have provided me with this potion so that I may alter my appearance," Kabilian said. "If I drink it, I can be transformed into a human for a short time, and then the slavers will be none the wiser."

"A most advantageous potion," Glynn said, admiringly.

Kabilian flicked the stopper off and drank the potion. He then did his best to put on a show for the avarians. He wanted them to think this looked good. He began convulsing and crying out in pain. His body began trembling, and then Kabilian hunched over, providing his audience with a clear view of his wings. He then concentrated on his appearance so that his magical pearl could do its trick, and made his wings slowly shrink until they were no more. Kabilian screamed the entire time as if the process were agonizing.

As a finale, Kabilian collapsed on the ground, panting and gasping for air. He looked up at the Captain, and with an overly exaggerated weakness, he asked, "Are they gone?"

"They are," Glynn whispered, amazed by the magic he just witnessed. He reached down and gently touched Kabilian's back where wings had just been. "Remarkable."

Kabilian stood up and rubbed his hands through his hair. "My strength already returns. I can go soon." He then glanced at Crick. "May we leave the armor behind as well? I fear that the slavers would recognize Crick's armor."

"Of course," Glynn said. "We shall guard it with our lives."

"We shall be back soon," promised Kabilian.

Crick glanced sadly at his armor. He did not like leaving it behind. The dwarves of Tregador had made the armor with such craftsmanship that he did not even like to take it off, much less leave it when he was going someplace that could potentially see him in battle.

"Take your swords," Kabilian said, seeing that Crick was upset.

Crick lifted his twin mystral drantanas and twirled them once each before slipping them into his belt. Without his armor and its built-in scabbards, he did not have anything to place the blades into.

"We shall be back shortly," Kabilian promised again. "We will seek information about the children and then return to keep you appraised."

"Good fortune," replied Glynn.

Kabilian and Crick began walking through the desert toward Zaman. Kabilian wondered if Crick were hot. Since he had drunk the Chill, he could not even feel the sun beating down on him.

After they were out of sight of the avarians, Kabilian removed the pearl from his forehead. The wardrobe of a member of the Aeronel instantly faded, replaced by his own wardrobe. "Much better," Kabilian said, rubbing his forehead. "I've never left it on that long before."

"What are we doing in Zaman?" Crick asked.

"Why, looking for a map to find the children, of course," grinned Kabilian.

"The children?" Crick asked, not amused.

"Don't you realize? They are slaves at Ramahatra," declared Kabilian. "That way, the avarians will take us all the way to our final destination."

"Is there really a map to Ramahatra?" asked Crick.

"Probably not too many that we can trust, but if we take the rumors and legends and put them together, with a Wind Soarer to cover more distance, we'll find it." His words were so certain that Crick trusted that Kabilian knew what he was doing. The two continued in silence to the city, where they would learn that before reaching Ramahatra and trying to ascertain their future, they still had to deal with their past.

❖ ❖ ❖ ❖ ❖

Rhyne watched Ilfanti as he climbed up onto a camel, supplies tied onto its hump, and rode off into the desert. He had thought that the dwarf would find a way to meddle in his affairs, but the Mage was too focused on his mission. It was a relief to see him depart, though as long as Rhyne still had some of the mists from the Gates of Tanorus, he knew that Ilfanti would pose little resistance to him.

As he turned to go back into the inner confines of Zaman, his heart

Kabilian confidently walked down the alley he had been told about. He could see the human vermin staring at him hungrily. Their eyes followed his every move, and Kabilian knew that they would strike in an instant if they saw even a hint of a weakness or fear. They would find none. If any were daring enough to strike, Kabilian knew that he and Crick would soon teach them not to set their sights so high. His demeanor must have been enough, because most people scurried back into the shadows, moving to avoid the pair.

At the end of the alley, Kabilian spotted a man who fit the description of Takelot. His eyes were sullen and drooping, his hair had abandoned him long ago, and his skin was burned and blistered by the desert sun. His wardrobe was in tatters, but Kabilian could see that the fabric had once been as fine as the tunic he himself wore. Takelot had fallen hard.

"Are you Takelot?" asked Kabilian.

The man glanced up, raising his arm to shield his eyes from the sun. He squinted as he tried to focus on Kabilian, then lowered his arm and drooped his head again.

"I asked you a question," sneered Kabilian.

"Spare some coins for a drink?" the man asked.

"If you do what I ask, I will provide you with many coins," Kabilian said, reaching into his satchel and pulling out a handful of his fake gold. If the story he heard was true, Takelot had most likely appropriated a true rendition of the map to Ramahatra. Though he did not hope that Takelot would still have a copy, perhaps he could look at the dozen maps already acquired and point out which ones were closest to being authentic, and which ones he could discard immediately.

The man reached his hand out toward the coins, but Kabilian pulled his hand back. "Who are you?"

"I was once the man you seek," Takelot replied, confirming his identity.

Kabilian lifted a trio of gold coins and dropped them at Takelot's feet. "There is more where that came from. I need information from you."

"I know very little that is going on, now," Takelot sighed. "Just leave enough for a drink, please."

"This is old information," Kabilian said. "Information from when you were still a trader."

"I am Takelot, but do not worry, I will not *take a lot*," Takelot giggled to himself, remembering his old spiel.

Kabilian lifted a gold coin and waved it in front of Takelot's eyes, gaining his attention. "You once sold a map that I have interest in."

"No," gasped Takelot. "Anything but that."

"Tell me what you know," instructed Kabilian.

"It is not a myth," gasped Takelot. "I tried to warn Djedhor that it was not a myth, but he would not listen."

"Why would it matter if he listened or not?" asked Kabilian.

"The place is cursed! The elf of darkness turned it into a place of death."

Kabilian glanced at Crick briefly at the mention of the elf of darkness. He had heard of dark elves in the Seven Kingdoms—Falestia specifically—though he had never actually seen one. They were known as the dalvor, and up until now, he thought that they were little more than nursery rhymes to frighten children into being good.

If the rumors of the dalvor were true, then they were magical creatures far different from the Mages of the realm. They used the magic of the time before the Mages, the magic of the time of wizards and sorcerers. If dalvor were here, then they could indeed have made Ramahatra appear cursed to those who were not experienced with magic. The possibilities of the dalvor being real, and of the potential enchanted items he might uncover, delighted Kabilian.

Kabilian handed the gold coins to Crick and then pulled out the maps. He set them down in front of Takelot, who was now staring at Crick's hands, and began unrolling them. "Do you remember the map? Could you point out which ones are closest to the one you had?"

Takelot slowly began to lick his dry and crusted lips, his eyes still on the gold.

"Takelot, you will answer, or the gold will leave with me," Kabilian sneered, grabbing the man by the chin and forcing him to look into Kabilian's eyes. "Look at the maps."

"I have map," Takelot said.

"Yes, right here," Kabilian said. "Which one is the most accurate?"

"No," protested Takelot. "I have map. Real map. I make copy to sell to others, but when Djedhor disappeared, none wanted it."

"Where is the copy?" asked Kabilian.

In that instant, Kabilian saw a hint of Takelot's old business savvy in his eyes. This was no longer the broken-down old drunk, but the master trader who had something that someone else desperately wanted. "How much is it worth to you?"

Kabilian beckoned Crick forward, and watched Takelot closely as the hobgoblin dropped the gold coins into the man's lap. "That is how much it is worth, nothing more."

"That was what you were going to give me to look at a map," shrugged Takelot. "Apparently that is all that you wish for me to do."

Kabilian's eyes narrowed into slits. He did not like the sudden rebirth of the trader.

"I could so use a bath," Takelot said.

"And much more," Kabilian replied, "but I will not be the one to finance it. You will answer my question, or I will take the gold and leave. You decide."

Kabilian could see that Takelot's newfound confidence was already waning. He wanted the gold, desperately, but he knew that his information was even more valuable.

"Crick, take it back," instructed Kabilian.

"No, no, wait," Takelot pleaded. "I will give you the map." He tore at his pants leg and pulled a strip off. A small diagram had been sewn to it. "Here, the true map. May you fare better than poor Djedhor and his tribe of nearly two hundred."

Rather than be deterred, the confirmation that so many had perished only inspired Kabilian more. The dalvor and his enchanted items must be quite powerful if he could make two hundred warriors disappear.

As Kabilian and Crick began to leave, they heard Takelot yelling out to them: "Beware the priestess, or else the elf of darkness will be the last thing you see."

Kabilian paused for a moment. The dalvor was a female? He had not expected that, but it changed nothing. He would find Ramahatra, find her, claim the Orb of Prophecy, and any other item that may be enchanted or of interest to him.

Mere feet from the main road, Kabilian tensed, and whirled around to see a small blade soaring toward him. Raising his arm, he flicked his wrist and sent a dart at the blade, intercepting it in mid-flight. So, one of the street vermin wished to test himself, he thought.

Kabilian reached into his belt and removed his pair of jewel-hilted daggers. With a quick incantation, they extended into full length swords. By his side, Crick drew his mystral drantanas as well.

"Show yourself," Kabilian challenged.

"Gladly," came a whisper that would send chills down a normal man's spine. Kabilian watched as a wraith stepped out, garbed in black with blades tucked away throughout his clothing. "Lady Salaman sends her condolences."

Kabilian grinned. So Lady Salaman was already coming after him. He didn't have to wait any longer. Now he knew what he had to do. "I'll be sure to return your tongue along with a message of thanks for her concern."

"Assassin extraordinaire," the wraith laughed. "A true assassin would not be so obvious and arrogant."

"So I should be more like you, then?" snickered Kabilian. "Thanks for the tip."

Kabilian watched the wraith as his hands grabbed several blades and threw them with such speed and accuracy that it almost took him by surprise. Kabilian twirled his swords quickly, deflecting each of the throwing knives.

"What's going on down there?"

Kabilian dared a glance back and saw a trio blocking the entrance to the alley. He easily marked them as patrolmen by their garments. They had white linen fringe hanging around their legs, beneath a white kilt held together by a linen sash. They were bare-chested, with white and gold head ornaments, and golden bracers upon their wrists. One was a human, one a giant, and the last a centaur.

"We were minding our own business, doing a little business with Takelot at the end of the alley, and this wraith began attacking us," Kabilian said.

"Takelot, eh?" the giant asked, snickering. "Must like throwing your money away."

"Something like that," Kabilian said, his back to the patrolmen so that he could keep his focus on the wraith.

"We'll handle this," the human said, stepping in front of Kabilian. The giant and centaur followed and stepped between Kabilian, Crick, and their adversary.

"What do we do?" Crick asked.

"We leave the bounty hunter up to the proper authorities," Kabilian said.

"Shouldn't we make sure he's beaten?" asked Crick.

"He won't be," said Kabilian. "Not by these three. Come. We must return to the *Passion*. Our time in Zaman has come to an end. Now that we know Lady Salaman is definitely after us, we'll be better prepared."

Crick could not understand why they did not just kill the wraith right then and there, but Kabilian always seemed to know what he was doing. Perhaps it was because the wraith had chosen the time and place of this confrontation, and not them. Perhaps it was because the guards were there and Kabilian did not want to become an outlaw in Egziard. Perhaps it was for some other reason that eluded the hobgoblin. Regardless, as long as Crick trusted Kabilian, he would follow where Kabilian led.

※ ※ ※ ※ ※

Rhyne glared with fury at the trio that had interrupted his confrontation. Even now, Kabilian and Crick were leaving. They were not retreating in fear, but slowly walking away and chatting, as if the arrival of Rhyne was inconsequential. They would learn not to turn their backs on him.

Since the patrolmen had gotten in his way, Rhyne decided that for the moment, he would have to take out his fury on them. Reaching into his cloak, he grabbed three throwing blades with each hand. The human was stepping closer to him, still now drawing his sword. Rhyne snorted at how pathetic the man was. A true warrior would come in with his weapon already drawn, just as Kabilian had done when he turned to face his attacker.

"Come with us peacefully, and there won't be any problems," the human said.

Rhyne was not one to taunt his prey. He did not need to make some kind of snide remark, or witty statement as he swept into action. That was just one area where he and Kabilian differed. Raising his arms, he threw both sets of blades at the human. The blades all dug into his chest, forcing him off of his feet and backwards in the throes of death.

"No!" the giant gasped, pulling out his club and preparing to swat at Rhyne. Rhyne was already in motion, lunging forward, grabbing the centaur, flipping over onto his back, and ramming a dagger into the base of his skull with all of his might. "No!" the giant screamed again as the centaur became limp and slumped to the ground.

Rhyne dropped to his knees, and glared expectantly at the giant. This was almost too easy. As the giant swung his club, Rhyne dodged aside, kicked off the alley wall, and climbed up the giant's arm. The giant tried to reach Rhyne, but he was standing on the giant's shoulders and moving from side to side.

Rhyne began pulling daggers, one at a time, and throwing them as hard as he could down at the giant. The blades kept digging into the giant's skull, his hands as he tried to dislodge the wraith, and the back of his neck. Rhyne did not slow down, sending dagger after dagger at the patrolman, making the giant's head look as if he were wearing a silver helmet.

The giant's motions began to slow. His protests lessened. The swipes of his hands would have had trouble dislodging a feather. He dropped to his knees, and then fell forward, his head resting in a pool of his own blood.

Rhyne stepped down from the giant and growled in frustration. He had used too many blades, but he had to move quickly if he hoped to catch Kabilian again. He ran after his quarry, pushing people aside with no regard for anything but his mission. He could not find the pair at first, but then saw two riders out on the desert, just heading over a bluff.

He ran over to a horse dealer, cut the reins of a horse, and galloped off into the desert after Kabilian. He heard the dealer crying out in protest behind him: "I've been robbed again! Thief! Come back! Thief!"

Rhyne barely managed to keep Kabilian and Crick in sight. They had stolen their horses first, taking the better steeds that the dealer had to offer. But Rhyne was lighter, and his horse managed to not lose too much ground. In the end, it would not matter. Rhyne saw the pair reach a boat that was sitting on the sand. They abandoned their steeds and stepped onto the ship.

Kicking his steed to speed up, Rhyne rushed as fast as he could. There were avarians aboard the ship. That meant that the vessel must be one of the avarian Wind Soarers, which would explain how a boat had gotten into the desert. He gritted his teeth with fury as he saw the ship rise into the air and soar away. Kabilian had escaped again.

Rhyne brought his horse to a halt. For a moment he was at a loss. How was he to proceed? He did not know where Ramahatra was, and with a Wind Soarer at Kabilian's disposal, waiting at Zaman would not yield results either. Clenching his fists, Rhyne knew that the only path left open to him was tracking Ilfanti. The dwarf would lead him to Ramahatra, and in doing so, to Kabilian.

CHAPTER 42

The trail to Memtorren took two weeks by camel, but was a relatively easy path to follow. Ilfanti was able to travel alongside the Sanjeez, the lone river in the midst of a vast desert, which brought life to desolation. For miles alongside the river, there were vegetation, trees, and irrigated farmland.

The cities of Egziard, for the most part, also were within the vicinity of the Sanjeez. Some were heavily populated and developed cities, with numerous outlying towns and villages, like Talhella. Others were smaller, such as the dwarven city of Memtorren, though it easily was several times the size of Vorstad, the largest dwarven city in the Seven Kingdoms.

Very few cities or towns in Egziard segregated the various creatures that populated them. Unlike the Seven Kingdoms, where the races had gone to war with each other, in Egziard, they all had to pull their resources together to fight the elements far more frequently than each other. Races that would be deadly enemies elsewhere were often close friends here.

Memtorren was one exception. The dwarves of Memtorren were certainly tolerant of visitors, but that was all. They took great pride in their heritage, and their city was built through millennia of dwarven struggles. This did not prevent the dwarves from living in other cities as well, but they refused to allow others to migrate into their home city.

As Ilfanti reached Memtorren, he admired the craftsmanship that he had not seen for over two centuries. Memtorren had been built into a mountain, though that description did not do justice to what the dwarves had done. They had actually flattened a mountain by cutting away at it and making the walls smooth, and then crafted an entrance to their city that would be a passageway through the mountain.

The entrance towered several stories high. The lowest level had stairs leading into the mountain, with spiraling pillars to the next level. The entrance was so tall that even a giant would be able to enter without having to crouch down. The next level above that had a dozen statues of dwarves crafted with such precision that the figures looked alive. The third and highest level had the largest statue, that of the first dwarven king of Memtorren, looking proud and holding his arms out in a welcoming gesture for all dwarves to enter this place and call it call their own.

Ilfanti hopped down off of his camel and took the reins, leading the camel up the stairs and into Memtorren. Inside the passage was a series of statues and paintings that would make even the Mage's Council museums envious. Rather than using torches to illuminate the passage, the dwarves had used a form of reflective stone that was built into the structure, bringing light through the passage from both sides of the mountain. It was so light inside that it was as if he were not in a mountain, but standing outside.

About half way through the passage, Ilfanti spotted stairwells leading to an upper level. He had never been up there before, but he knew from his last visit that the king and ruling families of Memtorren conducted all business within a protected area deep within the mountain. There was also a labyrinth built into the mountain that only the royal families knew how to navigate, so that if there ever were an attack, the rulers of Memtorren would be able to elude their foes.

Ilfanti passed several dwarves while he walked through the passage. A few were working on the statues, dusting them off and cleaning them with towels, a few were crossing the passage like he was, and a few were admiring the statues. Every dwarf, regardless of what they were doing, paused long enough to wave and greet Ilfanti as he walked by.

As he reached the other side, the true magnificence of Memtorren was before him. The city was enclosed within mountains, as if the mountains had risen in the form of a giant circle, and the dwarves had chosen the flatland to build their city. Of course, Ilfanti knew that it had actually taken generations to chisel away at the mountains and develop the foundation. The excess stone was what the dwarves had used to build other cities and structures, back when they were considered a lesser race and had been little more than slaves.

When the first dwarven king had freed his people, there was much skepticism about building a city where they would always remember the hardships that their ancestors had endured, but he had been adamant that they remember, and believed that their heritage and upbringing was what would make them strong and persevere. Most of the dwarves of Egziard have called this city their home ever since.

The dwarves were still heavily sought after to build other cities, but now they were hired and paid, not forced into labor. As Ilfanti thought about that, he decided that it was a miracle that the races had never gone to war in Egziard. When entire races were persecuted simply for existing and sold into slavery, there would naturally be animosity and hatred. But the dwarves were enough of an enlightened society not to strike back with outright hostility against their former masters.

The city of Memtorren had begun as a single layer, with small buildings throughout the clearing in the mountains. As dwarves continued to come to Memtorren, they ran out of room and had to redesign the city. They then began building large structures against the mountains that towered sometimes as high as a dozen levels, where the dwarves could reside. The middle of the city then had structures built for commerce and trade.

It was at one of these structures that Ilfanti had to stop first, to find a dwarf who would look after his camel. He found several stables close to the entrance and made his way to one where he saw a dwarf working. The dwarf was quite friendly, and with only a little bartering, agreed to feed, bathe, and watch the camel for him.

Before leaving, Ilfanti asked for directions to the residential archives. There was no guarantee that Osorkon still lived at the same place, and even if he did, Ilfanti doubted he could remember exactly where the residence was located. The residential archives helped take care of that. Every dwarf residing in Memtorren was listed, and for a small fee, you could find the proper residence.

Ilfanti found the building, which was domed, and entered it. A dwarf was standing on a small stool and putting a scroll back on a shelf. The entire structure was shelves, all along the walls, and in the middle as well. Somewhere, on one of these shelves, would be the information to find Osorkon.

"Good afternoon," Ilfanti said.

The dwarf glanced at the doorway, saw Ilfanti, and stepped down from the stepping stool. "I hope you were not waiting long?" the dwarf asked, apologetically.

"Just got here," Ilfanti said.

"What can I do for you then?" the dwarf asked.

"I'm looking for an old friend, Osorkon by name."

"Osorkon," the dwarf repeated as he headed over to a wall adjacent to where he had been working. "O-N, O-P, O-R, O-R, O-R, ah, here we go, O-S." He moved his fingers along the scrolls of the shelves and paused, pulling one out. He unfurled it and then began running his finger down the list. "Is it spelt with a 'c' or a 'k'?"

"A 'k'," Ilfanti said.

"Osorkon, here we are," the dwarf said. He transcribed a copy of the address and rang a bell. A young dwarf, probably not even in his teens yet, ran into the room. "Please escort our visitor to this address."

"Okay," the boy said, reading the address. "Follow me."

"Thank you," Ilfanti said to the dwarf. He reached inside his satchel and removed a trio of gold coins. He handed the first two to the dwarf who had helped him. The final one would go to the boy for bringing him up.

The boy led Ilfanti through a crowd of dwarves shopping and over to a stairwell made of the same rose-red rock that all of the buildings were constructed of. They ascended to the fifth level, and then headed down a platform walkway. Each level was slightly smaller than the one below it, allowing the walkway to be in the open air.

"This is it," the boy said, double-checking the note quickly.

Ilfanti flicked the coin in the air and watched the boy grab it. "Thanks."

"Thank you!" the boy said, who—Ilfanti surmised by his reaction—must not be used to getting gold coins for his work.

The doorways were covered by linens, but Ilfanti saw that there were dozens of small bells woven into each doorway. Ilfanti reached forward and shook the linen slightly, causing the bells to begin jingling.

"I'll see who it is," a voice had said from within.

The linen was pulled aside, and Ilfanti gasped. It was Osorkon, but he looked like he had all those years ago, not aged at all. His hair and beard was still as dark as the night sky, without even a single strand of gray to mark the passage of time. His eyes were a dark brown with an intensity that Ilfanti remembered all too well. His complexion was tanned and dark, as were most of the dwarves in Egziard. He had baggy white pants with black boots, and a black sash across his waist. His chest was bare and even more muscular than Ilfanti remembered.

"May I help you?"

The voice was deep, deeper than Ilfanti remembered. "Osorkon?" Ilfanti asked, hesitantly.

"Osorkon is my father," the dwarf said.

A son? Ilfanti sighed with relief. That made much more sense. Osorkon could not possibly still be the same age! "I'm sorry," Ilfanti apologized. "I'm staring. The resemblance to your father is uncanny."

"Inorus, who is it?" a feminine voice asked.

"May I help you?" Inorus asked again.

"Yes, I am an old friend of Osorkon's from a faraway land. I'm looking for him," Ilfanti said.

"An old friend?" Inorus asked, his face tightening as if he were growing angry.

"Yes, Ilfanti by name," Ilfanti said. "Is he here?"

"None of father's *old* friends are welcome here," growled Inorus. "Be gone!"

"Inorus, be nice," the same feminine voice said, as a female dwarf emerged. She was half a head shorter than Inorus, with auburn hair and light brown eyes. She wore a loose-fitting white linen dress with a red sash. "Did I hear right? Did you say you were Ilfanti?"

"That's right," Ilfanti said.

"Ilfanti, it's me, Dedi," the dwarf said.

"Dedi? *Little Dedi?*" gasped Ilfanti. "It can't be!"

"It has been too long!" Dedi said. "Come in, come in."

"Mother, this is an old friend of father's," Inorus protested.

"Don't worry, Ilfanti won't make your father rob tombs again. If it wasn't for your father and Ilfanti, I wouldn't be here right now, and none of you would either."

"That was a long time ago," said Ilfanti as he stepped inside and saw two other dwarves, both males around the age of one hundred. "You were just a child."

"I was," Dedi said.

"And you married Osorkon?" Ilfanti asked, shocked.

"I did," Dedi said. "Not right away, he was much older than me! But he stayed in touch and things just... well, they just happened."

"Well, good for you," Ilfanti said. "These are your sons?"

"Inorus is our oldest son, you met him at the door," Dedi said.

Ilfanti nodded to Inorus, who still looked skeptical, but he nodded back slightly, more to appease his mother than to welcome his guest.

"Our other boys are Meketre, and Sneferu," Dedi said.

Meketre was the same height as Inorus. His hair and beard were brown, though darker than his mother's. Unlike Inorus, he had a loose-fitting tunic covering his chest, and a kilt. Sneferu was the tallest of the trio, and also looked the most out of place. His hair and beard were blonde, his eyes as blue as the morning sky, and he was adorned with golden jewelry around his neck, on each of his fingers, the clip of his belt, and the lacing of his sandals.

"Pleased to meet you," Ilfanti said.

Sneferu stood up, waved briefly to Ilfanti, then faced his mother. "I need to get going."

"Of course," Dedi said. "Send our love to Amessis."

"I will," Sneferu said as he walked out of the room.

"A princess," Dedi whispered to Ilfanti. "We're so proud."

"That's wonderful," Ilfanti said. "Is Osorkon here?"

"No, he's in Talhella with our oldest child, Khonsu," replied Dedi. "He was commissioned by the Pharaoh."

"Oh?" asked Ilfanti, shocked by the news.

"Father has reformed from his tomb-robbing days," Inorus said.

Ilfanti glanced at Inorus and could see that the dwarf did not really welcome a blast from the past where his father was concerned.

"He has," Dedi said. "Instead of seeking buried treasure, now he protects it."

"Interesting," Ilfanti said, considering how much had changed. "You are all very fortunate."

"Will you be in Egziard long?" asked Dedi.

"There's something I came here to find," Ilfanti said. "I was hoping Osorkon could point me in the right direction."

"You were hoping he'd join you," Inorus said with no attempt to hide his scorn. The comment received a reprimanding glare from Dedi.

"He probably won't be back this way for several months," explained Dedi. "You can go see him in Talhella, though. Maybe he can take a little break to help you get started."

"That sounds like a plan," Ilfanti replied.

"Do you have time to stay for dinner?" Dedi asked.

"That would be wonderful," Ilfanti agreed. "I'm sure my camel could use the break."

"Then you'll be our guest for the night. In the morning, I'll have Inorus take you to Talhella."

"Mother!" Inorus protested.

Dedi gave him another look, and Inorus backed down. "It is settled, then," Dedi said happily. "We'll have a feast in the honor of the dwarf who helped save my life and bring this family together."

CHAPTER 43

Rhyne remained outside of Memtorren, watching the entrance closely. He did not know that it was an exclusively dwarven city, but he had seen several hundred dwarves coming and going since he had arrived, so he figured that a wraith probably would not be welcome.

If he were trying to kill Ilfanti, then he would not hesitate to venture into Memtorren to find the Mage, but all he was doing was following the dwarf, so in this instance, patience was key. He did not know how long Ilfanti would be, but he hoped that it would not be long. Wraiths liked the darkness, and preferred things cool. Here, the sun blazed down for sixteen hours a day, and it was always hot and dry. Perhaps he would ask Lady Salaman for a bonus for enduring these conditions.

When night did finally come, sleep would have been welcome, but Rhyne was afraid that he would then miss Ilfanti. He would have to force himself to remain awake for as long as he could. The last thing Rhyne wanted was for the dwarf to leave while he was unaware of the departure.

Rhyne considered going into Memtorren at night, just to try and find Ilfanti, but he knew that that would be a mistake. On the way here, he had managed to act like a shadow to Ilfanti, remaining slightly behind him at all times and never in sight. There were mornings when Ilfanti had left before him, but Rhyne could determine that right away and catch up easily enough.

He would be much happier when they were back on the open sands and trails again, rather than in a city where Ilfanti could lose him. Rhyne only hoped that Ilfanti would come out soon. He suspected that the dwarf would. After all, he was there to find Ramahatra and the Orb of Prophecy, which meant this was only a minor respite before the long journey. Even with his patience growing thin, Rhyne knew he could wait. If he somehow lost Ilfanti, then he would lose Kabilian, and that was not a viable outcome.

ILFANTI'S LOG

Osorkon and Dedi? Who ever would have thought? It was so long ago, yet I remember it as if it were just yesterday. Osorkon and I had been returning to Memtorren after finding the lost treasure of the thief Userhut, who gained his fame by plundering the tomb of Pharaoh Ramsyisies. It was remarkable to see, a cavern hidden by the sands, but filled from wall to wall with gold, magnificent artifacts, statues, and gemstones. In the midst of it all was the golden throne of Ramsyisies, and the decaying remains of Userhut.

We could not possibly carry all of the treasure ourselves, merely a few small items to prove that we actually managed to locate the stolen goods. So we were on our way home to find an entire expedition go back with us and collect things properly.

On the way back, we met a small hunting party of dwarves. They were part of the royal guard of King Nepitka, who was a direct descendent of the first dwarven king of Memtorren. They said that a young girl had been abducted from the home of the king. We didn't really care who the girl was, only that we rescue her. How exciting is going after the devilish fiend who dares to abduct a child before he brings harm to her? The child was the important thing, the adventure an added bonus.

The guards continued on their way, and Osorkon and I decided to do a little research ourselves. We found a few traders leaving Memtorren, and they said that the city was abuzz with talk that Nepitka's only daughter had been kidnapped. The princess!

I have always hated using my magical abilities when on a quest, but sometimes, a person had to use all of his powers to make sure that he was successful. Especially when a child's life was in jeopardy.

We went to the royal home, and I began focusing on the room where the princess had been abducted. It is a gift that not every Mage possesses, but it can come in quite handy for those of us that have it. By concentrating, I was able to visualize what had happened in the room I was in. I could create a small image for Osorkon to see as well, without the dialogue, and together, we were able to watch the kidnapper.

He looked like a beardless dwarf, but taller. We figured that he was probably some kind of dwarven hybrid with another race, either human or possibly sarnal. Turns out he was something called a halfling. The princess was sitting before reflective glass, adjusting a tiara on her head. The kidnapper came behind her and dropped a sack over her head, then pulled it up and hoisted it over his shoulder.

We then slowly made our way from the room, following the kidnapper as he put the sack in a wagon full of goods for trade. He then rode out, pleasantly waving and talking to everyone he passed.

We then knew who had abducted the princess, and which direction they had come. Of course, back in my Paladin years, enacting a spell such as that for as long as I did was draining and exhausting. I could barely keep my head up, but with Osorkon by my side, I really didn't need to. I slept and recuperated on the back of my camel as he led us in the direction of the kidnapper, which was the opposite direction from which we had seen the guards going!

After a couple of days' travel, I was back at full strength, and we began to see wagon tracks that had not yet been hidden by the blowing sands. We were getting close! The kidnapper was not too bright, either. He made a fire at night, giving us a beacon to follow right to him.

We found them that night—the girl was tied up and gagged. Her abductor was all mine. Osorkon made his way down to free the girl while I went to confront the kidnapper. Osorkon asked me to create a diversion, but I figured that we could do better than that.

By the time he had the girl cut and free, I had the kidnapper tied and gagged. Okay, so I used a little magic, but he deserved it! It turns out he was a real genius, too. The girl he kidnapped was not the princess, but the maid's daughter!

The girl was Dedi, and her mother had worked for King Nepitka for practically all of her life. Apparently, she brought Dedi with her one day, which was not her usual routine, and Dedi had found some of the princess's belongings, and was playing dress-up. That was when she was mistaken for the princess and snatched.

Nepitka had gone along with the mistaken identity, hiding his own daughter away, because he felt that those looking for Dedi would try harder thinking she was a princess, and the kidnapper would be less likely to harm the princess before getting whatever ransom he was looking for. To Osorkon and me, it didn't matter. We went in search of a kidnapped child, and we found her. Royalty or servant girl, it made no difference to us.

I wonder when Osorkon and Dedi began to become romantically involved? She was just a child back then, and he and I had already been in triple digits in age. But I guess age doesn't really matter if there is love involved. I'm glad they found each other. It is good to have a family and be happy. Osorkon's family seems very happy. I hate to admit it, but I am envious.

I know as a Mage that certain things are not for me as they are for others, like marriage and families, but there are still times I wish that I could be just like anyone else and have a family of my own. A child to watch grow and help guide through life. Would they seek adventure like me, or perhaps be an artist? Either way, I can imagine the pride I would feel in seeing them make those choices in life. Alas, it is something I can never have, so there is really no use in trying to visualize it.

I guess, in my own way, I do have family of my own. Cala and Herg are as close to me as any relatives could ever be. Even Osorkon is like a brother I have not seen in years. Perhaps I am the unofficial uncle to his children. Perhaps that is little more than fantasy, but at least I would feel a connection to something that will grow and continue beyond my mortal life.

CHAPTER 44

Normally, companionship on a three-week journey to another city would be a welcome thing. Someone to talk to, to joke with, and to share tales with. Someone who will help to pass the time. Ilfanti did not find this with Inorus at all.

Since leaving Memtorren, the only things Ilfanti had learned about Inorus was that he was extremely fit, he was much stronger than Ilfanti remembered Osorkon ever being, and he was able to endure the blazing sun without so much as a water break for hours at a time. Of course, Ilfanti also knew that Inorus was harboring some deep resentment toward him, but he had known that from the moment they had first met.

The first morning of their journey, Ilfanti woke up to the sweet smell of breakfast, made especially for him by Dedi. Inorus was already packed and ready to go, waiting by the camels. Ilfanti did not know what Inorus did for a living, but the dwarf certainly looked like a capable warrior.

He still wore predominantly white, but now had a white tunic and cloak, as well as a white turban wrapped around his head. Fastened to his sash was a pair of scimitars that had much wider blades than those he had seen used in the Seven Kingdoms. Inorus also had a dagger tucked into his boot, and Ilfanti spotted several other hilts of daggers attached to the packing on the back of the camel.

Other than that, Ilfanti knew very little. What did Inorus do? What did he like to do? Was he seeing anyone, like his brother Sneferu was? How did he feel about certain issues affecting Memtorren and Egziard? All of that remained a mystery. Ilfanti held out hope, though. Shimada had been like that when he had first secured passage to Egziard, but she eventually opened up to him, Inorus would too.

They reached Talhella on the eighteenth day after leaving Memtorren. One good thing about traveling with Inorus was that he did not waste time, and they managed to shave three days off of their journey. As Ilfanti reached the city walls, he marveled at the splendor of it all for a moment. Talhella was the largest, grandest, most splendid city in all of Egziard. It made Trespias look like a small summer retreat, rather than the capital of a great nation.

Like Memtorren, most of Talhella was built with the lasting stone structures that could endure the desert winds and sand storms that plagued the country. However, Talhella was capped with gold and golden structures, augmenting the style and appeal. Ilfanti thought it amazing that people did not try to steal parts of the road, chiseling out a golden brick and claiming it as their own.

The people of Talhella were also far more exquisitely dressed than those from either Memtorren or Zaman. Golden spirals of serpents or coils were wrapped up women's arms; tunics and gowns were silky and of finer quality than others; and the jewelry on people's hands, around their necks, dangling from ears, and in headpieces left little doubt that these people were wealthy and influential.

Ilfanti spotted dozens of patrols, usually in pairs, walking the paved streets and maintaining the peace. They were easily identified by sky-blue kilts and turbans, with weapons dangling from their sashes. There appeared to be no discrimination in the ranks, as Ilfanti identified at least half a dozen different races in uniform.

None of the guards paused to look at Ilfanti and Inorus as they rode in on their camels. Visitors were welcome at Talhella, as long as they did not break any rules. If Ilfanti remembered correctly, there were three punishments in Talhella, depending on the severity of the altercation. The first, for minor offenses, was the loss of freedom, where the guilty party would be sold into slavery, the proceeds of the sale benefiting the wronged party. The second, for more severe offenses, was banishment into the desert. But, they did not just turn you out of the city; instead, they brought the banished individual many days' journey into the open desert, removed all garments, weapons, and tools, and left them with enough water to fill both hands when cupped. Most people never survived their banishment. The third and final penalty, for major offenses, was instant death at the hands of the local executioner, an event that was made quite public to help deter future crime.

Perhaps fear of the justice system was why the gold woven into the design of the city was safe from even the beggars and peddlers of the city. They were merely more afraid of the penalty than they were hungry for food. Perhaps he was mistaken and this was an enlightened society now, but he doubted it. He had seen too much and been to too many places to believe that poverty did not breed desperation.

Inorus led Ilfanti through the city streets. If there was a section of Talhella that was full of the poor, beggars, and peddlers, he spotted no sign of them. Ilfanti could not conceive of the possibility of eliminating poverty, unless those without the resources to thrive here were not allowed admittance. If that were the case, then he would have thought that it would have been much more difficult to get into the city.

Inorus paused before a stairway made completely of gold, with dozens of guards standing at attention, and elaborate statues placed by the entrance. "This is the palace of Pharaoh Werirenptah, Father's employer."

Ilfanti was in awe of the structure. It was several times larger than the palace in Trespias, with such ornate detail in the design that it must have been the culmination of hundreds of architects' lives.

"Impressive," Ilfanti said. "Will Osorkon be here?"

"No," Inorus said, pulling the reins of his camel and moving on.

Ilfanti watched him leave and snickered to himself. "Guess not," he whispered, pulling his camel's reins and following Inorus further into the city.

Inorus led them through the rest of the city. It took slightly over two hours to travel from the northern to southern gates. For the past half hour, Ilfanti had seen the domiciles of the poor, and had seen people begging for food, money, or to purchase some good or service from them. He did not find it a relief to find them living in such dismal conditions, and wondered again at how those that lived outside of the Mage's Council really were dependent upon birthright and status. Those born to wealth and influence inherited everything, whereas those born to poverty often spent a lifetime struggling to survive. There were no dividing lines like that for Mages. Everyone, rich and poor, regardless of race, had been taken at birth and raised as equals.

After leaving the Southern gates of Talhella, Ilfanti spotted several pyramids in the distance: the eternal resting places of the past pharaohs. As Inorus led them over a dune, Ilfanti saw thousands of workers pulling stone tablets and working on the construction of a pyramid. It was far larger than any of the others, and with the top exposed, Ilfanti made out a virtual labyrinth inside the pyramid.

"There," Inorus said, pointing at a group circled around a dwarf scanning a scroll.

Ilfanti strained to see, and could not help but smile and laugh giddily when the dwarf lowered the scroll and his old friend Osorkon was revealed. Osorkon was barking and growling at those around him, pointing at the scroll, then at the pyramid, and shouting angrily. He still has his fire and spirit, Ilfanti thought.

Osorkon closely resembled Inorus, though there were signs of aging around his eyes, and his beard had faded from black to gray long ago. Ilfanti laughed slightly when he studied Osorkon's beard, which was separated at his chin, pulled around to the back of his head, and tied together. Any exposed skin was tan and dark, but a beige cloak, tunic, and baggy pants covered most of Osorkon's body. His feet were covered, not by boots, but some kind of fabric shoes that were the same color as his pants.

Ilfanti waited for the crowd around Osorkon to disperse, and then sneaked up on his old friend and slapped him on the back. "Osorkon, how's it hanging?"

Osorkon pivoted slowly, his face pale as he looked at Ilfanti. "Could it be? Is it Ilfanti? The friend I once knew?"

"It is I, old friend," Ilfanti said. "It has been far too long!"

"It has indeed," grinned Osorkon as he dropped his scroll and grabbed Ilfanti in a big bear hug.

As Osorkon set Ilfanti back down, Ilfanti grinned deviously. "So this is what has become of the great adventurer, eh? The dwarf that said that no tomb was ever safe when he put his mind to it, and now, you build tombs?"

Osorkon chuckled at the irony. "What can I say? Who better to build a tomb than one that knows how to overcome the defenses and steal the secrets and treasures contained within?"

"I suppose," shrugged Ilfanti. "I just never thought I would see you settle down in one place long enough to do something like this. You were always on the go."

"Just as you were, if I remember correctly," winked Osorkon.

"Kindred spirits," agreed Ilfanti.

"What can I say? The love of a beautiful dwarf and young ones of my own made me think about a great many things," explained Osorkon.

"I hope it didn't make you regret any of our adventures?"

"Of course not!" laughed Osorkon. "I wouldn't give up my memories for anything. I just have some new ideas about what makes good memories now. Right, Inorus?"

Inorus raised one eyebrow and peered at his father without replying.

"I don't think he likes me," whispered Ilfanti.

"He just thinks that you'll get me to run off on some adventure with you. He should know better," said Osorkon.

"Oh?" asked Ilfanti.

"We're already behind schedule," Osorkon moaned. "Werirenptah authorized hiring skilled labor, but the builders are looking to line their own pockets a bit, and acquired slave labor. They work the slaves day and night, but the poor souls are practically skin and bones. And don't even get me started on the group who call themselves artists. This supposed to be the grandest pyramid ever built, but I've broken into some with better art in the closet than what they are sculpting for the tomb room."

Ilfanti whistled, one long note. "You sure have changed, old friend. You've gone and gotten responsible on me."

"It happens," shrugged Osorkon. "But enough about me. What brings you back to Egziard after all of these years?"

"I'm afraid that I'm up to my old tricks, but for good reasons this time," said Ilfanti.

"We always had good reasons," snickered Osorkon. "But tell me these reasons."

Before Ilfanti began to talk about his quest for the Orb of Prophecy, he watched as a female dwarf leapt off of the top of the pyramid structure, her arms stretched to the sides, and soared down the side that was still smooth and not yet fully constructed. Ilfanti gasped, certain that the dwarf was committing suicide rather than remaining a slave.

Moments before hitting the ground, he watched the dwarf reach back and then yank her arms forward. In each hand she held an end of what looked like a tarp or sail, and then shook the fabric, creating a thunderous crack as the fabric snapped and expanded in the wind, slowing her descent.

She released the two ends and pulled a small hook from her belt, catching a line that was attached to the pyramid and angled down to the ground as a support line. She jerked slightly as the line bobbed up and down to support her weight, and then she began sliding down the line, holding onto the hook with both hands. As she sailed over Ilfanti, Osorkon, and Inorus, she released the hook, somersaulted twice, and landed on her feet next to Osorkon.

"Inorus," the dwarf said. "And who is this?"

"This is my old friend, Ilfanti," Osorkon said. "Ilfanti, allow me to introduce my firstborn, Khonsu."

"Ilfanti, eh? I've heard a lot about you," Khonsu said.

Khonsu was an inch shorter than her father, and like Inorus, had the same pitch-black hair and dark brown eyes that her father had in his youth. She was smiling, but although the look was warm and welcoming Ilfanti could see a deviousness that was burning to be free just under the surface. There was a look in her eye that reminded Ilfanti of Osorkon, when he was Khonsu's age.

She was wearing pants and a shirt similar to Inorus's, but hers were as dark as her hair. A violet sash was wrapped around her waist, and a light lavender cloak was clasped around her neck. Her pants tucked neatly into her black, knee-high boots.

"Impressive," Ilfanti said, his eyes rescanning the path she had just taken to reach them.

"If the stories I heard are true, you've done a lot more than that yourself," Khonsu said, admiration in her voice.

"Well, I have been known to jump off of a mountain or two," shrugged Ilfanti, suddenly feeling like he wanted to impress Khonsu. He paused for a moment and wondered why that was.

"Please, please, no stories," Osorkon pleaded. "Khonsu already takes after me a little too much for my liking. It took all of my persuasiveness to convince her to join me in building something impenetrable."

"What's your role?" Ilfanti asked.

"That's simple," grinned Khonsu. "Father designs the traps, and I try to crack them."

"If she can, then I design something else," sighed Osorkon. "Alas, she cracks most of my traps! She learned too well!"

Ilfanti laughed at the remark. Khonsu was the daughter of Osorkon, so it was natural that she would be drawn to the life that her father once had. Perhaps she would even surpass Osorkon in skill one day. Ilfanti wondered if that meant that Inorus was more like his mother than father.

"So what was it that brings you here, old friend?" Osorkon asked.

"In the realm I am from, an evil tyrant who had been banished long ago has returned. He has had millennia to devise his strategy for conquest, and has been doing so quite effectively. Everything we try, he is a step or two ahead of us. The Seven Kingdoms is quickly losing not only ground, but hope.

"One person had the foresight to try and unite the races in order to confront this tyrant. She is the daughter of a man that united humanity across the land, and now she hopes to do the same with all of the races, much like you have accomplished here in Egziard. Her name is Karleena, and she may just be the realm's last hope."

"Then why are you here, and not with this Karleena?" Osorkon asked.

"The tyrant had her abducted," explained Ilfanti. "He pointed us in the direction of a would-be ally in our struggle against him, and the humans fell for it, declaring war."

"Gullible fools," snorted Inorus.

"I have reason to believe that the Empress is not where we thought she was, but taken far away where she could not interfere. It is my hope to find her, rescue her, and bring her back to help unite the races against this common foe. She will be the beacon that all will follow.

"So I have come here as the first step in that journey. To find her, to save her, first I need to know where to look. Terra is too large to search for a lone individual. I have traveled here, faced a great number of perils, to obtain an artifact, one precious and rare, that will be a dangerous challenge just to find. But it also will be a quest full of excitement, unraveling an age-old mystery, and facing the ultimate test of skill and cunning."

"You're after the Orb of Prophecy," whispered Osorkon.

"I am," confirmed Ilfanti. "With it, I can determine where the Empress is, and hopefully retrieve her before it is too late."

"You are crazier than I remembered, old friend," scoffed Osorkon. "You think locating Ramahatra will be easy? You think stealing from it will be a simple matter? Maybe you are beginning to lose your good judgment in your old age."

"I'm not crazy," said Ilfanti. "I did my research before leaving. I have narrowed down where Ramahatra is located, and have learned that there is a mystical compass that points the way. I have a map indicating where this compass can be found. I intend to get the compass, and then go on to Ramahatra."

"Impossible," objected Osorkon. "Ramahatra is a hidden city, lost for all eternity. Even if you find it, it is cursed. You will die."

"But I shall try," declared Ilfanti.

"As shall I," said Khonsu. "Sounds like fun."

"Khonsu!" Osorkon shouted with disappointment. "Think of what you are saying! You heard the rumors of what happened to the Ptahhemat-Ty tribe!"

"It doesn't matter," Khonsu stubbornly replied. "I'm going."

"What happened to the Ptahhemat-Ty tribe?" asked Ilfanti.

"They were a group of nomads," Osorkon said. "The largest and most powerful to wander the deserts of Egziard. They came across this mystical compass of yours, and went searching for Ramahatra. Apparently, they found a powerful high priestess guarding the treasure, and most of the men perished, leaving the tribe in shambles."

"Don't forget, old friend, I have been known to dabble in mysticism myself every now and then," grinned Ilfanti.

"Quiet," warned Osorkon. "Things have changed since you were here last. It is now illegal to practice magic."

"Illegal to practice magic?" snorted Ilfanti. "That is ridiculous."

"It is not," pleaded Osorkon. "Bottles began popping up, and slavers were told that the bottle could bind a Mage with ease. The Mages did not go willingly, but they could not withstand the power of the bottles. It enslaved them!"

Ilfanti glanced at Khonsu and then Inorus, seeing on their faces that what Osorkon was saying was true. He had never heard of the ability to trap and enslave a Mage before. "Who designed these bottles?"

"I wish I knew," Osorkon sighed. "But be wary of revealing that you are a Mage, or you, too, will become a genie!"

"I'll keep that in mind," Ilfanti said, remembering seeing the peddler selling genies when he first arrived. He did not know what they were at the time, but now he was horrified. Imagine living a life being trapped in a bottle and only being released to do the bidding of your master.

"What will you do now, my friend?" Osorkon asked.

"If the compass has been found, then I no longer need to go to where I learned it would be kept. However, I must acquire the compass. Could you help me find a guide so that I can find whoever has it?"

"If you want a guide, then you have one," Khonsu boldly declared.

Osorkon bit his lip, clearly not happy with Khonsu's decision. "How can I let my only daughter and oldest friend face a threat alone? Count me in," he sighed.

"It will be good to travel by your side once more," said Ilfanti.

"Typical," growled Inorus.

"What is it, son?" Osorkon asked.

"I knew that he would only bring trouble," replied Inorus. "Mother will be most upset."

Osorkon laughed lightheartedly at the statement. "Perhaps," he shrugged. "But your mother doesn't have to know."

"Maybe," grinned Inorus. "Then again, I may tell her when we get back."

"We?" Osorkon asked.

Inorus grinned and nodded.

Khonsu punched him on the shoulder. "Well, all right!"

Ilfanti studied the three and nodded his approval. They would be a quartet setting out to help save the future of the Seven Kingdoms. If the mission was not so dire, and the result of failure not so grave, he was certain that he would actually be enjoying this.

CHAPTER 45

Sitting on the golden steps before the palace, Ilfanti and Inorus waited patiently for Osorkon and Khonsu to return. It was a glorious morning, and Ilfanti was anxious to be on their way. The quartet had been up most of the night reminiscing and preparing for their journey through the desert. As always, Ilfanti was impressed by the thoroughness and preparation of Osorkon. Somehow, in the midst of the night, he had managed to barter with peddlers and secure enough provisions to last them at least two weeks.

The palace was the last stop before leaving Talhella, allowing Osorkon and Khonsu the opportunity to tell Pharaoh Werirenptah that they would be leaving for a short time, and that the finalization of his sacred burial chamber would be delayed. The structure would still continue to be built while they were away, but Osorkon and Khonsu would need to be on hand later to test just how impenetrable it was, and make the necessary augmentations.

Osorkon also had promised Ilfanti that he would ask Werirenptah about sending some of their precious ore, adamantite, to Zaman for construction of barrels that could harness the power of the amphibier weapons. Ilfanti was not certain how successful Osorkon would be with having the ore donated. It was easily worth ten times as much as illistrium, the famed ore that the Tregador dwarves mined and crafted in the Seven Kingdoms. Where Ilfanti was from, illistrium was considered the strongest, most durable, and most desirable material that a weapon could be crafted from. The adamantite made illistrium look little better than steel.

In all of Ilfanti's travels, he had only come across adamantite twice. Egziard had a small supply that was uncovered, thought it was certainly possible that there were vast supplies buried over time in the sands of the desert. The only other place Ilfanti had ever even heard it referred to was in the Findalleyas, a mountain range with icy peaks and snow throughout the year. Trying to process the adamantite from the mountains where it was found was virtually impossible, even for dwarves.

"They come," Inorus said.

Ilfanti glanced up and saw Osorkon and Khonsu approaching. Khonsu was grinning, and Osorkon bobbing his head to relay the message that they were all set.

"It went well?" Ilfanti asked.

"Werirenptah is very reasonable," Osorkon said. "He granted us our leave, and has agreed to send an envoy of dwarves with some of his private supply of adamantite to Zaman to meet your Captain Augustus and design the weapon barrels for her."

"Wow," Ilfanti whistled in awe. "How did you manage all of that?"

"Simple, I told him that the threat would come and try to conquer here if efforts were not successful in your homeland," Osorkon said. "Conquerors are not typically satisfied unless they continue to expand their territory."

Ilfanti could not have planned it better if he had tried. The willingness of Pharaoh Werirenptah to offer so much meant that he was potentially an ally against Zoldex. Egziard was far from the Seven Kingdoms, but having allies from another continent could come in quite valuable if the war with Zoldex continued as it had been.

"He also offered to send a royal escort with us, but I figured that you'd prefer the group to remain small," Osorkon said.

"We'll have a better chance of sneaking into Ramahatra with a smaller group," said Ilfanti. "You made the right choice."

Inorus snorted at the comment. "Only you're forgetting that they already have the Orb of Prophecy. They'll know when we will get there before we will."

Osorkon and Ilfanti exchanged a knowing glance—Inorus had spoken wisely. The danger would increase the closer they got to their destination.

"Let them know," Khonsu boldly declared. "It will make stealing the Orb right out from under their noses that much sweeter."

"She has spirit," Ilfanti grinned. "I'll give her that."

"Spirit, and skill," Osorkon agreed proudly.

"Of course, I learned from the best," Khonsu said.

"Don't forget cockiness," teased Inorus.

"I love you too, brother dear," replied Khonsu.

"Well, we're ready," Osorkon declared. "Shall we go find the remnants of the Ptahhemat-Ty tribe and get the compass to Ramahatra?"

"Let's," nodded Ilfanti.

"It's about time," grinned Khonsu. "No more stories about the two of you. Now, I can see you both in action for real and live the adventure with you."

"And then you can watch mother tear into him far more viciously than any creature or blade ever could," predicted Inorus.

"Always the optimist," shrugged Osorkon. "Your mother wouldn't do that to me. Well, not *too* much."

As Inorus and Khonsu went to fetch the camels, Ilfanti leaned over and whispered to his friend: "You hope." He then left Osorkon scratching his head and wondering how Dedi really would react when she found out. With a shrug, Osorkon joined his children and friend, and their journey began.

CHAPTER 46

Rhyne was glad to see that Ilfanti was finally heading into the desert. Although Ilfanti now traveled with a trio of dwarves, he could track them more easily on the open desert and not have to worry as much about losing them in the midst of a vast city.

Thus far, Ilfanti had not detected Rhyne at all. Rhyne took pleasure in the fact that he was tracking not only a Mage, but also a member of the Council of Elders. Perhaps, with the mists of the Gates of Tanorus in his possession, and his natural abilities, he would begin hunting Mages when he returned home. There were always hefty bounties placed on the heads of Mages that interfered with the criminal underworld. He may as well tap into that lucrative income. If Ilfanti could not detect him, what hope would a Paladin have?

Rhyne dropped back to follow at a discreet distance. He was confident that he would not lose the quartet anytime soon, and decided not to risk being uncovered by traveling too closely. The vast desert was so open that the smallest shape on the horizon could be seen. It was his job to become invisible so that Ilfanti and the other dwarves would remain unaware of his presence.

Pausing, Rhyne saw a dozen individuals—all dressed in garments that blended into the sand quite expertly—between him and Ilfanti. He had tracked people long enough to know that this group was also following Ilfanti, but for what purpose?

The group moved as one, using hand signals and vocal sounds that were as soft as the wind. Rhyne was intrigued. Just who were these people? What were they after? Were they also searching for Ramahatra? Or were they perhaps following the dwarves that Ilfanti was traveling with?

One thing Rhyne did not like was having to guess. He would learn who these people were at the first opportunity. Undoubtedly, he would find one alone, and that individual would tell him everything, or suffer a very slow and painful death.

It was five days before Rhyne managed to get one of the creatures alone. A pair had been left behind, one had taken a nap, and the other was packing provisions. Rhyne selected the individual packing. He moved in swiftly, grabbed the creature by the throat, and slid a dagger up beneath its hooded cloak.

The creature was not only wearing garments to help blend into the desert, but also a mask that hid his true features. Rhyne had no clue what it was under the mask, but he felt confident that he could handle any surprises.

"Move, and die," whispered Rhyne.

The creature did more than move. He grabbed Rhyne's wrist holding the blade, twisted it so that Rhyne would drop his weapon, and then flipped Rhyne over his shoulder. Rhyne landed on his feet, crouching down, and in an instant propelled himself back at his adversary. As he connected with the creature's body, he heard a definite female gasp as the creature landed hard on its back.

Rhyne pulled the mask up, and saw what looked like a hybrid of a sabrenoh and an elf. It was definitely a female, closely resembling a sabrenoh in facial features, eyes, and fangs, but with the distinctive ears of an elf. Her form was also more nimble than that of a normal female sabrenoh. Upon her forehead, she had a tattoo of an ankh with a serpent wrapped around it.

"Unhand me, *Ra-tuk*!" she shouted.

Rhyne was not certain what "Ra-tuk" meant, but the way she had said it, he was certain that it was an insult. Pulling out a blade in each hand, he dug them down into her shoulders, pinning her into the sand below. The woman gritted her teeth, but did not scream.

"Who are you?" demanded Rhyne.

"I am your destroyer," the woman growled.

Rhyne twisted the blades, watching her wince, but still not scream out. "Who are you?"

"Die, Ra-tuk!"

"Not today," Rhyne said as he took several of his needle-sized blades and began slowly pushing them into her fingers. He finally got a moan of pain, and grinned delightedly. "Who are you?"

"Even if I tell you, Ra-tuk, it will do you no good."

"Then tell me," Rhyne said as he began pushing another needle into her finger.

He could see the turmoil on her face. She wished to be defiant and not speak, but she also wanted him to stop his torment.

"Speak!"

"I am Saj'haal, of the Co'iahla," she said.

"Why are you following the dwarves?" Rhyne asked.

"They seek that which must remain hidden," Saj'haal said.

"You intend to stop them from finding Ramahatra?" Rhyne asked.

"It is the sacred duty of the Co'iahla to keep Ramahatra hidden for all eternity," Saj'haal explained.

"Why?" Rhyne asked.

"Ramahatra has been consumed by darkness and can unleash untold tragedies upon the world. We are sworn to prevent that," said Saj'haal.

"Do you kill those that seek Ramahatra?" Rhyne asked.

"We deter," Saj'haal replied, cryptically.

"What does that mean?" demanded Rhyne, ramming another needle into her finger.

Saj'haal bit her lip; a trickle of blood began seeping down her chin. "We rarely strike outright, but we do cause accidents."

"Accidents," Rhyne repeated. "Fatal accidents?"

"At times," Saj'haal said.

"Then our mission is one and the same," Rhyne said, pulling one of the needles from Saj'haal. "I could care less about the secrets of Ramahatra, but I am here to stop a vile assassin from discovering Ramahatra and unleashing its evil on my own land."

"The dwarves?" Saj'haal asked.

"The dwarves are on a quest to steal a magical artifact from Ramahatra that will help them wage war in my homeland. They are not the one I am after, but they go to the same destination, and I am following them."

"If they seek artifacts to wage war, then they must be stopped," Saj'haal declared.

"If they are stopped, I will not find my way to Ramahatra in time to stop Kabilian," Rhyne growled in frustration. "I must prevent you from hurting the dwarves."

As Rhyne lifted his dagger to strike, Saj'haal's lips creased into a grin.

"You smile in the face of your death?" Rhyne asked, shocked.

"The Co'iahla are eternal," Saj'haal said. "You may strike this mortal coil down, but I shall remain. However, if you do not, then perhaps we will help stop the dwarves and then help you find this Kabilian that you are after."

Rhyne stared at Saj'haal for a long moment. He did not trust her, nor did he intend to keep her alive. But, if the Co'iahla actually knew where Ramahatra was already, then with their direction, he could reach the lost city before Kabilian. That was quite enticing.

"I accept," Rhyne said, removing the blades he had stuck Saj'haal with. "No hard feelings?"

"Ra-tuk, when your enemy has been silenced, then so too shall you," vowed Saj'haal.

"At least we know where we stand," Rhyne agreed.

ILFANTI'S LOG

We're close. I can feel it in my bones. I remember the sensation from when I was younger—the anticipation and certainty that I was almost at my destination. A couple of days ago we found the Yanhamu tribe. They knew of the survivors of the Ptahhemat-Ty tribe, and pointed us in the direction of a nomadic group that had taken them in. Unless the group has moved, which is quite possible, we'll reach them tomorrow.

I will be glad to have the compass and finally be on the right course to Ramahatra. Everything about this journey since the first day that the Soaring Mist departed Water Haven has been harder and taken me longer than I expected. Maybe I'm just getting too old to keep up the pace I did when I was young. There are many times I see Inorus and Khonsu pausing to wait for Osorkon and me to catch up. Maybe adventuring is better left to the next generation.

I can't accept that. I won't accept that. I made it this far. The Empress is counting on me. I'll find the Orb and complete my mission.

But thoughts of my age and my own mortality have gotten me thinking again. I see such pride and joy in Osorkon's eyes when he looks at Inorus and Khonsu. Is that a look I will never be able to share? One that I will never experience?

Perhaps the dictates of the Mages, and the doctrine of reproducing but not raising a family, are antiquated and need to be adjusted. We may have the greatest education in the land, but if we lose our hearts and souls in the process, what is the point?

If I were to ever consider taking a mate and trying to raise a family of my own, Khonsu would be the type of dwarf I would want to do it with. Khonsu herself is far too young for me, and Osorkon would probably kill me if I even looked at her that way, but she has a spirit and sense of adventure that rivals my own. I would want that. Someone who would not only understand me and why I do things, but also someone who could actually share my passions with me.

I hesitate to write this, but the more we travel, the more I do find myself drawn to Khonsu. It is taking almost every fiber of my being not to look at her fondly. I wonder what she thinks? Am I just an old friend of her father? Or does she see the fire inside of me and see someone that could be something more?

This is getting me nowhere. The mission is what is important. I need to focus on the mission. Good thing we'll find the mystical compass tomorrow. Nothing like progress to get your mind back on track.

CHAPTER 47

Shortly before nightfall, Khonsu appeared over a bluff and waved for her father, brother, and Ilfanti to join her. The group was weary, thirsty, and beginning to think that they would never find the nomadic group that had taken the survivors of the Ptahhemat-Ty tribe. The Yanhamu tribe had pointed them in this direction three days before, and still, there was no sign of the group they were looking for.

As Khonsu waved, the dwarves all hoped desperately that she had found something. They mounted their camels, moving sluggishly, and instructed the beasts to head to Khonsu. At this point, their water reserves were running dangerously low. They did not really care whether they found the survivors, or an oasis.

"What have you found?" Osorkon asked.

"Nomads," Khonsu said. "The Mokhtar tribe, led by Sheikh Nankitar."

"Is it the group we're looking for?" Ilfanti asked. "Are the survivors of the Ptahhemat-Ty tribe here?"

"Yes, and no," Khonsu said.

"Explain yourself," instructed Osorkon.

"There is only one," Khonsu said, her stern features showing a hint of fear.

"Only one?" gasped Osorkon. "The Ptahhemat-Ty are the largest nomadic tribe in Egziard!"

"The Mokhtar found only a dozen, and each of the others died shortly after," Khonsu said.

"Madness," Inorus whispered.

Osorkon turned and glanced at Ilfanti. "The curse?"

"We shall see," Ilfanti said. "If there really is a curse, I will not involve the three of you any longer."

"If you go, we go, old friend," Osorkon declared, speaking for his children. "Let us see this survivor and learn what happened for ourselves."

"This way," Khonsu said. "Sheikh Nankitar has offered us a place to stay for the night, and as much food and water as we can carry."

Ilfanti's eyebrow rose dubiously. "In exchange for what?"

"Our vow that we will break the curse," Khonsu replied. "He's afraid that what afflicted the Ptahhemat-Ty survivors will spread to his own tribe. He considered leaving Ptahetep behind to fend for himself."

"Ptahetep?" Osorkon asked. "He is the brother of Sheik Ptahmose."

"Then he should be well-informed," Ilfanti nodded enthusiastically.

Khonsu led them down into the encampment of the nomads, where several individuals greeted her and offered to look after their camels. A trio of women, their faces covered by veils, welcomed each of the male dwarves, and offered water and a platter of assorted fruits and cooked insects that they had acquired.

Ilfanti gladly accepted the water, and took a piece of fruit, which looked dried and shriveled, but tasted like a grape. He grinned and nodded to the woman to indicate that it was good.

Osorkon also tried some food, but Inorus only took the water, furling his nose at the plate before him.

"Eat up, boy," Osorkon said. "You need the energy."

Inorus reluctantly reached for a beetle, and watched as his father lifted it to his mouth and sucked on the tail. He did the same, feeling repulsed by what he was eating.

"Make sure you get it all," Osorkon said.

Inorus placed the beetle back on the tray tried his best to act thankful, but all he really wanted to do was vomit.

Ilfanti slapped him on the back and brushed one of the beetle's legs from Inorus's beard. "That's why I went with the fruit," he whispered.

"Wise advice," Inorus agreed.

"This way," Khonsu beckoned, leading the three to a tent that was further off from the camp than any other. "He is in there."

As they reached the tent, Ilfanti put his hand on Osorkon's shoulder to stop him. "I will go alone, in case he is cursed."

"I told you already, we are in this together," Osorkon replied, pulling the tent's doorway open and entering.

Ilfanti followed Osorkon inside, and saw Ptahetep lying on a carpet. His face was blistered and scarred, as if it had been badly scalded. His arms had small cracks all over them, as if his body were drying out and became brittle. His breathing was in gasps, with bouts of coughing every few seconds.

"By the gods," Inorus gasped, bringing his hand to his nose to try to block out the putrid scent.

Khonsu glanced at her brother, pulling his hand from his nose. She then began scanning the tent, studying every item within, her eyes dropping to a small box that was under one of Ptahetep's withered hands.

Ilfanti approached Ptahetep and kneeled down beside him. "You are Ptahetep?"

Ptahetep's eyes were open, but he stared at the ceiling of the tent. The only sign that he was even aware that he had visitors was a slight shudder when his name was spoken.

"Are you able to speak?" Ilfanti asked.

Osorkon began shaking his head. "This will get us nowhere. Let's just search him." As he reached down to take the box, Ptahetep's hand clamped down on it, his strength greater than it would seem from his appearance.

"No!" protested Ptahetep.

"He can talk," Osorkon said as he backed away from the box. "Just needed a little convincing was all."

"Are you Ptahetep, brother of Ptahmose, of the Ptahhemat-Ty tribe?" Ilfanti asked.

"Yes," replied Ptahetep, his voice as dry and weak as his body appeared.

"My name is Ilfanti. I am a Mage from a faraway land. I have traveled far to find something very particular. Your brother had found something of great value that would help me with my quest. Do you know what I am talking about?"

Ilfanti watched Ptahetep's eyes as they lowered from the ceiling of the tent and slowly made their way down to look at the box his arm was resting upon. "Yes."

"What is it I seek?" asked Ilfanti.

Ptahetep rose from the carpet, grabbed Ilfanti by the back of the head and pulled him closer. "The way to your death," he wheezed, then dropped back down as if the effort were too much for him.

Ilfanti glanced uneasily at Osorkon. "Are you sure you don't want to leave?"

"We're in this together," Osorkon quickly replied.

Ilfanti returned his focus on Ptahetep. "You found Ramahatra?"

"My brother, yes," Ptahetep returned.

"What did he find?" asked Ilfanti.

"He found that his greed and desire for wealth and power would be his downfall," Ptahetep said, his eyes beginning to mist at the memory.

"What happened?" Ilfanti asked.

"She happened," Ptahetep said.

"She?" Ilfanti asked.

"The dark-skinned witch," Ptahetep replied. "Beware the dark-skinned witch!"

"Did she do something to your brother?" asked Ilfanti.

"She did it to us all," moaned Ptahetep.

"What did she do to you all?" Ilfanti asked.

"She killed us all," Ptahetep replied.

Ilfanti turned and glanced at Osorkon. "The priestess, perhaps?"

"It must be," shrugged Osorkon. "I do not know how the priestess of legend could still be alive today unless she were a god."

"Or an eternal," suggested Ilfanti. "But eternals do not have dark skin."

"We'll figure it out when we get there," said Khonsu, confidently.

"No!" Ptahetep cried. "You must not go. She will do to you what she did to us. I watched my brother's skin melting from his body. There was nothing I could do. Nothing anyone could do but run."

"Sounds pleasant," Osorkon sarcastically grumbled.

"I must see this for myself," Ilfanti said. "Will you permit me?"

Ptahetep's eyes moved over to Ilfanti. "How?"

"It is an ability that Mages have. I will be able to send my consciousness into your mind and see your memories. Will you permit me?"

"No," Ptahetep said. "I no longer wish to remember it."

"You could just do it," Osorkon suggested. "He's too weak to argue."

"I won't force it," Ilfanti said. "He is not an enemy. I need permission."

"No," Ptahetep said again. "No more."

"Very well," Ilfanti sighed. "I understand. Do you remember where Ramahatra is, or do you still have the compass your brother found?"

Ptahetep's eyes lowered to the box again.

"Could we have it?" Ilfanti asked.

"No," Ptahetep said.

"Many lives depend on us getting to Ramahatra," Ilfanti said, his patience thinning.

"It is all I have left," Ptahetep said.

Osorkon kneeled down so that he was right before Ptahetep. "Then have the satisfaction of knowing that your brother and tribe would be avenged."

"You will fail," Ptahetep said. "Leave me. I must rest to regain my strength."

"He needs more than that," growled Inorus.

"You're not actually going to respect his wishes, are you?" asked Khonsu. "We searched to find him too long to just leave now."

"We'll try again later," shrugged Ilfanti. "Perhaps he will be more cooperative in the morning."

"Doubtful," sarcastically uttered Khonsu as she stepped out of the tent.

Inorus followed her, leaving Ilfanti and Osorkon behind with Ptahetep.

"They may have a point," Osorkon said. "We have come too far to let this stop us."

"We need rest," Ilfanti said. "If he still lives in the morning, we'll talk to him then. If he dies in his sleep, then we will just take the artifact he is guarding."

Ilfanti and Osorkon stepped out of the tent. Before they returned to the rest of the camp, Ilfanti heard a gasp from within. He peered back in, his eyes widening at the sight of a masked individual hovering over Ptahetep, and a dagger with a golden hilt shaped like an ankh with a serpent wrapped around it jutting from the nomad's chest.

The light of life was flickering, and Ptahetep was joining his brother in the ever-after.

CHAPTER 48

"What is this?" demanded Ilfanti as he rushed back into the tent.

The masked creature leapt out of the slit that it had created in the back, grabbing the dagger from Ptahetep's chest as it fled. Outside of the tent, Ilfanti heard Inorus and Khonsu shouting. They were in pursuit of the murderer.

Osorkon stepped inside the tent and glanced at the dying Ptahetep. "Guess we can take the box now, eh? Good thing we were still close enough for you to hear the murderer."

"There's not much time," said Ilfanti as he sat down and cross-legged before Ptahetep. "If he dies, his mind dies with him."

"What are you doing?" Osorkon asked.

"I am going to enter his mind and see if I can find out what actually happened when the Ptahhemat-Ty tribe reached Ramahatra," Ilfanti explained. "If Ptahetep dies before I can get out, though, I too shall die."

"It's not worth the risk, old friend," Osorkon said.

"I have to try," Ilfanti replied. "We have to see what we're really up against."

With the words out of his mouth, Ilfanti closed his eyes and began to concentrate. It had been a long time since he had used the Mage mental abilities—the rare and elusive gift of Mind Magic—but he felt that what he could learn from Ptahetep far outweighed the risk of the man dying before he could get out.

When Ilfanti opened his eyes again, he was no longer sitting in a tent, but instead was at another encampment with hundreds of nomads. Ilfanti saw himself as Ptahetep, or rather the way Ptahetep had been before he had escaped Ramahatra. It was a night, just like this one, and the nomads were alarmed. Something was happening.

"My Sheikh!" a man cried out as he sprinted toward the nomads.

"Bek!" the man next to Ptahetep shouted.

"Beware the witch!" It was the same warning that Ptahetep had given to Ilfanti. Ilfanti wondered how many people received this warning, and how many ended up like Ptahetep.

"Bek?" the man gasped.

Ilfanti watched as Bek began to convulse and scream in agony. The sand around him burst skyward and he began clawing at his skin as if something was crawling on him and he was desperate to get it off. There were small orange and black snake-like creature that swirled all over Bek's body like quicksilver. As Ilfanti watched, he knew that the creatures were devouring the flesh of Bek in seconds.

"What madness is this?"

Bek's body fell to the ground, only dried and crusted skeletal remains left behind. The creatures dropped back into the sand from which they had come, and Ilfanti watched as the sand moved with hundreds of tiny bulges until it settled down to its normal desert calmness.

"What madness is this?" the man repeated. "What just happened?"

Ptahetep stepped forward cautiously and jabbed the skeletal remains of Bek with his saber. The bones disintegrated with his touch. "The curse," he spat as he jumped back.

The man who looked like he was in command, who Ilfanti assumed was Ptahmose, turned away from Bek and returned to the encampment.

"Brother!" Ptahetep shouted as he raced to catch up with Ptahmose. "We must abandon this desire of yours to find Ramahatra. It will be our end!"

"Abandon?" Ptahmose laughed. He held up a triangular black onyx with golden markings around the edge and a single golden serpent in the middle. "Coward, Ramahatra has been found. Now, we take it!"

"Brother, don't be foolish," pleaded Ptahetep. "Remember the curse!"

"I will not see my men die in vain," growled Ptahmose angrily. "We will go to Ramahatra, learn its secrets, and then Bek and all of the others who perished to bring me this will be vindicated!"

Ptahetep watched Ptahmose walk away. Ptahmose began barking orders to prepare the expedition to Ramahatra. Ptahetep's head drooped: "We're doomed," he whispered.

Ilfanti frowned at the scene. If Ptahmose had listened to his brother, then they would all still be alive today. Perhaps he was acting like Ptahmose himself, stubbornly pushing forward when it could mean his own demise. He hoped that Osorkon and his family did not pay the ultimate price because he was too focused on his vision of how he could win the fight against Zoldex.

All around Ilfanti, everything suddenly got very dark. He raised his hand, but could not even see it in front of his eyes. Ptahetep was slipping away. Perhaps it was too late already.

The shroud of darkness lifted, and Ilfanti sighed a breath of relief. Ptahetep was at least taking another breath. Deciding to risk it, Ilfanti concentrated on Ramahatra, and he saw the images around him begin to swirl, speeding up. As Ilfanti watched Ptahmose walk up to the gates of Ramahatra, Ilfanti concentrated to slow back down to watch the events unfold properly.

Three of the mighty abuephas were driven up to the gates and made to batter them, moving back and hammering forward again, splintering the gates and leaving Ramahatra open. Ilfanti walked into the hidden city, amazed to see that people were actually living there.

The warriors of the Ptahhemat-Ty tribe charged into the city, which Ilfanti saw had a vast courtyard where the nomads were gathering. Ptahmose glared at the people of Ramahatra – a combination of elves, sabrenoh, and hybrids of the two – who were all garbed in loose silk garments, with golden jewelry and elaborate headpieces adorned with serpents.

The people of Ramahatra all glared at the newcomers. One of the elves stepped forward and screamed: "Get out!" Ilfanti shuddered at the face of the elf as it distorted into that of a hideous decaying skeletal beast. All of the residents began showing similar features, causing the nomads to shriek in fear and confusion. The ranks faltered and chaos ensued.

Ilfanti watched as the residents of Ramahatra killed hundreds of nomads. Then, at the end of the courtyard, before the stairs leading up to the temple, a black hole opened in space, and an elf, her skin as dark as the hole, emerged. The first thing Ilfanti could see was her eyes, which glowed with an eerie ghostlike blue-green hue. Her hair was also dark, and was woven into a braid that touched the ground behind her. She wore an elegant gown that wrapped around her like a shroud of darkness, and held a golden staff with a black stone adorned with gold at the head.

All of the combatants stopped and watched her. The elf looked out over the heads of the nomads and rested her eyes on Ptahmose. "You are the leader."

"I am," Ptahmose said.

"You are here to plunder my city," the elf accused.

"I am here to expand our wealth and power," Ptahmose said. "An alliance would serve those ends."

"Bold statement, from one whose forces have already been decimated," the elf said.

Ilfanti could not deny the words. The battle had not been going in Ptahmose's favor. The tide had quickly turned against them.

"I am Ptahmose, sheikh of the Ptahhemat-Ty tribe, largest and strongest of Egziard's nomadic tribes. An alliance with me would be most beneficial."

"Then I shall have you and yours serve me, as the largest and strongest of Ramahatra's defenders," the elf said.

"You do not understand," Ptahmose sneered.

"It is you who do not understand," the elf said. "But you shall."

Ilfanti watched as she lowered her staff to point at Ptahmose. Ptahmose began to scream in agony, his flesh becoming distorted and flowing from his bones as if it were little more than clay. It was over in an instant, from the moment he began screaming to the moment his flesh bubbled at his feet.

Ptahmose had been carrying two items before his death. In one hand he had his saber, and in the other, the mystical compass that led them to Ramahatra. As his skin slid from his body, so too did the two items. The compass hit the ground and rolled on the sand, landing at the feet of Ptahetep, who stared in disbelief at what was happening to his brother.

"Ptahmose?" Ptahetep gasped. "Brother?"

The skeletal remains of Ptahmose reached down and lifted the sword that had fallen while in the throes of agony. A yellow glow appeared in the eye sockets and mouth, and the skeleton of Ptahmose rammed one of the nomads through with his sword.

"No," Ptahetep cried. He reached down and picked up the compass that his brother had dropped. "Flee!"

The elf raised an open hand and began to close her fist. All around the courtyard, the nomads began to sink into the sand, their struggles to find freedom only hastening their descent into the ground.

The warriors that had already been slain began twitching and convulsing. Ilfanti watched as the battered bodies with lifeless eyes lifted themselves up, armed themselves, and began marching on their allies who were trapped in the sand. It was a slaughter that forced Ilfanti to turn his head away.

Ptahetep fled from Ramahatra, those who had not yet entered the city quickly retreating along with him. Bulges in the sand followed, and Ilfanti watched the snake-like creatures bursting from the ground and swirling over nomad after nomad, leaving only the skeletal remains behind.

Above them, the blue sky darkened, and caustic rain began pouring down. The rain struck the fleeing nomads and burned their skins. Ptahetep glanced up, the rain striking his head and making him cry out in agony. He lifted his tunic overhead to try to stop the rain, but it only burned through.

Most of the abuephas, camels, and horses were also burning, lying on the desert sand and dying. Ptahetep found some the rain had not yet reached, and he and a little over a dozen others managed to reach their steeds. They fled as quickly as they could, leaving the cries and screams of their people behind. The last thing Ilfanti saw was the faces of children watching in terror as the rain reached them, and they too began to burn.

Realizing that he had seen all that Ptahetep could show him, Ilfanti concentrated on breaking contact. The world around him grew dark again, but this time there was also a chill so cold that Ilfanti felt like he would never be warm again. For an instant, the world returned, and with a flutter of his eyes, Ilfanti was back in his own body, looking at the dying nomad.

Osorkon had two fingers on Ptahetep's throat. He glanced at Ilfanti and shook his head. "I think he waited to take his dying breath until after you got out."

"Then I am fortunate," Ilfanti said. "I was almost trapped."

Osorkon moved Ptahetep's hand away and opened the box. Inside was the compass that pointed the way to Ramahatra. "At least we know the way."

"After what I saw, we may not want to go," Ilfanti said, still stunned by the experience.

Osorkon took a deep breath and held it for a moment. After letting it out, he sighed. "So you know what they went through?"

"I do," Ilfanti said.

"It is horrible?"

"It is," confirmed Ilfanti.

"Then we'll know how not to proceed," Osorkon said. "No worries."

"If you saw what I saw, you wouldn't be saying that," Ilfanti said.

"Hey, this is us," Osorkon shrugged. "We'll get through it."

Ilfanti heard shouts and crying, and headed over to the opening of the tent. When he looked out, he was shocked to see the encampment in complete and utter chaos. Tents were on fire, people were running aimlessly, and in the midst of it all, Ilfanti spotted several individuals garbed like the murderer.

Inorus ran over to them and paused, a scimitar in each hand. "We must get out of here."

"What happened to the murderer?" Ilfanti asked.

"She escaped," Inorus said.

"She?" Osorkon asked.

"She looked like a sabrenoh, but not as big and strong," Inorus explained.

Ilfanti's eyes widened at the statement. Perhaps she was like the hybrid sabrenoh and elves he had seen when Ptahetep had first arrived at Ramahatra. They had been adorned with jewelry fashioned to look like serpents, and the hilt of the murderer's blade was that of a snake. She had to be from Ramahatra.

"Where is your sister?" Osorkon asked.

"Getting the camels," Inorus said. "There!"

Khonsu rode through the smoke of burning tents, the reins of three camels in her hands. She did not slow down as she passed her companions, having them rush to grab the camels and pull themselves up as she rode by.

Osorkon laughed joyously.

"What is it?" Ilfanti asked.

"The camels," Osorkon said. "They have been reprovisioned!"

The quartet rode away, leaving the carnage and confusion behind. They did not care which way they went, as long as they got away from the encampment. Now, not only were they searching for Ramahatra, but the denizens of Ramahatra might be searching for them.

CHAPTER 49

Aboard the *Passion*, Kabilian saw the glow of the flames in the distance. They had been searching the area for several days, and had been about to move on to the next spot that Kabilian had identified as a possible location for Ramahatra, when the fire made them stop to look. If there was fire, there might be a city.

"Captain, can you get us there?" Kabilian asked.

"Of course," Glynn replied with a chortle. He lowered his scepter and touched the orb on the bridge, and the Wind Soarer hummed to life and soared to the glowing lights in the distance. They reached the light in minutes, a journey that would have taken hours by camel, and saw an encampment below burning.

People were all about, running in chaos and confusion. A few were fighting, engaged in duels, but most were trying to escape or salvage items before they burned. Kabilian pondered briefly who the combatants were, but quickly lost interest. This was clearly not Ramahatra, so whatever they were fighting over, it was irrelevant to his search.

Taking a quill, he crossed off this location on the map, and glared at it angrily. He then tossed it aside and pulled another. He was beginning to run out of maps. Hopefully, this would be the true map to Ramahatra. If not, they were almost out of places to look.

"Let's try north," Kabilian said as he studied the map.

Glynn studied the orb and shook his head. "If north is the way we must go, then we will have to delay."

"Why?" asked Kabilian, glaring at the Captain scornfully.

"A sand storm is brewing," Glynn explained.

Kabilian glanced at Crick, who was still watching the battle below. He then nodded. "Bring us around the storm, then."

The Wind Soarer arched and began flying away. Kabilian spotted four camels riding north, leaving the encampment behind. "Good luck," he snickered. "Fools!"

❋ ❋ ❋ ❋ ❋

In the encampment of the Mokhtar tribe, Rhyne had lost himself in the chaos, enjoying the ability to kill randomly for a change. He had been so focused of late that he almost forgot how it felt to slaughter people merely for being in your way. A nomad charged him, screaming at him in a tongue that Rhyne did not comprehend. Perhaps the man was trying to avenge a mate, such as the pregnant woman lying lifeless at Rhyne's feet. Rhyne lifted three throwing blades and sent them at the nomad, halting his advance and prematurely ending his life.

Rhyne reached down and recovered his blades from the woman, then walked over to the man and pulled his blades from the lifeless body. He had been away from the Hidden Empire so long that his supply of weapons was beginning to run thin. He had to be more careful with how he used them. After all, he would need them when he finally confronted Kabilian.

In his peripheral vision, Rhyne glanced skyward and saw the familiar glow of a Wind Soarer. He tightened his hand into a fist as he watched it turn and soar away. Kabilian was here, he was close, but still too far out of reach. This chase would have to end soon. Rhyne was growing weary of it. It was time to confront Kabilian, and then return home to collect his reward.

CHAPTER 50

The quartet rode through the night, hoping to put as much distance as possible between themselves and those attacking the Mokhtar tribe. They all hoped that Sheikh Nankitar and his people would be all right. He had been kind and generous to them, even if they were not able to enjoy his hospitality for too long. On the open desert, life was harsh and survival was a daily challenge. To offer to share with strangers the supplies that would feed his own people was enough to show that Nankitar was a good man.

There had been more attackers than merely the murderess. The encampment had been chaotic, but they had seen several similarly-garbed attackers striking the other nomads. Ilfanti and Osorkon remained convinced that the attackers had something to do with Ramahatra. Either they were from there, or served the lost city in some capacity.

As the morning sun shone on the horizon, they slowed their camels and dismounted to give them a rest. Ilfanti strained to see in the distance. Even with the sun rising, the sky to the north remained dark. There was an ominous feel to the sight, and Ilfanti felt a cold shudder running down his back.

Osorkon reached into his pocket and produced the compass that he had taken from Ptahetep. "Shall we see what our direction is?" He held it out in his palm, and watched as the small arrow pointed north.

Ilfanti pulled his eyes from the darkness beyond them, and glanced down at the compass. "Figures," he grunted.

"What is wrong?" Khonsu asked as she peered over her father's shoulder.

"That's our direction," Ilfanti said. "Look in the distance. What is that?"

"A storm, maybe?" Inorus suggested.

"It blankets the sky," Osorkon said. "We should seek shelter and see what happens."

Ilfanti closed his eyes and took a deep breath, concentrating. One of the first lessons a Mage learned when they began exploring magical abilities was focus and concentration. A Mage had the ability to see beyond the limits of normal sight, and become aware of even minute shifts in patterns around them, such as the gentle blowing of the wind.

Ilfanti focused on the darkness before him, the distance between him and the darkness dwindling, as if he were soaring toward it faster than the fastest bird. As he reached the darkness, he saw hundreds of thousands of tiny insects flying toward him. Ilfanti maintained his focus, allowing the locusts to pass by him, and then saw what had stirred them—a sand storm!

The winds were blowing at hurricane velocities, lifting sand up for miles around, high into the sky, and flowing with tidal-wave force forward. The wall was nearly impassable, and Ilfanti doubted that much would survive if the sand struck them.

Ilfanti began slowly turning in a circle, searching for any sign of a haven that could safeguard them from the storm. To the west, he saw dozens of vessels that looked like boats—but not nearly as bulky—riding the sands as easily as a seafaring vessel would ride the waves. They were traveling away from the sand storm and would be of no help. To the south, he saw the remains of the Mokhtar tribe salvaging what they could from the night's ordeal. There was no sign of the attackers that Ilfanti could see without specifically looking for them and focusing on them. To the east, Ilfanti spotted some rocks and ridges. Nothing grand that would have caves for them to seek shelter in, but perhaps enough to help with the storm.

"We go east," Ilfanti said. "Quickly."

"What is it?" Osorkon asked.

"Sand storm," Ilfanti tersely replied. "Coming soon."

The four mounted their fatigued camels, and pushed east. The beasts were weary and needed rest, moving far more slowly than usual, but they did go onward. In the distance, the darkness was growing closer. By high noon, they could hear the fluttering of wings of the locusts fleeing the storm.

"We're not going to make it!" Osorkon shouted as the locusts bore down on them. The swarm was so thick that one could not even see. The grasshoppers felt like stones pelting the dwarves.

Ilfanti strained to see ahead, his head turning involuntarily as he was struck again and again by the bugs. The rocks were still at least an hour away; too far to make it with the locusts already upon them.

"Everyone together!" Ilfanti shouted, but the sound of the wings fluttering was so loud that he could hardly even hear himself speaking. He concentrated on his three companions, and thought the words instead. The message was sent directly into the minds of the trio, as if Ilfanti were speaking to them directly on a clear day.

Khonsu was too far away, but Ilfanti, Osorkon, and Inorus were all together. Ilfanti raised his arms, and from his fingertips a light gleamed through the darkness of the insects, flowing and forming a bubble around the three dwarves and their camels. The locusts struck the light with soft bangs, dying instantly as they met an irresistible barrier.

"Uncanny," Inorus said, watching hundreds of the locusts strike the mystical forcefield. "What of Khonsu?"

Ilfanti concentrated on Khonsu. She was trying to make her way back to them, but she could not find her bearings as the locusts continued to strike her. Her arm was before her eyes, and she was moving blindly. Her camel toppled over and Khonsu fell to the ground, hard.

"No!" Ilfanti shouted.

"What is it?" demanded Osorkon.

Ilfanti turned and looked at Inorus. "How fast can you run?"

"As fast as is needed," Inorus vowed.

Ilfanti swiped one arm to the side of the forcefield closest to Khonsu, and a small tunnel appeared, though nowhere near as strong as the bubble that the main group was in. "Run, I cannot hold it long!"

Inorus nodded and sprinted through the tunnel, his head ducked down because the tunnel was not large enough to run upright. The locusts struck all around him, but unlike the main bubble, not every one was stopped. Inorus gritted his teeth as several began pelting his body again. He would not be deterred.

He pushed himself, running faster than he ever had before in his life. His lungs felt like they were going to burst, but he forced his feet to keep going, moving faster and faster. More of the locusts were hitting him now. The shield that Ilfanti erected around the tunnel was beginning to fail. There was not much time left.

Inorus lost track of time. Had he run for seconds, or minutes? He was not certain. In the distance, he spotted Khonsu lying limply. She was unconscious. He slid down the last few feet, reaching her and checking her quickly for any kind of injury that would prevent him from moving her. She had welts on her face and hands, and he was certain under her sleeves as well, but she did not seem to have any broken bones or damage that would be life-threatening.

Lifting her and cradling her in his muscular arms, Inorus began heading back to his father, Ilfanti, and the protective bubble. Each step was agony as more and more of the locusts broke through the failing tunnel and struck him. Inorus growled in rage and began moving more quickly, defying the locusts to keep pelting him and his sister.

The shields flickered out completely, and the swarm hit them all at once. Inorus fell to his knees, straining just to remain upright. Then, the swarm stopped, and the way was clear again. Inorus's eyes had been struck so many times that he had the bodies and organs of the locusts blocking his sight. He did not need to see to walk straight though, and the swarm was no longer striking him, giving him an opening to move more quickly.

"You did it!"

The voice shocked him. Inorus had thought that he was still too far away from the bubble, but his father was taking Khonsu from his arms. Inorus wiped at his eyes, repulsed at the sight of what now covered his body. He felt as if he would never be clean again.

He glanced over at Ilfanti, and saw the dwarf with both arms up to keep the barrier erect. His hair was drenched and matted to his head, his forehead poured sweat, and his tunic was wet around his neck.

"Can you hold it?" Inorus asked, remembering the failing shield.

"I will," vowed Ilfanti. "The tunnel was more of a strain. Sorry about it weakening while you were out there."

"You did fine," Inorus said. "My sister has been recovered."

Ilfanti glanced over at Khonsu, who was being tended to by her father. Osorkon looked up and nodded—Khonsu was fine.

The locusts stopped hitting the barrier, suddenly leaving those within silent. The dwarves turned to look outward, and saw the sand storm raging before them. The sand struck like a fist, jolting the shield. Ilfanti tried his best to hold it, but the shield began rocking and blowing in the wind.

There was no rhyme or reason to the movement. The dwarves and surviving camels stumbled and fell, trying desperately to remain upright. It took all of Ilfanti's concentration to keep the bubble erect. The force was tremendous. Then, they struck something and lurched to a halt. The raging sand continued pounding on the barrier, but they were safe and no longer moving.

"That was interesting," Ilfanti groaned. "Is everyone alright?"

"Fine," Osorkon said. "We're both fine."

"As am I," Inorus said. "One of the camels has a broken leg."

Ilfanti and Osorkon shared a worried look. Even if they could mend the leg, the camel would most likely not be able to support the weight of a rider for quite some time. They would probably have to do the merciful thing and put it down.

Inorus shook his head. "I will tend to the camel," he said. "Hopefully it will still be able to carry provisions for us."

"We shall hope," Osorkon said. After wiping Khonsu's face clean, he walked over to Ilfanti and kneeled down. "How long do you think it will last?"

"I have no way of knowing," Ilfanti said.

"Are you sure you can keep this little mystical barrier up?" Osorkon asked, whispering so that Inorus would not overhear.

"As long as you keep giving me water, I should," shrugged Ilfanti. "I think."

"That last part is what worries me," Osorkon sighed.

"How is she?" Ilfanti asked.

"The two of you saved her," Osorkon said. "She'll be up and about soon. Thank you."

"You don't have to thank me," Ilfanti said. "I wish I could have found a way to help even more."

"Even you, oh mighty and powerful Council of Elders member, have your limits," reminded Osorkon.

"So I do," reluctantly agreed Ilfanti. "So I do."

"What do you want me to do?" asked Osorkon.

"Get some rest," suggested Ilfanti. "If I fall asleep, the shield will fade along with my consciousness. I'll need you up later to help keep me alert."

"I can do that," Osorkon agreed.

Ilfanti watched his friend put his head down and begin snoring within minutes, confident that no harm would come to him. Khonsu remained unconscious, but she was tossing and turning, which Ilfanti was somewhat appeased by, knowing that she was alive and would be well soon. Inorus tended to the injured camel, and then wiped himself down with a towel as much as he could. He tossed his tunic and cloak away, too dirty to even consider wearing further.

When Inorus was done, he too put his head down and went to sleep, leaving Ilfanti alone with his thoughts and the storm. Both seemed endless, and both troubled him a great deal.

CHAPTER 51

The minutes turned into hours, which turned into days. Ilfanti did not know how much longer he could keep the barrier up. The storm had not abated at all, and every muscle in the dwarf's body ached with the strain of keeping this single spell functional for so long. He prayed that the end was almost in sight.

Khonsu was up and about again, disgusted by the small wounds on her body, but otherwise not harmed. She had spent many hours with Ilfanti, asking him to tell tales of his Paladin years and helping to keep his mind occupied. Ilfanti was not positive whether she was just doing it for his benefit, but she seemed to absorb his every word, giggling at his oversold jokes, and smiling encouragingly.

If he had been three hundred years younger, then he probably would look at Khonsu's behavior as not-so-subtle flirtations. Now, she had to just be humoring him so that he would not fall asleep and allow the shield to fail. Their lives all depended on that.

Yet there was something in her eyes; something that told him that perhaps she was really interested in him. Ilfanti quickly buried the thought. He was an old dwarf seeing things in the eyes of the beautiful daughter of an old friend. He should not have such thoughts.

But Khonsu made it very difficult for him to not think about her. As he finished another story, and it was time for her to switch with Osorkon and get some rest, she stood up, brushed against Ilfanti, ever so slightly, and trailed her fingers slowly up his arm. Ilfanti smiled warmly as their eyes met, saw longing looking back at him, and wished her a good night's sleep. Khonsu sighed, as if disappointed, and went over to lie next to her brother and go to sleep.

Osorkon sat down and slapped Ilfanti on the back. "How are you holding up?"

"Let's just hope that this storm is almost over," croaked Ilfanti.

"I've never known a sand storm to last for so long," Osorkon said.

"It is not natural."

Ilfanti knew the implications of the statement. When he was in Pta-hetep's mind, he had seen the dark-skinned elf that the nomad was so scared of. Could she have somehow summoned the storm and unleashed it on Egziard like a wave of destruction?

"Khonsu has taken a fondness to you," Osorkon said, staring at his daughter.

Ilfanti was taken aback by the forwardness of the statement. "I...I hadn't noticed."

"Sure you did," Osorkon said. "I see the way you look at her, too."

"I will not act on any impulse I may have," Ilfanti promised.

Osorkon stared at the sand whirling beyond the barrier. The dust was so thick that he really could not see anything.

"What of your other children?" Ilfanti asked. "Sneferu may be-come the next King of Memtorren? Aren't you proud?"

"Sure, sure," Osorkon said, his eyes shifting to look at Inorus and make sure he was asleep.

"What is it?" Ilfanti asked.

"Nothing, just a family matter," Osorkon said.

"You can tell me," Ilfanti prompted.

"I must deal with this on my own," Osorkon said.

"You know I am always here to listen if you need me," offered Il-fanti.

Osorkon sighed. "I know. It's just, if this gets out, so much could happen. I do not wish to even put it into words."

"What could happen?" Ilfanti asked.

"Sneferu and Amessis would come to an end to start off with," Osorkon said. "Khonsu and I would also suddenly find that we were no longer welcome to build the pyramid for Pharaoh Werirenptah. Dedi would be ridiculed by her peers, and even Meketre would probably find himself struggling for opportunities."

"You left out Inorus," pointed out Ilfanti.

"Inorus would be banished," Osorkon said.

Ilfanti studied the sleeping dwarf. *Why would he ever be banished?* he wondered. Inorus certainly had not been inviting when Ilfanti first arrived, but he had merely been looking out for his father as any son would. Since leaving Talhalla, Ilfanti had been impressed with Inorus on more than one occasion. Not only was he strong and capable, but he also had a quick wit about him.

"If you do not wish to tell me, I understand, but I admit, I am curious as to what could possibly cause all that you just said," replied Ilfanti.

"Certain things in Egziard are forbidden," Osorkon said cryptically.

"Like being a free Mage?" asked Ilfanti, not certain he knew what Osorkon was trying to get at. If Inorus were a Mage, he would know it.

"Not like that," Osorkon said. "It has to do with certain, shall we say, preferences."

"What kind of preferences?" Ilfanti asked.

Osorkon sighed and then stared blankly at the sand again. "About thirty years ago, Inorus was the brother seeing Amessis. Dedi and I were so proud—our eldest son and the King's daughter! But Inorus did not seem interested.

"When the King invited us for a formal dinner in honor of their relationship, Inorus did not show up. The King was insulted and forbade Amessis to ever see Inorus again. Dedi was crushed. As for me, I was confused. I went to find Inorus to demand an explanation, and that was when I found him kissing another dwarf. A bearded dwarf, if you get my meaning."

"I do," Ilfanti said. "How did you handle it?"

"Not very well," Osorkon shrugged. "I was enraged. I hit my boy, thinking he needed to have some smarts beat into him. What he was doing was forbidden, but even worse, he was risking the scorn of the king! How he could ever hope to keep his secret was beyond me. So I told him that he was no longer a member of this family unless he began behaving like a proper son should."

"I'm sure that went over well," said Ilfanti.

"Real well," Osorkon sighed. "He left home for two decades before Dedi's begging made me go after him. I can't say that I condone his choices. I certainly don't understand them, but he is my boy. I have been struggling to accept it for almost thirty years now, and the day that his preferences become public knowledge, I will stand by his side and support him, even if that means losing everything I spent my life building."

"There are other places that may be more tolerant than Memtorren," Ilfanti said.

"Yes, and we shall relocate if we need to," Osorkon replied. "I have been trying to spread my money around. Every coin I make from Werirenptah has remained in Talhella with a group of gnomes that promise that they can take my money and double it in a year's time. A risk, perhaps, but the gnomes would not have a problem if Inorus's secret came out."

"Well, when his secret does become known, and undoubtedly it will, hopefully he, and all of you, will be judged by your actions, not by your personal preferences," Ilfanti said.

"Let us hope," Osorkon agreed. "Look, the wind has shifted."

Ilfanti followed Osorkon's gaze, and saw that he was right. The sand was now moving not in a southerly direction, but north. He hoped that this did not mean that they would be stuck here for several more days as the storm reversed direction. Staying, as it turned out, would not be a problem.

The bubble shifted and they began rolling as the wind reversed direction. Khonsu and Inorus were both awakened as they slid around and stumbled inside the protective shield.

"Try to brace yourselves!" Ilfanti shouted.

The storm raged again, dragging them along. Ilfanti realized that they would not be wedged to a stop anytime soon, and tried to alter the form of their shield. He thought of some kind of brace to hold everyone in place, both the dwarves and the camels, and then brought his creation to life, expanding his bubble inwards to grasp onto those inside.

Fastened securely to the edge of the bubble, they no longer slid and moved, but they were restrained as the bubble rolled end over end in the storm. Khonsu was laughing; Osorkon was looking pale, as if becoming sick; Inorus actually closed his eyes and went back to sleep.

Ilfanti did not know how long they were rolling around, but he could feel the storm dissipating around them. The rolling slowed to a gentle rocking, and then the bubble remained stationary, the light of the blazing sun baking down instead of the darkness of the sand.

"It's over," Ilfanti whispered, not wanting to jinx their good fortune. He closed his hands, and the bubble faded away, leaving the dwarves and camels on the now-calm sands. Ilfanti's eyes blurred almost instantly, and he allowed his fatigue to overwhelm him. They had survived the storm. He would face his next challenge whenever it was that he awoke. For now, all he could do was sleep.

ILFANTI'S LOG

Five days? I find that nearly impossible, improbable even, but who am I to argue with three dwarves telling me that it is so. I have been sleeping for five full days! I was starving when I awoke, but fortunately Inorus had done some hunting while I was asleep, and I had meat and, ugh, cooked locusts as my meal.

The sleep worked wonders. My body is still a little stiff, but I feel good. It is almost like I had not been straining to keep that spell going for so long. Not that I'll be forgetting that little act anytime soon. I wonder how the nomads handle storms like that? They have to have some secret. Nobody should be able to survive a sand storm that lasts days!

Osorkon showed me the compass to Ramahatra. It doesn't tell us how close we are, but it looks like we were blown closer to our destination. That's always a good thing. Moving when you weren't even trying!

We did lose a quarter of our provisions due to the storm. We figured after the storm we would go back for Khonsu's camel, but apparently the storm blew us far from where we had started, so there is no chance of recovering anything.

I wonder if the storm really was natural, or mystical in nature. The dark elf could have manipulated the winds and weather, though magic of that scale is unheard of. But Inorus's words still linger in the back of my mind: "Only you're forgetting that they already have the Orb of Prophecy. They'll probably know when we will get there before we will."

The dark elf could know we're coming. She might have sent the storm to dissuade us from trying to take the Orb. The creatures that murdered Ptahetep were the first wave, and when they failed to stop us, she took matters into her own hands. If that is true, and that is the power she wields, then that prospect is terrifying.

I guess we'll find out soon enough. No use worrying needlessly about something that cannot be changed. Whatever happens, we'll face it as we come to it.

CHAPTER 52

In large part due to Inorus's continued care, the injured camel had survived and was walking again, albeit more slowly and without carrying any supplies. However, Inorus was pleased that he was able to save the camel, and had been happier than Ilfanti had ever seen him.

They traveled for days through the desert, the sun beating down on them, and over every dune, there were miles and miles of sand as far as the eye could see. They only had two camels remaining that could carry them, so the dwarves split time between walking and riding, with short distances after the sun went down with two dwarves riding each camel.

As they approached yet another dune, on yet another day with the sun endlessly baking down on them, Ilfanti tensed and strained to hear. "Do my ears deceive me?"

Osorkon listened as well, shrugging. "You need water, my friend. The sun is making you hallucinate."

"No," Ilfanti said. "I hear water. A light trickling, but water. Can't you hear it?"

Khonsu's smile widened. "He is right! I hear it too!"

"As do I," Inorus agreed.

Osorkon glanced back and forth blankly at his children and friend, then took his index finger and rubbed his ear to try and clear it. He still heard nothing. "You're all hallucinating!"

"Come!" Khonsu said as she ran up the dune. As she reached the top, she giggled excitedly. On the other side, rather than the endless sea of sand as they had come to expect, she saw signs of vegetation, and further down, water flowing. "There is water!"

The other dwarves left their camels behind, running to see. The sight was beautiful to behold for the weary travelers.

"Water," gasped Osorkon. "You were right!"

"Inorus, let's get the camels. They could use a good drink," suggested Ilfanti.

Inorus and Ilfanti returned to the three camels, taking the reins and leading the camels over the dune. The camels saw the water and moved toward it quickly, dipping their heads beneath the surface and drinking. Osorkon and Khonsu were in the midst of the river, splashing water at each other.

"Ilfanti, Inorus, join us!" Osorkon shouted gleefully.

"Yes, join us," Khonsu said, her eyes fixed on Ilfanti.

Ilfanti took his satchel off and placed it on a large rock that was jutting from the ground. He removed his outer layers of clothing, shaking each several times to free it of the sand that managed to get everywhere, and then folded it and placed it with the satchel. In only his underdrawers, Ilfanti leapt into the water, landing between Osorkon and Khonsu, splashing both of them.

As he surfaced, he heard Khonsu laughing, a sound that was more pleasing than even the most elegant symphony. She lunged for him, grabbed him by the head, and pushed him back underwater. She did not hold him down long, allowing Ilfanti to reach the surface again.

Khonsu winked playfully. Ilfanti rounded his lips and a stream of water sprayed out at her. Osorkon and Inorus both began laughing as Khonsu began shouting for Ilfanti to stop.

The four dwarves played like children, as if they did not have a care in the world. Of course, as with most things, it was only a minor respite before the burden of the mission and their responsibilities would begin to weigh them down again.

Lying on the sand, his feet still dangling in the water, Ilfanti glanced at Osorkon. "What do you think this is?"

"The Sanjeez," Osorkon said. "It has to be."

"Then we are lost," Inorus sighed, frustrated by the prospect.

"Not necessarily," Ilfanti said. "We followed the compass, and it points a little further north, but upstream."

"If Ramahatra is near the river, then how come it remains a hidden city?" Khonsu asked.

"Good question," Ilfanti replied. "But I think we're close."

"You've thought that for days now, my friend," Osorkon teased.

Ilfanti shrugged. Finding the Sanjeez was unexpected, but it did weave its way through Egziard. Perhaps Ramahatra was simply further north than had currently been developed and settled.

As Ilfanti stared skyward, he saw a shadow cover him momentarily. The soft hum was a familiar one—a Wind Soarer! Ilfanti jumped up and studied the sky, spotting the avarian vessel flying north.

"Look," Ilfanti said excitedly. "A Wind Soarer!"

"Perhaps it is going to Ramahatra," Osorkon speculated.

"Let's follow it," Ilfanti suggested. He rushed to the rock with his clothing and put it back on. As he was sliding his feet into his boots, he was already hopping in the direction that the Wind Soarer had gone.

"Leave the camels for now," Osorkon said. "We'll be back for them and stay here for the night."

Inorus nodded his assent and ran after his father and Ilfanti. Khonsu was the last to leave, grabbing a pack from one of the camels and slinging it over her back. Just in case she wanted her tools with her.

The dwarves ran, moving with renewed vigor and vitality. They knew that they had no hope of catching a flying ship, but as long as they kept it in sight, they ran as quickly as they could, refusing to give up hope.

In the distance, the Wind Soarer slowed, and then began circling around. As the fastest in the group, Khonsu sprinted ahead of the others. She reached the top of a dune, and dropped to her knees, then crouched down and slid backwards slightly. She rolled over and held her hands up for the others to slow down.

"What is it?" Osorkon asked.

"Careful," Khonsu advised.

Ilfanti got down on his belly and slid forward, reaching the top of the dune, he looked out, and saw their destination before them. It was the same as in the memory he shared with Ptahetep—Ramahatra!

CHAPTER 53

Ramahatra was exactly as Ilfanti had seen it when he had viewed it through the mind of Ptahetep, but somehow even more massive and eerie. The city was undoubtedly made of the same stone as everything else in Egziard, but it was layered with shiny black obsidian.

The wall and gates of Ramahatra barred their path. From their angle, the dwarves could see somewhat over the wall and into the lost city. They spotted movement in the open courtyard and upon the walls. Numerous buildings that looked to be residences outlined the inner walls. Vast statues of immaculate design could be seen built into the bases of structures.

In the center of the city stood a temple, a small obsidian pyramid. A stairway led to an opening halfway up, a pair of obsidian statues of sabrenoh with serpents wrapped around one arm and a halberd in the other stood at each side of the doorway. The top of the temple, rather than being pointed like a pyramid, was a glass dome with a golden cobra wrapped around the base, with its head raised and overlooking the city, its fangs bared.

The Wind Soarer stopped circling and flew to the other side of the city, landing beyond the walls, nearly an hour's walk away from Ramahatra. Ilfanti gritted his teeth in frustration. Someone in the Wind Soarer might be after the same prize he was. If it became a race, then he might be forced to do something foolish that he normally would not even consider. He did not like the thought of getting this far only to meet a foolish demise.

"In Ptahetep's memory, the people of Ramahatra were somehow demonic, as if possessed. Even their features changed when they were in combat," Ilfanti explained. "We should avoid them if we can."

"Agreed," Osorkon said.

"The dark elf, the priestess, is the one that ended the nomads' advance, single-handedly. If you see her, try to hide. I am the only one that may stand a chance against her," Ilfanti said.

"Perhaps we will be able to avoid her too," Osorkon chimed in, hopeful.

"Doubtful," Ilfanti said. "I would think that the Orb of Prophecy is in the temple. The priestess will be there as well. We will encounter her before this is over. Just be prepared for anything. If I fall trying to stop her, I only ask that you bring the Orb to Zaman and ask Captain Augustus of the Soaring Mist to see it safely to Faylinn."

"None of that," Osorkon growled. "You'll be delivering the Orb yourself. We've shared many adventures, old friend. I have faith that we will succeed. Our tales don't end here."

"I pray that you are right," Ilfanti replied.

"What is our strategy?" Inorus asked, still studying the city.

"See the dome at the top of the temple?" Khonsu asked.

"Yes," Ilfanti acknowledged.

"That is my way in," Khonsu said.

"Wait, that's too dangerous," Ilfanti protested. "You'll be seen scaling the walls and temple."

"Aw, that's sweet," Khonsu grinned. She leaned over and kissed Ilfanti passionately. The kiss was a shock at first, but then embraced by both, as if finally finding water when parched for days. The moment became surreal, even the blowing sand beginning to slow as the dwarves continued their kiss. Then, Khonsu pulled away, grinning. "You do care."

Osorkon's mouth had dropped open, staring at his daughter and old friend, his eyes moving back and forth between the two. He tried to speak and protest, but the words eluded him, coming out only as a grunt and deep coughs.

Inorus did not seem to care, his attention still on the city below. "I will create a distraction for you," he offered. "They won't see you."

"I have no doubt," Khonsu said. She then stood up and began running down the dune, heading for the east wall that she planned on scaling. The pack she had taken from the back of the camel was slung over her shoulder.

"Um, she, um, will be fine," said Ilfanti, his eyes following Khonsu and his thoughts unusually clouded.

Osorkon was turning bright red, glaring at Ilfanti and then at the departing Khonsu. "My daughter?" he finally gasped.

"She kissed me," Ilfanti quickly retorted, holding his hands up innocently, though both could see the longing that Ilfanti had. He had enjoyed the kiss. He wanted more.

"Focus," Inorus said. "We have a mission to complete."

"We do," Ilfanti agreed. "My apologies. Osorkon, how do you think we should get in?"

Osorkon did not seem as willing to drop the subject, but he had been in enough dangerous situations to know that one did need to stay alert and focused. He would confront his old friend about his intentions when this was over. "There," Osorkon pointed. "See how the river flows by the western wall?"

"I do," Ilfanti said.

"Well, see the water inside Ramahatra?" Osorkon asked, pointing out numerous fountains. "My bet is that we'll find a way in by the river."

"Agreed," Ilfanti said. "Inorus, you said that you were creating a diversion? How do you plan on going?"

"I've always preferred the direct approach," Inorus replied with a grin.

"Boy, you heard Ilfanti. Avoid and evade the enemy," Osorkon barked.

"The three of you will do that," Inorus said. "I'll draw their attention so that you'll all succeed."

"My son will not be a martyr!" Osorkon protested.

Inorus stood up and drew his two scimitars. "You better hurry," he said. "The diversion will start soon."

"Inorus!" Osorkon cried. "Don't do this."

"Do not fear, father, I have no intentions of dying here. But I will create the opening that you need. Go." With this final word, Inorus turned and ran down the dune as Khonsu had done.

Ilfanti watched the headstrong dwarf dash for the main gate and sighed. Perhaps it was not he who would do something foolish, but those that he was with. There was no use saying anything else—they were committed to the plan. Ilfanti only hoped that somehow the four of them would manage to find the Orb and make it out safely again. Deep down, he doubted that that hope would become reality.

CHAPTER 54

Running to the eastern wall, Khonsu kept her eyes on the top to make certain that there were no prying eyes to spot her. She slid into the wall, and leaned back against it, glancing upwards. The wall was at least five times her height; not a problem for a dwarf who had been scaling walls and breaking into places she should not be since she became old enough to carry a pickaxe.

Khonsu slid her pack off her shoulder and untied the strings that fastened it. She looked inside and rummaged through the supplies, pulling out several items that would be ideal for this particular task. The pack contained most of the items that she used to use when breaking into tombs and searching for hidden artifacts. The rest of her supplies were lost to the desert, wherever her camel had been buried during the sandstorm. Fortunately, Osorkon had taught her the idea of always being prepared and ready for the worst. Her tools had been split up just in case some of them were lost.

She studied each item as she took it out of the pack. She had a pair of pickaxes, climbing claws, rope, hooks, a dagger, and a hand-held crossbow. She spread each out in front of her, and then tied the pack back up. She then took her sash off, flipped it over, revealing a harness with loops for her items, and then put it back on. Each of the pickaxes and hooks went into the loops; her dagger she slid into her boot; the rope she wound from her left shoulder down to her right hip; and the crossbow she hung over her right shoulder, first lifting the tail end and removing a dozen bolts which went into a small holder that fastened to her leg.

Khonsu checked her gear one last time, and was satisfied that she was ready. Picking up her final items, the climbing claws, she slid them onto her hands, the claws resting in her palms and fastened around the back. She then stood up and lifted her left arm up, digging the bladed claws into the obsidian.

The obsidian cracked slightly, small chips falling down and hitting Khonsu on the head. She was used to the dust and debris of older temples and tombs, but this would not be too much of an obstacle. Raising her right arm up slightly higher than her left, she dug those claws into the wall as well, using her grip to pull herself up.

If she had not lost her other pack, then she would also have claws for the bottom of her feet, making her ascent much easier. It would also be easier if she could just throw the rope up with a hook and try to latch on to something. However, the risk of discovery would be too great.

The surface of the wall was smooth, far smoother than most surfaces that she had encountered. When it had been constructed, the designer probably thought that it would be impossible to scale his wall. If so, he had not counted on the pride and determination of a dwarf.

Khonsu's ascent was slow, but she was making progress. Her arms could really feel the strain as she held on, unable to grip with her legs at all. She trained regularly, even if the tomb-raiding lifestyle was behind her—she just never could tell when her skills would be needed.

Khonsu reached the top and remained there, listening. If there was anyone near the eastern wall, she could not hear them. Deciding that it was worth the risk, Khonsu lifted herself up and glanced over the wall. There was nobody near her. Pulling herself over the wall, Khonsu dropped and knelt on the top, studying her surroundings.

The sun was beginning to go down, giving them the cover of darkness, at least for the next seven and a half to eight hours. Khonsu was confident that they would find the Orb of Prophecy and be gone before the morning sun shone on the horizon.

Without dallying, she found a stairwell down to the main grounds, and made her way to it. She would rather not be so out in the open, but she did not see anyone nearby, and her dwarven eyes saw just as clearly in the dark as daylight. As she reached the bottom, an elf stepped out of a small building and walked directly past her. Khonsu flattened against the wall, the tip of one hand brushing against the head of her pickaxe in case she needed it. The elf did not pause to look her way, and did not discover her.

Sighing with relief, Khonsu slid behind a large statue of some hideous two-headed beast, and searched the grounds for any other sign of life. Satisfied that there was none, she sprinted forth to the temple, reaching the lower blocks of the pyramid structure.

Khonsu climbed up the first level, and then paused to kneel and study her surroundings again. So far, things had been too easy. She hoped that fortune would continue to shine on her, but deep down, a lingering thought was screaming for her to be cautious. Over the past century, Khonsu had learned to trust that inner voice. This night would not remain as quiet as it was now.

❀ ❀ ❀ ❀ ❀

Ilfanti and Osorkon waded through the Sanjeez River, searching for some sign of an opening. They had found some bamboo and taken it with them, an act that had already saved them from discovery. Several times since walking past the walls of Ramahatra, they had come across individuals talking, guards patrolling, and in one instance, a guard snoring. The two dwarves quickly moved beneath the surface of the water when they heard anything, lifting the bamboo up to breathe.

Moving beyond the guards, Ilfanti stiffened, listening. A grin widened on his face as he turned and looked at Osorkon. "Hear that?" he whispered.

Osorkon nodded. The trickling water was flowing more quickly up ahead. The two followed the current and found a small grate in the wall of Ramahatra. Water was pouring down the grate like a miniature waterfall, going into some cavern beneath the city.

"This is our way in," Ilfanti said. He reached into his satchel and removed a dagger, beginning to slide the blade back and forth above the metal bars. The stone that the bar was built into was not as strong as the obsidian, and chiseled easily. Within minutes, Ilfanti and Osorkon had removed a pair of bars, making an opening large enough to squeeze through.

"After you," Osorkon offered.

Ilfanti slipped through the bars, dangling down from the top one. He could not see how deep the hole was, and concentrated on using his innate mystical abilities—his fingers began glowing as brightly as a star, and the entire cavern lit up. The drop was only about seven feet, certainly survivable.

Ilfanti dropped down and tried to land feet first, allowing the water to break his fall. The water was deeper than he expected, and Ilfanti was completely submerged, going deeper and deeper with each second. As his descent slowed, Ilfanti began kicking and made his way back to the surface, reaching the top and gasping for air. Even the stale, musty air of this cavern tasted and smelled wonderful to him at that moment.

"You all right?" Osorkon asked.

"Fine, just jump in. The water is pretty deep," Ilfanti said.

Osorkon squeezed through the bars and jumped forward, not quite having enough room to form a dive, and instead landing on his belly. When Osorkon returned to the surface, he screamed and cried out in pain.

"Stop whining," snickered Ilfanti. "I told you to jump, not try to dive."

"Where are we?" Osorkon asked.

Ilfanti illuminated his hand again, allowing both to see clearly. There were dozens of tunnels that spread out from this cavern, each bringing water to a different part of Ramahatra. Several passages could also be seen, if they chose to get out of the water.

"We can probably follow one of these passages straight into the temple," Ilfanti speculated.

"Fortune shines on us," agreed Osorkon. "Let us pray that it stays that way."

The two agreed on a particular tunnel, one that they felt would most likely head to the temple, and they swam through the water down the tunnel. Once they were in the tunnel, they were able to touch bottom again. Further ahead, the tunnel was illuminated by torchlight. They were on their way, and Osorkon seemed to be right; so far fortune was shining on them. Ilfanti only hoped that the same could be said for Khonsu and Inorus.

❖ ❖ ❖ ❖ ❖

Inorus boldly approached the front gate of Ramahatra. The gate was made of the same obsidian material as the rest of the wall, but was double layered here. He had tried to wait for about an hour before approaching, giving both groups time to try and get into position. Now, it was time for the direct approach, and the distraction.

Khonsu and Osorkon were good at subterfuge and misdirection. For as long as Inorus could remember, he had preferred a more physical way of dealing with things. He watched his father one time brushing away sand with a small brush, trying to uncover something below. Inorus would rather dig and if something was found, they could clean it afterwards.

Without pause, Inorus pounded the hilt of one of his scimitars on the obsidian gate three times. He waited, and then pounded again. Someone, he was certain, would answer his call.

A small window slid open in the gate. An elf glared at him through it. "Now who in Tanorus are you supposed to be?"

Inorus smiled deviously as he glared threateningly at the elf. "I am the distraction." Twirling his sword so that the pommel faced the elf, Inorus rammed it forward and struck the elf in the nose, breaking it instantly.

The elf stumbled backwards, the window remaining open so that Inorus could see inside. He stepped as close to it as he could and shouted for all to hear: "Servants and soldiers of Ramahatra, face me, Inorus, and face your death!"

Inorus did not have long to wait for a reply. He felt the vibration of the gate as it began to move, and he jumped back, twirling both scimitars and preparing for whatever might come. The gate opened and Inorus came face-to-face with dozens of elves and sabrenoh—all armed with scimitars, smaller swords, spears, and axes—and charging for him.

For most, the sight would be terrifying. Inorus' smile only broadened further.

CHAPTER 55

Khonsu heard the grinding of the gates as dozens of sabrenoh and elves turned the massive wheel that opened the mighty obsidian barrier. Pausing in her ascent, Khonsu watched as dozens of the people of Ramahatra gathered before the gate, waiting for the attack.

They probably expected an army to confront them, or at least a large force. Instead, they would fine only a lone dwarf. Khonsu watched as the gates opened enough for her to see her brother standing there, defying the odds, his scimitars twirling. With a feral war-cry, Inorus did not wait to be attacked, he charged headlong into Ramahatra, his blades moving as swiftly as if wielded by an elf, but with the strength and ferocity of a dwarf.

As she watched, Khonsu's admiration and respect for her brother grew. She had read the tales of old, of the dwarves who resisted their masters rather than endure the bonds of slavery. The tales told of warriors unlike any other, who would face down legions and charge forward with a spirit and vigor that was unmatched anywhere in the land.

The dwarves of Memtorren that they had grown up with were workers, miners, builders, and weapon smiths. They had not seen war in this land for many generations. There were still guards to defend the city, but they typically dealt more with thieves and beggars than with foreign aggression.

Inorus, though, looked every bit like the legends of old. His feet did not stop moving, even though, by all rights, elves and sabrenoh both should be swifter than he. He already was leaving a pile of bodies in his wake. His skill and proficiency were remarkable. His spirit and determination were inspiring.

Khonsu took her eyes from her brother, and returned to her task. She was about halfway up the eastern side of the temple. So far, she had not been spotted. The higher she went, the less likely it was that others would interfere with her. Not only were they busy with her brother, but someone would also have to really be looking for an intruder to see her, the way she was moving. After each level she climbed, she flattened on the stone precipice and paused before moving on.

The climb was slow, but steady. Khonsu wondered how her father and Ilfanti were faring. It had already taken her an hour to reach the point she was at. Perhaps they already had the prize that they were all seeking. If not, she thought, then the shroud of night would abandon them just in time for their attempt to escape in the morning.

❁ ❁ ❁ ❁ ❁

As Khonsu continued climbing the temple, her father and Ilfanti reached the end of the tunnel, with the water leading into a round pool lined in gold. The two dwarves cautiously emerged from the water, studying their surroundings.

There were large statues along the walls of the chamber, each designed with such precision that they looked like they could have been living and breathing individuals. Most were elves, but there were a couple of sabrenoh as well. Only a few faces appeared serene, the others were in various stages of fury or anguish.

"What do you make of them?" Osorkon asked as he approached one of the statues and rubbed his palm along the cheek of an elf. He then knocked on it with the back of his knuckles several times. "They look real."

"Perhaps they were," replied Ilfanti as he lifted a torch from the wall and brought it closer to one of the statues. The one he looked at was a female elf with a tattoo of an ankh with a serpent wrapped around it on her forehead. He was not sure what the symbol represented, but as he studied it, he felt that it had some significance.

He stepped over to another statue, this one a male sabrenoh, and raised the torch up to his forehead. He had an identical marking above his brow. "Curious," Ilfanti said.

"What is?" Osorkon asked.

"These markings on their heads. Do you know what they represent?"

Osorkon also took a torch from the wall and raised it to see that the elf he was looking at had the same markings. "I have never seen this marking before," Osorkon said. "The ankh typically is the symbol of life, but with the serpent wrapped around it, I am not certain."

"We should move on," Ilfanti said.

"Agreed," Osorkon replied, lowering the torch and following his friend.

Ilfanti led them through a doorway and down a narrow corridor. As they walked past, he tilted his torch to the wall and saw that the entire corridor, including the walls, floor, and ceiling, all had hieroglyphs. Ilfanti moved his finger from top to bottom to read one line. "It reads like the wisdom of the ages."

Osorkon read a line and nodded. "This is a recounting of the history of Egziard."

"I wonder if every passage we saw has corridors like this," speculated Ilfanti.

"Perhaps," Osorkon said.

"Then scholars could spend a lifetime here and still not learn everything," explained Ilfanti. "Even if this is all that Ramahatra has, it is rich beyond our imagination."

"Rich in words?" Osorkon dubiously asked.

"Rich in history," Ilfanti said. "The knowledge that comes from experience. This is priceless. I know quite a few Mages back home that would love the opportunity to spend a century here studying the markings."

"Not you?"

"No, not me," Ilfanti admitted. "I prefer the excitement of the discovery. Someone else can take the time to analyze and study it."

"That goes for me as well," Osorkon said. "Let's move on."

Ilfanti continued down the corridor, which opened into a vast chamber. Before stepping inside, Ilfanti lowered the torch and saw that there was a very narrow walkway, the rest of the room open to a deep pit.

"Careful," Ilfanti said. "Make sure you stay right behind me."

Ilfanti stepped onto the walkway, feeling a slight vibration as if it were not entirely stable. "On second thought, stay here until I get across."

"Good luck," Osorkon said.

Ilfanti took each step pensively; lowering his toe down to tap the rock walkway first, and then applying his weight. Sand and debris kept raining down every time he took a step, falling into the darkness below. He reached the other side, and peered into the next corridor to make certain that there was no danger before turning back to beckon Osorkon to follow him.

Osorkon began making his way across, and then stopped, halfway to Ilfanti. "What is that?"

"What is what?" Ilfanti asked.

"The floor, it is moving!" Osorkon shouted.

Ilfanti tossed his torch down into the depths of the room. It struck the ground where the two dwarves saw a swarm of small orange and black snake-like creatures. They varied in size, but most were tiny, like worms. They were swirling over the floor like quicksilver, soon burying and extinguishing the torch.

"Be very careful not to fall," Ilfanti cautioned.

"What are they?" gasped Osorkon as he took another step toward Ilfanti.

"I will tell you when you are here," Ilfanti promised.

"That bad?" gulped Osorkon. As he took his next step, he slipped on some of the sand on the bridge, and fell.

"Osorkon!" Ilfanti shouted.

Osorkon reached out with his hand, grabbing the walkway. He could feel the stone beginning to crumble under his grip. Below him, his torch had fallen, and soon that light was also extinguished.

"It is up to you, old friend," Osorkon said, straining to maintain his grasp. "Tell Dedi I love her." He could no longer maintain his grip, and felt his fingers slipping from the ledge. It had all happened so quickly. He had done so much in his life, and now it had come to an end. He always suspected that one of his foolhardy quests would be his end, but he never expected the end to come because he slipped on some sand. Foolish.

As soon as Osorkon had tripped, Ilfanti rushed back onto the walkway, lunging for his friend as his precarious grip faltered. As Osorkon began to fall into the midst of the creatures below, Ilfanti reached out and caught his friend's hand. The weight almost pulled Ilfanti from the bridge, but he managed to maintain his leverage and hold on.

"You're not done yet," wheezed Ilfanti, holding his friend tight. He tried to pull Osorkon, but every time he did so, he began to slide closer to the edge himself. There was no way to pull his friend up without risking both of their lives. That is, no way for someone who was not a Mage.

Ilfanti closed his eyes and concentrated on their surroundings. Everything became clear to him. He could see every inch of the room, from the highly ornate ceiling, to the bridge with him holding Osorkon, down to the creatures swirling below. He even saw small particles of sand floating in the air, moving slowly as if time had stopped existing all around them.

"Leave me, old friend," protested Osorkon. "I am too heavy."

"None of that," Ilfanti said, trying not to break his concentration. In his mind, he focused on Osorkon, and only on Osorkon.

Osorkon began floating, rising higher and higher. "Whoa! What is happening?" gasped the shocked dwarf.

Ilfanti did not respond, trying not to break his concentration. He kept his eyes closed, watching in his mind as his friend lifted up, floated over the bridge, and then landed safely upon it. He then opened his eyes and saw Osorkon checking himself, stunned by the fact that he was still alive.

"See, you can tell Dedi yourself," Ilfanti said.

"I owe you, old friend," Osorkon said. "My words will not give justice to what I am feeling. Thank you."

"Anytime," Ilfanti replied. "Let's get off of this thing before one of us falls again."

"Good idea," Osorkon agreed.

They made their way off of the walkway, hearing stone crumble behind them as they reached the other end. "We're not going back that way," grunted Ilfanti.

"Hopefully we will not need to," Osorkon said. He then went to take a step into the next corridor, when Ilfanti grabbed his shoulder. "What is it?"

"Careful," Ilfanti said. He pulled his dagger from his satchel and poked it on a tile in front of them. A trio of darts launched and struck the wall where Osorkon would have been standing. "Booby-trap."

"Great," sarcastically muttered Osorkon. "Now the fun really begins."

✸ ✸ ✸ ✸ ✸

Inorus crouched down, swiping his blades and striking the hamstrings of two foes, and then lunged forward, digging both blades into the chest of the largest sabrenoh that he was fighting. He somersaulted over his foe, pulling his blades with him, and then stood defensively as several elves and sabrenoh moved to attack him.

Ilfanti had warned him that these people were somehow possessed, or were demonic in nature. He had seen their other faces while they were in the throes of death. Their features were distorted, revealing a look that could only be considered demonic and evil. He was grateful that they did not always look that way, or else his fear might get the better of him.

Inorus was not afraid of elves, sabrenoh, or the hybrids of the two. He was not afraid of the vast number of foes he faced. He was not even afraid of the dark elf he had been warned about. He was confident in his own abilities, and if it was his time to die, then he would do so fighting, helping his father and sister accomplish their task.

What he did fear was the unknown of the afterlife. Spirits, ghosts, demons, and the agonizing fire pits of Tanorus terrified him. These creatures he was facing were not normal foes, but somehow creatures of the afterlife in the material world. To see them would be to acknowledge that his fears existed. To fight them was a torment he did not think that he could bear for long.

A sabrenoh lunged at Inorus, grabbing him and trying to drag him down. Inorus twirled his blades and rammed them into the creature's back, trying to pull away from its grip, which even in death seemed as strong as iron.

The other elves and sabrenoh began circling around. They knew he was partially trapped. They sensed that the battle was almost over. Inorus pulled his blades free of the dead sabrenoh and glared defiantly. If this were to be his end, he would face it with both bravery and honor.

As his foes began closing in on him, Inorus thought that perhaps the very pits of Tanorus were rising to claim him, and flames streamed out and everything around him was engulfed.

CHAPTER 56

The Co'iahla led Rhyne to the camels that Ilfanti's group had left behind at the river. They examined the supplies and packs, searching for signs of the dwarves' intentions. Rhyne watched them working with mild annoyance. They were wasting time. Kabilian was close, he could feel it.

"Ra-tuk, the dwarves you follow are lost," Saj'haal said.

"Lost?" Rhyne asked.

"They have traveled on foot to Ramahatra. There, they shall remain," Saj'haal replied.

"Why?" pressed Rhyne.

"I told you, Ra-tuk, Ramahatra has been corrupted by darkness. None that enter may survive."

Rhyne did not like the answers that he was getting. He needed to find Kabilian and have confirmation that the assassin would trouble Lady Salaman no more. He would not leave that up to some myth or fear that these Co'iahla had.

Deciding to leave his traveling companions, Rhyne followed the tracks that were left behind by the dwarves. A trio of Co'iahla rushed to block his path.

"Out of my way," growled Rhyne, his tone leaving little doubt that the words were an order.

"You must not go," Saj'haal said. "The elf of darkness will claim you."

"Who is this elf of darkness?" demanded Rhyne.

"She is the destroyer of dreams, the corrupter of innocence, and the collector of souls," Saj'haal said. "She was a visitor from far away, searching for the truths that were Ramahatra. In the beforetime, those seeking knowledge were welcome in Ramahatra. The elf of darkness preyed upon that, destroying all of the innocence and purity that Ramahatra had to offer.

"Only a few managed to flee Ramahatra and the clutches of the elf of darkness. Those of us that did, became the Co'iahla. It is our mission to keep others from ever going to Ramahatra and being destroyed as we were," Saj'haal said.

"You once told me that you were sworn to prevent the darkness from spreading," Rhyne said.

"That is so," Saj'haal replied. "As long as the elf of darkness and those that she touches live, we shall not allow any to go to Ramahatra again."

"But people have," said Rhyne.

"That is so," Saj'haal solemnly nodded. "None who have lived. The dwarves are lost. If you go, you too shall be lost."

"Who is this elf of darkness? Where did she come from?" Rhyne asked.

"Who she was and where she came from have been lost in the sands of time. Now, we know her only as the elf of darkness, the High Priestess, Nefrukakashta."

Rhyne had heard enough. He was not one to believe in superstition. This priestess must be a Mage, and as long as he had mists from the Gates of Tanorus, he did not fear the abilities of a Mage. "Out of my way," Rhyne said again, glaring at the Co'iahla in front of him.

One of the Co'iahla looked over at Saj'haal, whose eyes dropped in sorrow. "Let him pass."

The Co'iahla separated, allowing Rhyne to make his way up the dune and over the bluff, seeing Ramahatra in the distance. As soon as he saw it, his lips creased into a smile—his quest was almost at an end. Kabilian and Crick were standing just outside of the entrance.

Saj'haal walked up to the top of the dune—the rest of her faction of the Co'iahla joining her. She watched Rhyne rushing headlong into his fate. She sighed with resignation before addressing the others, "His fate is sealed, as are the fates of them all. If any of them manage to walk out alive, we must make certain that the evil of Ramahatra does not walk out with them."

CHAPTER 57

The golden serpent coiled around the top of the temple was remarkably smooth and hard to hold on to. Khonsu slipped her climbing claws back on and tried digging them into the golden-scaled statue. It was not as easy as the outer wall to Ramahatra, but she did manage to gain a grip and hoist herself up.

Khonsu placed her feet firmly on the golden coils, removed her climbing claws, and then studied the dome at the top of the temple. The material was shaded and dark, but it was smooth to the touch and felt like ordinary glass. She rubbed her fingers along the edges of one of the panes, searching for a weak spot where she could pry it loose—she would hate to announce her presence to anyone inside by shattering it— but she found no faults anywhere.

Khonsu paused, listening. Something had changed. She was not sure exactly what it was, but something was definitely different. Glancing around, she realized what it was—the clanging of blades had ceased! She looked down and saw Inorus standing, a sabrenoh lying dead at his feet, and dozens of his foes circling him, closing in on him.

"No," gasped Khonsu. She pulled her crossbow, ready to launch a bolt. As she took aim, she realized that she was too far and the bolt could not possibly hit what she was aiming for. Still, she had to try something!

A human and hobgoblin appeared at the gate. Khonsu had to rub her eyes to see if she was imagining things, because they had just materialized out of the air. They were both completely overdressed for Egziard. The hobgoblin was even wearing a full suit of armor! He must be frying in that, Khonsu thought.

The human reached into a satchel and pulled out a golden scepter with a ruby tip. Khonsu watched the pair curiously. She had seen Ilfanti with a satchel just like that. Perhaps these were allies of Ilfanti, Mages from his homeland. The human pointed the scepter at the foes surrounding Inorus, and a rapid succession of fireballs lanced from the ruby tip, igniting with such intensity that Khonsu had to turn away from the glare in the midst of the night.

She strained to see what was happening, hearing screams of pain and agony as the creatures below were consumed in flames. The human and hobgoblin entered the gates, acting as if the lives they just claimed were nothing more than a mere distraction.

Khonsu waited, hoping that the flames had spared Inorus, praying that her brother was all right. If these were allies of Ilfanti, as she hoped, then her brother would not be harmed. He would emerge from the flames unscathed. Khonsu bit her lip while she tensely waited to see if her brother was alive or dead. To her dismay, the human and hobgoblin walked past the fire, and Inorus did not emerge.

❋ ❋ ❋ ❋ ❋

Unaware of Inorus's plight, deep within the passages of the temple, Ilfanti and Osorkon cautiously continued advancing. They remained in the lower levels of the temple, beneath the ground, and traversed areas that looked untouched for millennia.

The walls were covered with cobwebs and dust so thick that they needed to brush away the top layers to see the hieroglyphs beneath. In one tunnel they went through they had to cut their way through spiderwebs so thick that they could actually hear the webs cracking as their daggers cut them down.

Throughout the passages torches were lit—regardless of how abandoned the area seemed. Even rooms that looked as if they had been undisturbed for over three thousand years had torches blazing on the walls. Osorkon found it somewhat eerie, but Ilfanti decided that the torches must have been magically lit and maintained.

Ilfanti strained to see ahead of them through the cobwebs. There was a door that spanned the entire width of the corridor that was not made out of stone, but gold. The two dwarves approached it, studying the markings on the door.

"What does it say?" asked Ilfanti.

Osorkon wiped some of the cobwebs and dust away, focusing on the writing on the door. "I'm a little fuzzy with some of the words, but if I am reading this right, it says something to the effect of: 'Herein lies the glory of our God.'

"The glory?" asked Ilfanti. "What does that mean?"

"You've got me," shrugged Osorkon. He studied the markings some more, and then reached out and touched a golden serpent that was curled in a circle, the tip of its tail in its mouth. As he touched it, the snake moved out of the door, and began revolving in a circle.

"What did you do?" Ilfanti shouted as he heard clanking and clanging within the wall.

"I just touched the snake!" Osorkon replied, tossing his arms in the air to feign innocence.

With a hiss of air, the door unlatched and slowly opened. The door was easily as thick as the dwarves were wide. Behind the door, the room slowly illuminated with bursts of flame that began by the door and extended into the chamber—which seemed to go on and on.

Ilfanti and Osorkon peered inside, their mouths dropping. For two dwarves who had spent years searching for buried treasure and lost artifacts, what rested before them would have served as the culmination of their lives' work. Piles of gold in all shapes and sizes—coins, mugs, plates, swords, shields, helms, armor, statues, and chariots—extended all the way to the ceiling. Chests of jewels and gemstones were open and sparkled in the torchlight. Everywhere they looked, as far as the eye could see, were mounds and mounds of treasure.

"I've died and gone to Wolhollm," gasped Osorkon. "Could even the great hall of immortality be so beautiful?"

"We're still alive," Ilfanti said. "I wonder if the Orb of Prophecy is in here?"

"Perhaps," Osorkon said. "We should explore this room and see."

Ilfanti glanced at his old friend, and saw a hunger on Osorkon's face that he had not seen in many years. Osorkon may have given up his old ways to reform and build better and more secure tombs, but his heart still yearned for the time when he could open a tomb up and find a treasure that had been lost to the ages.

The two entered the room, heading down a gold-plated walkway that stretched the length of the room. They glanced back and forth, scanning as much of the room as they could, but neither saw any sign of an item that could be a magical orb. It took them nearly half an hour just to walk the length of the room. At the end, the two paused before giant pillars with hieroglyphics, and a dais with dozens of statues before a throne with the largest statue in the entire chamber.

"What is it?" Ilfanti asked as Osorkon studied the writing on the pillars.

"According to this, our friend up there is some kind of serpent demon," Osorkon said. "If I'm reading this right, his name is Akeneh."

Ilfanti studied the statue sitting on the throne. It was not entirely human. It had the body of a man, but the head of a cobra. In the statue's right hand was an ankh. Ilfanti wondered if the tattoos on the statues' heads that they had seen earlier were related to this supposed serpent demon.

The other statues that stood before Akeneh were all elves, with various serpents wrapped around them. At the base of the dais, there were images of sabrenoh painted, bowing down to Akeneh.

"The elves look like guards," Ilfanti said. "The sabrenoh, servants?"

"Close," Osorkon said as he studied a second pillar. "According to this, Akeneh despised felidae above all else, considering them the minions of his greatest enemy. He enslaved the entire race so that they would be forced to do his bidding, increasing his power and diminishing his rivals'."

"So the sabrenoh were slaves," Ilfanti nodded. "What of the elves?"

"This is confusing," growled Osorkon. "This can't be right."

"What does it say?" Ilfanti asked as he studied the hieroglyphs. Unfortunately, the symbols had little meaning to him. The Mage's Council provided the best education in the world, but even they did not teach ancient Egziardian.

"The elves were the willing hosts of Akeneh's minions and children," Osorkon said. "What does it mean by 'hosts'?"

"Maybe the elves were possessed?" guessed Ilfanti. "Come on. Other than explaining why Ramahatra is full of elves and sabrenoh, this isn't helping us."

Osorkon could not seem to take his eyes off of the statue of Akeneh, as if the ancient image of the serpent demon were calling to him. As Ilfanti grabbed him by the shoulder and prompted him to go, Osorkon forced his gaze away. Some things were better left buried.

As they began to leave, neither dwarf noticed that the eyes of each of the statues had begun to glow. A presence that had lain dormant for many millennia had been disturbed and was awakening. Neither dwarf would know what had truly happened that night, but in the years to come, all of Egziard would suffer for the dwarves' violation of the tomb of Akeneh.

❁ ❁ ❁ ❁ ❁

Inorus could feel the heat of the flames; his body was perspiring and the sweat evaporating before it could even hit the sand. He struggled to free himself, twisting and pulling to get away from the deceased sabrenoh, but no matter how hard he tried, he could not free himself.

Swiping his blades out, Inorus brought them slicing in and struck the sabrenoh's arms. He repeated his efforts several times, doing his best to strike the arms in the same spot. Finally, the arms were severed and the body fell limply to the ground. Inorus tried to pry the hand off, but still could not remove it. At least even if he could not get the hands off, he was free to try and escape the flames.

He pivoted, turning in a circle, searching for the best place to try to escape the flames. He was certain that the pits of Tanorus were claiming him, but he would not go willingly. Through the flames, to his right, he could barely make out the wall of the city. If he could see through the flames, then he could get through the flames.

Inorus crouched down and braced himself. Being lower helped him breathe, without as much smoke filling his lungs. He then sprang for the opening, leaping through the fire. He reached the other side—his clothing ablaze—and rolled on the ground, trying to douse the flame.

He dropped his blades so that he would not risk cutting himself, and did his best to roll around close to them in case an enemy tried to strike.

After only a few seconds, he felt a chill that penetrated him to the core. His entire body seemed to slow, and he began shivering. His teeth were chattering as he tried to see what was happening.

A human with long auburn hair, a brown brigandine, gloves, and pants, with a sea-blue shirt and black boots was crouched in front of him. "Sorry about the ice. Blizzard doesn't really give me degrees of effectiveness." As he said it, he tapped a silver scepter with a diamond at the tip in his other hand.

"W-w-w-who a-r-r-re y-y-y-ou?" Inorus stammered through chattering teeth. He had lived in the desert and in the heat of Egziard his entire life. He saw the thin layer of ice covering his body. It was a cold more intense than anything he had ever experienced.

"Kabilian is the name," Kabilian replied, practically singing his introduction. "You're not one of the residents of this place, I take it?"

"N-n-no," Inorus said.

"In that case..." Kabilian reached into his pouch and withdrew a small vial with a sparkling whitish-orange liquid. He pulled the cork off of the top and lowered it to Inorus's lips, pouring some of the potion into his mouth.

Inorus tried to resist, but he could hardly move. The potion flowed into him, and there was nothing he could do to stop it.

"Drink," Kabilian ordered. "This will help."

Inorus stopped shaking. His teeth slowly began to stop chattering. The coldness was leaving him. "What was that?"

"The potion of Warmth," Kabilian said. "It will keep your body warm even in the harshest sub-arctic temperatures. It certainly is effective enough to warm you up from the effects of Blizzard."

Inorus raised his arm and saw that the ice had already turned to water and was dripping off of him. He was still wet, but he no longer felt cold at all. He was not certain who Kabilian and his armored hobgoblin companion were, but they had just saved his life. First by killing his foes, then by dousing the flames that were on him, and finally by warming him back up from the frostbite and ice that layered his skin.

"I am Inorus," Inorus said. "You have my gratitude for your assistance." After the pleasantry, Inorus bent down and recovered his scimitars, keeping his eyes on Kabilian to make certain that the human would not do something unexpected.

"So this is Ramahatra?" Kabilian asked.

"It is," confirmed Inorus.

"Kabilian," Crick called, pointing at more elves and sabrenoh emerging from buildings.

Kabilian dropped his silver scepter into his satchel, and lifted a pair of jewel-hilted daggers from his belt. With a wry grin, he glanced at Inorus and said, "Is this a private party, or can anyone join in?"

"Let's do it," Inorus growled as he raised both blades and charged headlong at the new foes. His new companions were in step alongside him. Now, there were three.

CHAPTER 58

Before Inorus leapt from the flames, Khonsu had already averted her eyes, fearing that she had lost her brother. The moment was overwhelming, the feelings of remorse and loss brewing within her. Her fingers tightened their grip around her pickaxe so tightly that they became white as circulation was cut off.

In that moment of anger and frustration, Khonsu slammed the blade of her axe down on the glass. The glass spidered, but did not shatter. Khonsu struck it a second time, and then a third. Finally, the pane shattered and fell into the temple, striking the ground of the temple and shattering.

Khonsu looked inside, and saw an obsidian dais with a single object resting in the center of the temple—an orb that glowed and radiated an aura of light. The rest of the temple was enshrouded in darkness, even more so than the night that Khonsu had become accustomed to. As a dwarf, her eyes would usually adjust and she would be able to see, but she found herself straining to adjust to the darkness inside, as if it were more than shadows, but actually devoid of light at all. Only the orb could shine in such an environment.

Removing the rope from her shoulder, Khonsu unfurled it and tossed one end into the temple, securing the other around the neck of the golden cobra. She grabbed hold of the rope and leapt into the temple, falling through the air down to the waiting orb. As she neared it, she tightened her grip and slowed her descent. She then gently lowered herself down further, taking her right hand from the rope and reaching for the orb. If she could reach it, she could climb right back up the line and be out of the temple with none the wiser.

Her fingers brushed against the orb, and as soon as they did so, torches all around the chamber burst to life, igniting on their own.

Khonsu jerked her head back and forth, studying the room and trying to determine what had happened. The walls had giant obsidian statues of creatures with the heads of snakes holding staffs with an axe head on both ends. Along the walls, she saw the remains of bodies. They were mostly skeletons, but some still looked as if they were dried-up flesh. The sight sent a shiver down Khonsu's spine.

Deciding not to dally, Khonsu reached for the orb again, only to find that this time she could not touch it. Some kind of barrier had been erected around it, preventing her from reaching her goal.

"Foolish mortal," a voice said with a laugh that made every hair on Khonsu's body stand on end. "I have been expecting you, Khonsu."

Khonsu searched for the speaker, a woman by the sound of it, but she saw no one else in the room. "Show yourself," Khonsu challenged as she dropped from the rope and landed on her feet. She pulled her two pickaxes and stood in a defensive posture, pivoting around to see if she could find her opponent.

"Those will not help you, Khonsu," the voice said.

"You know me, who are you?" Khonsu demanded, her tone unwavering.

A wave of black light cascaded over the room. Energy cracked and sizzled. A black orb bubbled from the ground, and then dripped away, leaving a lone figure in its wake. It was an elf with skin and hair that were as black as the darkness Khonsu had first peered into here. She wore a gown that clung to her body, of a dark purple and black fabric. Golden serpents coiled around her arms, with ruby eyes that moved as if they were alive. In her black fingers, she held a gold staff with a black stone at the tip that was encased in gold.

Her face was gentle, almost angelic, with smooth features, and a prettiness that was almost siren-like. Her eyes were glowing, almost as bright as the Orb of Prophecy, with a blue-green hue. She grinned deviously, and in that instant, Khonsu could see that this dark elf was not pretty and angelic, but as evil as a creature could be.

"What are you?" growled Khonsu, not really expecting an answer.

"I am your death," the elf of darkness replied. "As the orb prophesied, so it shall be!"

Khonsu gulped at the comment. If the orb had already foreseen her demise, then would it not be so? She watched as the elf lowered the staff in her direction, unleashing a beam of pure darkness that struck her with an intensity so powerful it hurled her backwards and into one of the pillars many feet away.

Khonsu slumped to the ground, hearing the sinister cackle of her foe. If she were to survive this, she had to fight magic with magic. She needed Ilfanti!

The elf would not give her the time to wait for her champion. With a swiftness that defied the senses, suddenly the elf was behind Khonsu, lifting her up by the throat, and hurling her back across the room again. Khonsu was completely disoriented, not knowing how the elf could have sneaked up on her so easily.

As she strained to lift herself up from the ground, she felt herself suddenly becoming very light and was lifted all the way to the ceiling of the temple, rushing faster and faster. She struck the top and felt herself bruise with the impact. Then, with the pain threatening to overcome her, she felt herself falling, just as quickly, to what would certainly be her death. Khonsu's eyes blurred as the air rushed past her head—she never felt the final blow.

❂ ❂ ❂ ❂ ❂

After wandering the lower depths of the temple for what seemed like an eternity, the anxious Ilfanti finally spotted a stone stairwell that ascended to the next level. The two dwarves walked over to it and began studying the stairs for any sign of booby-traps. A few stone steps were brittle and crumbling, but there was nothing else that would hinder their progress.

As they were climbing the stairs, both dwarves paused and flattened against the wall, hearing shouts and screaming. Osorkon paled as he listened, and then gasped, "Khonsu."

The two ran up the rest of the stairs, but the top was blocked, preventing them from entering the next level. Beyond the barrier, they could both hear Khonsu moaning as if in pain.

"There's no time for subtlety!" shouted Osorkon.

Ilfanti had to agree. He raised his hands at the pile of bricks and stone that barred their path and sent a wave of pulsating power through his fingertips and into the obstacle. With a brilliant explosion and scattering of dust, the two dwarves emerged and found themselves in the main hall of the temple.

The dark elf that Ilfanti had seen when he joined minds with Ptahemet stood before them—her arms raised as if casting a spell; a sinister grin on her face. Ilfanti looked up, knowing what he would see, and felt his heart skip a beat as the elf lowered her arms and Khonsu fell from the ceiling, plummeting to what would be her certain death.

Ilfanti raised his arms, using the magic built up within him, trying to slow Khonsu's descent and ease her landing. The strain was much more intense than he would have guessed, the power of the priestess countering his own. Ilfanti refused to succumb to her powers, asserting his own will and trying to save Khonsu. As she slowed down and gently reached the ground, as light as a feather, Ilfanti sighed with relief.

Glancing at where the priestess was, Ilfanti's glee quickly abandoned him when he saw that she had vanished. "Osorkon, watch yourself."

Osorkon did not heed the warning. His daughter was lying still on the floor, and he could only think of one thing—was Khonsu all right? He was a father; he needed to protect his baby.

A black mist swirled in front of Osorkon, halting his advance. The glowing blue-green eyes of the dark elf glared hungrily at him. She jabbed with her hand, her palm stretched open, clutching Osorkon's chest. The dwarf was taken completely by surprise, and then, for some reason, he found that no matter how hard he tried, he could not move.

"Osorkon!" Ilfanti shouted.

The dark elf began licking her lips, her mouth opening as if in ecstasy as she held onto Osorkon. From her hand, a cloud of smoke began rising. Osorkon tried to scream in agony, his blood beginning to boil within his body, but no sound could escape his lips. His eyes and mouth began emitting smoke as his body burned from within.

Ilfanti ran to help his friend—his hand balling into a fist, creating a projectile of pure magical force. Ilfanti reared back and threw the ball, sending a globe of red energy at the dark elf. The elf raised her staff with a sidelong swipe and deflected the ball, sending it wildly at one of the walls and causing an explosion that opened part of the temple to the outside.

The dark elf glared at Ilfanti, then grinned tauntingly. "Come, Mage, and see how helpless you are."

Ilfanti was not just a Mage. He was a member of the Council of Elders, the leaders of the entire Mage's Council. Of all those in their order, there were perhaps only two that could rival him for pure prowess and magical acuity: Pierce, the leader of the Council, and Kyria, a child who defied reason with the amount of power at her disposal. Out of thousands of Mages, he was one of the three most powerful. He was not just a Mage, and this priestess would soon learn that.

"Let's see, shall we?" Stepping forward, Ilfanti thrust his arms toward the dark elf and Osorkon, and sent hurricane-force winds at the two. Osorkon was swept away, tumbling over until he struck a pillar. The dark elf stood her ground, her smile only broadening.

❁ ❁ ❁ ❁ ❁

The sabrenoh and elves were not fighting with passion. As Inorus, Kabilian, and Crick killed their foes, they all found their adversaries to be somewhat lackadaisical. They fought as if they had to, but not as if they wanted to, or as if they even knew how.

For Kabilian, the confrontation was almost laughable. He may not normally engage in fights of this magnitude, preferring instead the gentle subterfuge that comes from sneaking up on a foe, but he had been in enough encounters to master his own abilities, and fighting foes such as these somehow diminished him. However, these elves and sabrenoh dared to stand in the way of obtaining the Orb of Prophecy, so he had little regret for striking down so many.

Crick was more cumbersome than Kabilian, larger and bulkier, and far slower with his attacks, especially with the armor that he wore. However, he too was beginning to leave a pile of bodies around him, and if not for the desert heat, would not have even been working up a sweat.

Inorus viewed the battle somewhat differently. Unlike his newfound allies, he had not led a life of combat and swordplay. He found a gift for it, but not because he had gained decades of skill and experience. He took his time with his strikes, making certain that he hit his mark. Whereas, he noted, Kabilian seemed to be able to dance around his foes, striking fluidly and always hitting his mark, even when he did not appear to be paying attention. Inorus decided that he could learn a lot from a swordsman like Kabilian.

Inorus also knew that regardless of skill, the sheer quantity of adversaries could find a way to overcome you. That was what had happened before Kabilian and Crick had arrived. He had been doing well, but one sabrenoh had given his life to nearly claim victory for his kinsmen. As Inorus struck another elf down, he wondered if the sabrenoh even knew what he had been doing. Every now and then, Inorus would see the faces of their foes contort into some demonic image, but otherwise, their eyes were lifeless.

"We must find a way through!" Inorus shouted.

Kabilian glanced at the temple, and realized that they were no closer to reaching the stairs than they had been when they first began this battle. If nothing else, the mob of elves and sabrenoh were delaying them. Kabilian grinned as he came up with an idea. "Crick, cover me."

Crick stepped in front of Kabilian, twirling his twin mystral drantanas, and struck down any foe that came close to his companion. Kabilian threw his two swords into the ground so that the hilts were sticking up and waiting for him to retrieve them, and then reached into his satchel. He pulled his hand out with three different items, a piece of hair, a tooth, and a claw.

Kabilian held the hair in his open palm and whispered an incantation. Before his eyes, the hair transformed into one of the most vicious and uncontrollable creatures in the Seven Kingdoms—a lupan. The beast stood fourteen feet tall, and was completely white-furred with a white mane trailing from its head. Its fangs and claws were almost as large as Kabilian's entire hand. It growled with such primal ferocity that every combatant paused to look at the creature now in their midst.

"Destroy them," Kabilian ordered.

The lupan, standing erect, stepped forward, clutched the nearest sabrenoh with its massive hand, lifted him into the air, grabbed both the sabrenoh's arms and legs, and began pulling until it ripped the felidae creature in half. If the elves and sabrenoh had shown no life before, they did now, withdrawing as quickly as they could from the ferocious beast.

Kabilian watched as the lupan chased its prey—each step for the beast matched three of those fleeing from it—grabbing elves and sabrenoh, clawing them, squeezing them, biting them, and battering them aside with its tail. The creature was unstoppable, but Kabilian was not yet satisfied.

He lifted the claw he had taken from his pouch, dropped it on the ground before him, and whispered another incantation. Just as the lupan hair had, the claw began to spin and crack, and a koxlen sprang from the claw, growing in instants to its full size of eight feet. Like the lupan, the koxlen was one of the most ferocious beasts in the Seven Kingdoms. It was more cat-like, standing on all four razor-sharp clawed paws, with a massive lion-like frame, and two pairs of terrifying teeth jutting up and down from its mouth.

In Kabilian's homeland, to come across either a lupan or a koxlen would almost certainly be a fatal encounter. Even the bravest and most cunning hunters of Dartie had found that these two beasts were to be respected and avoided whenever possible. The elves and sabrenoh of Ramahatra were quickly going to learn that as well.

"Attack," Kabilian instructed the koxlen.

With a leap, the koxlen landed on the back of a sabrenoh, digging its claws into his back, and then leaving a bleeding and dying warrior on the ground as it sought its next prey.

Kabilian grinned at the chaos and devastation his beasts were causing. He glanced at the last item in his hand, the tooth of a dragon, and decided to return it to his satchel. He had recently lost a tooth of a dragon—his beautiful forty-foot silver dragon—at the lair of the Hidden Empire. The lair had been burning to the ground around him, and the foes he was facing were quite skilled and had mystical weapons to augment their already formidable abilities. Rather than risk his own demise, Kabilian had summoned his dragon and used the distraction to flee. He had hoped that he could claim some of the mystical weapons after the fire had died down, but the heroes had bested his dragon and escaped. Worthy adversaries that he looked forward to fighting again one day.

Rather than risk losing his last dragon's tooth, Kabilian dropped it back into his satchel. He would save summoning the dragon for a time when he really needed it. His lupan and koxlen were more than capable of creating the diversion he wanted. The dragon would be overkill.

An explosion shook the ground, and Kabilian turned to see a gaping hole in the pyramid of the temple. Dust and debris were raining down on the courtyard; the obsidian that had been there was completely incinerated.

"They need me!" Inorus shouted, running for the temple. Several elves and sabrenoh attempted to thwart his advance, grabbing onto his back and trying to drag him down. Inorus would not be swayed. He took step after step, forcing his way forward until he reached the double doors leading into the temple. With a push, the doors slowly swung open and he made his way inside, a trio of foes still clinging to his back.

Inorus was horrified at what he saw. His sister was lying upon the ground, unmoving. His father was clutching his chest, smoke flowing from his eyes and mouth. Ilfanti and a dark elf were facing each other, magnificent colors swirling about them as they dueled with magic.

Forcing his shoulder down, Inorus swung two of his three foes over his shoulder. He dug both blades down into their stomachs, and then brought his blades back and slashed them across the shoulders of his last foe—who was still desperately clinging to him. As the final elf slid lifelessly from him, Inorus twirled his blades and made his way toward his family, desperate to help them.

Kabilian—who had reclaimed his two swords—and Crick stepped into the doorway of the temple. His eyes immediately found the Orb of Prophecy resting upon a dais in the center of the chamber. He licked his lips with anticipation—soon, his future would be clear to him, and then, he would know what it was that he and Crick were supposed to do in the battle with Zoldex. If their roles were truly predetermined, the orb would reveal that to him.

As he took a step toward it, he could not help but see the dark elf fighting Ilfanti in his peripheral vision. The sight made his blood nearly freeze. "The rumors are true," he gasped. "A dalvor!"

CHAPTER 59

Rhyne reached the gate to Ramahatra and peered inside. The fire that Kabilian had started was still blazing. He lifted a trio of throwing blades in each hand, and cautiously made his way around the flames. If Kabilian were upon the other side, Rhyne would end this quickly.

As he circled the fire, he saw no sign of Kabilian, only elf and sabrenoh bodies. They were scattered everywhere. Most had sword wounds, but some, Rhyne saw, looked as if they had been ripped apart.

A growl startled him. Rhyne recognized the sound of a lupan, but had been unaware that any existed in Egziard. He searched for the source and spotted a koxlen leaping onto a pair of sabrenoh, dragging them to the ground and biting them. Further into the courtyard, the unmistakable form of a lupan grabbed an elf by the head, lifted him from the ground, and then threw him at others as they fled.

Rhyne was glad that the beasts were chasing the elves and sabrenoh further into Ramahatra, leaving a clear path for him to reach the temple. Rhyne saw Kabilian and Crick stepping inside the temple's doorway. He would have them soon. They would not escape him this time.

An elf jumped out at him, and Rhyne tossed a trio of blades, striking the elf in the chest. The elf staggered for a moment, and then dropped to his knees. Rhyne saw the face of the elf contort and look almost demonic before falling headfirst into the sand. Perhaps Saj'haal had been right about curses and warnings about entering Ramahatra.

Rhyne decided that he would remain only as long as he needed to to kill Kabilian. Once the assassin was dead, he would leave this place and never look back. No curse would be his undoing.

❀ ❀ ❀ ❀ ❀

Saj'haal and the rest of her sect of the Co'iahla watched as Rhyne made his way to the temple and entered it. The elves and sabrenoh of Ramahatra were running rampant, though silently, trying to escape from the pursuing beasts.

Before long, Saj'haal's group was joined by another, and then another. The Co'iahla from all over Egziard had returned to Ramahatra, as if summoned for some grand purpose. A virtual army waited upon the dunes watching the city below. They could all feel it—this night was bringing about changes. They all had to be there to experience it for themselves.

"They are doomed," Saj'haal said as Rhyne vanished within the temple.

"Only the sands of time shall determine that," Ra'veez—one of the oldest and most prominent members of the Co'iahla—said. His eyes remained on Ramahatra, searching for the reason that they were all summoned there. After centuries of hopelessness, Ra'veez suddenly felt hope welling up inside of him once more.

The mood was contagious. The Co'iahla watched silently, but even skeptical Saj'haal had to admit: none had ever survived this long within the confines of Ramahatra since Nefrukakashta had arrived. Perhaps this group would finally succeed where so many others had failed. If not, then she vowed that she would kill them personally for their failure. None would leave Ramahatra alive, unless they manage to lift the curse that had condemned the once-prosperous city.

CHAPTER 60

A dalvor? Ilfanti studied his opponent and wondered how he could not have seen it before. It was shortly before his first century of being a Paladin had past, when he was exploring caverns in northern Falestia, that he had first heard the name 'dalvor.'

He had put together an expedition to look for the lost lair of a pair of the most renowned dragon and mystral warriors. They had been lost well before the end of the Age of the Dragon, and legend had them in the Falestian Mountains fighting invaders from Darnak. The invasion was halted, but the saviors were also lost. Ilfanti had thought for certain that he had uncovered information about their final resting place.

While exploring, members of his expedition began to abandon him, terrified of the "dark ones," the dalvor. He remembered never hearing of them before, but tried to learn as much as he could. Allegedly, the dalvor were dark elves that lived beneath the surface and were considered by those on the surface to be inherently evil. Beyond that, if he accepted that to be factual, there was very little that he could determine. There was no reference to the dalvor in any text in the Mage's library, and even those in the expedition all had varying stories. Ilfanti forgot about the dalvor, assuming that they were little more than myth.

Until today. The elf before him certainly fit the description. She was as dark as night, and he could somehow feel that she was evil. He tried desperately to remember the stories that the expedition team had told him—dalvor came and stole children that did not listen to their parents in the night; dalvor were from a time before Mages; dalvor were so evil that brothers would plot against each other to rise in stature; and his particular favorite: dalvor will turn to stone in sunlight! How laughable. Would any of that would help him win this encounter?

Since some of the stories indicated that the dalvor only come out at night, live in the darkness, and possibly could turn to stone in daylight, Ilfanti decided that light might be his best weapon against the priestess. She seemed able to counter all of his attacks, shielding herself from them, redirecting them, or somehow absorbing them with her staff. How could she defend against light, though?

Raising his hands, palms out, Ilfanti emitted several bursts of high-intensity, short-duration pulses of pure light. Even with his eyes closed and expecting the bursts, he could see spots in his eyes after doing it. That was nothing compared to the reaction for the dalvor! She screamed, as if in agony, lifting her arms to try and cover her eyes, and now, after the lightshow ended, was stumbling, her eyes staring blankly.

"Very clever, Mage," the priestess growled. "You may have blinded me, but still do not have what it takes to defeat me."

"I'm glad you think so," Ilfanti taunted as he launched lightning, not at the dalvor, but at the floor beneath her, shattering her foothold and toppling her to her knees. "From where I stand, you suddenly seem weakened."

The priestess raised her hand, waggled her fingers, and whispered an incantation. The shadows came alive, binding Ilfanti by the wrists and ankles. She then stood up, her maniacal grin widening as she slowly approached Ilfanti, ready to end his quest prematurely.

Ilfanti struggled against the bonds, pulling at them and trying to gain leverage, but he was trapped and could not move. Quite an effective spell. Perhaps the last spell Ilfanti would ever see.

❈ ❈ ❈ ❈ ❈

Inorus slid down when he reached Osorkon, horrified by the smoke that was emanating from his eyes and mouth. Upon his father's chest was a palm print, burned right through all of Osorkon's clothing and glowing brightly.

"Father!" gasped Inorus.

"It burns," wheezed Osorkon.

"I know what can help," Inorus said, confidently. "Wait here. I shall return." He then stood up and searched for Kabilian, seeing the human and hobgoblin making their way over to the dais with the Orb of Prophecy upon it.

Inorus ran after them, praying that they could save his father as easily as they had saved him. "Kabilian!"

Kabilian skidded to a halt, turned and glared at the dwarf that dared to disturb him when he was so close to his goal.

"Kabilian, I need your assistance," Inorus shouted.

Kabilian glanced at the Orb of Prophecy, so close, and then at Inorus, his eyes trailing over to Osorkon. What did he care for a dwarf from this land? His own future was at stake here. The Orb of Prophecy was within his grasp. But even as those thoughts flowed through his mind, he could not find the energy to turn and claim the Orb. Instead, he found his feet moving in the wrong direction, speeding up and running to the side of Osorkon. Even as he bent down to help, Kabilian was scolding himself for losing sight of why he was there, and hoping that this random act of kindness did not come back to haunt him.

"It is my father," Inorus said as Kabilian studied the smoking dwarf. "Can you help him?"

Kabilian studied the hand print burned onto Osorkon, and then looked into the dwarf's mouth. "It burns inside?"

"Yes," wheezed Osorkon.

"Can your scepter not cool him down as it did for me?" Inorus asked.

"No," Kabilian replied. "You were being burned from the outside. Your father's blood is burning. The scepter will not help."

"What then?" pleaded Inorus. "There must be something!"

"Perhaps," Kabilian began, shaking his head as he even thought it.

"Perhaps what?" demanded Inorus.

"The Potion of Immunity," Kabilian said. "When drunk, it makes you immune to magical spells. For a time. I've never taken it after fighting a Mage though, only before. I do not know if it will work."

"What about a healing potion?" Crick suggested.

"He has no broken bones or ailments," Kabilian said. "The healing potion would just be a wasted attempt. It is the Potion of Immunity or nothing."

"Let us try," Inorus said.

Kabilian reached into his satchel, thought about the Potion of Immunity, and produced a vial of a sparkling green liquid. Of all of his potions, this one tasted the worst, one of the reasons Kabilian preferred facing foes with enchanted items and not actually going up against magic users.

"Drink this," he said, tilting the vial so that some of the liquid went into Osorkon's mouth. The potion was very dense, and felt slimy as it slowly made its way down Osorkon's throat.

Inorus glanced impatiently back and forth between his father and Kabilian. "Well?"

"It may take time," Kabilian said. "*If* it works."

"Help Khonsu," Osorkon wheezed.

Inorus looked over at his sister, still unmoving where she lay.

"I'll get her," Crick offered.

"Thank you," Inorus said.

While they were waiting, Kabilian reached into his pouch and produced a small red ruby. He lifted it to his eye and stared at the dalvor. The ruby allowed him to see magic and enchanted items clearly, making them radiate a brighter red than everything around it. The dalvor's staff, bracelets, and necklace were all radiating.

"It's working," cheered Inorus.

Kabilian removed the ruby from his eye and watched as the smoke coming from Osorkon began lessening, and soon stopped completely. The palmprint on his chest was also no longer as inflamed, and soon even that vanished. Within minutes Osorkon was up and ready for action once more.

Crick returned with Khonsu and set her down between Osorkon and Inorus. Inorus glanced at Kabilian to see if there was anything that he could do.

Kabilian shrugged: "A bucket of water to toss on her?"

"What?" Inorus asked.

"She is unconscious, but looks otherwise unharmed. She will be fine," Kabilian said.

"It warms my heart to hear that," Osorkon said.

"Not too much, I hope," Kabilian quickly retorted. "We just got through cooling your heart down."

"Very funny," sarcastically growled Osorkon. "How fares Ilfanti?"

"He's not going to make it," Kabilian said as he prompted them to look at the dwarf, bound by the dalvor.

"No!" Osorkon shouted. "We must help!"

"She is a sorceress," Kabilian said. "Not a Mage like your friend, but something from before the dawn of Mages."

"How would you know that?" asked Osorkon, his patience thin.

"Trust me, I would know," Kabilian said, thinking back to his fairly recent vision of his own father, Sabourin, the Sorcerer Slayer.

"We must still help," Osorkon said, definitively. "Come, boy, we'll take her down."

Inorus nodded his assent, then glanced at Kabilian. "If you will not help, will you at least protect my sister?"

Sabourin would have liked these dwarves, Kabilian decided. "Crick, watch the dwarf. We'll be back."

"So, you're not yellow after all, eh?" Osorkon taunted. "Good."

Kabilian's eyes narrowed to slits as he glared at Osorkon. He was beginning to regret using some of his potion to help the ornery dwarf. "Remember this, you are immune to magic spells, but not everything that she could send at you."

"What do you mean?" Osorkon asked, suddenly interested.

"She could stab you, bite you, use her magic to drop the ceiling on you. All of that would kill you, but with an energy strike, such as lightning or fire, you would be unharmed."

"For how long?" Osorkon asked.

Kabilian shrugged. "It took a lot of the potion to counter the effects of what she already did to you, but it should remain in your body for at least the next hour. Maybe a little longer if you are lucky."

Osorkon pulled a curved dagger from his belt, his eyes firmly on the dark elf binding his friend. "Let's do this."

Inorus twirled both scimitars and followed his father. Kabilian extended his daggers into full-length swords again and followed as well, leaving Crick and Khonsu behind. Soon they would be in the battle of their lives, and all Kabilian could wonder was—why was he even involved?

❀ ❀ ❀ ❀ ❀

Rhyne emerged from the shadows and watched as Kabilian made his way toward the priestess who could only be Nefrukakashta. She was standing before Ilfanti, her hand holding his chin, the Mage bound and unable to move. Ilfanti's male companions, along with Kabilian, were trying to intervene and save the Mage.

Rhyne found the situation somewhat unusual. He could not understand why Kabilian would be helping these dwarves. There must be something in it for him. Some way that he was manipulating them and trying to con them. Whatever it was, his attempts would not succeed.

Reaching beneath his cloak, Rhyne produced the vapor that he had collected in the Gates of Tanorus. The mist blocked the power of a Mage, leaving them vulnerable. If Kabilian was trying to help Ilfanti, then he must be hoping to use the Mage's abilities to help defend himself. Rhyne was not about to let that happen.

Leaping forward, he tossed the container at the feet of Ilfanti and Nefrukakashta, shattering it and releasing the mist. He watched as the shadow bonds holding Ilfanti dissipated, and the dwarf stumbled to the floor. They were powerless now, and could not help Kabilian.

Rhyne lifted a blade, only one, and hurled it at Kabilian. The assassin deflected the blade with ease, knocking it aside with one of his swords. Rhyne grinned, revealing his fanged teeth. "The time has come for you to pay for your insolence and betrayal of Lady Salaman."

Kabilian turned to face Rhyne, his swords held before him in a defensive posture. "Looks like you're on your own, boys. I have some business to attend to."

Rhyne saw the dwarves acknowledge the statement, and then continue on to Ilfanti, leaving Kabilian alone to face him. It was time for the endgame. Kabilian's life was about to come to an end. This months-long hunt would finally be over.

CHAPTER 61

Ilfanti dropped to the ground, a mixture of emotions flowing through him. He was glad to be free of the priestess, but he also remembered the Gates of Tanorus well, and without his magical abilities, he was not sure how he could defeat his foe. He only hoped that she too was without her magic.

The person who freed him shocked him—it was Alaran, the wraith who was pursuing a mutineer. Ilfanti spotted a human preparing to fight Alaran, and he wondered if this was the foe that he had been so determined to find and kill. If so, why were they both here?

Deep down, Ilfanti had never trusted Alaran. He trusted him even less showing up here and now, like this. Something about the wraith had made the little hairs on the back of his neck rise, a sure sign of danger.

Those same hairs were rising now. Ilfanti glanced back at the dalvor, silently berating himself for being startled by the sudden arrival of Alaran. He did not have to wait too long to learn that the dalvor had already regained command of her magic. She pointed a finger at him, and it began glowing as a beam of destructive force lanced out at him.

Ilfanti lunged away, landing on his shoulder, rolling, and then leaping back to his feet. It was hard enough fighting the priestess when he had his magic; how was he supposed to fight her now? As long as air still filled his lungs, he would try to find the answer to that.

Osorkon reached the dalvor and jabbed his blade into her hip. The priestess shrieked in pain, bringing her staff down and cracking it over his head. With her other hand, she felt the wound, the blood flowing through her fingers, and sneered with contempt at the dwarves raiding her temple.

Inorus charged and struck a magically erected barrier when he swung his blades at her. The priestess offered him a snort of derision, letting him know that his advance was so loud that she had all the time in the world to defend herself against him.

"You no longer amuse me," the dalvor said. "It is time for you all to die." With a wave of her staff and a silent incantation, the entire temple burst to life. From the ground, hands burst to the surface as mummies forced their way to freedom. Along the walls, the skeletal and dried remains of the nomads stood up, claiming the weapons they had wielded prior to their deaths, and advanced upon those in the room. The statues along the walls cracked and groaned, coming to life and stepping from their stone resting places, each step shaking the entire temple.

"Oh crud," groaned Ilfanti.

※ ※ ※ ※ ※

Kabilian glared at Rhyne, waiting for the wraith to make the first move. If Rhyne was here and had been following him, then Lady Salaman had acted quickly in placing a contract on his head. After all the years he had served her, she certainly did not forgive a sole indiscretion. After dealing with her minion, he knew he would have to track down the crime lord and properly end his employ with her, in the only method he knew that she would understand.

"Lady Salaman sends her greetings, eh?" Kabilian asked, quoting the phrase that he had used so many times when trying to intimidate those that the crime lord wanted something from. It was a phrase he vowed never to say again.

Rhyne reached into his cloak and removed three throwing knives for each hand, his eyes fixed on Kabilian, blocking out everything else that was going on in the temple. His goal was in sight. The confrontation had begun. It was the only thing that demanded his attention. Let the dwarves and priestess kill each other—he had Kabilian at last.

"The silent type, eh?" Kabilian shrugged. "Lady Salaman either thinks you're very good, or doesn't like you very much."

"I'm very good, I assure you," Rhyne growled as he brought his arms forward and released the six blades.

The wraith's aim was unflawed, but Kabilian moved his swords with such ease and quickness that he managed to deflect five, and sidestep the sixth. A taunting grin never left his face as he glared at Rhyne, a look of: "Is that the best you've got?"

Rhyne leapt into the air, pulling several more throwing blades and hurling them at Kabilian. As soon as the blades were thrown, he reached into his cloak as he reached the ground, rolled, came back up with new blades in his hand and threw them as well.

Kabilian was impressed by Rhyne's swiftness and skill. He definitely was as good as claimed. It did not really matter in the end, Kabilian knew, he would win and Lady Salaman would just keep sending more bounty hunters, assassins, and mercenaries after him. Both people who already had a name and people who were looking to make a name.

Rhyne was not ceasing his attack, reaching into his cloak and removing more of his blades, hurling them at Kabilian. Kabilian deflected them all, looking as if the effort were not even a strain. As Rhyne paused, removing several needles, Kabilian flicked his wrist and small darts soared at the wraith. Unlike Kabilian, Rhyne did not have a sword to deflect the projectiles. He threw the needles, sending one of the arrows off of its trajectory, but the other still soared straight at him. Rhyne swatted both hands together, smothering the arrow between them.

"Not bad," Kabilian said, impressed by the wraith's response.

Rhyne opened his hands and glanced at the arrow. Perhaps he had been too smart for his own good—there was some blood on his palm where he had pushed the tip into himself. Without knowing why, he suddenly felt a bout of dizziness, and became nauseous. "It was drugged?"

"Of course," Kabilian grinned.

"I will kill you for that," growled Rhyne.

"Thought you were already trying to kill me for Lady Salaman?" shrugged Kabilian. "Better be careful, thinking for yourself is what got you sent after me!"

Rhyne twirled the arrow that Kabilian had launched at him and sent it hurtling back at the assassin. The bolt never reached Kabilian, instead, striking the decayed remains of a human male who wandered into the midst of their battle. The arrow struck his head, and the undead creature fell to the ground with the impact.

"What madness is this?" Rhyne demanded. For that instant, the two risked looking around to see what was happening. Dozens of these undead creatures were approaching them. Their duel would have to wait.

CHAPTER 62

Ilfanti pulled his dagger from his belt, looked at it with a frown, and then held it defensively. Against the undead, he would need something a bit more effective than a dagger. He backed over to Osorkon and Inorus, the three dwarves creating a defensive triangle. Osorkon was in the same position, armed only with a dagger.

"Thanks for the assist," Ilfanti said, never taking his eyes off of the skeleton creature that was closest to him.

Osorkon rubbed his head and looked at the blood on his hands. The priestess had struck him pretty hard. He was just glad that he had not lost consciousness. "What are friends for?"

"This kind of reminds me of that time we found the tomb of Anknutahtet," Ilfanti said.

"At least there the mummies did not come to life," snickered Osorkon.

"Do you two ever stop your incessant chatter?" barked Inorus. "We are fighting for our lives here. This is not some childish game. Ilfanti, can your magic help?"

"Harsh, boy, harsh," growled Osorkon.

"What Alaran threw at me blocked my powers," Ilfanti answered. "It wasn't much, so hopefully they will return soon."

"Yes, hopefully," Osorkon said, his eyes focused on the dalvor who was using the distraction to try and regain her vision. "We need to defeat the priestess."

"The priestess is mine," Ilfanti said. "Let's just take down some of these creatures, even the odds until my powers return, and then you focus on the Orb, and I'll focus on the priestess."

"Agreed," Osorkon said.

"You both make this sound so easy," Inorus sighed.

"Isn't it?" Ilfanti asked, his elbow nudging Inorus to try and lighten the mood. The skeleton was almost upon them now, wielding a scimitar. Ilfanti wanted that scimitar. Sliding his dagger back into his belt, he offered a final sentiment: "See you when this is done."

He leapt at the skeleton, landing directly before it on his hands, and kicking his legs up into the skeleton's chest. The skeleton stumbled backwards and fell. Ilfanti quickly drew his dagger again, jumped atop the skeleton warrior, and rammed the dagger into its skull. The bones crumpled lifelessly and scattered with the strike.

Ilfanti lifted the scimitar, twirling it a couple of times to check the balance, and then glanced at Osorkon and Inorus. "There may be a lot of them, but they go down pretty quickly."

A mummy lunged at Ilfanti, trying to grab him. Ilfanti dodged out of the way, and then struck with the scimitar, slashing the creature in the chest. As the body was cleaved in two, it burst into dust, leaving little more than a pile of soot and ash where the creature had been.

Ilfanti grinned at how easily these creatures were being vanquished—never before had he fought undead that were so easy to best—even without his magic, he was confident that they could handle the odds. Then an axe blade the size of Ilfanti struck the gound right behind him, forcing him to scurry away. Turning back around and viewing his newest foe, he saw one of the massive statues confronting him. Perhaps this would not be so easy after all, he thought.

❋ ❋ ❋ ❋ ❋

Osorkon and Inorus acknowledged Ilfanti's comment about the ease of defeating these foes by charging headlong into the midst of the skeleton creatures and mummies. Inorus, who had handled himself well against the living creatures beyond the temple walls, did even better against the undead. There was no doubt that these creatures were unholy, and he did not hold back at all, cutting lose and giving in to his instincts.

His scimitars flashed in the torchlight from one foe to another, leaving bones and dust behind him, without pause or thought for his effectiveness. Only Osorkon seemed to acknowledge Inorus's ferocity, wondering where his son had learned to be a warrior, but filling with pride at the sight of his son in action.

Osorkon lifted a spear from one of the fallen skeletons and twirled it around like a staff, striking creatures with both ends. A swipe of the legs would quite often separate the skeleton at the knees, forcing it to crawl to fight. Thrusts at the heads and battering the skulls were the fatal strikes. Osorkon jabbed the spear end into the ribcage of one of the skeletons, and then slashed with all of his might, scattering the bones over the floor.

"Father! Watch out!" Inorus shouted.

Osorkon pivoted and watched as one of the statues charged at him. The statue was similar to the one of Akeneh that he and Ilfanti had found. It had the body of a man, and the head of a snake, though the head of this one was longer, like a giraffe's with the snake's head at the top.

The statue was swinging its double-bladed staff and striking skeleton creatures and mummies as it ran by, leaving more debris in seconds than Osorkon and Inorus had managed in minutes. It brought the staff back and began swinging for Osorkon. Osorkon hoped that he was still as nimble as he was in his youth, and waited for the strike. At the last instant, he jumped and landed on the massive blade, though he quickly lost his balance and fell off.

"Father!" Inorus shouted.

Lying on his back, Osorkon glared at the statue, wondering whether adventuring was something better left to the younger generation. He had once been as swift and nimble as Khonsu, and as strong as Inorus. Now, he was lying helplessly on his back, and though he did not want to admit it, something had cracked when he landed. Time was catching up with Osorkon.

❋ ❋ ❋ ❋ ❋

Crick was conflicted. Kabilian was under attack from the wraith, and then from the creatures around them. His loyalty was to his companion first, but he had promised to watch and protect the unconscious dwarf. Should he leave to fight alongside Kabilian or remain and guard the dwarf?

A mummy grabbed him from behind, trying to squeeze his illistrium armor. If not for the decayed flesh and wrappings dirtying his armor, Crick probably would not have even taken notice, such was the protection of the Tregador dwarf's suit of armor. Reaching down, he drew his two mystral drantanas and shoved them backwards, striking the mummy with both blades.

Growling in disgust, Crick tried to shake the dust of the dead mummy off of himself. It would probably take hours to clean his armor after this little encounter. An odd thought for a hobgoblin, but Crick definitely preferred things to be pristine and maintained.

Kneeling back down, Crick dropped the two swords by his side and grasped Khonsu by the shoulders. He began shaking her, trying to force her to wake up. The undead were coming their way in greater numbers. Even if he did remain to defend her rather than join Kabilian, he did not think that he could fend off all of them before one managed to do something to the dwarf.

Crick shook harder and harder, Khonsu's head dangling. "Wake up!" he shouted with another succession of shakes.

Khonsu's head was the first indication that she was coming out of it. It began to rise as her neck became less limp. Then slowly, her eyes began to open. She was groggy, and still in pain, but Khonsu was awake.

She glanced up at Crick, and lost all sense of where she was and what she was doing. The last thing she remembered, she had been trying to defend herself from the elf of darkness. Now, some orange-furred creature in dragon-designed armor was shaking her violently and screaming at her.

Reaching for her pickaxe, Khonsu found the grip and brought the blade swinging into Crick's armored scalp. "Leave me alone!" she shouted.

Crick dropped her with the blow, looking confused, and even angrier. "I'm not your enemy," he growled bitterly. He then grabbed her head between his two armored gauntlets and forced her to look at the advancing skeletons and mummies. "They are!"

Khonsu's mouth hung open, shocked by what she was seeing.

Were those really skeletons preparing to attack, or was she dead and this was some kind of tormenting limbo, forcing her to spend eternity fighting unimaginable odds in the place she had perished?

Crick lifted his drantanas from the ground and stood up, leaving Khonsu on the ground. "My oath to protect you is done. You are awake. If you choose to remain there, then I shall not be responsible for your death."

The argument was compelling. If he would not be responsible for her death, then she must not yet be dead. Khonsu did not know who the armored orange-furred creature was, but he was at least defending against the creatures she knew were evil. For now, at least, until she figured out what was going on, they were allies.

She tried getting to her feet, and found that her entire body ached. She remembered the elf of darkness battering her into the ceiling, and wondered how bruised her entire body was beneath her clothing. That was for another time. She spotted her second pickaxe, and picked it up, twirling the two and preparing to fight the undead bearing down on her. If she could still move, she could still fight. It was time to not only think that, but prove it.

❂ ❂ ❂ ❂ ❂

Kabilian weaved in and out of the undead creatures, cutting them down quickly and easily. His movements were constrained, though, for with each step he found himself searching for Rhyne to make certain that the wraith would not sneak up on him to stab him in the back. He would not put it past one of Lady Salaman's minions to take advantage of a distraction. He may have worked for her for some time, but he rarely saw eye to eye with others in the Hidden Empire.

There was a certain code and honor that should be upheld amongst professionals. He was an assassin, *the* assassin extraordinaire. He knew that things had to be done in certain ways, and respected that. If one did not adhere to that, then they were little more than a bully or thug, which seemed to be the type of enforcer Lady Salaman preferred. Unfortunately for her, they rarely managed to last long when facing a professional.

Kabilian was still not certain what to make of Rhyne. He definitely was skilled with throwing knives, and was swift and hard to track. Since he had managed to follow Kabilian this far, in a Wind Soarer most of the way, he was a masterful tracker as well. However, Kabilian did not trust that the wraith would adhere to the codes of a professional, and fully expected a dagger hurled at his back.

The best thing that he could do, Kabilian decided, was deal with Rhyne without the added distraction of all of these creatures. There was one thing that could potentially help him with that. The beasts he had summoned—the lupan and the koxlen—were bound to him psychically until he dismissed them. If he thought about them, commanding them to come to the temple, they would.

As Kabilian sent the mental image to his two beasts, he wondered if their arrival would also mean that the remaining sabrenoh and elves would enter the temple and strike. If so, then the added allies might be insufficient when the foes were doubled. It was a concern that he would have to worry about when the time came.

Kabilian severed the head of a mummy, which burst into dust as a result, and twirled around to look at Rhyne again. The wraith was throwing knives at foes of his own, and far enough away from Kabilian to be unable to strike at the moment. He wondered just how many blades Rhyne had, and whether the wraith would have enough to continue fighting after the undead creatures were dealt with.

Whispering the incantation to change one of his swords back to a dagger, Kabilian tucked it into his belt. He then reached into his pouch and removed his scepter, Inferno. Pointing it at the nearest foe, a series of flames lanced out and struck the skeleton, setting it ablaze. Kabilian grinned as the body stopped moving and the bones fell to the ground, still burning.

Pivoting, he sent flames at as many of the undead creatures as he could. He held his other sword in defense in case any creature got close enough to him, but after several strikes, he was attacking all his foes from a distance. With his magical weapons, perhaps he would not need his summoned beasts. As he heard the familiar growl of the lupan, his grin grew even wider—he might not need them, but they certainly were a welcome addition to the battle.

❀ ❀ ❀ ❀ ❀

Rhyne was growing impatient. Kabilian had been in his grasp, and now, the distance between them was growing. These undead creatures kept advancing, and he could not see an end in sight. When he thought that they were almost defeated, he saw more walking into the chamber from other passages and up stairs. How many skeletons and mummies could one temple have buried?

He too heard the growl of the lupan, and watched as the mighty white-furred beast burst into the temple, grabbing skeleton warriors and mummies and tossing them aside with ease. The koxlen leapt in after him, biting and slashing at anything that moved. He had seen them on the common grounds of Ramahatra, and hoped to avoid them. That would probably be far less likely now that they shared the same confined space.

Rhyne tensed with frustration. Every time he thought that the end was almost in sight, something happened to offset it. He could not do anything at the moment to stop the two beasts from his homeland, but he might be able to do something about the undead creatures. They had been raised by Nefrukakashta. If he could kill her, then the undead would most likely revert to their previous state, leaving him free to deal with Kabilian and leave this place before something else happened.

He spotted Nefrukakashta, rubbing her eyes and standing near the shining Orb on the dais. Seeing that she was blinded, he decided that he would not waste any more of his throwing blades, and would instead just slit her throat.

Several skeleton creatures got in his way as he approached Nefrukakashta, but he dealt with them quickly, refusing to be swayed. First he would kill the priestess, and then he would finally be done with Kabilian. There was not a moment's hesitation in his actions. He was certain that his plan would work.

He reached the priestess, stepped behind her, and brought his dagger to her throat. Rhyne had learned decades ago how to be silent and stealthy when assassinating someone, and he did not make a sound. Even his heart slowed so that its beating would not give him away.

As he went to slit her throat, one of the golden snakes coiled around Nefrukakashta's arm turned and looked straight at him. Rhyne paused, startled. It jerked at him, biting his arm with its golden teeth. Rhyne dropped his blade and pulled his arm away, cradling the injured forearm.

Nefrukakashta spun around, her blind eyes glaring directly at him as if she could see. "Foolish slave."

"Slave?" growled Rhyne, confused by the comment.

Nefrukakashta raised her hand and pointed her index finger at the wraith. "Ash'na tel'oh sid'rel."

A purple mist swirled from her finger and began wrapping around Rhyne. The mist entered his nose, his mouth, and his ears. It began to cling to his body and harden, shredding his clothing and creating wounds all over the wraith as if he had been pricked by thousands of little thorns. Rhyne screamed in agony as he experienced pain more intense than anything he had ever endured in his life.

From his skin, in the wounds, small spikes began to form. They came from deep within his body, as well as without. Those within pierced organs, ripped through his flesh, and shattered bones. The torment was intense, and as his life left his body it was as if he were finally free—released from the agony into his death.

Nefrukakashta moaned in ecstasy as Rhyne's body fell lifelessly to the ground. She could feel the agony that he had felt, and it invigorated her. She had taken strength from the death of Rhyne, and her own powers grew. Her eyesight had also returned in the moment that Rhyne's life left him. Now, she was unstoppable.

She stared at the dead wraith, accepting the sacrifice of a member of the race that had once been slaves to the dalvor, and cackled with amusement. Lowering her staff, Nefrukakashta touched Rhyne's forehead with the black gem at the tip. Rhyne's body jerked and convulsed, life reentering it. Not the life of Rhyne, but of a demonic disciple of the priestess.

"Go, my pet. Destroy them all," she instructed, amused as the wraith lifted himself from the ground, hissed with obedience, and ran to find a foe so that he could comply.

CHAPTER 63

The animated statue struck at Ilfanti again, bringing the massive blade slicing down where the dwarf had been standing. Ilfanti rolled out of the way, leapt toward its legs, and slashed his scimitar at its ankle with all of his might. As the blade struck the obsidian leg, it shattered to the hilt.

"Crud," Ilfanti groaned as he tossed the useless hilt aside.

A massive stone hand whipped out and wrapped around Ilfanti before he could even react, holding him so tightly that he could not move, and brought him up to its serpent head. The statue lowered its head to glare directly at Ilfanti, and hissed with a stone-tongue.

"You're not just going to kill me, you're going to torture me with your breath? Gross," Ilfanti taunted, knowing that his words would have no effect on the lifeless statue, but needing to hear them anyway. If only he had not been robbed of the powers of a Mage, he could probably find a way through this.

The fist around him began to squeeze, forcing the air from his lungs. Ilfanti strained to move, but knew that his strength was abandoning him. His consciousness was almost lost. Before blacking out, he felt a familiar surge of power that was as familiar to him as one of his limbs. Its return fueled him, filled him, but had his magical powers returned too late to save him?

❊ ❊ ❊ ❊ ❊

Lying upon the ground, Osorkon stared at the serpent-man statue above him. It lifted its leg into the air, raising it over his body, and began to lower it. Osorkon could hardly believe that after all of his adventures, being stepped upon would bring about his demise.

Inorus hastened to his father's side, standing with his father between his legs, both swords pointed up at the stone statue that was lowering toward them.

"Inorus, no, save yourself!" Osorkon pleaded.

"I shall not abandon you," Inorus vowed.

Osorkon was not about to let his son face the statue alone. He pulled himself up, using Inorus's leg as support, and felt a stabbing pain in his chest—at least one rib had been broken. He reached his feet and lifted his spear, pointing it at the lowering foot.

The two stared at the foot, defying it to step down and face their blades, although they suspected it would be their final act together. Then they heard a mighty growl and the foot did not descend on them but instead pivoted and turned. The dwarves were shocked to see the white-furred lupan leap onto the statue and begin clawing at it. Its attack was somewhat effective, stone crumbling from the body as it tore away at it.

"I'd advise getting away from that thing," Inorus said.

"I couldn't agree more," Osorkon agreed. He searched the chamber and saw skeleton warriors and mummies approaching Khonsu and Crick. No oversized statues fighting them, which meant that a pair of dwarves could still help out. "Let's go to fight by your sister's side."

"Agreed," Inorus said, taking one last look at the lupan fighting the statue. The ferocious beast was actually winning. The statue's arm was ripped from its shoulder, and large chunks of its chest were also torn away. Kabilian's beasts had come through again.

❁ ❁ ❁ ❁ ❁

Crick and Khonsu met the attack of the skeleton creatures and mummies without hesitation. Khonsu's actions were a bit sluggish, but Crick managed to position himself so that he took the bulk of the blows. Both his drantanas and her pickaxes were quite effective against their foes, turning them to dust and a pile of bones with little more than a swing.

Khonsu saw her father and brother heading their way, beginning to strike the creatures from behind. Soon, the undead forces split, some fighting her and Crick, and some fighting Osorkon and Inorus.

A burst of pure blue flame struck one of the mummies before her and ignited it, incinerating it in seconds. Khonsu searched for Ilfanti, presuming that it had been he who had launched the fireball, but instead spotted a shadowy-skinned creature with thorns and spikes jutting from its entire body. The creature wore only tattered clothing, and had open wounds all around its body. As it glared at her, it breathed heavily, every exhale sounding like a hiss.

It raised its hand, a blade of fire forming, and hurled it at Khonsu. Khonsu shrieked and tried to dodge, the blade striking one of her pickaxes and melting the weapon before her eyes.

Khonsu lifted her crossbow and sent a bolt at the creature, watching it ignite and turn to ash before even reaching it.

Crick pushed Khonsu aside, stepping in between her and the creature. He raised his drantanas and approached it, hoping that the armor of the dwarves would somehow protect him. In the creature's hand, another fiery blade formed, one that raged with the intensity of hellfire, and was thrown at the hobgoblin.

❄ ❄ ❄ ❄ ❄

Kabilian had seen the death of Rhyne with his own eyes. What he had seen next had shaken him to his core with pure dread—she had resurrected him and made him a puppet in her hands. The creature that had been Rhyne was now fighting Crick and the dwarf, and Kabilian saw that the wraith had been augmented and transformed in more ways than one.

The bolt that was incinerated before it even struck him meant that the wraith had some kind of heat-shield surrounding him. The blades he was wielding were also hot enough to melt an axe, no easy task. If this was the power of the dalvor, then this may have been a futile mission.

Kabilian had a moment to breathe. His lupan and koxlen had done well, clearing a path of the undead creatures. Far fewer of them were still standing and fighting. He counted half a dozen of the massive statues, one being shredded by his lupan, and another looking like it was about to kill one of the dwarves. The dalvor was watching as well, like a predator waiting to swoop down and select her prey. Kabilian had no desire to be her next victim.

The dwarf being killed by the statue had been fighting the dalvor and doing well. If they were to survive this night, he had to be rescued. But, Kabilian could not leave Crick to face the demonic Rhyne by himself. Focusing on his lupan, he sent his beast after the wraith, hoping that his summoned creature could get there first and defeat Rhyne. The koxlen he left finishing off the undead creatures. He, in the meantime, had to help Ilfanti.

CHAPTER 64

As the darkness began to overwhelm Ilfanti, he tried one last act of desperation, summoning his innate mystical powers. It began as a gentle vibration, his hands shaking slightly, then it grew, and Ilfanti felt the grip around him beginning to loosen. He gasped for air, tasting it and thinking that air had never tasted so good.

Even then, he did not stop, continuing to send pulsating waves of energy through his hands and into the animated obsidian statue. Soon, the statue began trembling, and then large chunks of rock began falling from it as the shockwave vibrated it until it had been destroyed.

Ilfanti fell to the ground, trying to position himself to cushion the blow, and landing on his right arm. It hurt, but he did not hear anything break. He could deal with the pain until the job was done.

"Very impressive."

Ilfanti turned to see the speaker, studying the man before him for a moment. "We have met, have we not?"

"In another land, another time, nearly a lifetime ago, perhaps," the man said. "Kabilian's the name."

"Ilfanti," Ilfanti replied. "I saw that you helped Osorkon. You have my gratitude."

"You can save it until we survive this night," Kabilian said. "Then I'll accept your gratitude by taking the Orb of Prophecy."

Ilfanti's eyes narrowed as he glared at Kabilian. "That, I cannot allow."

"You may not have a choice," Kabilian said. "Then again, I may not have a choice either."

"The fate of the Seven Kingdoms hangs in the balance," argued Ilfanti. "I must obtain the Orb."

"Something as dear to me as that is to you is why I need it as well,"

Kabilian said, his tone and body language shifting from friendly to threatening.

Ilfanti did not like where this was going. This man was the one that Alaran had been after. Though Ilfanti did not trust Alaran, he wondered if Kabilian really might be a mutineer and cutthroat. Was Kabilian truly an ally, or was this some elaborate deception? Over the years, Ilfanti had learned to trust his instincts, and they were telling him that Kabilian could be trusted. Ironic that they were both here for the same thing and would ultimately be at odds.

"Perhaps when this is done, we can work out a...shall we say, an arrangement?" Kabilian offered.

"I need the Orb," Ilfanti adamantly replied.

"I have something in my possession that may help you more," Kabilian grinned, knowing that what he had would be far too alluring for any Mage to give up.

"We will discuss this when we claim the Orb," Ilfanti said, not being tempted in the least or finding himself curious as to what the assassin had to offer. "For now, our companions need assistance."

Kabilian reached into his satchel and removed the tooth of the dragon. "I could not agree more." He whispered the incantation to summon the beast, and it enlarged to a thirty-five-foot silver dragon—the smaller of the two he once had. A shame that he had lost the male.

The silver dragon was almost identical to its mate in every feature, including the horns upon its head, and down its back to its tail; the thick silver-scaled armor that served as its skin; the wings that would allow it to fly vast distances in short spans of time; and the claws at the end of each of its fingers and toes.

Kabilian admired his dragon for a moment, fondly remembering when he had two of the mighty beasts. If it were possible, perhaps one day he would try to sift through the wreckage of the Hidden Empire lair and try to recover his other dragon's tooth. That venture would probably take years of his life, considering how much destruction and debris had buried his dragon.

"Destroy the stone statues and the remaining undead warriors," instructed Kabilian. The dragon roared in acknowledgement, and flapping its wings, began soaring through the chamber and collided with the closest stone warrior, sinking its claws into it and biting the stone neck.

Kabilian watched with pride, then glanced at Ilfanti, whose eyes were following the dragon in awe.

"You can control a dragon," Ilfanti said, impressed.

"And more," Kabilian grinned.

"Let us go now to help our allies," Ilfanti said. The two rushed through the piles of bones, obsidian, and dust to where they saw their companions facing the demonic wraith. Ilfanti risked a sidelong glance at the dalvor, knowing that this night was far from over.

❀ ❀ ❀ ❀ ❀

Osorkon and Inorus saw Crick leap in front of Khonsu and begin fighting the shadow-creature. They hastened their pace, trying to get into the battle, but found that reaching Khonsu was nearly impossible with all of the undead barring their path. They heard a ferocious growl behind them and saw the koxlen pounce on top of several skeleton warriors at once, sending their bones shattering in all directions.

"Come, we can make it," Inorus said.

Osorkon had to admire the enthusiasm of youth. If he survived this quest, it would certainly be his last. At his age, he decided that living the rest of his days with his beloved Dedi and children, and building tombs for Pharaoh Werirenptah, would be a life worth living.

Crick shrieked in pain as a hellfire dagger struck his armor and began melting through it—though the illistrium did not melt nearly as fast as Khonsu's pickaxe. Crick gritted his teeth and tried to reach the wraith, his drantanas jabbing, but he pulled back when he saw that the tip of his blades were starting to darken when he got close. How could you defeat something that you could not even touch?

Osorkon took his spear and threw it at the wraith, watching it have the same effect that Khonsu's crossbow bolt had. It burst into flame and turned to ash before striking its mark.

Inorus stepped beside Crick, the two holding a pair of swords each, and hoping to defend Khonsu and Osorkon. Osorkon rushed to his daughter's side.

"Are you harmed?" Osorkon asked.

"I'm fine," Khonsu said. "That beast, how can we beat it?"

"If I have learned anything over the years, it is that there is always a way," Osorkon said.

He heard another growl and watched as the white-haired lupan pushed its way through the few remaining undead creatures and went to attack the wraith. The wraith spun around, more of its hellfire blades forming in its hand, and throwing them at the lupan. The flaming blades burned right through the beast, dropping it to its knees as it cried out in animalistic fury.

The lupan forced itself back up and reached out its muscular arms, grabbing Rhyne by the throat. The arms of the lupan began to burn, but the beast did not let go, trying to squeeze further.

With a hiss, Rhyne opened his mouth and a stream of acidic mist sprayed out, striking the lupan in the face. The lupan pulled away, the fur on its arms gone, its skin blistered and burned, and its face bubbling and burning as well. Rhyne formed a new hellfire dagger, and sent it at the lupan, the flames burning through its heart.

As the blade went through, the lupan began to glow a blinding blue, and then burst, leaving only a lone hair, somewhat singed, floating to the ground. Crick reached out and picked it up, certain that his companion would want the hair back, even if the lupan were destroyed.

Before Crick fully righted his posture, he felt a burning sensation as Rhyne backhanded him across the face. Where the hand hit, his fur began to sizzle and burn, but the strength behind the slap was far greater than any wraith ever possessed, sending Crick hurtling into a stone pillar, and rendering him unconscious. The last thing he saw before blacking out was Kabilian running toward him.

CHAPTER 65

As they were racing toward the battle with their companions, Kabilian returned Inferno to his Mage's satchel and reached for his second scepter, Blizzard. Kabilian banked on the theory that if Rhyne burned then perhaps ice could somehow cool him down. He was the first to engage the wraith, sending ice shards at Rhyne and gaining the wraith's attention.

Kabilian lowered Blizzard with determination, sending succession after succession of ice shards at the demonic wraith. Rhyne merely hissed challengingly and charged Kabilian, leaving the dwarves behind as an afterthought.

Ilfanti used the distraction to race to his friends. Osorkon was wheezing and panting heavily, but he nodded to assure Ilfanti that he was fine. Inorus appeared unscathed, and Khonsu was bruised and battered a bit, but ready to resume the fight.

"This is almost over," Ilfanti promised.

Inorus glanced around the chamber, seeing the dragon and koxlen finishing the final few statues and undead creatures. That left the priestess and her demon as the only remaining adversaries. "We will triumph," he said, confidently.

"The morning sun will shine on us and our victory," Khonsu added.

"Such spirit," Osorkon chortled. "Ilfanti, remember when we were that young?"

"I remember, old friend," Ilfanti said. "They are right, but none of you will be here to see it."

"What?" protested Khonsu.

"Kabilian will face the demon, and I shall face the priestess," Ilfanti said. "I want the three of you to get the hobgoblin and get out of here."

"We're not leaving," Khonsu growled stubbornly.

"You must," Ilfanti said. "I do not wish to be distracted by having to worry about all of you."

Osorkon's eyebrow lifted with the comment. "Trying to force us to leave by angering us? It won't work."

"Father is right," Inorus said. "We agreed to see you through this mission, and we shall."

"I for one will not go home and have my reputation sullied because I failed to acquire the Orb of Prophecy," Khonsu said nonchalantly. "That Orb is mine."

"Osorkon, you have one stubborn family," growled Ilfanti. "Won't you all just do what you're told for once?"

"No," Osorkon said. "We'll see this through."

Ilfanti sighed, revising his strategy to somehow include the others. "How about this? Inorus and Khonsu will take the hobgoblin out to safety, and Osorkon can snag the Orb of Prophecy, and then join you. If I defeat the priestess I'll join you, too. If not, get the Orb to the *Soaring Mist*."

"One change," Khonsu said. "I'll get the Orb. Father is hurt."

"And not too proud to admit that his daughter has surpassed him in skill," Osorkon added with a sigh. "She'll get the Orb just fine. Are you sure you want us to leave, though?"

"Yes," Ilfanti said. "The Orb is all that is important here. It doesn't matter what happens to me."

"It matters to me," Khonsu whispered.

"And to me," Osorkon quickly added.

"To us all," Inorus admitted.

Ilfanti was at a loss of words for a moment. His heart filled with warmth and a sense of appreciation that he had never experienced before. Was this love? "Don't worry, I don't plan on dying tonight. Too much I want to do."

"Then get to it," Osorkon said, his head nodding to beckon the priestess. "Good luck, old friend."

"To us all," Ilfanti said. He then turned and faced the dalvor, openly challenging her and feeling ready for anything. This was it. This is what it would all come down to. He had something to live for and a goal to achieve. No matter how powerful she was—or thought she was—he would find a way past her defenses to claim victory. He was Ilfanti, and it was time that the priestess learned exactly what that meant.

❋ ❋ ❋ ❋ ❋

The dwarves watched Ilfanti as he made his way across the chamber. His hands were clenched, and soon began to glow as he built up a charge of mystical energy. They all wanted to help, but in battles between a sorceress priestess and a Mage, they would just get in the way.

Osorkon pulled his gaze away from Ilfanti and stared at Crick. "You heard what we need to do, so let's do it."

"Are we really going to leave him?" Inorus asked, twirling his blades and still ready to fight.

"We're really leaving him," Osorkon said. "Khonsu, can you get the Orb?"

"There was some kind of barrier around it," Khonsu said.

"Go at it from below," Osorkon suggested. "Find a way."

"I will," Khonsu promised.

"Get going, then," Osorkon instructed. "We'll see you outside."

After Khonsu ran to the dais holding the Orb of Prophecy, Osorkon and Inorus headed over to where Crick had collapsed. Inorus returned his swords to their scabbards, and the two dwarves lifted an arm each, trying to drag the armored hobgoblin.

"Ugh," groaned Osorkon. "He's heavier than he looks."

"The armor is heavy," Inorus said. "Far too heavy for the desert."

"Good thing he doesn't stay here longer then," Osorkon said. "No use complaining, let's start moving!"

The two dwarves forced their first step, the armored form of Crick barely dragging behind them, but then with the second step, they saw progress. Crick was heavy, but together they could move him. The battles with Kabilian and the wraith; Ilfanti and the priestess; and the summoned beasts and the remaining undead of Ramahatra raged around them as they moved, but they ultimately reached the steps leading out of the temple and the courtyard.

Osorkon dropped Crick's arm and stretched his back, wincing at the pain from his broken ribs. He pointed at the horizon: "Daylight is upon us."

✦ ✦ ✦ ✦ ✦

Khonsu raced over to the dais where the Orb was positioned and reached for it once more, feeling the same barrier prevent her from touching it. Reaching down, Khonsu picked up a handful of sand and tossed it in the air over the dais. The sand slid down as if a dome was covering the Orb.

Glancing at Ilfanti and the priestess, Khonsu wondered if she would have to wait until the priestess was dead or unconscious before the spell would be broken. If so, then she might be here for a while.

Thinking of her father's suggestion, Khonsu took her remaining pickaxe and began chiseling at the obsidian dais. Chunks of rock shattered beneath her strikes, bringing a slight grin to her face as she realized that the barrier did not protect the entire display.

Khonsu kept working at it until there was an opening in the dais. She then used her dagger and tried to pry in further, forcing it up and under the protective barrier. When her dagger broke the top of the dais and jabbed the air next to the Orb of Prophecy, Khonsu pumped her fist triumphantly. It was only a matter of time before she would have it.

CHAPTER 66

Ilfanti bit his lip, oblivious to the slow trickle of blood that began dripping from it until the unmistakable taste reached his tongue. The priestess required every ounce of his attention, and the slightest misstep or hesitation seemed to give her the upper hand. As the blood in Ilfanti's mouth registered, in the split second that it took him to ponder what it was, he knew he would suffer for it.

The dalvor lowered her staff, sending a continuous stream of black light at Ilfanti. As Ilfanti erected a barrier to deflect the darkness, and focused on his bit lip, he missed the subtle gesture that the priestess had made. It was not much, nothing fatal, but still a mistake. From beneath Ilfanti, behind his protective shield, a magical gust of wind blew, sending sand and stone at the dwarf, pelting him and momentarily blinding him. As Ilfanti reacted, the black light struck him on the chest and burned through to his skin.

Ilfanti fell to the ground and slid away from the dalvor with the force of her strike. His eyes rolled in the back of his head for a moment as the black light began waging a battle within Ilfanti. Ilfanti could feel it inside of him, like a cloud trying to cut off his mystical powers at the source.

He knew he could not focus solely on the battle within, the cackling priestess already closing in on him to strike a deathblow. Forcing himself to his feet, Ilfanti strained to regain his focus, which remained dizzy and hazy, and spotted a blur that had to be the dalvor. Unable to really think about what he was doing, Ilfanti tried to create a powerful surge with every ounce of magic that his body could still muster in his condition, and then brought his fist slamming down on the ground, releasing the magical onslaught.

From his fist, the ground began to tremble, and then split—small cracks at first and then a widening chasm that made its way toward the dalvor. Ilfanti hated that he had to split his focus, and not make certain that the priestess would at least be distracted for a few moments, but if he did not deal with the darkness that was corrupting his body, then he would no longer be able to defend himself.

Sitting on the ground, cross-legged, Ilfanti closed his eyes and began to concentrate. His surroundings, the tremors of the ground, the cackling of the dalvor, the roars of the dragon and the koxlen, and the battle between Kabilian and the demonic Alaran faded away as if they were nonexistent. Ilfanti sent his consciousness within, searching for what he thought of as a virus.

When he opened his eyes, he was no longer in the temple of Ramahatra, but was deep within his own mind, on a plane of existence that only the most focused and talented Mages could reach. It was a world where physical prowess and magical abilities were meaningless. Here, only the acuity and sophistication of the mind were important. The only boundaries imposed on a Mage were those that they imposed on themselves. Even knowing this, very few Mages were able to master mind magic.

Ilfanti was wise enough to know that mind magic was not his forte. The Mages that excelled at this often spent their entire lives learning to manipulate and control their abilities and the environments created by their minds. Rather than doing that, Ilfanti had been traveling the world seeking thrills and adventure. Even so, he knew enough to perhaps halt the flow of darkness within his body.

When using mind magic, Ilfanti saw himself encased in a suit of elegant white armor. The armor was elaborately decorated with elven designs, something Ilfanti always thought a bit unusual since he was a dwarf. In his hand he held a sword, but not a real sword—he held a hilt, and from the hilt there was a humming blade that emitted an aura of pure white light.

His surroundings were unexpected, but felt quite familiar. As Ilfanti glanced around, he recognized Otarima, the legendary Aezian city that was paved in gold. If Ilfanti had completely mastered the ability to mind walk, he could manipulate his surroundings, but instead he accepted them as familiar, and, he had to admit, far more pleasant than Ramahatra.

In the distance, he saw the day had turned into night, as a wall of darkness was approaching him, consuming everything that it passed. Ilfanti studied the image, and searched for some kind of consciousness within the shadows, but found none. If there was no consciousness guiding the wave, then he hoped that he could deal with it far more easily. After all, there was no real foe.

Ilfanti charged forward, running straight for the wall of darkness. He tightened his grip on his sword, and then leapt into the air. From his armor, wings sprouted and Ilfanti soared to the top of the dark cluster, wondering if everything that the wave touched had turned dark. Behind the wave, Ilfanti saw Otarima as it would be at night, but otherwise undisturbed.

Diving down before the wave of darkness, Ilfanti soared to the ground, taking his sword and slicing into the earth. With the power of his mind, he forced the ground to open into a bottomless pit, where the wave would fall endlessly and cease to trouble him. Ilfanti stood on the other side of the chasm, watching the darkness approach.

As it reached the opening, the darkness began flowing into the opening, bringing a smile to Ilfanti's face as he saw that it was working. Perhaps, he thought, he was better at mind magic than he thought.

Reaching down, he touched the ground and willed the chasm to close, trapping the invading darkness in an endless abyss forevermore. The ground sealed together, leaving a single black dot that Ilfanti could not get rid of no matter how much he rubbed at it. Deciding to leave it for the moment, Ilfanti studied the darkened Otarima, and sensed that he had to not only destroy the wave of darkness, but reverse its effect as well. Taking his sword, he dug it into the ground, and watched as light began streaking through the ground like veins; bringing color and illumination back to the environment.

Satisfied with his effort, Ilfanti returned one last time to look at the black dot. It began to bubble, and Ilfanti scurried back when he saw the dalvor emerge before him, dressed entirely in black-snake-scaled armor. As soon as she emerged, dozens of snakes also crawled from the dot, slithering along the ground and leaving a trail of darkness on whatever they touched.

Ilfanti was at a loss. Was the dalvor a Mage? She certainly commanded magic, but her methods were different than his—casting spells and using incantations instead of instinctively feeling and performing magic. Having her in his mind was disturbing, and brought to question the fact that only Mages could walk the paths of the mind. If this battle became one of wills, Ilfanti doubted that he had the experience to defeat his foe. On the physical plane, he was holding his own, and doing his best. Here, the outcome was far less favorable.

❁ ❁ ❁ ❁ ❁

Khonsu kept cutting at the stone, working her dagger frantically up and into the protective barrier. As chunks fell, she reached in with her other hand and cleared the debris, not letting it get in her way. She was almost there. She could feel the orb, its radiance, and its pulsating power beckoning her to claim it. With one last thrust of her dagger, the dais crumbled enough for the orb to fall through the hole, and land safely in Khonsu's waiting palm.

Lifting the Orb of Prophecy, Khonsu, who was inexperienced with enchanted items, suddenly found herself lost. The iridescent glow of the orb increased and consumed her. Khonsu felt nauseated as she saw herself moving over the sand more swiftly than the fastest animal, reaching her home of Memtorren, and seeing the dwarven city in shambles. Khonsu gasped at the destruction, unable to comprehend what it could possibly mean.

She saw the bodies of her people lying everywhere, their lifeless eyes all staring at her pleadingly. She knew, instinctively, that they wanted her to perform the burial rites so that they could join their ancestors in Wolhollm. There were so many, though, too many. What could possibly have caused this?

The thought sent her soaring again, this time reaching Talhella. It too looked in shambles. Buildings shattered, bodies lying lifelessly, water flowing crimson in the aqueducts, and no apparent signs of life. With the thought of life, the image shifted to the palace of Pharaoh Werirenptah, and Khonsu saw the ruler of Egziard in the air, being held motionless by a beast that had the body of a man and the head of a cobra. Werirenptah was gagging, as if he were being strangled. The creature was glaring at him, his right arm outstretched, but not physically touching the Pharaoh. Somehow, he must have been magically holding the Pharaoh in place.

"This is for your defiance of the Gods," the creature said, slowly, menacingly.

Khonsu shrieked, and in that instant, she dropped the Orb of Prophecy. As the orb hit the sand and rolled, Khonsu lost the image, and found herself back in Ramahatra, in the temple, standing next to the dais. She felt disoriented, and could not help but bend over and vomit. Was that her future? The future of Egziard? This country had lived in peace for generations. What could happen that would cause such mayhem and destruction? Who was the man with the head of a beast? Khonsu feared that the answers to those questions had to be answered, or the future of her homeland would be in peril.

Not wanting to touch the orb again, Khonsu tore some of the fabric from her tunic and used it to lift the orb, wrapping it so that she could hold it without falling victim to its magical effects again.

As Khonsu held the wrapped orb up, she felt the ground begin to shake as tremors filled the temple. She searched for the source of the quake, and saw Ilfanti lifting his hand from a crevice growing in the ground. He then sat down cross-legged, his eyes closed. Khonsu found the position quite unusual, but wondered if it had something to do with the black stain on his chest—a mark that was smoking much like her father's had been doing earlier.

Focusing on the priestess, Khonsu watched the crevice grow, sand and obsidian dropping into it. The dalvor backed away, not taking her gaze from Ilfanti as the ground opened before her, swallowing everything. Finally, the temple stopped shaking, and the ground stopped splitting. The dalvor glared at Ilfanti, hatred evident in her glowing eyes, and sat down opposite Ilfanti, a wide chasm between them. She too closed her eyes, and Khonsu wondered exactly what was going on.

As the priestess's head drooped, Khonsu wondered if she could perhaps sneak up upon the dalvor and end this struggle with one slash of her blade. Remembering that Ilfanti had said that the orb was all that was important, she growled in frustration, and made her way to the doorway leading out of the temple. With a final glance back at Ilfanti,

Khonsu prayed that it was not the last time she would see the dwarf alive.

❀ ❀ ❀ ❀ ❀

After sparring with the demonic Rhyne for what seemed like the longest battle he had ever been in, Kabilian wished that he could go back and just kill the bounty hunter before he had been possessed. This demonic version was a creature of few words, only hissing, growling, and foaming at the mouth, but it was also faster, stronger, and could endure more pain than its host could when alive.

The ice shards, to Kabilian's dismay, had not worked. He then tried his enchanted bracers, sending drugged darts at the wraith, but even though the darts somehow managed to pierce its skin, unlike the wooden arrows, it had no effect on the wraith. Kabilian considered briefly summoning his dragon or koxlen to assist him, but they were still finishing off the undead creatures, and though there were only a few remaining, Kabilian did not want to have to split his attention between them and this demon.

In his peripheral vision Kabilian saw the dwarf claim the Orb of Prophecy and run from the temple. For the briefest of moments, Kabilian pondered using his amulet to transport him outside, leaving Ilfanti alone to deal with both Rhyne and the priestess. What did he care if the Mage lived or died, as long as he got the Orb of Prophecy from the dwarf? The thought left his mind as quickly as it had arrived. He might be an assassin, but he always maintained an ethical standard. Sometimes that seemed a bit contradictory—especially considering his preferred occupation—but he would not abandon an ally in need for personal gain.

Retrieving his second dagger from his belt, Kabilian whispered the incantation to enlarge it into a full-length sword. Twirling the two, he grinned knowingly at the demon. This fight would only have one conclusion—the death of the demonic Rhyne.

CHAPTER 67

"Foolish Mage, the outcome of this battle was decided before it even began," the priestess taunted.

Ilfanti tightened his grip on his sword, his eyes never leaving that of his foe. There were far too many questions that he did not have the answers to, and this certainly was not the time to try and get them. Before his eyes, the dalvor began to grow, her body widening and leaving the boundaries of her mortal form behind. As he watched, she turned into a snake that towered over him, its glowing eyes glaring down hungrily.

"Oh, crud," grumbled Ilfanti. He knew that he could take any form, and manipulate his surroundings in this landscape. It was how he had grown wings to fight the wave of darkness. All he had to do was think of the form he wanted, and then have the willpower to force the transformation. Suddenly, Ilfanti found his mind quite blank.

Several of the smaller snakes slithered around Ilfanti, wrapping around his legs and moving up them. Ilfanti swiped his blade down, striking the shadow-serpents and severing them in half. When they fell, they vanished completely.

The mouth of the giant snake came down, gnashing in the air where Ilfanti had stood. Ilfanti rolled out of the way, then swooped into the air upon his wings. He circled the head of the snake, jabbing with his sword whenever he could. He saw the darkness of the snake begin to illuminate momentarily, but then fade back into shadows as if he had no effect.

Lifting higher into the sky, Ilfanti tried to think about what to do. So far, his tactics were not working at all. The priestess was not about to let him have the time he needed. From the back of her serpent body, she grew massive wings—like those of a dragon—and swooped into the air after Ilfanti.

Ilfanti's eyes widened momentarily, but the shock only lasted an instant, and then he was in control again. He wished that Master Ariness of the Council of Elders, Master Aravinda of the Drannin, or Master Cali of the Mage's Academy were here. They were the most prominent Mind Mages that he knew of, and he bet that they could swat the snake down without hesitation.

As he thought of his colleagues, Ilfanti wondered if that were the answer. Did he just need to think about swatting the snake? If so, he would need a pretty large instrument to do so. Ilfanti grinned, knowingly, as he soared away from the flying priestess. He knew exactly what to do. After all, the setting was his. He was in Otarima. The answer lay by the southern wall.

Ilfanti glanced back, making certain that the dalvor was following him. He grimaced to see that she was gaining—and why not? Her wings were larger! Ilfanti held his wings close to his body, darting through the sky as quickly as he could. He was almost there.

"You cannot flee," the priestess hissed behind him. "Wherever you go, I shall follow."

Ilfanti certainly hoped so. Ahead, he knew what was waiting for him. Before Otarima had been lost, warlords of the south that rode dragons into combat had plagued the city. At least once a week, according to scrolls that Ilfanti had discovered, the warlords would strike to try and steal the gold of Otarima. At least once a week, the people of Otarima would thwart the assault. Defending against dragons was something they had become quite skilled at, more skilled than any other civilization that Ilfanti had ever come across, even the dreaded dragon hunters who had brought about the end of the Age of the Dragon in the Seven Kingdoms.

Ilfanti could visualize the vast weapons on and behind the southern wall. There were a dozen ballistae to send a barrage into the air that dragons were hard-pressed to dodge all at once. Upon towers, they had created massive harpoons that were launched like arrows to strike the wings and bodies of dragons and drag them down with reinforced lines. Otarima also had gifted warriors who wielded bows that were more powerful than those designed by elves, sending their arrows at a velocity much faster than the warlords would expect. Otarima also boasted a legion of Mahotsukai, the Aezian spellcasters.

As Ilfanti thought of these, he visualized the defenses being prepared, and Otarima coming to life to repel another warlord invader. Soaring over the defenses, Ilfanti pumped his fist in triumph, seeing that the southern wall was ready to strike the priestess, just as he wanted—and had created.

The dalvor flew past one of the sacred temples, and spotted the defenses aligned against her. She hesitated, momentarily, and then laughed at Ilfanti's effort. Her laughter quickly faded as the ballistae snapped and the air was full of jagged projectiles, flaming oil-lined cloths that would explode and scatter on contact, and balls of concrete.

She tried to evade the incoming arsenal, but found herself struck in several places, her wings ablaze. As she shrieked in anger, several harpoons were launched, two striking her left wing, and the third her right, trapping her where she was.

Hundreds of archers lined the wall, their arrows already nocked as they waited for the command. Ilfanti soared over the archers, and as he reached the end of their ranks, he slashed his sword down and shouted, "Fire!" Arrows filled the air, striking the giant serpent, piercing her dark scales with such force that she shuddered with each impact.

"Mahotsukai!" Ilfanti shouted.

In the courtyard, a dozen elegantly dressed older men and women began moving their arms in unison, creating identical gestures as they began chanting the same phrase. Ilfanti listened, but knew that the words were coming from his imagination and did not necessarily mean anything.

"Sin, cha, who, la, ti, fahn, to, chell," they all said as one. Their bodies then rose into the air, moving vertically atop a portion of sod torn out of the ground. They all floated before the serpent, their arms still moving in unison. "Fah, tis, toh, ge, ak, nel!"

As their chant ended, the ground began trembling, and giant boulders burst from beneath, leaving building-sized craters where they had been. The boulders soared high into the sky, much higher than the bound serpent and the Mahotsukai. In the air, they ceased their ascent, and then began falling back down, all aimed directly at the bound snake. As the boulders closed in, they burst into flames as their speed broke the sound barrier.

The bound dalvor pushed and pulled, struggling to move with all of her might. In the end, she lowered her gaze at Ilfanti, and Ilfanti swore that she actually grinned and snickered as the boulders began striking her, tearing her body to pieces with the impact. After the second strike, the snake lost cohesion and appeared to evaporate.

Ilfanti raised his hand and saluted the Mahotsukai. They were not real, he knew, but his ability to conjure them in his mind had saved his life. For that, he was grateful. Focusing on leaving his mind, Ilfanti closed his eyes, and when he opened them, he was back in the temple of Ramahatra. Across from him was the priestess, her staff shattered in half, her arm hanging limply, and blood flowing like a river from her nose.

"You will suffer for that, Mage," she snarled.

Ilfanti's grin widened. He had hurt her in their telepathic battle, and now they were back on a plane of existence he was much more comfortable with. If she had truly known the outcome of this battle, then she would not be so angry and surprised that he had harmed her. The Orb may have warned her that he was coming, but the future was still an open book.

❉ ❉ ❉ ❉ ❉

Khonsu stepped outside of the tunnel, shielding her eyes from the glaring morning sun. When they had arrived last night, she had hoped to be gone before the sun rose, but now, it really did not matter. The entire city knew that it had been under siege. She could see that just by looking around.

Osorkon, Inorus, and Crick were at the bottom of the temple steps, her father tending to the hobgoblin and trying to rouse him. When Khonsu joined them, the armored Crick was conscious, but certainly not coherent.

Inorus was standing—his arms crossed while he waited—above his father and Crick. He watched her closely from the moment she left the temple. "Did you get it?"

Khonsu lifted the torn tunic to show that the orb was wrapped within. Her face was expressionless, and her posture looked fatigued. The effort to even hold up the orb was a struggle. Inorus noticed and took the orb from his sister.

"What troubles you? Ilfanti?" Inorus asked.

Osorkon glanced up from Crick to see his daughter's reply.

"We're doomed," Khonsu whispered, the words so soft that the dwarves had to strain to hear her.

"We'll make it," Osorkon said, reassuringly. "And if I know Ilfanti, he'll make it too."

"No," Khonsu protested, her face pale. "You don't understand. We're doomed. All of us."

"That's nonsense," Osorkon said, standing up and embracing his daughter.

"I saw it," admitted Khonsu.

Inorus lifted the orb, and wondered if his sister had seen the future by using it. Perhaps he too should look, just to see what had spooked Khonsu so badly. Osorkon shook his head back and forth, knowing what his son was contemplating.

"We should leave," Osorkon said. "Put some distance between us and Ramahatra. Ilfanti will catch up."

Inorus obediently nodded, bending down and helping Crick to his feet. "Time to go."

"Flying," moaned Crick. "Like mystral."

"Sure you are," Inorus said. "One foot in front of the other, come on." As Crick shuffled his feet, holding onto Inorus for support, and moving slowly for the gates of Ramahatra, Inorus nodded approvingly. "That's it, you're doing it."

Osorkon took Khonsu in his arms, leaning her head onto his shoulder, and followed Inorus. His ribs were aching, but he would not give in to the pain when his daughter needed him as she did now. He wondered what exactly Khonsu could possibly have seen that would have terrified her so. She was such a strong-willed daughter, he did not think that anything could breach her defenses. But something had, and it had devastated her. Whatever it was, he would be there, and he would be strong for her, as a father should be for his daughter.

❋ ❋ ❋ ❋ ❋

Deflecting another hellfire dagger, Kabilian wondered if he should try to find some way to delay Rhyne long enough to drink a potion, such as Quicksilver—a potion that would allow him to move so quickly that he appeared to almost be a blur to those around him. Of course, that particular potion always left Kabilian feeling dizzy and disoriented when it wore off, but hopefully Rhyne would have been killed by then.

If not a potion, then perhaps an enchanted ring. The Ring of Power would provide him with increased physical strength, possibly enough to match the newfound power of the wraith. That, or the Ring of Dexterity, which would increase his skill and movement of his hands and body.

Even if he did decide to drink a potion or put on a ring, Kabilian would need time to do so. It would take only a few seconds to extract it from his Mage's satchel and use it, but the demonic Rhyne would not allow him those precious moments. His daggers may be enchanted, but other than his Xylona honor blade, they were the least mystical items in his repertoire. It had been a long time since Kabilian had fought without relying upon his potions, rings, scepters, bracers, and numerous other magical items.

Kabilian deflected another hellfire dagger, and as he went to counter the attack, Rhyne leapt overhead, tossing hellfire daggers down as he did so. Kabilian dropped and tried to deflect the flaming blades, but at that angle, could not do so. One struck his right shoulder, the other grazed his waist on the left.

Kabilian rolled on the ground, trying to douse the flames in the sand, and also to separate himself from the wraith, who was already attacking again. Even with his shoulder wound, Kabilian refused to drop his sword, knowing that without it, he would not be able to beat the demon.

When the flames went out, Kabilian moved into a crouching position, and then propelled himself at Rhyne, bringing his blades forward and burying them deep into Rhyne's chest. The demon had been careless, assuming that Kabilian could not counterattack after that last maneuver. The demon was wrong.

As Kabilian buried his blades to the hilt, he could feel the intense heat blazing around the skin of the wraith. His hands were tingling and felt as if they were burning just as much as his shoulder and side had been when struck by flames. Kabilian refused to yield, twisting the blades from side to side to try and do as much damage as possible.

The wraith hissed, and then began snickering, as if amused.

"That's not good," groaned Kabilian as he searched the demon's eyes for signs of pain. The wraith glared back at him, no hint of injury at all. Instead, it reached out and grabbed Kabilian by the collar, pulling him closer, making the aura of heat around him singe bare skin.

Kabilian rammed his knee up, striking the wraith and yelping with the impact. He managed to free himself, but the wraith's new spikes had shredded his pants and dug into his flesh. With the heat of the wraith, the wound had instantly cauterized, leaving a hole just above his knee.

Kabilian stumbled backwards, pulling his swords from the wraith as he fell, and landing on his backside. The demon hissed delightedly as it stepped closer to Kabilian, who could not take his eyes from his leg, the open wound and the blistered skin. Reaching for Kabilian's throat, the demon hissed triumphantly. It would tighten its hands around his throat, strangling him and burning the life from him at the same time.

The black fingers of the wraith touched Kabilian's throat, burning it instantly, and then his whole hand was upon the assassin. Kabilian, who seemingly had not noticed, and showed no apparent reaction to the pain he was undoubtedly feeling, waited, staring blankly at his knee. Then, without any hint of retaliation evident, he brought his two swords slashing up and dug them into the wraith's arms, pulling his blades with all of his might until he forced the blades through the wraith, severing his arms.

Rhyne leapt back, hissing angrily at the attack, and glared menacingly at Kabilian. Kabilian knocked the arms from his throat, not wanting to even look at the damage that the wraith had caused. His whole body felt like it was burning. Every breath tasted like smoke, and he felt more parched than he ever remembered being.

"Game over," Kabilian whispered in a weak and scratchy voice as he used his swords to help lift himself back up. His knee objected, sending waves of pain cascading through his nerves, but he had the initiative now. It was time to end this battle once and for all.

The demon hissed again, and to Kabilian's dismay, flames sprang from the stumps of its arms, and took the form of arms. The flames faded, and before Kabilian's eyes, bones were forged, quickly covered with muscle, and finally skin began to flow from his body down the arms.

Kabilian limped toward Rhyne, stopping when he was face-to-face with the creature, feeling the heat emanating from the demon. His burns felt intensely worse this close to heat, but Kabilian bore the pain without flinching or pulling away. His eyes flickered to Rhyne's arms, which were almost completely reformed. When they were, then the demon would be back to full strength, and Kabilian would be little more than a hobbling victim, waiting to be killed.

He was not going to let that happen. Using the distraction to his advantage, Kabilian swiped both blades up, striking Rhyne on both sides of his neck and severing his head. His body slumped to the ground, lifeless. His head rolled along the sand, stopping face up.

"Regrow that," growled Kabilian, defiantly. He whispered the silent incantation to transform his swords back into daggers, and slid them into his belt. He then reached into his satchel, thinking of a Healing Potion, and produced the glass vial. As he brought it to his lips, feeling the coolness of the glass and the potion, he heard a sound that sent shivers down his spine—the hissing of the demon.

Kabilian stared in shock at the decapitated head, smiling deviously and hissing. If severing a head did not kill it, then what possibly could? Kabilian drank the remaining contents of his Healing Potion in one swig, and then threw the empty vial away from him. Reaching into his satchel, he removed one of his scepters, Inferno.

Blizzard had had no effect, and Kabilian was running out of options. With the heat and flames that Rhyne was emitting, launching more fire at him may not be the best decision, but Kabilian had to at least try it.

Lowering the tip of Inferno at Rhyne's head, he unleashed a succession of fire-blasts at the demon. Even in the midst of the blazing fire, Kabilian could still hear the unmistakable hissing of his foe. If decapitating it and burning it did not work, then Kabilian was at a loss. How could he defeat it?

As he considered his options, he paused, listening. The hissing had ceased. Kabilian halted the fire bursts, and looked at the smoldering head. Only a charred skull remained where the demonic head had fallen. Kabilian sighed, thankful that the beast was finally dead.

After returning his scepter to his satchel, Kabilian rubbed his fingers along the wound on his leg. The potion was already doing its job, knitting the injury. The blistering and redness around the wound was also fading, but not quickly enough. He would need several more potions to eliminate the scarring completely. He did not intend to keep a memento from this place.

With the demon dead, Kabilian searched first for the Orb, making certain that Khonsu had left with it. Satisfied that she had not been stopped at the door, he assumed that the dwarf had taken it from the temple. He then summoned his dragon and koxlen to him. The undead that they were facing had been defeated. With a wave of his hand and a quick incantation, the dragon faded into a tooth, and the koxlen into a claw. Kabilian placed both back in his satchel, thankful that his beasts had been able to help him in this encounter.

Now that his own concerns were addressed, Kabilian turned his attention on Ilfanti and the dalvor. The two were fighting, sending bolts of magic at each other, each deflecting the strikes in what looked like an endless battle. If not for the sight of the dalvor's blood and limp arm, Kabilian would have thought that the battle was a stalemate. However, Ilfanti had hurt the priestess. In time, he would win. With a grin, Kabilian's decision was made—he would help bring about the demise of the priestess a bit sooner, and then, Ilfanti would have to let him use the Orb of Prophecy, especially if he thought Kabilian had saved his life.

CHAPTER 68

Ilfanti wanted to find a quick way out of the temple. He did not have a desire to kill his opponent, only to escape and find his companions, who already had the Orb of Prophecy. The priestess was extremely powerful, and, Ilfanti had discovered, quite innovative and resourceful. He was amazed by some of the spells that she had used to attack him. The ground beneath him had turned to quicksand; the weapons of the fallen undead soared to life to strike; illusions were cast to try and deceive him; and she even used a spell that made Ilfanti itch incessantly from the sensation of hundreds of small insects crawling over him.

As a burst of lightning lanced out at him, easily deflected by the dwarf, Ilfanti wondered if the spell that had defeated the dalvor in their mind magic duel would also be able to do so in the physical plane. Ilfanti concentrated on the ground, and all around the temple, stones and sand began rising into the air. They were not quite the boulders of the Mahotsukai, but this was a desert, after all.

Deciding to alter his strategy slightly, Ilfanti created hurricane-force winds to sweep up what he had lifted, and sent sand, dust, and debris spiraling around the dalvor. He could hear her muffled screams as sand filled her mouth, and everything was soaring so quickly that he was certain it was tearing her skin to shreds.

Lowering the velocity of the winds, Ilfanti grimaced when he saw the dalvor, staring at him with hatred, but for the most part unharmed. Her hair was in disarray, her clothing now in tatters, and her exposed skin bleeding, but she had also managed to erect a small shield—which was probably the only reason she was still conscious.

As Ilfanti returned her gaze, he flinched as a fireball struck the dalvor. The priestess fell backwards, raising her good arm to defend herself as a shard of ice struck her arm. Kabilian!

Ilfanti took the respite to take a deep breath and try to regain his focus and composure. For a dwarf who didn't like to use magic when on a quest, he certainly had used plenty on this one. As Ilfanti watched the dalvor defend herself from Kabilian, he saw her sidestep a ray of light that was coming from the dome above. Ilfanti glanced up and saw the rope dangling from it, and knew that it must have been where Khonsu had entered the temple.

The dalvor stepped forward, trying to claim the initiative against Kabilian, raising her bleeding arm and sending streamers of darkness floating through the air. They touched Kabilian and began to bind him where he was. The assassin struggled, but the streamers constricted and forced him to the ground, cussing as he fell.

Ilfanti ignored the plight of the assassin, focusing instead on the priestess's movements. Once again, she avoided the beam of sunlight. Remembering Khonsu's words, "The morning sun will shine on us and our victory," and the rumor that dalvor turned to stone in daylight, Ilfanti suddenly wondered if the secret to defeating her was within his grasp.

He looked up at the dome, and then at the priestess again. She would have to be in the perfect position for him to try it. All he had to do was convince her to go where he wanted. Stepping to the center of the temple, directly beneath the dome, Ilfanti took a deep breath. He was ready. Now, he had a plan. A dangerous one, perhaps, but a plan.

❋ ❋ ❋ ❋ ❋

The dwarves and Crick—who was now finally back to normal—made their way out of Ramahatra and back up the dune they had come down the night before. The camels would be further down the slope, and then they would follow the Sanjeez all the way back to Talhella, a much easier trip than wandering the vast sea of sand.

As they reached the top of the dune, all four stopped, staring in shock at the hundreds of cloaked and hooded people on the other side. One of the people spotted them and shouted out, sending dozens running at the dwarves and hobgoblin.

What were they to do? Fight hundreds again? In their condition? Osorkon let Khonsu go and stepped forward, his palms held up to show that he was not going to be a threat or give them any trouble. With a sidelong glance at Inorus, who had his hands on his hilts, he showed his displeasure, and that was enough for Inorus to raise his arms as well.

The people grabbed them and roughly took them down the slope to where others had gathered. Each of the dwarves was pushed down to the ground. Crick tried to defy them and refused to kneel, but they kicked his knees from behind so that he too was forced down.

One individual stepped forward, pulling his cloak down. He had the face of a sabrenoh, with short gray fur, large incisors, and catlike eyes. But, he also had the ears of an elf, and a familiar tattoo upon his forehead. The same tattoo, Osorkon remembered, as those he had seen in the depths of Ramahatra when he and Ilfanti first arrived.

"You survived Ramahatra?" the gray-furred creature asked. "Survived Nefrukakashta?"

Osorkon was not certain about the name, but assumed that it must be the priestess. "We have," Osorkon said.

"You bring ruin to us all," the creature said.

"We do not," Osorkon replied. "We escaped the dalvor priestess, this Nefrukakashta as you call her, and one of our own, even now, is trying to bring about her demise."

"He will fail," the creature said. "As do all who try."

"You do not know my friend," Osorkon grinned, proudly.

"All those that visit Ramahatra suffer an excruciating death," the creature said. "We shall spare you of that."

"Wait just one second!" Crick growled as he began to stand up. Several hooded creatures from behind forced him back down.

"Silence," the gray-furred creature growled. "You have all been cursed. If you were to live, you would spread the curse."

Khonsu gasped, wondering if what she had seen when she touched the Orb of Prophecy was her fault. Were they cursed? Was it possible that the destruction of Memtorren and Talhella was directly related to their departure of Ramahatra?

"Who are you to determine our fate?" Osorkon asked challengingly.

"I am Ra'veez, elder of the sacred order of the Co'iahla," the gray furred one replied. "It is our duty to keep Ramahatra hidden so that the curse will not spread, and then deal with the consequences if we fail."

"We're the consequences, eh?" Osorkon asked.

"You are," Ra'veez replied matter-of-factly. "I am sorry. Your fate was sealed the moment you set foot inside of Ramahatra. I assure you, your death at our hands will be far more lenient and quick than that which the curse would see you have."

"Death is death," growled Osorkon. "I don't think I'll like it however it happens."

CHAPTER 69

The priestess walked over to Kabilian, and reached down to touch him. Ilfanti had seen her do the same thing to Osorkon when she burned his chest. The fact that she appeared to enjoy being close to her enemies as she killed them increased Ilfanti's confidence in his plan.

"Hey, you forget about me?" Ilfanti shouted, sending a low-energy magical ball at the dalvor, striking her on her side with minimal force.

The dalvor jerked upright, sneering, and turned away from Kabilian, focusing on Ilfanti once more. Ilfanti knew that she was too smart and cunning to have forgotten about him, so he wondered why she left herself open like that. Perhaps, he speculated, she could somehow absorb Kabilian's life to help restore her own health and vitality. Looking at her, she certainly appeared to need medical treatment. Still, Ilfanti was not going to underestimate his foe.

"I forget nothing, *Mage*," she growled, nearly spitting the word Mage. As she made the comment, she narrowed her glowing eyes and two beams lanced out and struck Ilfanti on the chest.

Ilfanti toppled to the ground, in agony. This was what he wanted, and he had braced himself for it, but he did not expect the pain to be so excruciating. He was not certain if he blacked out or not, but the dalvor had been across the chamber, and suddenly, she was atop him, her hand reaching down to his chest.

Ilfanti, lying on his back, looked up. Not at the priestess who was about to end his life, but at the shaded glass dome at the top of the temple. Raising his arm, which took far more effort than it should have, Ilfanti used all of his remaining strength to send one last burst of magical power shooting upwards. The stream was silver, and burned like fire, streaking skywards.

The priestess backed away, thinking that the dwarf was trying to strike her. She glanced, perplexed, at the dwarf, who was grinning triumphantly, and then followed his gaze up to the dome of the temple.

The silver beam struck the dome and shattered it, soaring directly through it and into the sky—the sunlit sky. Shards of glass exploded, flying away from the temple and raining down upon them inside.

Ilfanti tried to erect a protective barrier over himself, and saw that his hand was trembling as he did so. The shield formed, but kept crackling as it faded in and out of existence.

The dalvor waved her arms and most of the shards were redirected. As soon as she did, she realized her mistake—a fatal error for a dalvor. With the shaded glass out of the way, rays of sunlight shone down directly upon her. She tried to move, to run out of the way, but her legs were slow and sluggish, stiffening beneath her. She tried to lift her arm to block the rays with her arm, but it solidified where it was. She tried to pull her eyes away from the light and look elsewhere, but her head would not obey her command.

Ilfanti stared at the transformation. It took only seconds from when the dalvor was first exposed to sunlight for her entire body to turn to stone, creating a lifelike statue where the deadly priestess had stood. As Ilfanti slowly managed to get to his feet, the statue was already beginning to crumble and decay, as if it were many millennia old. Before Ilfanti reached Kabilian's side, the dalvor was little more than a pile of dust blowing in the wind.

❊ ❊ ❊ ❊ ❊

On the open sands, the Co'iahla were preparing to execute the dwarves and hobgoblin. They lowered the heads of the cursed ones onto large stones, and a Co'iahla stood beside each of them with an axe, waiting to receive the final command to decapitate them and insure that the curse would not spread.

Ra'veez watched the final moments with silent resolve. This was his mission, as it had been for generations, and so it would be for many more. With a nod, the executioners lifted their weapons, ready to carry out the verdict of the elder.

In the sky, a silver light lanced up, bursting all the way to the clouds. The Co'iahla were confused, many running to the top of the dune to see what had caused the effect. Ra'veez stared in the sky, and then watched his kin on the dune, wondering what possibly could be happening now. In all of his years, he had never seen a silver light such as that. It was radiant and beautiful, but powerful beyond imagining.

Saj'haal ran back down the dune. "It was from Ramahatra," she shouted. "The beam burst through the dome."

"Ilfanti," whispered Osorkon, knowingly. He then shouted for Ra'veez to hear: "That came from our friend. Would you wish to incur his wrath by killing us?"

"Is he a God?" Ra'veez asked. "Such power could only be wielded by a God!"

"A God that would be angry if you killed us," Osorkon said, going with the flow.

"Let them up," Ra'veez instructed. "But keep them bound until we learn what this means."

The Co'iahla executioners lowered their weapons and let the dwarves and hobgoblin up. Osorkon sighed with relief. They may not be free, but as long as they lived, there was still hope.

❊ ❊ ❊ ❊ ❊

Deep within Ramahatra, in the passages that Ilfanti and Osorkon had visited, and in hundreds of other tunnels in a vast labyrinth that ran beneath the temple and city, statues began to vibrate. Pieces of stone broke off of the statues, large chunks at a time, leaving living tissue behind.

From inside the casings of the statues, sabrenoh and elven hybrids with tattoos upon their foreheads stepped out, freeing themselves of their prisons. Some had been encased in stone for centuries. Others, not so long. Old allies rejoiced when they saw each other. Sons and daughters were dumbfounded to see parents and grandparents that had been lost centuries before.

All were citizens of Ramahatra from before Nefrukakashta had arrived to plague them, or members of the Co'iahla that had been resisting her and trying to safeguard the city ever since. In their stone prisons, the dalvor priestess was able to absorb their life energy and augment her own, keeping her alive for generations.

As the true inhabitants of Ramahatra emerged, they all prayed that the curse that had been Nefrukakashta had finally been ended. Some were curious, and went to the temple; some were afraid and remained where they were; some were frantic to reach the surface and see daylight for the first time in countless years. They all made their way, like a swarm, searching for the answer, and the freedom, that they desired.

❀ ❀ ❀ ❀ ❀

Ilfanti saw the creatures entering the temple, and tried to brace himself for another attack. At this point, without rest, he doubted he could last for long. The creatures were not hostile, though. They asked about the priestess, and when Ilfanti told them that he had killed her, they lifted him onto their shoulders and shouted triumphantly, promising to make this day a holiday in honor of their liberation.

Ilfanti directed them to Kabilian, and with their help, they freed him of the strands binding him. Kabilian was grumpy, to say the least. He told Ilfanti that he used to have a scar that when tossed at someone, would bind them in a similar fashion. After being bound himself, he said he was glad that he lost the scar in the lair of the Hidden Empire. Nobody should suffer like that.

With the emergence of the victims of Nefrukakashta, the Co'iahla guarding Ramahatra had a reunion with their former colleagues and family members. The dwarves and hobgoblin were immediately released, and the grateful Co'iahla tended to those injured.

True to their word, a holiday was established to honor Ilfanti and his triumph over the priestess. The celebration lasted for seven days and seven nights, with the Co'iahla adamant that everyone remain. They even sought the avarians from Kabilian's Wind Soarer and brought them back to Ramahatra as well.

The occasion was joyous, but for those not from Ramahatra, their impatience and sense of dread was growing. Khonsu had been quiet, and in a constant state of despair since she had touched the Orb. She would not talk to anyone, lost in her own thoughts and fears.

Osorkon harbored many doubts about his ability to adventure any longer. They had won, and that pleased him, but he was more proud of his children than he was at his own performance. Perhaps old adventurers were not supposed to get old, he decided.

Inorus remained stern and silent, constantly watching over his sister to make sure that nothing else happened to her. He was as Ilfanti remembered from the day he first met him. The bold sentinel refusing to let harm come to his family. Admirable.

Crick was quite bored, and refused to remove his armor, damp with sweat. He could not understand why they were remaining. They found what they had come after, now it should be time to return home. He voiced this opinion many times, but the words always fell on deaf ears.

Kabilian seemed almost as anxious to go, as if he had important business waiting for him back in the Seven Kingdoms, but he was also being patient. He had come for the Orb of Prophecy, and though it was in Ilfanti's possession, he was still determined to unlock its secrets and discover what he had traveled so far to learn.

Ilfanti watched Kabilian closely. On that final night, he knew the assassin was ready to approach him. Ilfanti knew that whatever Kabilian said, he could not relinquish the Orb of Prophecy. He had already asked the Orb to show him Karleena, and what he saw broke his heart. To find her, though, he needed to hold onto the Orb so that it could guide him. Kabilian would just have to accept that and live without it.

Kabilian stood up from where he was resting, leaving Crick behind, and walked over to Ilfanti. "That was some adventure, eh?"

"It was," Ilfanti concurred.

"I saved your life, you know, and those of your friends," Kabilian said.

"As I saved yours, and my friends saved your companion," Ilfanti quickly pointed out, knowing that Kabilian was trying to create an argument to persuade Ilfanti to relinquish the Orb.

"That you did," Kabilian said. "Well, we leave in the morning. The avarians are already preparing the ship."

"It would be appreciated if your Wind Soarer could drop us off in Zaman," Ilfanti suggested.

"Perhaps," Kabilian shrugged. "I'm not sure that Captain Glynn would be too enthusiastic about that. It's a small ship, after all."

"I understand," Ilfanti said. "Well, good journey, then."

Kabilian grinned, a wide, knowing, confident grin. "Before I go, I have an offer that I don't think you can refuse."

"Oh?" Ilfanti asked, skeptically.

"Oh," Kabilian said.

An offer I can't refuse? How laughable? How insane? How true! All Kabilian wanted was to use the Orb of Prophecy once. He promised not to deceive me, and to let me keep it. I was skeptical, and doubted him completely. If I gave it to him, he would try to steal it. But, then he made me the offer. In exchange for letting him borrow the Orb for several minutes, he would give me a prize beyond prizes. The reward greater than any reward. A Zecarath!

I couldn't believe my ears at first, but he reached into his satchel and pulled one of the mystical orbs of immortality from it. He said that it was useless to him, since he was not a Mage, but it would be quite useful for me. Useful enough to let him borrow the Orb.

That was an understatement if I ever heard one! My skin absorbed the Zecarath when I touched it, and I feel completely different now. I feel stronger than I have ever been in my life. The power of my magic has increased tenfold. All of my injuries were healed as well, even the scars!

I'll have to explore this more, find out my limitations, but this is magnificent! The legends were true. I have a Zecarath. That means that there are others out there. With this one, and maybe some of those, Zoldex would not stand a chance against us! Though, now that I have a Zecarath, I can hear voices in my mind, and one of them, I think, is Zoldex. I fear that he too may be a Zecarath bearer. Either that, or I'm losing my mind. That's one experience I don't want to go through again. I shudder to think of the repeating verse: "then Ilfanti Day 133, then Ilfanti Day 134, then Ilfanti Day 135, then Ilfanti Day 136..." Bah!

I don't think that is the case. My mind is clearer than it has been in at least a century. I see everything that I need to do, and know how I have to do it.

According to the Orb of Prophecy, Karleena is north, in the land of the bloodgetts. Even with the Zecarath, I'll need allies to free her. Centain should be waiting for me at Faylinn. I'll have to stop there first, and then assemble the heroes and leaders of the realm. Some will join me on an expedition to find the Empress. The others will have to remain behind on a mission that is just as vital—protecting the realm from Zoldex and trying to maintain the rebellion as long as they can. We'll need an army when we return with Karleena.

I wonder who will join me. Some seem obvious. Centain and Adonis are near certainties. There will be others. Maybe I can persuade Captain Augustus to bring us north in the Soaring Mist after we return home. The crew is a capable one. I might as well take advantage of that if I can.

But I am getting ahead of myself. Sure, it's good to plan ahead, but I'm still months away from returning to the Seven Kingdoms. And, as always, this log serves as my reflections on what happened for future prosperity, which means I should stop thinking ahead and planning, and record what actually happened.

Which brings me back to Kabilian. We exchanged orbs, the Zecarath for the Orb of Prophecy, and Kabilian used it at once. He seemed genuinely surprised when he had his mystical vision, and mentioned something about a crown and a gorn child along with a derisive snort, as if he did not believe what he saw. He then tossed the Orb back to me, and with a quick comment of "Until next time," he touched an amulet around his neck and vanished. He reappeared next to Crick, and then both vanished.

Until next time, indeed. At least he gave me the Orb back before he vanished! I wonder if he got what he was looking for? He gave up a Zecarath, an item that would be the most sought-after prize for any Mage, and in exchange, got to use the Orb of Prophecy for a matter of minutes. An interesting exchange, but at least it left us civil, and possibly as allies.

Allied with an assassin. War makes strange bedfellows.

With the Orb of Prophecy in my possession, and the Zecarath within me, I find myself in a position where I have achieved far more than I had even dreamed of when I first decided to come here. Yet, I am also saddened because of the inexplicable behavior of Khonsu.

She has been quiet, sulky, depressed. She must have seen something when she first touched the Orb of Prophecy, but whatever it is, she is not talking about it. Whatever it was, it terrified her and shook her world to the ground. I've wanted to talk to her about it, but never seemed to be able to find time alone with her. Inorus has been watching her like a hawk, and probably would want to stay by her side even if she were willing to talk.

She's a strong girl, though. Whatever she saw, I'm sure she'll come to terms with it. Perhaps after I save the Empress and help bring down Zoldex, I'll return here and see if there is something that I can do to help. If there is danger, then she'll face it with me by her side. If there is none, well, I admit that I would at least like to see her again.

I wonder how Osorkon would feel about that? With the Zecarath, I'm no longer as old as I should be. Well, I am, but it's called a Mystical Orb of Immortality for a reason. Before, why would Khonsu want to really explore relations with me, when I was in the twilight of my life? Now, though, provided that someone doesn't reach into my chest and pull the Zecarath out of my heart, I may have an endless amount of tomorrows. How to spend them will be an interesting challenge.

Perhaps I have time to repair the mistakes of my life. I do not want to change anything. There was no right when I should have gone left. I accept what I have done and cherish my memories. But, I do think I missed out on certain things. I see the pride in Osorkon's eyes as he looks at Khonsu and Inorus. I would like that for myself. Now, I have the time. Someday, maybe I'll have Khonsu.

First thing's first, though—Zoldex. I wonder if he can hear my thoughts, like I think I can hear his. If so, then he probably knows that I am coming. He knows what I have planned. I'll have to see if Master Ariness can teach me to shield my thoughts, because I'd hate to think that the advantage of the Zecarath could become one of our greatest shortcomings as well.

No use worrying about that now. I'll face that as I come to it. Tonight, we celebrate. Tomorrow, we return to Zaman. With the Sanjeez, our return trip should be much quicker. I anticipate reaching Zaman no later than the 1ˢᵗ of Jurgeleit, two full months before Captain Augustus said that they would be forced to leave.

It is time to go home. It is time to bring the Empress home. Soon it will be time to face Zoldex once and for all. I've never been one to believe in the Gods, but if they exist, may they have mercy on us and see us through this one. We can use all the help we can get.

EPILOGUE

Almost eleven full months after embarking on the journey to find the Orb of Prophecy, Ilfanti stood at the stern of the *Soaring Mist*, watching Zaman and Egziard shrinking in the background behind him. The voyage home would still be long and potentially full of peril, but Ilfanti felt that this particular adventure had already come to an end.

He was leaving Zaman yet again, and his friend Osorkon behind. He wondered if he would be able to return in Osorkon's lifetime, and hoped that he would see his friend again. Especially if he were returning to ask Osorkon's permission for Khonsu's hand in marriage. He was not certain that Khonsu felt the way he did, nor did he know if she wanted the same things he did, but there were times he looked in her eyes and thought that he saw her looking back with just as much passion. One day, he hoped to explore that further.

As always, Captain Augustus and the crew of the *Soaring Mist* were at the peak of efficiency, preparing to leave and setting sail within hours of Ilfanti's arrival. On their way to Egziard, the crew was efficient, and professional. On their way home, they seemed a bit more jubilant and excited. And why not? They too had been gone for almost eleven months.

If their voyage was a smooth one—and when on this journey was anything smooth?—they would reach the Seven Kingdoms by late spring. Ilfanti wondered briefly if Kabilian would fly the entire way home in a Wind Soarer. That would cut his voyage considerably, but without one of the avarians' flying vessels, there was no greater ship than the *Soaring Mist*.

Ilfanti stepped away from the stern, leaving Egziard behind him, and returned to his cabin so that he could think and reflect upon his journey. So much had stood in his way, beginning with his own self-doubts and fears, all the way to the dalvor priestess. It was a miracle that he had managed to actually find and claim the Orb of Prophecy for his own.

And, Ilfanti thought, that was the easy part! The danger was what was to come. With Karleena in the clutches of the bloodgetts, Ilfanti did not see how he could rescue her, even with the Zecarath. The bloodgetts were a ruthless and bloodthirsty race that survived by feeding on the blood of others—cannibalistic and wild. They would not fear a magic user, but continue swarming until finally one got through and struck him. Yes, the search for Karleena was far from over, and certainly would be full of peril.

Ilfanti was confident that he would have many volunteers to help search for Karleena. Finding her was crucial to the survival of the Imperium, both for the humans that ruled it, and for all of the races that had been subjugated for centuries. With Karleena in command, the future was bright and optimistic. Without her, it was a future hardly worth living—a nightmare that one would never awaken from.

Ilfanti's resolve was strong. He had found the Orb, now he would find the Empress. Let Zoldex, bloodgetts, armies, and more stand in his way. He would find her, and he would bring her home. This, he swore.

The Imperium Saga

And find out what happens next to Ilfanti in. . .

THE SIEGE OF ZOLDEX

The war for the Imperium has begun!

A year has passed since the forces of Zoldex first began arriving in Trespias. The time for his conquest has come! The dark Mage has waited long enough. His forces are vast and strong, and he is confident that nothing will stand in his path.

Follow the adventures of the heroes of the realm as they try to preserve the Imperium and confront Zoldex's forces. Their hearts are true and their intentions noble, but will that be enough to overcome such overwhelming odds?

Find out as this epic saga continues.

Now Available!

For more details and information,
visit www.SilverLeafBooks.com

Also available from Silver Leaf Books:

CLIFFORD B. BOWYER

Fall of the Imperium Trilogy

An evil tyrant weaves a tapestry of deception as he plots to conquer the Imperium. Only a few heroes are brave enough to uncover the mystery and face Zoldex directly. Follow the adventures of the heroes of the realm as they try to preserve the Imperium and confront Zoldex's forces. Their hearts are true and their intentions noble, but will that be enough to overcome such overwhelming odds? Find out in the *Fall of the Imperium Trilogy*.

The Impending Storm, 0974435449, $27.95
The Changing Tides, 0974435457, $27.95
The Siege of Zoldex, 0974435465, $29.95

The Adventures of Kyria

In a time of great darkness, when evil sweeps the land, a prophecy foretells the coming of a savior, a child that will defeat the forces of evil and save the world. She is Kyria, the Chosen One.

From the pages of the Imperium Saga, *The Adventures of Kyria* follows the child destined to save the world as she tries to live up to her destiny.

The Child of Prophecy, 0974435406, $5.99
The Awakening, 0974435414, $5.99
The Mage's Council, 0974435422, $5.99
The Shard of Time, 0974435430, $5.99
Trapped in Time, 0974435473, $5.99
Quest for the Shard, 0974435481, $5.99
The Spread of Darkness, 0978778219, $5.99
The Apprentice of Zoldex, 0978778227, $5.99
The Darkness Within, 0978778243, $5.99
The Rescue of Nezbith, 0978778251, $7.99
and more to come!

ILFANTI

Known as an adventurer, the dwarven Council of Elders member Ilfanti is one of the most famous Mages in the realm. Everyone knows his name, and others flock around his charisma. But even Ilfanti is at a loss for why the Mage's Council is ignoring the fact that Zoldex has returned and none are safe as his plans go unchallenged.

The Empress has been kidnapped while in the midst of trying to unite the races. Her true whereabouts are unknown, but her return is vital to the survival of the Seven Kingdoms. The Mages are doing nothing, and Ilfanti can no longer condone avoiding the obvious signs that are plaguing the realm.

Follow Ilfanti as he returns to a life of an adventurer and battles against time to save the Imperium. Experience the adventure and learn if the charismatic adventurer can complete one last mission in time to save the realm.

Ilfanti and the Orb of Prophecy, 0978778278, $19.95
and more to come!

CLIFFORD B. BOWYER
CONTINUING THE PASSION

Continuing the Passion follows the story of Connor Edmond Blake, a best-selling novelist who, after suffering the tragic and unexpected loss of his father decides that the best way to honor the memory of his father is by carrying on the legacy that his father left behind.

Connor's father, William Edward Blake, a Hall of Fame High School Baseball Coach had led his team to numerous state championships. Most of Connor's memories and moments he shared with his father have something to do with and revolve around the sport of baseball. As a former coach himself, of a men's softball team, Connor decides to at least make the attempt to coach a High School team in attempt to honor his father.

Continuing the Passion is seen through the eyes of Connor Blake as he experiences the tragedy of the loss of his father, and his pursuit to help his family find a way to overcome the loss.

Continuing the Passion, 097877826X, $18.95